BLOOD MOON
REDEMPTION

Judy DuCharme has given us a story woven together with the historical blood moons past. *Blood Moon Redemption* takes the reader into a captivating drama, drawing from her rich knowledge of the ancient land of Israel.

—Trina Hankins
Mark Hankins Ministries

While the Bible makes it clear that no one knows the hour of Jesus' return, it also gives us signs of His coming and tells us to be prepared. In *Blood Moon Redemption*, Judy DuCharme weaves together the biblical signs of the coming of Jesus with today's news headlines to craft a page-turning tale of mystery and suspense. At the same time she delicately tells the story of a modern-day Jewish family grappling with the question of the Messiah, while interacting with Christians, Muslims, and Jews along the journey. With unexpected turns along the way, this story will surprise and delight, while inviting you to view today's news headlines in a whole new light.

—Dr. Craig von Buseck
Editor of Inspiration.org and author of *I Am Cyrus: Harry S. Truman and the Rebirth of Israel*

It is a very pleasant surprise to find a fictional story that is based in reality. Judy DuCharme's novel *Blood Moon Redemption* explains a difficult spiritual truth in an extremely entertaining way.

The convergence of the modern blood moon quartet on Jewish Holy Days is of profound significance, and it is imperative to have a handle on it. This story will help you to do just that.

—J.R. Brestin
Master Control, WHMB TV-40, Indianapolis, IN

BLOOD MOON REDEMPTION

JUDY DUCHARME

AMBASSADOR INTERNATIONAL
GREENVILLE, SOUTH CAROLINA & BELFAST, NORTHERN IRELAND

www.ambassador-international.com

Blood Moon Redemption

ISBN: 978-1-62020-822-9
eISBN: 978-1-62020-828-1

Cover Design and Page Layout by Hannah Nichols
eBook Conversion by Anna Riebe Raats

AMBASSADOR INTERNATIONAL
Emerald House
411 University Ridge, Suite B14
Greenville, SC 29601, USA
www.ambassador-international.com

AMBASSADOR BOOKS
The Mount
2 Woodstock Link
Belfast, BT6 8DD, Northern Ireland, UK
www.ambassadormedia.co.uk

The colophon is a trademark of Ambassador, a Christian publishing company.

DEDICATION

I would like to dedicate *Blood Moon Redemption* to all those who were such great influencers in the writing of my book. My husband Lee sowed the original idea and some key concepts, and he gave a few gentle nudges to get it done. Our son Chris plays a big part in the actual story and what you read is who Chris is. These two guys are the loves of my life. Thank you.

Then there are so many from my church and extended family who encouraged and exhorted me as well as prayed for me . . . so essential. Thank you to each of you. Christians United for Israel and Billye Brim Ministries were two places that provided understanding of and background information for the subject matter of the book. They also fostered my great love of Israel. The persistence of my agent, Joyce Hart, the readiness to publish of Ambassador International, the patience and oversight of my editor Daphne Self, and the beautiful cover creativity of Hannah Nichols have so blessed me. Of course, without the steadfastness of the Lord in my life, this work would never have been completed.

Our first grandchild was born this summer and though my excitement for the release of *Blood Moon Redemption* is so high, that little boy stole my heart. And as he grows and continues to bless my heart and be the focus of my love and prayers, I pray this book will bless and grow you.

PROLOGUE

Terror. Fingers of fear constricted her throat. "Papa." The word barely escaped Lydia's lips.

Papa scooped her up, eyes wide, and held her close. The smell of anger filled the air. She did not understand it.

The warm summer evening now held a chill that penetrated her. Never had she known her little home to be full of people shouting.

Her father's ever-present prayer shawl slipped off his shoulder. Lydia grabbed the tassel as he pulled her closer. Men—angry men—shoved Papa and Mama out the door. Lydia took one final look at the home she loved, the place she felt safe and free, the place where now people broke windows and smashed furniture.

The men yelled and yanked the prayer shawl. They ripped and tore it and laughed. Lydia buried her head in her father's chest. His heart beat so loudly, but he said nothing. She gripped the tassel still wedged between them as the awful men shoved her Papa again, and her family stumbled away.

When she finally felt Papa's hold on her lessen, the darkness of late evening settled around them. They were in the woods with a gentle rain falling as if the sky didn't feel the fear.

Lydia screwed up her nose. The smoldering smell made her feel a little sick. She tried to understand the events of this day. In recent weeks fewer people walked the streets and visited their home. Usually guests came often to counsel with her father, the rabbi. She asked her father why one day. He told her times were hard and many moved away.

Papa always spoke with calmness and strength, and his answers satisfied Lydia's curiosity. But nothing made sense now. Just a few weeks before she and her best friend Gabe whispered that everyone appeared fearful. Where they played they saw broken windows and scattered furniture. Soon she was confined to playing at home, seeing Gabe only at Shabbat. Plus, Shabbat wasn't even in the synagogue any more since a fire had destroyed their lovely building.

"Papa, where is your prayer shawl?"

"Oh, sweetheart, they took it, but God's Word is in our hearts and we are alive." His deep brown eyes looked sad, but Lydia, even in the dark, could see the ever-present peace she loved.

"Papa, look!" Lydia opened her hand. She held the tassel from the prayer shawl.

"Oh, Lydia, we are blessed. God has given us a piece of Himself to take with us wherever we go."

Lydia wasn't sure if she saw tears or rain on his face. "Where can we go? Is our house still there? Mama, why are you crying?"

Mama put her face in her hands. Water droplets dripped from her hair as it fell forward. "Reuben, what can I say?"

Papa set Lydia down and wiped his wife's tears. "We must always tell the truth, my dear Esther. Lydi must know, hard as it is. In the long run, it is always better. No matter how hard, we have God's promise that He will bring us through."

They continued through the woods as the shadows lengthened and disappeared. Mama took her hand. "My sweet Lydia, we will be strong even though our house is no longer there." Mama's voice shook. "They burned all the houses in our neighborhood. See, look there." They paused and peered through the darkening woods. Glimpses of flames darted before their eyes. "We are too far to see well, but those are the houses of our friends."

Lydia strained to see the houses, but the smoke and darkness made her view hazy. "I smell smoke, Papa. Perhaps there is a camp fire and neighbors nearby to keep us warm." Lydia looked first to her mother and then her father.

"That smoke is from the burning houses, sweetheart." Papa stooped down and picked Lydia up again. "Lydi, they would find us and hurt us if we started a fire. We must trust God to keep us warm tonight."

Lydia looked her father in the eye. "Gabe told me they cut people open because they thought they had jewels in them."

Mama gasped. Papa held Lydia close. "Yes, yes, they did that. It was evil, Lydi." He gulped. "It was evil, but we must take comfort that those friends are now in Abraham's bosom and free from all pain." He stopped and peered through the woods. Then he spoke in his stern voice. "We need to find a place to hide and then get ourselves out of Spain. There is no mercy here for Jews."

Mama put her hand on Papa's arm. "No. We must travel as far as possible now and then hide in the daylight. They will find us easily if we hide nearby and travel in the morning. Look there is a partial moon to give us enough light to travel."

"But, Mama, there are so many clouds. They block the light of the moon."

Mama touched Lydia's head. "Yes, but that is good. The evil men will perhaps not follow us, because of the clouds and rain. We can go on the little light we get. We know these woods better than they do."

"Papa, I can walk. I will pretend we are playing a game and Gabe is trying to catch us. Papa, is Gabe okay?"

Papa sighed. "Truthfully, Lydi, I do not know. I pray he and his family are alive."

There was a shuffle of leaves and the breaking of a branch behind them. A voice nearby, pierced the air around Lydia's family. "We are well, but if you insist on being so noisy, we will all be dead, dear Rabbi."

A muffled scream left Mama's mouth. In the attempt to quiet herself, she tripped and fell. Papa threw his body over Mama. Lydia dropped next to them before she realized they heard friendly voices.

"Esther, Reuben, I am so sorry. I did not mean to frighten you. I thought you heard us as well as we heard you. Are you hurt?" Mr. Goldman, Gabe's father, hurried to assist Papa and Mama from their crumpled positions on the ground.

"I landed on this branch full force on my ribs." Mama groaned as she accepted the hand extended and struggled to rise. "I must look a sight, covered with dirt." She attempted to laugh but sucked in her breath. "I perhaps bruised my rib."

Papa put his arm around her to help her stand upright. "You look wonderful, Esther. You are alive. You will heal." He turned to the Goldmans. "Dear friends, we are so encouraged to see you alive."

Papa always had good words to say. That was why he was such a good rabbi.

Gabe's father kissed Papa on each cheek. "Oh, Rabbi, we have lost all, but now that we see you and your family, we have proof that God is still with us."

Lydia pushed herself between the two men. "And look, we still have Papa's tassel. The bad people took everything else."

"Let me see that, Lydi." Gabe held it in his hand. He was a little taller than Lydia and almost a whole year older. The nine-year-old looked up. "What is the prayer, Father? 'The Lord our God is one . . .'" As Gabe said the words, everyone echoed the refrain, visibly relaxing as peace settled on the small bedraggled group. Gabe smiled as he looked at Lydia's father. "I want to be a rabbi someday."

Papa ruffled the boy's hair. "You'll make a fine one."

The boy handed him the tassel. "Come on, Lydi, we know where we can go. Mama's cousin is sailing to find new land, and he is taking all of us with him."

Gabe's mother hushed him. "Do not speak loudly, son. The trees have ears."

Lydia and Gabe laughed. "I don't think that's true, Mrs. Goldman." Lydia paused. "Is it, Papa? You said it's better to know the truth."

Papa chuckled. "She means there could be bad people hiding and listening to us. But, Anna, what does Gabe mean?"

In the ever-darkening haze, Gabe's mother held her finger to her lips and looked around. Everyone stood still and followed her gaze. She moved close and indicated with her arms for them to draw close in a huddle. "My cousin is Cristobal Colombo. The queen knows only he is Spanish and Italian. She does not know he is Jewish as well."

"He denies his faith?" Mama rubbed her ribs.

"He only appears to do so, so he isn't evicted as are we. He has won the favor of the queen and king and been given permission to set sail with three ships. He is smuggling many Jews out of the country and we are able to go. You will come with us, Reuben. We need a rabbi."

Lydia jumped up and down. She was about to squeal but was quickly shushed by all the adults.

"This is truly amazing." Papa placed his hands together in front of his face and sighed deeply. "How soon does he sail? You're sure there will be room for us?"

"There is room for every displaced Jew, every Jew that has been forced to convert to Catholicism, and every Gentile who is willing to let the Jews live." Gabe's father, Joseph Goldman, placed his hand on Papa's shoulder. "Rabbi Reuben Liebermann, we need you. We sail in three days. We must be on the ship in two. Praise be to God that we have found you."

Gabe grabbed Lydia's hand. "Let's go, Lydi. We will sail to a new land and grow up together. I will be a rabbi and you will be my wife."

Lydia pulled her hand away. "Will not. Gabe, I will hit you if you try to marry me."

"Shh, children." Gabe's father took them each by the hand. "Let's get to the boat. There will be plenty of time to talk of marriage. Now we must concentrate on staying alive."

They proceeded carefully through the woods, occasionally tripping on roots and rocks, but staying close enough to catch each other before anyone else could fall. Lydia and Gabe yawned and rubbed their eyes but did not complain. She could hear Gabe's mother and Mama as they whispered about the homes and friends now lost, the children, and their wonderings of what sailing would be like.

Gabe's father and Papa diligently watched for any other people who might be in the woods. Mr. Goldman was in the front of the group with her and Gabe. Mama and Mrs. Goldman walked behind him with arms locked while Papa followed directly behind them, praying and quoting Scripture.

They neared the edge of the woods, and Lydia could see roofs of houses in the distance. Mr. Goldman turned. "Praise God we've made it safely this far. We know the way to another cousin's house not far from here."

Papa came close to Mr. Goldman. "Joseph, how is it they have not been evicted or killed. Are they not Jews?"

Mrs. Goldman laid her hand on Reuben's arm. "Rabbi, they are, but they have pretended to become Catholic."

Papa pulled his arm away and placed his hand over his mouth. He looked away. "We are forbidden."

Mrs. Goldman stepped around to see Papa's face. "No, Rabbi, it was for life. It was for our lives. They remain Jews to the core. This is simply to protect the many who must escape. Please understand. It was not easy." She implored him with her eyes.

Mama took Papa's hand. "Reuben, she is right. God has made a way of escape for us. Anna, is that why you remained when you could have left earlier when the decree was given?"

Anna nodded, and Mr. Goldman placed his arm around her. "Anna has worked closely with her cousin and kept in touch with many who pretended to convert. She was able to make lists for Cristobal. He used them to hire crew and create a list of passengers for the queen. Anna was not able to talk directly with him, but another cousin 'converted' as soon as all this began to be discussed so that he could be the go-between. It is to his home we must go now."

Papa shook his head. "Yes, yes, mysterious are His ways. Sometimes past finding out. Anna, thank you for your faithfulness. I never knew and often wondered why you stayed so long."

Mrs. Goldman smiled. "We wondered the same about you, Rabbi."

"I could not leave my flock. I knew I must stay as long as possible. Esther and I knew the danger but felt we must do it." Papa rubbed his hand on his face, then nodded. "We will go."

"But won't soldiers be around?" Mama wrapped her arms around herself and rocked.

Mr. Goldman touched Mama's shoulder. "Because this is a Catholic area, there are fewer soldiers. They will be checking, but since all the Catholics are either Jews, or Catholics who wish us no harm, I think we'll be safe. I have been here many times with Anna. We must hurry, though, so we don't draw unnecessary attention to ourselves."

The small group held hands and prayed for protection. As they were about to exit the woods, a man stepped out from the shadows nearby. His hair was long and white, sprinkled with gray. His nose was large and his deep-set eyes kind. A few missing teeth were revealed when he smiled, but the most notable aspect of this man was the uncanny glow. Did it emanate from within or without?

"May I be of assistance, my friends?" His voice was strong, but kind.

Mr. Goldman whirled around. "Put out your flame, man." His voice was a hiss. "You'll get us all killed."

The strange man held out his arms. "I'm here to protect you."

Papa hesitated and grabbed Lydia's hand. Mama's hands were over her eyes as tears streamed down her face. Peeking out through her fingers, she stepped behind her husband.

"Who . . . who are you?" Papa took a step toward the man then stopped. Lydia wondered if Papa felt what she felt, an overwhelming impulse to kneel.

Lydia studied the man. "Papa, it's okay. He is here to help us. I think that's God shining out of him." She felt her father relax.

"Lydia is right. Rabbi Liebermann, Mr. Goldman, have no fear. My name is Hernando Wental." His eyes emanated peace. "Follow me. I will escort you all safely to your friend's house."

Papa hesitated. "But the light. It will expose us."

"Stay close. It will keep us hidden." The man's voice resonated inside Lydia.

Mr. Goldman shook his head as he took his wife's hand.

"Come along, children." The man's voice commanded authority along with a great gentleness. Gabe and Lydia giggled and ran over, each taking one of Hernando's hands.

Papa slipped his hand around Mama, and they began following the strange man. Wonderment filled Lydia's soul. The soft light around Hernando was like a lantern exposing roots and rocks in the path.

Upon reaching the cluster of homes and roads, they paused. Papa whispered. "It is certain death if we're seen."

Hernando turned. "No fear, my friends, we'll be there shortly."

The streets were deserted. Mama still shook. Mr. Goldman kept looking in every direction. Papa did not take his eyes off Hernando. Lydia and Gabe giggled and skipped, and Hernando did not shush them. Lydia wondered why the adults were so nervous. After all the fear and anger of the early evening, she felt safe again.

As they turned a corner, Papa gasped and stopped short. Mama's hands went to her face. There were Queen's guards, clubs ready, canvassing the street. Hernando simply turned to the others and smiled. The slightest shake of his head indicated they should not worry or speak.

Mrs. Goldman stood frozen. Her husband wrapped his arm around her and pulled her close. She buried her face in his shoulder as they stayed close to Hernando.

The guards, not twenty feet away, looked directly at them, almost through them. Lydia heard her father whisper, "How can this be?"

"See anything?" one of them called to the other.

"Thought I heard something down this way." He walked toward the group.

The first guard called, "Let's go. There's nothing here." Their footsteps faded in the distance.

Papa doubled over and placed his hands on his knees. "Did they not see us? How is that possible?" His voice was hoarse.

Mr. Goldman scrutinized Hernando. "How did that happen?"

"I am sent to protect you." Hernando smiled.

Gabe looked at Lydia. "I wasn't afraid a moment."

Lydia pushed him. "Were too. I was."

Papa gazed around. "So was I. I think we all were. Esther, are you okay?"

Mama held her hands over her face. "I'm still petrified."

Mrs. Goldman put her arms around Mama. "But God, blessed be His Name, has again kept us safe."

Hernando's voice was a blanket of calm. "Come. We must continue."

Moments later, they arrived at the small stucco house, surrounded by gracious gardens. Hernando laid his hand on Papa's arm. "Rabbi Liebermann, your descendants are set to influence the blessing and rise of Israel in the end days."

Papa stared at the little man. "Israel?"

"The land of your fathers, the land of your people to come."

The door opened. With big eyes, the man looked at Mr. and Mrs. Goldman. "How did you get here? Come in, come in, quickly."

"Hernando brought us safely, praise to the Almighty." Mr. Goldman turned to introduce him to Hernando, but no one was there.

Papa scanned the area. "Where did he go? We were just speaking to each other. Lydi, did you see him?"

"Yes, Papa. He smiled, patted my head, and disappeared. I think he went back to heaven."

"Rabbi, all of you, we must shut the door. It is not safe."

CHAPTER 1

Tassie Stevens ran her hand over the leather arm of the chair and inhaled the professional fragrance of wood, leather, and power in her new office. First day on the job. Get the paperwork over and dive in. She was so ready.

"So, Tassie, is that your real name? I mean, full name?" The young file clerk looked up and waved his hand. "I mean, is Tassie a nickname?" He looked back at the form ready to write.

Tassie smiled, wishing she could grimace. She straightened her black suit jacket and crossed her legs in order to keep from tapping her sling-backed heel on the polished floor. She'd been answering this question all her life. "No, it's Tassel."

His head came up, eyebrows arched. Just like a dog with his ears up. He just needs to tilt his head now. The rueful thought amused Tassie, but she was so tired of the joke of her name.

"Yes, Tassel." She half-smiled and looked down. "It's from a story in my family's history. Now, what else do you need?" The curt explanation effectively stopped any further questioning. The young man continued through the basic paperwork process.

How dare her parents saddle her with the legend! Fine if they wanted to believe it, but to name her Tassel Lydia after the magical remnant of a prayer shawl and the name of the little girl who saved it was ludicrous. A children's story! That's all it was. Who cared about a tassel from 1492? Her brother was stuck being named Reuben Liebermann, the name of Lydia's father, the rabbi.

At least he didn't have to explain his name every time he turned around. He just went by Rube and no one questioned it.

From childhood all she wanted was to be a lawyer. A high powered, high-stakes lawyer that people respected and feared. She had gotten the second highest score on the bar exam and landed this position with the best law firm in Chicago.

She wished she could lie about her name—that Tassie was her legal name, but she couldn't. She had vowed to be honest as well. That was her upbringing and that was okay. It was just the tassel story. She could still hear him snickering silently.

———

Full of stories to share with her parents about her entry into the legal profession, Tassie made her weekly visit to the home where she'd grown up. As soon as she walked through the door, her mother began the conversation.

"Darling, I have been working on our family history, and I think you—"

Tassie groaned. "Mother, I really don't have time."

Her mother spread out several sheets of paper, not looking at Tassie. "It will take only a few minutes. I think the most interesting—"

Tassie stood straight. It served her well as an attorney. It accomplished nothing with her mother. "Mother, look at me. I don't want to look at your papers. I don't care about our history."

Her mother sat in the chair. She brushed her slightly graying hair off her face and looked up at Tassie with a gentle smile. "Sweetheart, you were a history major."

"World history, not family history." Tassie shook her head. "Besides, it was a good base for law."

"I'm quite sure Christopher Columbus, well Cristobal Colombo, is in our family tree."

Tassie gazed at the ceiling. "Oh, please. Perhaps we came over with him, but if the story is true, Lydia Liebermann was only eight years old. I highly doubt she married Columbus."

"Oh, no, of course not. But his cousin traveled with the Lierbermanns and her son married Lydia. Isn't that amazing!"

"Mother, how many generations ago is that? Wait. No. Don't answer that. It was over five hundred years ago. It's not really history. It's speculation. Why should I be interested?"

"Tassie, you are named for—"

"I know, I know, and I love you, Mother, but if this name sinks my career, I just . . . I just . . . I don't . . . " Tassie faltered and didn't finish.

Her mother stood and came around the table. She embraced Tassie. "Nothing will sink you, Tassie Stevens. Don't you worry. When you want to talk about this, just let me know." Scooping up the papers, she walked out of the living room into the small study that served as her office.

Tassie followed. "Mother, I . . . I'm sorry." She glanced at her mother's favorite books lining the walls interspersed with sculptures and vases she collected from trips all over the world. The mahogany desk was immaculate except for upholstery fabric samples that covered one end.

"Oh, no need to fuss." Mother carefully placed her papers in a file and set it on the side cabinet. She slid an arm around Tassie and guided her back into the living room. "You have a lot on your plate. I understand." Her mother stepped back and looked at Tassie. "I love your hair down like that. My beautiful brown-eyed girl. And that dress is very flattering. Stylish and professional. I think you need a little more lipstick to bring out the highlights in that gorgeous auburn hair, though. Jack, what do you think?"

Tassie's father glanced up from his easy chair and from the football game. He held out his arms to Tassie. "You always look wonderful. If I were the other lawyer, I'd just rest my case and give you the win."

Tassie hurried over and sat on his lap. She fell into her father's hug just like she'd done since she was a little girl.

Her father pressed his lips to her forehead. "How's it going, girl? Got any questions for me?"

"I do have a couple situations, Daddy." Tassie loved to discuss case studies and sticky law questions with her dad, a retired judge. And she had never stopped calling him 'Daddy'. She always thought he was the epitome of a teddy bear and an encyclopedia. As a judge he had been both approachable and exacting in his judgements resulting in high regard throughout his profession.

Father and daughter climbed out of the chair with a few chuckles and headed into Jack's den. "We won't be too long, Mother."

Tassie heard her mom chuckle as she closed the door. She could easily spend hours with her dad, yet Mother never complained.

"Daddy, Mother kind of drives me nuts with all this Columbus stuff. I'd much rather discuss law."

Her dad patted her hand. "When we married, she was as exacting as you. Except it was in her study and love for archaeology. She gave up her career dreams to raise you and Rube."

"Did that upset her? That would be so hard for me."

"Well, she just transferred that gifting to decorating our home with artifacts and furnishings from around the world." He grinned. "And . . . she included you in the search for pieces of art from almost every time period. She fed you an appreciation for art and history, which prepared you for the study of law."

"Oh, Daddy, I think your love and understanding of the law did it."

Her father tapped her nose. "Tassie, I worked long hours when you were little. I spent every moment I could with you and your mom and Rube, but those moments were too few for many years. Give your mom some credit.

And let her tell you her discoveries. They're significant. Some day you should ask her about the dream she had when she was pregnant with you."

Tassie squinted her eyes at her dad but said nothing.

Her dad sat up straighter. "Now, let's hear about your cases. I'm all ears."

The next morning in court, Tassie noticed him immediately. As the attorney turned from the opposing lawyer's bench, his eyes caressed her from her head to the floor. Tassie was glad she did not blush easily, but she felt a warm electricity flow through her. *I must be slipping or he's really good at this.*

The opposing counsel's face was angular and incredibly handsome. Dark skin with deep set eyes. Close cropped hair with just the slightest curl. Probably had adorable curls as a little boy.

Tassie smiled before realizing he still gazed at her. She slowly swiveled her head to her fellow attorneys and began talking as if her smile was solely intended for them.

Two hours later when the judge recessed proceedings until the next day, Tassie glanced one more time in the handsome man's direction. He nodded at her with the slightest of smiles.

Smooth. He was very smooth, and because of it, she was not quite sure if she trusted him. Not that she needed to. Rarely did she trust the defense lawyers. His tone was firm when speaking to the witness and the jury, giving him a professional respect in the court, and an underlying kindness that made witnesses open up to him.

It was the slightest bit of disdain she detected beneath the handsomeness, the professionalism, the kindness that unsettled her. During court proceedings it seemed no one else picked up on it. She watched for skepticism, a slight tilting down of the chin, narrowing of the eyes, but saw not one bit of any of those reactions. Her father always told her she read people well and to trust those instincts implicitly.

Lost in thought, analyzing every step of procedure in the day's case, Tassie almost ran into the man as she passed through the courtroom doors.

"I am so sorry." Tassie looked directly into his eyes. Deep green, beautiful. Quickly she turned to go past him, fighting a school girl tendency to sigh at his beauty.

"No need to apologize. I was waiting for you." He bowed slightly and flashed a beautiful smile. "I'm Omar . . . Omar Tugani. You are very impressive in the courtroom."

Tassie paused. "Thank you. You were succinct and put the witness at ease. Now, if you'll excuse me."

The man touched her arm and shivers ran though her. "Miss Stevens, would you do the honor of allowing me to take you to dinner?"

Tassie stood straight. "I can't discuss the case with defense. You know that."

The deep green eyes sparkled, and little crinkles formed at the corners of his eyes. "I'm quite sure we can find many things to converse about other than our jobs."

Tassie cleared her throat and repositioned her purse on her shoulder.

"I'll take that as a yes." He took her by the elbow and guided her to the elevator. "Chicago Pizza sound good? There's one just down the street."

Tassie laughed. "Excellent choice. Only good things happen over pizza." Mr. Green Eyes was a little too smooth, but she could handle him.

———

Even though her mother sometimes drove her crazy, Tassie enjoyed her Sunday evening visits to her parents.

"I made ravioli. Would you get the wine, Tassie?"

Dinner conversation covered court issues, the weather, the neighbor's sick cat, and plans to remodel the guest room. When dinner was over, her mother brought out her folder.

Expecting to see remodeling fabric and wallpaper samples, Tassie's eyes fell on a thick stack of papers, entitled, 'Four Blood Red Moons: Columbus to Now'.

"What in the world!" Tassie pursed her lips and turned toward her mother.

"My latest research about lunar eclipses falling on the Jewish feast days."

Tassie shook her head and began clearing the table. "Can I get you coffee, Daddy?"

"Please."

Tassie went to the kitchen, returning with a steaming cup of coffee which she set before her dad. She then poured another glass of wine for her mother and herself. "You . . . this . . . it's superstitious, Mother. Are you getting into astrology?"

"Do you remember Uncle Rupert?"

"Vaguely. He always played with me, but I remember everyone thinking he was crazy."

Her dad laughed. "That's true. A kind old man, but a little off."

"Maybe not." Her mother took a sip of wine. "Do you remember, Jack, what he always talked about?"

"Yes, yes." Her father nodded his head. "Lunar eclipses. They started calling him Professor Luney."

Tassie laughed. "Oh, my goodness. I remember that. I thought his name was Rupert Luney."

Marge groaned and then began to giggle. Soon they were all guffawing.

"Okay, I'll bite." Tassie wiped the tears from her eyes. "What was the reason he was called Professor Luney?"

"He was obsessed with lunar eclipses." Her father shrugged his shoulders. "Astrology?"

"No, actually he'd been a science teacher and loved studying and teaching about space. He was really interested in eclipses and began charting them. He was also quite a devout Jew and served as an officer in World War Two. He was able to visit Israel and met David Ben Gurion right when they were struggling as a new nation. He was quite an impressive man." He sipped his coffee before continuing. "So, anyway, in his study of eclipses, he saw that around 1948 and 1967 there were four lunar eclipses in a row that fell on Jewish feast days."

"Well, I suppose that's not so unusual. Aren't there about seven lunar eclipses every year?" Tassie sat down at the table and lifted her wine glass to her lips.

"Yes, there are." Her mother shuffled the papers. "However, to land on feast days was considered highly significant and seemed to tell of upheaval and harm to the Jews."

"Sounds like old wives' tales."

"That's why he was called Professor Luney. But, look what happened. Israel became a nation in 1948 and regained Jerusalem in 1967." Marge pointed at one of her papers.

"Well, that's interesting, Mother, but it wouldn't hold up in court. It's anecdotal, not direct cause and effect."

"Perhaps, darling. But this is very interesting because there were also four lunar eclipses on four Jewish feast days near 1492."

Tassie rolled her eyes. "And I suppose they're on Christian holidays in 1776 and 1863. There are probably a dozen of these incidents. It's all conjecture, Mother."

Her dad set down his coffee cup. "It actually is interesting, Tassie, although I must remind everyone that Uncle Rupert Luney was on your mother's side of the family." He winked at his wife. "These alignments occurred on Jewish feast days in 1493-94, and then not again until 1949 and 1967. That's it. Uncle Rupert also studied rabbinical teachings and the rabbis always predicted great upheaval followed by great provision when the lunar eclipses were on feast days." He spread his hands. "So now Mama Marge has taken up the baton."

Tassie groaned. "Okay, it's history, a little luney, but history. And, we love history in this family, but this stays here . . . in the family. You're not going to share this with the synagogue and the neighborhood." Tassie tipped her head at her mother.

"It's not just history, Tass, it's future too, almost present."

"Whatever do you mean?"

"It's happening this year and next. Four lunar eclipses on four Jewish feast days."

Tassie poured another glass of wine and walked over to the window. "Mother, you're smarter than this. Life is full of interesting coincidences, but you can't make connections with, with, well, whatever it is. Actually, I don't want to know what you are trying to say. I have to go."

Tassie set down her glass without taking a sip and kissed her mother on the cheek. Her father stood and gave her a big hug. "Goodnight, Daddy. Love you." She picked up her jacket and purse and walked out.

CHAPTER 2

The ship gently rocked as Lydia drifted off to sleep. Most of her fears had subsided and she enjoyed the excitement of traveling on the ocean. She missed her home and neighborhood terribly. She chose her happiest memory to be the last thing she thought about each night as sleep came, and fear tried knocking on the door of her mind.

It had been her eighth birthday just a month before their eviction from their home at the edict of the Queen of Spain.

"Lydi Liebermann, what an impact on the world you will make! The most beautiful daughter ever!" Papa had beamed as he handed Lydia her present.

"Ha, ha, Papa, so funny. I am the *only* daughter of the Liebermanns. That would make me most beautiful and the smartest."

Papa's eyes had twinkled. "Ah, Lydi, there has never been a more beautiful Liebermann daughter ever. Just as the Psalmist said, 'Many daughters have done beautifully, but you outshine them all.' Is it not true, my dear wife?" Papa bowed and swept his hand in the direction from Lydia to his wife.

"True, it is," laughed Mama. She picked up the towel draped over the chair and swatted her husband. "But, it is also true, dear husband, that you have only one daughter, your brothers have only sons, and your papa had only sons."

Papa extended his hands, raising his arms. "As I said, never a wiser, smarter daughter than mine. She will be remembered as were Rachel and Sarah. I know it!"

Lydia ran her fingers over the luxurious texture of the brocade bag before peeking inside. Reaching in, she pulled out a small cloth doll with a beautiful porcelain face. She loved the lacy dress her mother had sewn. It was the best present ever.

The three held hands and danced in a circle, a traditional Jewish dance. Papa gave his wife a kiss on the cheek and his daughter a kiss on her head.

Lydia lay quietly and smiled as the memory faded. *I don't have that doll anymore, but I have my Mama and Papa, so I am okay.*

———

A few days later Papa reached down and felt Mama's brow. Lydia knew it was too warm. She had also touched her forehead.

"Is she okay, Papa?" Lydia sat at the foot of her mother's bunk.

"I think it is just the sea and the rocking. It makes one dizzy sometimes." He dipped a cloth into a bucket of water, wrung it out, and laid it on her forehead. Mama moaned.

She opened her eyes and looked at her husband. Lydia could see the fear screaming out of her mother's eyes. Papa swallowed and patted her hands. "Esther, all will be well. God is with us." He closed his eyes and Lydia wondered if he, too, was afraid.

Lydia heard what sounded like mumbling from her father. She knew he was praying. *Good, Papa doesn't fear anything. He knows how to pray. Mama will get well.*

Mama moaned again and placed her hand on Papa's arm. "My ribs. Such pain. Can't get my breath."

Papa's voice was full of compassion. "You bruised them, dear wife, when you fell in the woods. Remember when I bruised myself after falling while building the house?" Mama nodded, and a slight smile crossed her lips. Papa laughed. "Yes, I was not a good builder, now was I? Why did I bring that up?"

He looked at Lydia. "I am a better Rabbi than I am a carpenter. I will tell you that story someday."

Lydia nodded. She took a deep breath. Her parents were smiling and laughing. Surely all would be well now.

Papa touched Mama's ribs gently. She winced. "It will take time to heal, dear one. We will be patient. It took me quite a while to heal." Mama smiled again. Papa chuckled. "I know you think I nursed that too long, so our friends would do the building for us. But a bruised rib takes a long time. You just need to rest." He leaned over and kissed her lightly on the lips.

"Come, Lydi, let's let your mother sleep a while."

"Love you, Mama." Lydia paused and gazed at her mother. She kissed her mama's cheek, took her papa's hand, and walked to the upper deck where Gabe and the other children played.

Gabe called to her to join them. Papa smiled and nodded, and she ran over to see what her friends were doing to pass the time.

A FEW WEEKS LATER

"I am so sorry about your mama, Lydi. I will say the Prayer of Mercy for her."

A tear ran down Lydia's cheek. She didn't speak but nodded.

Gabe put an arm around her. "I will take care of you, Lydi. I promise."

Lydi stiffened and pushed Gabe with both hands. "No, Gabe, my papa will take care of me. And I want my mama." Her little chest convulsed, and she ran from the lower deck sobbing. She found Papa on the upper deck just staring at the ocean. Blinded by her tears she slid into the railing.

"Lydi, Lydi, you must be careful. I cannot lose you as well." He scooped her up and the two wrapped their arms around each other and sobbed.

"Papa, why did they drop her in the ocean? How will we find her for a proper burial?"

"We won't, little one, but even in the ocean, she is in Abraham's bosom. And, we will see her again."

Lydia stopped sobbing. Putting both hands on her papa's chest she pushed back so she could see his eyes. "What do you mean? She lives? How will we see her? When?"

Papa set her down, took her hand and walked along the deck. "Lydi, the Torah tells us we will all be in heaven with Father God one day. That is where we will see her."

Lydia stopped and pulled her hand from Papa's. "No, Papa, not when we die. I want her now."

Papa stooped to eye level with Lydia. "So, do I, my sweet Lydi, but we must know and accept the truth. Mama will always be in your heart, but you will see her no more in this life. We must take care of each other, my sweet Lydi."

Everything was blurry. Wiping her eyes did not help. "I will always take care of you, Papa. But not Gabe." Lydia stamped her foot. "He thinks he can marry me."

Papa laughed a big laugh. It was so good to hear that Lydia stopped crying and smiled at Papa.

"Maybe someday, Lydi, he will marry you, but not for a long, long time."

EARLY 1493, NEW WORLD

Rabbi Liebermann stood with Lydia on the sandy shore and waved as Christopher Columbus sailed away on his return trip to Spain. Lydia missed him already. Not long into the voyage, she started to call him Uncle Colombo. She and Gabe had loved to stand with him as he steered the ship.

Gabe's mother, Anna Goldman, wiped a tear from her eye, as she turned to her husband and the rabbi. "May God give my cousin safe travels. I wonder if we shall ever see him again. I did not know him that well growing up, but watching him as the admiral of our ship, stirred great respect. Now, he goes back with reports of ways through the sea, the lay of the land, the peoples, the riches." She scowled. "I think all Queen Isabella and King Ferdinand want to know about are the riches . . . whether there are gold and spices. Wouldn't she be surprised to know this journey opened a whole new world for the Jews of Spain? Perhaps the Jews from all over the world will come here, too."

Mr. Goldman placed his arm around his wife. "Yes, a whole new world and we must explore it as well."

"Look what he gave me before he sailed." She pulled a small cloth package from her pocket. Unwrapping it revealed a small coin. On one side was the image of Queen Isabella.

Her husband raised his eyebrows. "Truth be told, I don't care for that image, dear wife."

"Ahhh." Anna smiled. "Study the other side."

Mr. Goldman turned the coin over and there was the image and name of Cristobal Colombo, 1492. Lydia stood close to Mr. Goldman. "Ooh, look. Papa, look. It looks like Uncle Colombo. What a nice gift."

The Rabbi leaned in. "Right you are young lady. It is a wonderful gift. Joseph, this is a wonderful memorial of how God Almighty, blessed be He, has taken care of us."

They gazed out at the water and watched the ship get smaller and smaller as the sails billowed and the ship flowed with the wind. The sky was blue and feathery clouds lazed about the sky. Small birds graced the air above them and they all just stood and soaked in the beauty.

"Papa, Papa." Lydia tugged on her father's sleeve.

He reached down and patted her head. "What is it, Lydi?"

Lydia pointed at the sky. "Papa, how far is the sky blue?"

"Oh my, Lydi, I guess forever." Each person crooked their neck and peered into the heavens. "What do you think . . . as far as heaven?"

Lydia placed her hands on her hips, tilted her head, and scrunched up her lips and nose. "I think it's as far as God will take care of us." She turned to her father. "Because He will."

Rabbi Liebermann reached down and picked up his daughter and held her close. His words were choked. "Yes, Lydi, He will."

———————

PASSOVER, SPRING 1493

"Papa, Papa!! Look!" Lydia's face was aglow with excitement even in the dark. "The moon's face is moving!"

Rabbi Liebermann and his daughter stepped outside and stood next to the little home they now shared with the Goldmans. His dear wife was gone, but Lydia filled his life with delight. The Goldmans daily provided love and strength as the rabbi worked to set up a simple synagogue for all the Jews displaced by the edict of Spain.

As Rabbi Liebermann looked up, his stomach churned. He stepped back and gulped. "Oh my. Oh my."

The night was cool and clear. But the sight before him sent shivers up and down his spine.

"What is it, Papa?" Lydia stiffened as she watched her father. "Is it bad?" Tears formed in her eyes.

"Oh, not to fear, sweet one, not to fear. It's one of God's majestic events in His creation. I learned about this as a young man in my studies of the Talmud and about the heavens. The earth gets between the sun and the moon and makes a shadow on the moon." He took her hand. "Isn't it amazing?"

Lydi looked at the moon, then gazed up at her father's face. "But it looks red, Papa. Our shadows aren't red, are they?"

"No, they are not. You are so smart. They call it a Blood Moon because it's red."

"Why did you look so surprised, Papa? You almost looked scared. Were you scared?"

"I was surprised, sweet one, because this is Passover. And a blood moon on a holy day is very important to the Jewish people."

"What does it mean?"

"I am not quite sure. I must pray and seek His face. Times and seasons are in His hand, bless His holy name. Our people in Spain just came out of horrendous pain and suffering, and now we are in a new land. Perhaps this is His sovereign plan." The rabbi took his daughter's hand and bent over to kiss the top of her head. "He does know the end from the beginning. So, it is our duty to seek the wisdom revealed in His Word and hidden from those who do not seek His face."

"Maybe it's like the blood sacrifices in the temple so long ago, Papa." Lydia's face lit up. "Remember those?"

"Oh yes, Lydi. God commanded the blood sacrifice for the removal of sin."

"Oh, Papa!" Lydia squeezed her papa's hand and signaled with her finger for him to come closer. He kneeled on one knee and Lydi put her mouth to his ear. "Maybe He's showing all the people who left Spain, wherever they are, that He has forgiven the sin of the whole world. Cause that was a big sin, Papa, what they did in Spain."

Rabbi Liebermann coughed and cleared his throat. A single tear ran down his face. In barely a whisper, he said, "Out of the mouth of babes." He stood slowly and picked up Lydia. "Oh Lord, what wisdom You place in little ones. My heart is overrun with Your presence. You have forgiven the world. You have forgiven Spain. I, too, will forgive."

He grasped the tassel that he wore on a loosely woven rope about his neck like a pendant. It had been lovingly kept and held in high honor as they crossed the ocean and settled in a new land. "Blessed are You, God of the universe. I will walk in forgiveness, and every time I see a blood red moon, I will perceive that You have done sacrifice and forgiven the world."

The rabbi shared the story with his small but always growing congregation. "We have lost much and yet we have gained a whole world in which to live and grow. Let us always be mindful of the lovingkindness of our God, not just toward us, but to all those, good and bad, who live in this world."

CHAPTER 3

"Tassie, this man asked for you."

Tassie held up one finger as she finished writing her closing remarks. *I need to practice this. Almost have this thought down.*

"Miss Stevens?"

"Uh-huh, Uh-huh." Tassie nodded. Satisfied she had the wording correct, she looked up. "Yes?"

"I do apologize, Miss Stevens. The man insists he wants you to represent him."

"Certainly, send him in."

"You may want to come out, Tass."

Tass? Tassie frowned. Normally Teresa maintained proper decorum and called everyone Mr. or Ms. To call her Tass? Something must be wrong.

"What is it?"

"See for yourself, Ms. Stevens. Please."

Tassie sighed. So focused on her closing arguments, but always willing to add a client. Why in the world did she need to go out there?

Tassie smelled him before she saw him. She raised her eyebrows as she looked at Teresa. Teresa ran her hand over her face and returned to her desk.

"Aah, Miss Stevens. Thank you for seeing me."

Tassie wanted to run. This was not the type of client her firm attracted or serviced. The older man ran his fingers down his long gray beard.

Oh, no, his eyes twinkle like Santa Clause in Miracle on 34ᵗʰ Street. She had watched that movie every year with her mom while growing up. It was a

Christmas movie, but her parents always taught her to appreciate the culture she lived in. But the man in the movie didn't wear a plaid shirt and she doubted he smelled.

She glanced over to Teresa's desk, hoping she would intervene. Teresa smiled, winked, and looked down. Then it dawned on Tassie: this was a trick to embarrass the rookie. *Okay, I'll play along.*

"How may I help you, sir?"

"I would like to discuss a case with you. I've met your mother."

Sure you have.

Tassie kept seeing images of her cousin's farm, and she was reminded of the smells of cows, pigs, and sheep. It didn't fit in this high-class office. But this must be her initiation. They would all have a laugh over drinks about what a good sport she was.

"Certainly, please come to my office, and we'll talk." *Okay, Tass, don't sound too cheery. Everyone is looking, big eyes, smiling, some even holding their nose. Well, it was fun at my cousin's farm.*

Tassie opened her office door and held out her arm inviting Santa Claus from the farm into her office. She paused before following him in, smiling at everyone observing her.

Trying not to chuckle, knowing she was passing the initiation test with flying colors, Tassie started around her desk. She hesitated, then grabbed her legal pad from her desk, rolled the pages to an empty sheet, and sat down facing the man on the same side of the desk. *I'll be kinder, be at his level.*

Picking up her pen, she smiled. *Hope I can get the smell out of my office.* "So, you know my parents, Mr. . . . I'm sorry, I didn't get your name."

"Hector, Hector Woodley." He reached out and patted her arm. Tassie fought not to recoil. "Your father is a very kind man."

"That, he is," Tassie agreed. "You know him well?"

Mr. Woodley rubbed his chin. "He may not recall me. Your mother probably would though."

"Oh."

"Your mother and I visited many years ago, but enough of that. Today is your day."

"My day?" Tassie crossed her legs and wrote *Hector Woodley* at the top of the page.

"Yes, you need to pay attention to your mother's interest in the blood moons."

"What?" Tassie leaned back in her chair and looked straight at Hector. "Who are you and why are you here?" Her face heated.

"Tassie, don't get upset."

"Mr. Woodley, you may call me Ms. Stevens. You said you needed to speak to me about a case."

"Yes, yes." He leaned forward. "There is a very strong case for you to play an important part in keeping this nation safe."

Tassie stood up. "Mr. Woodley, I will convey your greeting to my parents. I do believe our conversation is over."

Trying not to march, she strode to the door and opened it. Hector remained sitting. "Have a nice day, Mr. Woodley." She tipped her head toward him.

Nodding, he stood up, ran his hand down his beard again and smiled sweetly. *Santa Claus.* "Don't forget, Tassie." He walked out the door and down the hall.

She stood with her hand on the door knob for a minute, shook her head, and shut the door.

What was that? How did he know my mom was into blood moons? Wait, maybe he's a security breach.

Tassie started to open the door and call for security. *Wait, get a grip, Tass. This is not a company issue.*

She walked around her desk and sat down.

How did he know? Is he a hacker? That doesn't even make sense. I've never writ-ten down the words 'blood moons'. Did my mother put him up to this? Mother drives me nuts at times, but she is too classy to send smelly Santa to my office.

A noise brought Tassie out of her musings. Teresa stood in front of her desk.

"Ms. Stevens, are you okay? I'm so sorry I let him in."

Tassie looked hard at Teresa. "This wasn't a rookie lawyer initiation? A good laugh for everyone?"

"That has never happened here, Ms. Stevens. Did he scare you?"

"No, he just made no sense. Must have wandered in from the street."

"I won't let it happen again. So sorry."

Teresa excused herself, leaving Tassie to her thoughts.

Walking over to the window, Tassie studied the gray sky. *Well, no blood moons tonight.*

A knock came on the door. Tassie turned. The glass window revealed it was the senior partner. She quickly put Hector Woodley out of her mind and opened the door.

"Mr. James, I have my closing arguments almost complete. Would you like to look them over?"

———

Tassie loved being able to take walks along the water on her lunch hour. It happened only a couple times a week as lunch time often involved meeting with a client or discussing cases at a local restaurant with the bosses. When not engaged in work, she would sit on a bench near the fountain at Grant Park and eat her lunch.

She had done this with her dad many times when she was little. Her mother would pack a sandwich lunch and they would walk along the lake and then wait on a bench for her dad to join them on his lunch break. To this day, a sandwich lunch on a bench near the fountain tasted better than any meal she could have in the classiest restaurant in the world.

She had to close her eyes. It was part of the ritual. Her dad would say, "Tassie, close your eyes. Now, if you could go anywhere in the world where would it be?"

At first, she named Hawaii and China and Switzerland, but she finally came to the only answer she would give. "Right here with you, Daddy." He would squeeze her, give a hearty laugh, and then kiss the top of her head. After kissing her mother on the cheek, he would head back to the court room.

Yes, right here with you, Daddy, even if you're eating lunch at home right now with Mother. This is my favorite place, my happy place.

"You look very happy, Tassie. You must like it here."

Tassie startled. There was Santa Claus, Hector Woodley. She stood quickly. "Mr. Woodley, it's a free world, and you have every right to be here, but I do not have to converse with you."

"Tassie, you're right, but I would so appreciate a few minutes of your time. Have you been studying the four blood moons prophecies?"

"No, I have not. My mother loves that. Perhaps you should talk to her."

"Israel is key to what is happening in the world and how world policies and politics will proceed."

"I'm sorry. This doesn't really apply to me."

"Don't you see, Tassie, the Israelis are coming to God."

"That doesn't make sense. The Jews are already known for knowing God."

"True, but now they are finding their Messiah, truly knowing 'God with us'."

"With us? You mean with them."

"Immanuel, the name for Jesus. It means 'God with us'."

Tassie paused. She looked down and scuffed her foot against the concrete. "Well, that would certainly be a big change."

"Yes, Tassie, my point."

The fountain, thirty feet in diameter, sparkled in the sunlight. Dancing streams of water created small rainbows that shimmered in the afternoon sun.

"I don't believe it, though. There's no evidence. I'm a Jew, but that's just my background. It's not who I am. I'm not a Christian, so I don't relate to Jesus. And, I'm dating a Muslim and none of this pertains to him."

"It most certainly pertains to Omar."

Contempt swept through her. *Why am I even talking to this man and how can he know Omar's name?* "How so?"

"You know how to investigate."

Tassie clenched her fists. *This little man . . .* "Of course, I'm a lawyer."

Hector took a step closer to Tassie and lowered his voice. "Then do the background check on Omar."

"You have got to be kidding!" Tassie almost hissed.

"You might be surprised, Tassie."

Tassie shook her head. "I'm surprised I'm standing here talking to you."

"It's a wise choice on your part." Hector reached out and patted her hand.

Tassie quickly crossed her arms. "Whatever."

Suddenly, Tassie felt chilled. She hadn't noticed the breeze that picked up until now. She kept her arms wrapped around herself and resisted looking at this strange little man in front of her. Memories of her fifth-grade substitute teacher reminding her to quit acting superior to the other students floated into her mind. That had been a tough year. She loved her teacher but when she took maternity leave, the class had Mr. Woodson.

Geez, it was Harry Woodson, and now it's Hector Woodley.

Her teacher, Mrs. Cousins had understood her, recognizing her high intelligence, guiding her into challenging projects and reading material. And, when Tassie got out of line, as she often did, Mrs. C. could just give her that look. How did she do it? That look told Tassie she understood but had to bring it down at the same time. Mr. Woodson would stand in front of her and say Tassie's name. She knew it meant 'settle down' but she resented it. If Mrs. Cousins hadn't come back when she did, Tassie doubted she would be a successful lawyer today.

Why am I going there? She glanced back to Hector. He actually resembled Mr. Woodson. "Are you . . . ?"

A small smile creased his face and his eyes twinkled.

Santa Claus. Mr. Woodson had made her think of Santa Claus, too, except when he was getting after her attitude.

"Tassie." He turned his head slightly. "Don't slip into superiority."

Tassie shook her head and groaned. *He's back.*

She lifted her chin and closed her eyes. Taking a deep breath, she met his eyes again. "Okay, what do I need to do?"

"Investigate Omar, do a background check."

"Why?"

"You need to see his connections back in Syria."

The breeze grew stronger and she wrapped her arms more tightly around herself. "He already told me he has family in Syria. What of it? People are related to people all over the world."

Hector shifted his feet, ran his hand over his beard. Mr. Woodson was looking at her again, giving her an assignment she felt was beneath her.

"Be careful, Tassie. He has powerful connections influencing oil in the Middle East."

She gave a rueful laugh. "What Middle Eastern Arab doesn't have strong connections to oil?"

"Follow the oil, Tassie. There are bigger, more subversive things going on than anyone here knows about."

"Oh, please. Some subversive plot? Why am I even talking to you? I need to go."

"Be the investigator you are."

Tassie spent the whole walk back to her office trying to put her conversation with Hector Woodley and her memories of that teacher, Harry Woodson, out of her mind. It was difficult.

Back in her office, Tassie dove into her current case, trying to put the disturbing encounter with the scraggly old man out of her thoughts. Her case involved a Jewish man, seeking mediation in a potentially ugly custody battle. Her job on this one was background investigation. It was what she did well.

Mr. Goldman arrived shortly after she returned from lunch and lost no time in describing his situation. His wife had moved to the States from Israel. Her grandfather was part of an oil company drilling for oil in Israel. The man had spent all of his own money as well as money he'd been able to get from the Israeli government. Apparently, he had at least one friend in high places. He also had Christian financiers in the States. They thought oil in Israel fulfilled some Biblical prophecy.

As Tassie listened to Mr. Goldman, she felt like Hector was also sitting in the room. She glanced around expecting to see him. *Crazy.*

Mr. Goldman continued, "My wife's grandfather was about to close down the company. It would have created a lot of debt for all those involved financially: the Christian groups, the Israeli government, and my wife's family. We were embarrassed, and Sally didn't even want anyone to know who her grandfather was."

"Okay." Tassie waited. *That's it. They went bankrupt and now Mr. Goldman doesn't want to carry any of the debt.*

Goldman sighed. "But he hit oil. It wasn't a big strike, but everyone thought they could at least break even."

Tassie shifted in her seat. *We Jews are storytellers. I just want the facts. This is like listening to my mother.*

She took a sip of her coffee and then smiled at Mr. Goldman. *Don't offend the client. Polite, gracious, listen.* She put her pen to the notebook and looked up.

Mr. Goldman droned on. "Well, within two months a well already drilled, one that had not produced before, began to produce. It provided enough revenue to drill one last place. The family wanted him to stop. They would break even. Don't risk more. But her grandfather was not that type. He'd been high military. He was a calculator, a risk taker."

And probably not a storyteller. Please, Mr. Goldman. Tassie kept her face down as she took notes. She would reveal her weariness with the story if she looked up. She silently willed him to finish the thing, so she could get to the custody issue.

Mr. Goldman spread his hands. "Her grandfather said he had a dream. A dream." He shook his head. "Can you believe it? Everybody's livelihoods on a dream! What, you ask, was he thinking? I ask that question myself. I don't know the answer. And what was the dream? That I can tell you. He saw the location of a new well. It was where some old Israeli map showed Asher dipping his toe."

"What? Who? Asher?"

"Jewish prophecy. Moses telling the children of Israel about their futures. It was the tradition of the patriarchs before they died, and it's recorded in the Torah."

Tassie nodded but did not reveal her own Jewish roots. *Not necessary. Don't get involved.*

"So, what is that story? I tell you, that's a story in itself." Mr. Goldman wiped his forehead with his hand. "Anyway, he felt he had to drill this one last well. He had drilled in this area before. Did he know the map from the Torah? Yes? Yes, of course yes, but this was more specific. They did their soil samples and it looked good, but what they got was almost a gusher. Somehow, they kept it out of the press for a while, or else nobody thought much of it. All the surrounding nations had the oil advantage. Israel was a small gamer in oil. No one really expected much."

Tassie remembered hearing reports of Israel's oil, but it sounded laughable. The consensus was that Israel couldn't be an oil power. Not when the little country was surrounded by such giants in the oil business.

"Israel's government became more involved, as did the Christian financiers, yet they somehow managed to keep it under the radar. We didn't even hear about it. But then my wife's aunt began letting Sally know that this was growing far beyond expectations. More oil wells, more drilling, more profit."

Mr. Goldman took a breath. "Because they want to keep this undercover, they want only trusted family members in the business. So, Sally's aunt offered her a position in the company."

"Not you, though, Mr. Goldman?"

"Oh, yes, me too. You think I don't belong to the family? Of course I belong, but the job is in Israel. Me, live in Israel? What are they thinking? It's dangerous there, no? And I like it here. I like my job here."

"So, bottom line, your wife wants to move to Israel and take your daughter, and you want to stay here?"

"Yes, of course, yes. My daughter, Josie, what a joy she is to me. She is happy here, and she doesn't want her mom to leave. Do I want her mom to leave? No, of course not."

"Leave, as in go to Israel, or leave, as in divorce?"

"Well, go to Israel. My wife isn't thinking divorce, but my wife has made up her mind to go and insists on taking Josie, the joy of my heart."

Tassie picked up her cup of coffee. She shook her foot as she often did when her legs were crossed. *Don't get involved, Tassie. Just gather the facts.*

"You know, mothers are usually granted custody."

"Yes, yes, I know, but I can't let Josie leave the country."

"When did Sally move here from Israel?"

Mr. Goldman sighed. "When we got married. We met when I traveled to Israel on business. I'm in marketing for a fine arts and relics gallery."

Probably knows my mother. I might need to recuse myself.

"So, you couldn't transfer to Israel?"

"You know, yes. Yes, of course. I'm Jewish in case you haven't noticed." He chuckled, then groaned. "But, just because I'm Jewish doesn't mean I love Israel, may I not be struck with lightning."

Tassie smiled. *I get it.*

"I love my wife. She loves me, of course, but I think she loves Israel more than me." He looked down and clasped his hands together.

"Well, often in custody cases, the custodial parent can't leave the state, at least for a while."

"She never became a U.S. citizen. She's still an Israeli, and because of that, so is Josie."

"I see. The senior partners will strategize with you on all the ramifications. I'm here mainly to lay out the background. You've been very thorough, Mr. Goldman. Is there anything else we should know?"

He wrung his hands and then rubbed his chin as he looked over at the window. "Yes, yes, perhaps. This is a bit odd, but because my company deals in relics this caught my attention. Problem is, Sally doesn't know I know this. Is this trouble, yes? Yes, I think it is." Mr. Goldman wiped his forehead again with his hand. "I picked up her phone the other day by mistake and swiped it open. Her emails came up and it was open to her aunt's latest email. Sally's grandfather, her aunt's father, had revealed more about finding the location." He stopped and studied the room and the surface of the desk. "You are recording this, no?"

"No, Mr. Goldman, no recorders, just taking notes."

"Of course. Of course."

"Would you like me to record this."

"Oh, God forbid. Forgive me, no recording."

"All right, no recording."

"They were out surveying and did a little digging. They unearthed a glass bottle sealed with wax and fully intact. Inside was a tassel, probably from a prayer shawl."

Tassie coughed. The blood drained from her face and light-headedness took over. *I'm going to pass out.*

She reached for her cup but had no strength. *The story of the tassel is true? How can that be?* She tried to stand but was too woozy.

"Are you okay?" Mr. Goldman jumped up to steady her.

Tassie sat back down. "I'm okay, okay. Forgot to eat breakfast today." It was a lie. "Continue, continue."

"You're sure? Can I get you something, yes?"

Tassie shook her head and signaled for him to go on. "The relic." Her voice was a whisper.

"Well, apparently, this bottle with the tassel came on the boat with Christopher Columbus."

Tassie looked up. Mr. Goldman's hands were shaking.

"I know. I know. It's like an urban legend, but it's an Israeli legend. Somehow it represents God's provision in tough times, so Sally's aunt and grandfather think this is a sign of God's plan for them and for Israel. I'm sure that's why Sally wants to return. She thinks it's the safest place to be. But do I think that? No, of course not, no. I think she's crazy. However, what do I know of relics? They bring in a handsome price, yes? Of course yes." His eyes lit up. "A very handsome price, indeed." He shook his head. "But, I am not supposed to know about it. I mean, Sally hasn't told me this. I can't tell my company. I would like to, yes. Even if she told me, she would think I was only interested in making money. Big money." He sighed.

"I'm obviously not a therapist, Mr. Goldman, but have you considered going to Israel with her for at least a while to see if it would work, and then . . . ?" Tassie left it open.

"And then . . . I could find out more about the bottle, yes. And then . . . "

"You love your wife and daughter?"

"Yes, of course yes. I can't bear the thought of losing Josie, and I really do love Sally."

"It's an option."

Mr. Goldman drummed his fingers on the arm of the chair and stared out the window.

"So, you think the relic is bigger news or bigger profit than the oil?"

Mr. Goldman didn't answer right away. Tassie actually looked around the room, half expecting to see Hector sitting in the corner.

"Of course it would be bigger for my company. I think the oil is bigger for Israel, but there is significance about the relic that's connected to the oil. Like it promises Israel great provision and protection. Sally's uncle, husband to the aunt, is a rabbi, and so he's studied this. And then there's something about . . . " He caught himself. "Well, I think you've gotten the background, yes. I want to keep my daughter here. She was born here. She's happy. My wife is an Israeli citizen and actually can go if she wants, but I should get a portion of the oil proceeds."

"Yes, yes, the financial end. So, you would want alimony support from your wife. She'll be making more than you?"

"Okay, that's the rub. She technically will take an official amount less than what I make, but she'll be a part of this great windfall."

"I think that can be proven, don't you?"

"Yes, of course, yes, and my daughter deserves it, even if I don't."

"You make a handsome salary, no doubt."

"I do, but she'll make a lot more."

"In another country."

"I don't know the laws."

"Nor do I, at the moment, Mr. Goldman, but that is what this firm does, and we are good at it."

"But, see, the relic plays into this. Sally doesn't know I saw the email."

"Do you think it matters?"

Mr. Goldman sat up straight. "Oh, I do. I don't follow or depend on prophecy, but I do know the stock people put into that and into relics. It's part and parcel of relics and archaeology. It influences and becomes almost self-fulfilling because the people buy into it and work harder to make it happen. Because of my business, Sally may not want me to know."

"But it would be a way for her to get you to move to Israel, wouldn't it?" Tassie wondered if she could ask these questions when she was simply the background investigator. *I'm getting involved. Not good. But I have understanding because I'm Jewish. Probably why they put me on this.*

"Yes, but she'd know I'd have an ulterior motive . . . that I wasn't going because I love and understand her."

"Do you think she has an ulterior motive?"

"Uh, what? I . . . " Mr. Goldman shrugged. His brow furrowed. "I don't know. What possible—"

"Somebody else in Grandfather's company?"

"Sally, unfaithful? I don't think so. I mean . . . " Mr. Goldman blew air out of his mouth causing the hair on his forehead to flutter. He squeezed his eyes shut. "Have I ever considered that, no? Of course not, no." He was visibly shaken. "It doesn't compute."

"Well, it does seem there is some family tradition or secret that has a strong pull on her. Did they want her to move away with you?"

"They gave her their blessing and she seemed happy to go with me. I just don't get it. Can you help me?"

"The firm can. And will. Not me personally. I'm the background investigator."

"So now what?"

Tassie covered the official filing procedure and set up an appointment for Mr. Goldman with one of the senior partners. She shook hands with the man and turned back to her desk as he opened the door to leave.

"Ummm."

Tassie looked up.

Mr. Goldman closed the door. "Do you think I should tell her I saw the email?"

"I can't tell you that. It was inadvertent, and it seems to have a lot of weight on the case. It would probably come out in court."

"You would tell her?" His eyes were big, and Tassie saw moisture forming over his eyebrows.

"Your attorney would not tell her, but court has a way of exposing all the secrets. You should know that."

"Oh my. Thank you."

Tassie felt sorry for him as she watched him walk slowly down the hall. *Tough position.* She went over her notes, filling in some details, his body language, and a few of her conclusions.

What a dilemma for me. If he only knew. If the firm only knew. If my mother knew. Tassie propped her elbows on the desk and cradled her chin with her hands.

My mother told me about the bottle. And I couldn't care less. I hated that she named me after the thing. And now it's been found. I wonder what the exact date of discovery was. I should have asked.

CHAPTER 4

The first blood moon Lydia and her father saw occurred in 1493 on Passover. Several months later, in the fall, as they established temple worship, places to live, community, and the desire to continue traveling north, they beheld a blood moon on the first of Sukkoth. It was the beginning of the Feast of Tabernacles, when the Jews remembered their time of wandering in the wilderness.

The small congregation laughed that they did not need to set up little tabernacles to remember the time in the wilderness as they were now in the wilderness living in very humble homes. They sensed, though, that the time would come when they would prosper and multiply and continue to see God's hand do wonderful things for them.

When another blood moon occurred on Passover, 1494, they watched in awe. Rabbi again taught God's forgiveness of the world as Lydia perceived it the year previous.

A few weeks after Passover, Mr. Goldman sat down with Rabbi Liebermann. "Reuben, I think the tassel needs to be preserved. It has held up so well, but it won't last forever, and we have nothing else from our synagogue to keep and remember. I feel we must remember this way that God has provided."

"I believe you are right, my friend. The tassel should be protected. But it is not the only thing we brought." He reached down and removed his shoe. Tucked into the toe he pulled out three gold rings.

"Rabbi, how in the world? I am amazed. If they had thought you had anything, they would have cut you open. How did you do it?"

"It has been in my shoe forever. I do not know how they missed it, and yes, it was perhaps foolish not to turn it over." Rabbi Liebermann rolled the two rings between his thumb and fingers. "But I felt this strong urgency . . . I trust it was from God . . . to keep these and to simply place them in my shoe."

"Well, we serve the same God." Goldman grinned and his whole face lit up. He reached down and pulled the tiniest of bags from his shoe. Opening it up, he poured several small diamonds into the palm of his hand.

Rabbi clapped him on the back. Soon both were laughing so hard that tears rolled down their cheeks. Esther, Lydia, and Gabe came into the small room.

"Papa, why are you laughing so?" Lydia climbed up into her father's lap.

Rabbi and Goldman showed their families the treasures that had made the journey.

"Father, what shall we do with these?" Gabe picked up one of the rings and felt the smoothness of the gold.

"We need to preserve them with the tassel. What can we use?"

Gabe reached into his pocket. "I just found this bottle on the beach."

The rabbi examined the bottle. It was a square bottle though the corners were slightly rounded. The glass was fairly thick, and the bottle stood about seven inches tall. The neck was a little over an inch in diameter and an inch in length.

Mr. Goldman reached over to take the bottle from the rabbi. "I think this is perfect. We can make it sterile by placing it briefly in the flame of the fire. We can use wax from our candles to seal it securely. I do believe this was a medicine bottle of some sort."

Rabbi Liebermann chuckled. "The tassel will be our medicine. There is a proverb that the Word of God is health to our body, so when we look at the tassel, we will remember and speak His Word and we shall be made well."

"Rabbi, I remember a story that I had almost forgotten, passed down through my family, about Yeshua, the prophet that many thought was the Messiah." Mr. Goldman turned to face the little group. "He died a gruesome death. But one day it is told that as He traveled down a road with His followers, a woman very sick with a bleeding condition followed Him."

Anna put her hands up to her face. "Oh my, wasn't that forbidden? She would be unclean."

"Yes, that is so." Mr. Goldman extended his hands. "Apparently, she had spent all her money on physicians and was none the better. She heard about the Prophet Healer and went out to find him. She said to herself, 'I must just touch His tzitzit, the tassel of His prayer shawl, and I will be well.' And she did just that."

"What happened?" Lydia sat with her elbows on her knees and her chin resting in her hands.

"She was healed of her condition. And Yeshua turned and said, 'Woman your faith has made you whole.' Isn't that amazing? The tassel. He did not even see her coming."

Rabbi said nothing for a few seconds. He gazed off to the side. "It truly is amazing, my friend. God told us in the Torah that He would bless our bread and our water and take sickness away from us. This woman must have known that and knew the tassel was a symbol of all the law and promises of Almighty God, blessed be He. Thank you, Joseph, for sharing that story. Once we have the tassel sealed, let us pray that God's blessing of wholeness will always follow it."

Lydia laid her head against her father. "I wish Mama had touched the tassel when she was sick."

Rabbi Liebermann placed both arms around his daughter. "Oh, Lydi, so do I. Perhaps we did not trust enough at the time. We were all so shaken. Your mother was not only sick and injured, but was so fearful of the ocean, the voyage, of leaving her home. She wanted to be strong for us, but she knew you, Lydi, and I would be strong and brave. So, she went to Abraham's bosom, and we will see her again someday."

"I know, Papa. I just so miss her some days."

Mrs. Goldman came over and took Lydia's hand. "I miss your mama, too, and I will do everything I can to provide you the comfort and guidance that a young woman needs from her mother. I cannot take her place, but I already love you as if you were my own."

Lydia hugged Mrs. Goldman. "I know, Auntie Anna, I know."

The men sterilized the bottle by holding it in a fire flame on the end of a fire poker. They allowed it to sit and cool and then took a white cloth to wipe out any blackening that formed on the glass. At the same time, they took the finest candles Colombo had given them from their ship and melted them.

Joseph Goldman suggested they put a layer of wax in the bottom and then place the diamonds into the wax and place another layer of wax over it. Esther Goldman suggested they add the memorial coin to the bottle as well. It was placed under the diamonds with another layer of wax. Then they looped the end of the tassel through the three rings and covered the rings with wax as well. Laying the bottle on its side they inserted the tassel into the bottle and filled the neck with wax, so the rings were completely invisible. The wax then was used to completely cover the outside of the neck so that no air could enter or escape the bottle. Each of these steps was done over a few days to make sure that every part was secure.

The Goldmans and the Liebermanns agreed that they would never reveal the presence of the diamonds, the coin, or the gold rings. It should only be revealed in a time of extraordinary need or at God's command. Each person, adults and children, pledged this to the others.

Then they held hands and prayed that God's blessing of wholeness and safety would dwell with the tassel bottle as it would with the holy temple of God.

The Liebermanns and the Goldmans traveled together and set up synagogue and temple worship along the islands for those who desired to know the God Jehovah. Many from the original journey with Colombo journeyed with them. They lived in humility and kindness, believing that God had ordained their travel in this new land. They learned from the natives to garden and hunt and told the story of the Tassel of the Tallith, the Jewish prayer shawl. The five knots of the tassel they equated with the five books of the Torah.

"Five in Hebrew, the language of God, blessed be He, gives the meaning of grace. Such grace that we can know the Torah, that we can belong to the God of the universe, that we have His commandments and can know them, that we can obey His commandments." Rabbi Liebermann smiled at his little congregation.

"The Hebrew word for tassel is tzitzit. All letters in Hebrew have a numerical value and the letters in Hebrew for tzitzit add up to 600. There are eight strands here with five knots. 600 plus eight plus five equals 613, which is the number of the commandments that God has given us. So, this tassel, this tzitzit, which was attached to my prayer shawl, my tallith, is a reminder to know, honor, and obey the commandments which the great God, blessed be He, gave us for our good."

Lydia stood up and walked over to her father. She gazed up at him with big eyes. "Papa, how can we know all of them and obey them here if we don't have the Torah scrolls?"

"Our God, blessed be He, knows our plight. He has given us the tassel as a reminder. Many of us have God's Word written in our hearts and minds. We will pass on what we know and pray that one day we will again have the Torah for our eyes."

Lydia returned to her seat satisfied.

"The prayer shawl, the tallith, which we no longer have, also represents God's amazing and infinite light, greater even than the light of day from the sun which our God, blessed be He, hung in the sky . . . for us." The rabbi bowed his head and shook it slightly. "Oh, the things He has done for us." He looked back to his attendant group. "The fringe of the tallith, the tassel, points as well to that divine light that permeates every single portion of creation."

Gabe raised his hand. "Rabbi, so our tassel tells us of God's commandments, 613 of them, and is a reminder of all that God has given us and a reminder to obey His commandments?"

"That is so, Gabe."

"And it also tells us that God's light is in every part of creation?"

Rabbi Liebermann walked over and patted Gabe on his head. "You have learned well, today, young man. You will make a fine rabbi someday."

Rabbi Liebermann turned to those gathered. "Let us now recite the shema, the call to hear."

The small congregation of believers stood. Rabbi began and each one joined in as much as they had memorized the prayer. "Hear, O Israel, the Lord is our God, the Lord is One. Blessed be the Name of His glorious kingdom for ever and ever. And you shall love the Lord your God with all your heart and with all your soul and with all your might. And these words that I command you today shall be in your heart. And you shall teach them diligently to your children, and you shall speak of them when you sit at home, and when you walk along the way, and when you lie down and when you rise up.

"And you shall bind them as a sign on your hand, and they shall be for frontlets between your eyes. And you shall write them on the doorposts of your house and on your gates. And it shall come to pass if you surely listen to the commandments that I command you today to love the Lord your God and to serve Him with all your heart and all your soul, that I will give rain to your land, the early and the late rains that you may gather in your grain, your wine and your oil. And I will give grass in your fields for your cattle and you will eat and you will be satisfied. Beware, lest your heart be deceived and you turn and serve other gods and worship them. And the anger of the Lord will blaze against you, and He will close the heavens and there will not be rain, and the earth will not give you its fullness, and you will perish quickly from the good land that the Lord gives you.

"So, you shall put these, my words, on your heart and on your soul; and you shall bind them for signs on your hands, and they shall be for frontlets between your eyes. And you shall teach them to your children, and you shall speak of them when you sit at home, and when you walk along the way, and when you lie down and when you rise up. And you shall write them on the doorposts of your house and on your gates, in order to prolong your days and the days of your children on the land that the Lord promised your fathers that He would give them, as long as the days that the heavens are over the earth.

"And the Lord spoke to Moses, saying: Speak to the children of Israel and say to them they should make themselves tzitzit on the corners of their clothing throughout their generations, and give the tzitzit of each corner a thread of blue. And they shall be tzitzit for you, and when you look at them you will remember all of the Lord's commandments and do them and not follow after your heart and after your eyes which lead you astray in order to remember and do all My commandments, and be holy for your God. I am the Lord, your God who leads you from the land of Egypt to be a God to you. I am the Lord, your God."

CHAPTER 5

The day of Mr. Goldman's visit with the senior partners had come and gone. Tassie looked forward to hearing what had transpired in the morning meeting. As she gathered her files and notebooks for the meeting, she turned back to grab her coffee cup. She was ready. Before she could turn back to the door of the office, there was a knock.

Odd, Teresa knows I have a meeting in ten minutes. "Yes, come in."

Mr. James walked in and he didn't look happy. Tassie raised her eyebrows. "Good morning Mr. James. I was just heading down to the conference room for our meeting. Can I get you something?" Tassie tried to sound cheerful but her voice had a nervous quality to it.

"We need to talk a few minutes, first. Take a seat Tassie."

She set her items on the desk and sat down quickly on the client's side of the desk. Mr. James sat next to her in the other chair.

"Yesterday was Mr. Goldman's appointment."

Tassie breathed. "Yes, I was wondering how that is proceeding."

"It isn't." Mr. James' voice was flat.

"Pardon? What do you mean?"

"You didn't know he wouldn't follow through?"

"He isn't following through?" Tassie widened her eyes and her hands felt sweaty.

"He called ten minutes before his appointment and said he'd changed his mind, that he was moving to Israel, and would not be pursuing the case."

"He's going to go?" *Of course he's going to go.* Tassie wanted to smile, thinking like Mr. Goldman talked, but this was not the time to smile with Mr. James staring her down.

"Did you advise him to go, Ms. Stevens?"

Blood drained from her face. He called her Ms. Stevens, not Tassie. "I presented a few options as he asked questions while he gave me his background. His wife . . . "

"Yes, I know the case. Your background notes were very thorough. I just want to know if you inserted your own speculation into his situation to persuade him to move in a certain direction. These cases bring in a lot of revenue, Tassie. Yes, it is unfortunate from one point of view that we profit over someone else's troubles, but we provide a service at their request. Did he request it? Did you advise against it?"

"Sir, he asked at the end if we could help him. I very specifically told him I could not, but our firm most certainly could, that you or Mr. Connors would find out everything necessary to assist him in his particular situation."

"You did not advise him to move to Israel and drop the whole thing?"

"I discussed moving to Israel as an option, temporarily to find out if it would work. He was rather distraught at the thought of losing his daughter."

"This would have been a good case, an interesting case, and a case we believe we could win."

"Yes, sir." Tassie had no idea what else to say.

Mr. James sat for a few moments. Tassie didn't breathe.

"Ms. Stevens. Tassie. You will learn. You're still new. And we are pleased with your work so far." Tassie breathed. "When you do background, you do not interject your own opinion. You do not get involved, other than to promise our unmitigated assistance to take up their cause and win. Are we clear?"

"Crystal." It came out before Tassie could stop it. "I mean, yes sir, we are clear. I will be totally objective."

Mr. James had a slight smile on his face. "Haven't heard 'crystal' in a long time. I believe we have a briefing meeting to get to. Let's go, Tassie."

———————

"How was your day?" Omar smiled at Tassie.

She slumped into the chair and pretended she was going to slide out.

"That bad, huh?" Omar chuckled. "Well, you look lovely, and you don't have any pressure on you now."

"I do appreciate that." Tassie took his hand and straightened in the chair. "How was your day?"

He picked up the glass of wine that Tassie had waiting for him and swirled it gently. "Always fantastic." He smiled. "Actually, financial law is a great field. Opened two new accounts today. You?"

"Well, we actually lost one. It's good in the long run. But the firm wanted to make sure I wasn't the cause."

Omar glanced up from the menu and scanned her eyes. "Ouch. Tell me about it."

Tassie shook her head. "You know, attorney-client privilege."

"Don't give me the details or names, just the general gist of the thing." He placed his hand on his heart. "I promise to never breathe a word of it."

Tassie smiled. "It was a custody battle, an international one."

"Hmmm, sounds big."

The waiter arrived, and they ordered. Omar chose the lobster Alfredo while Tassie had the beef bourguignon.

"So, an international custody case. Sounds juicy." Omar put his fingers to his lips then opened his hand and made a puckering sound.

Tassie laughed. "Yes, but it seems they chose to stay together. She wanted to return to Israel where her family has possibly hit it big in oil."

Omar's eyebrows went up. "Oil? Israel? Isn't that an oxymoron?"

"Most would agree, but the husband was quite convinced." Tassie looked down, then turned her head as she looked back at Omar. "Remember, this conversation never took place. You can't use it in your financing." She felt Hector needling the back of her mind about Omar and the oil business.

Omar guffawed and then took another sip of wine. "Oh, never fear. I would never recommend that even if I thought it was a great idea. So, that's it, case closed?"

"Well, his business was archaeology and relics, like my mother, and these people had also discovered some relic."

"Really, I always thought it kind of odd that people get so into that. I mean, history is interesting, but you have to live in the here and now. But go on. Was it like those urns with the Dead Sea scrolls in them? That was a big find."

"No, it was a bottle . . . one they thought came from Spain to America with Christopher Columbus."

The food arrived. The aromas so tantalized Tassie's nose that she just sat and enjoyed the savory scents for a minute.

"Are you praying?" Omar winked.

"Oh, it's just a family thing. We had to appreciate everything so whenever the meal is served we have to pause and inhale. I guess it's a part of me now."

"Okay, now I'm intrigued. A bottle from Spain to America found in Israel. Sounds far-fetched."

"My mother has studied this a bit." Tassie looked up. "It's her field." She took another bite. "This is so good."

Omar smiled. His eyes were warm. "So tough on the outside, so sweet on the inside. I may just keep you."

Tassie almost choked as she laughed heartily.

"But if you self-destruct, I'm sending you back." Omar reached across the table and squeezed Tassie's hand. "So, your mom has studied this bottle?"

"Yes, we are actually descendants of Christopher Columbus."

Omar paused and let go of her hand. As Tassie looked up, she detected a flicker of . . . what? Disdain? But, almost as instantaneously as it appeared it was gone. He stabbed a piece of lobster with his fork.

"So, you're Jewish?" He put the lobster in his mouth and waited.

"Well yes . . . but how did . . . I mean why would . . . I mean what differ-ence does it . . . " She put her fork down. "Is that a problem, and how did you deduce that?"

"It's not a problem. I knew Columbus was part Jewish, so if you're a descen-dant that seems a likely conclusion. It is not a problem. I'm totally contemporary."

Tassie detected a bit of humor in his voice, but something felt unsettling. "You knew Columbus was a Jew? Not that many know that."

"It was in a class I took or . . . " Omar looked upward, his eye going back and forth for a moment. "Perhaps it was on the news." He shrugged. "Don't quite remember, just thought it interesting. How did you know? Wait, is it common knowledge in the Jewish community?"

"Jewish community?" Tassie raised her eyebrows. *Stereotypes. Ugh.* "Actually, I don't think most people, Jews included, realize it. But, as you know, this is my mother's area, history and archaeology."

"Well, all that is very interesting." Omar reached across the table and gently took Tassie's hand in his again. "But on another note, how would you like to go up north to Door County for a weekend." Omar searched her eyes. "Together, of course. Some friends I work with said it's a place well worth seeing."

Tassie swallowed. "I love Door County. My family has gone there many times. You say a weekend? The two of us?"

"Is it too soon?" Omar smiled and took Tassie's other hand in his. His green eyes sparkled. "I think we could both use a break from work. I'd like to get to know you better."

Tassie shook her head, then nodded. Laughing, she said, "I like the sound of that. I think I'm free weekend after next."

Omar let go of her hand and took a sip of wine, all the while holding her eyes with his. "Then it's settled."

Tassie let go of her concerns as they talked about Door County until a voice interrupted.

"Why, Tassie, hello. We didn't see you here." Her dad stood next to their table. "Marge just went to the ladies' room and we're about to leave. What a wonderful dinner we had."

"Daddy." Tassie stood and gave her dad a hug. Over his shoulder she saw her mother walking their way. "Daddy, this is Omar. I've mentioned him to you. Omar, this is my father, Judge Stevens and this is my mother, Marge. Hi, Mother." Tassie reached out and took her mother's hand. "We are just finishing dinner."

Omar rose to his feet and shook her dad's hand, and then took her mother's hand and lightly kissed it. "So very nice to meet you. Won't you join us, perhaps for dessert."

"That would be wonderful." Mother smiled and tilted her head toward Tassie raising her eyebrows.

Her dad shrugged. "Certainly, but you may want the evening to yourselves."

"Nonsense." Omar held out the chair for Tassie's mom.

"Such chivalry. Thank you, Omar."

Tassie's dad sat down as the waiter arrived, as if on cue, with a dessert tray. "Well, that was well timed." He chuckled and selected a carrot cake.

"Mother, shall we share a carrot cake?"

"Love to, that's plenty."

Omar laughed. "Looks like it's carrot cake all around. It's always been my favorite." He gestured to the waiter. "And do put it all on my tab."

Her dad started to protest, but Omar waved him off. "I'm delighted to treat the parents of this amazing lawyer. You have obviously raised her well."

Tassie laughed. "Oh, my goodness, Omar. I'm starting to blush."

"Well, we do agree that she is amazing." Her dad patted her hand.

"Mrs. Stevens, I understand you are quite the expert on archaeology and relics."

Marge nodded as the waiter returned with the cake. "It's always been my love and my field of choice."

"And you are a descendant of Cristobal Colombo."

Each one of the Stevens family coughed, covering their mouths. Tassie froze and then closed her eyes. *No, Omar, don't get her going.*

"I'm impressed you know the Spanish name of Christopher Columbus and that Tassie has discussed our connection with him. Are you a student of the bl—"

"Mother, we haven't discussed your studies, just a little family background."

"Did you enjoy history growing up?" Marge winked at Tassie.

"Well, I enjoyed studying every subject. My family really promoted getting a good education to get a good job. But, back to Columbus, not many realize Columbus was Jewish." Omar smiled. "One of those little-known facts."

There was a moment of silence. Tassie glanced from mother to father. "Daddy, Omar is a financial lawyer with Crowder and Langdon. You probably tried some of their cases in the past, didn't you?"

"Oh yes, a fine company. Lamar Janbry was with them for many years. Is he still practicing law?"

The conversation continued a few minutes between Omar and her dad. Tassie warned her mother with her eyes to go no further.

Her mother nodded and when the conversation lulled, she took her husband's hand. "We really should go. Let's let these two have the rest of their evening without us."

Her dad stood up and shook Omar's hand. "So nice to meet you. Stop over anytime with Tassie and thank you for the treat of dessert." He bent over and gave Tassie a kiss on her head. "See you later, Sweetie."

As they walked off, Omar took Tassie's hand. "Nice parents. Glad I met them."

———————

"Mother, I love you and of course, I would like you to approve. But it is my life and my choice."

"Tassie, dear, there is something that just troubles me. He seems to adore you on the one hand, but on the other, there's something in his eyes . . . disdain? I don't know. Oh, do be careful, darling."

"Mother!" Tassie rolled her eyes. "Daddy, you like him, don't you?"

"He's very savvy, and, yes, he seems like a good man."

"Seems? Daddy, what are you saying?"

He looked at Tassie and allowed his shoulders to slump. "Oh, it's the elephant in the room, Tassie. We're Jewish and he's . . . "

"Not. He's not Jewish. So what? We are beyond that. Daddy, I can't believe you . . . "

"Tassie, he's Muslim. Many Muslims despise Jews." Her dad closed his eyes and looked down.

"And many Jews despise Muslims." Heat rose in Tassie's face and her voice became louder. "I am not one of them, and I cannot believe my parents, who raised me to respect every person, no matter their place in life, their color, their religion, are talking to me like this." Tassie placed her hands on her hips and shook her head.

"Whoa, whoa." Her dad reached out and grabbed her hand. He pulled her to his lap, but she sat stiffly and refused to look in his eyes. "Tassie, we have no problem with Muslims."

"Although, my research . . . "

"Not now, Marge." He and Tassie both turned toward her. Her mother said no more.

"We have no problem, even if you marry a Muslim." He cast a warning glance toward Marge. "However," he waited and took a deep breath, "we just wonder if perhaps he has something against us because we are Jews."

"Just be careful, Tassie. We don't want you to be hurt."

Tassie put her face in her hands. "Oh, Mother."

Her dad patted her back. "Do be careful, Tassie. He's handsome and smooth. That doesn't mean he's up to no good. You're a good discerner, Sweetheart. Don't drop your guard too much."

CHAPTER 6

NEAR ISRAEL, 1948

"I am so thrilled." Sophie's hair blew away from her face.

Samuel gazed at her in the predawn light. "I will be thrilled if your father consents to our marriage."

Sophie gave him her sweetest smile. "Me too, and now, Samuel, we get to return the tassel! Eretz-Israel, the land of Israel, will have the blessing, the protection. Oh, I can hardly contain myself."

"Look, is that it?" Samuel squinted his eyes and pointed to land barely coming into view off the starboard bow. "Are we really almost there? Praise God, I believe the British will allow us in. It's taken so long, but now we're here. It'll be full daylight in an hour. This will be a day to remember."

Sophie stood as close to Samuel as she dared. Her father was so protective and she, of course, thanked God he was. But more than anything she wanted to wed Samuel Orbin and she wanted their marriage to be in Eretz-Israel, the land of promise, according to all the Jewish traditions.

Coming here posed many dangers. The war had ended, but the British still made it difficult for Jewish people to return to their homeland. So many from concentration camps and those ousted by their countries had nowhere else to go.

Sophie looked around. Few stood at the bow of the ship. Most huddled out of the wind and wrapped threadbare coats and blankets around themselves. Sophie still detected little hope in their sunken eyes and frail bodies. Even when she smiled, most looked away not sure if they could trust anyone to be kind. The children flocked around her, though. Hardly anyone had energy to enjoy or play with the children. Sophie and Samuel spent much of each day holding hands and playing games with the little ones.

Sophie told them the story of Christopher Columbus, the man who provided safe passage for so many Jews across a much bigger sea than the Mediterranean. The Jews had been made to suffer and leave a land called Spain and one of those had been her grandfather many generations before. He was a rabbi and preserved a tassel from his prayer shawl.

"Actually . . ." Sophie would pause and touch the little girls on the nose, before continuing. "It was a little girl named Lydia who kept the tassel when everything else they had was stolen. And God took care of them, and wherever that tassel was, they were safe."

One of the older girls looked at Sophie. "We know of people that got almost to Eretz-Israel and they wouldn't let them in. Do you think we'll get in, that we'll be safe like Lydia?"

Sophie would then pull out the bottle. "This is the tassel that belonged to Rabbi Liebermann 450 years ago. It's preserved in this bottle and God has blessed it. They always arrived safely with this tassel. It has been in our family all this time, and now we are taking it to Eretz-Israel. We will get there, sweethearts, because it is with us, because God Almighty has blessed it and He is with us. I'm sure we'll arrive safely."

Each child would come to Sophie and touch the bottle and gaze at the tassel. They went back to their parents or whoever was caring for them and told them the story of the bottle. Many had lost one or both parents in the concentration camps. Some were only with siblings, some with aunts and uncles. Most had seen or experienced unspeakable horrors and now feared they would be turned away at the shores of Eretz-Israel. It had happened to so many. Hope was a rare commodity, so when the children told them of Sophie's tassel in a bottle that had God's protective blessing on it, they were drawn to see this thing.

Sophie delighted in telling the story over and over. It had not just been on Columbus' voyage, but on other sea voyages. Ships were often lost on the great ocean, but not those that carried the tassel. As the family traveled north, often on the water, they always made it safely. When the pioneers ventured west in wagon trains many suffered attacks by marauders, thieves, wildcats, and even great storms. Those that carried the bottle, however, were always safe. In fact, it was the only reason that Sophie's family now felt assured that they would be able to settle in Eretz-Israel when the British turned so many away. They carried the God-blessed bottle, His tassel of promise.

The tale traveled to the Captain, and this morning he'd invited Sophie, Samuel, and Sophie's father, Rabbi Jonathan Steele, to the steering room as dawn whispered its presence. After holding the bottle and praying with her father, he radioed the tugboat pilot who would escort them into port.

"We're coming in."

"There are a lot of British stopping passenger ships right now."

"I know, but they'll let us in."

"I pray you're right."

"God be praised, I am confident."

Many ships came in under cover of darkness unloading passengers into small boats owned by people who honored the Jews, whether Jewish or not. Those who thought of themselves as freedom fighters used clandestine methods to find openings for as many Jews as they could that wanted to be in Eretz-Israel.

The captain shook his head. "Against all sensibility, the Brits prevent displaced Jews from settling in their homeland. Britain thinks it has to limit the numbers, keep a lid on the population. So many people have been turned away with no place to go, so others have worked hard to secret them in." He paused as he peered into the waters before them. "People died, some were arrested, but many Jews made it to Israel. Life has not been easy for them. Arabs still feel it should be their land. They with their Mahdi, as they call the

Arab ruler, even now are plotting against the Jews. You may encounter bombs, sniper attacks, and beatings. Do be wise. Do be careful, my friends."

Sophie and Samuel returned to the bow. The morning dawned red and bright. The sky streaked rays of scarlet on clouds that hung out in the eastern sky. Sophie and Samuel held hands as they beheld the sun rise, a golden orb that glistened with ripples of fire on its outer edges.

"Landing Day!" Sophie's father walked up behind Sophie and Samuel, clapping a hand on each shoulder. Both froze. Her father boomed with laughter. "This is as good a time as any, children, to tell you we must most certainly have a great wedding as soon as we can in Eretz-Israel. We will land today, and we will invite all on this ship to share with us in our great joy."

"Oh, Daddy, this is the most exciting moment of my life." Sophie threw her arms around her father's neck.

Samuel just grinned, and when Sophie released her dad, he grasped the older man's hand, shaking it vigorously. "I will work so hard to take care of your daughter and to honor you, sir. Thank you."

The captain's voice came across the loudspeaker. "We are cleared to dock. Please gather your belongings. You will have to go through processing. It will be perhaps long and arduous, but we have made it. Some ships have actually been blown up and sunk. God has brought us through safely, blessed be He. So, stay strong, work hard, and honor God. He will stand by you."

A cheer rose. It was weak, as the people were not strong, but it was a cheer.

─────────

The story of Sophie's tassel in a bottle spread throughout Eretz-Israel. The Jews had their land back, but survival was tough. The Brits and the Arabs worked against them. The blessing of God's protection was sought after by everyone called Jewish.

Sophie and Samuel displayed the bottle prominently in their small home on the mantel of the fireplace. Hospitality arose as a natural and necessary fact in the life of a Jew. Sophie and Samuel were masters of it. Rabbi Steele had accumulated a great deal of wealth, and when his wife passed away he joined Sophie and Samuel's dream of going to Eretz-Israel. He committed himself heart and soul to help every Jew be fed, housed, and cared for. He funded Sophie's love for cooking, and their home was a place of caring, helping, and lots of eating.

The bottle encasing the tassel became like a mezuzah, the small metal tube which held Scripture passages attached to the door frame on Jewish homes. Jews traditionally touched it as they entered and exited a home and then would kiss their fingers. After touching the mezuzah at the door as they entered, guests would often do the same with the bottle: touch, kiss their fingers and then bring the fingers to their forehead to receive a blessing.

At least once a week, a guest would watch this ritual, shake his head, and look askance at the rabbi. "Rabbi, the holy writ states, 'Thou shalt have no idols'."

Rabbi always smiled and shook his head just the slightest. "My friend, the holy writ says, 'Thou shalt have no gods before me.' The tassel is a relic from 1492 when God, blessed be He, showed Himself strong on behalf of His people. He has done that ever since for those in possession of it. But it is not the tassel, it is the remembrance and honor of the great almighty God. Him only we serve and by His mandate and blessing we also serve you."

At that, all would embrace, and the eating would begin. The little house reverberated with joy.

———————

Nadir could not believe he was being given an audience with the Mahdi. His whole body shook as he walked in, keeping his head down and praying that he would not offend in any way.

"Mahdi, my ruler, we have heard of a relic with protection properties. It is nearby in the home of Jews."

"Go on." The Mahdi did not look up but focused on his food as he reclined on his exquisite rugs. As ruler of the Arabs in the area known as Palestine, he held great power and was not known for patience.

"They say the God of Israel protects those that have it and all situations around it."

The Mahdi paused, his wine glass almost to his lips. His dark eyes stared straight ahead for a full minute. "So, if we remove it, perhaps this land will be ours, as it rightfully should be."

The young messenger shifted his feet. "A correct conclusion, sir, I, uh, presume."

The Mahdi turned toward the young man, who now felt the sweat dripping down the side of his face. "Go carefully. Is the relic protected?"

"Not really. It is on display in the home of a young couple who are doing their best to feed everyone who passes by."

The Mahdi cut a piece of meat and noisily sucked it. He chewed slowly and burped after swallowing. "Do they ask each guest if they are Jewish." He spat.

"No, but they all partake of a ritual of touching the relic, kissing their fingers, and then rubbing the forehead."

"You could do that?"

"Yes, sir."

"And eat?"

"Yes, and, sir, if they do ask if I'm Jewish?"

Mahdi took another sip of his wine. "Make up a story of how hard it was to get here, how Jewish friends helped you, and now you want to help settle their land and protect it. Ask questions about the relic and get the details so we know. Go a few times before you take it, so it isn't too obvious. Then hide it so nothing can be traced to you. We'll retrieve it later, so we can use it to help us obtain more land."

Her Nadir, chosen by the Arab ruler, the Mahdi himself, to steal the relic from the infidel's home was ecstatic. "My dear wife, we will become wealthy if I accomplish this task."

"And if you don't. . ." Bashra looked him straight in the eye and then down. She wrung her hands. "Dear husband, what if . . ."

The house was plain, but warm from the cold and cool from the heat. Only two rooms were sufficient. Most cooking was done on the roof or outside the living room that held a few chairs and a box for a table. The bedroom was just a bit smaller than the living room, and Bashra knew she could bed down a few children in the room when the time came. The mat that served as a bed was comfortable and was easily moved to the roof on those beautiful nights when they loved to gaze at the stars before sleeping. It was sufficient.

Bashra walked close to her husband. "What if you don't?"

"Do not speak of it." Nadir's eyes flashed, and he raised his hand.

Bashra stepped back. "Do not strike me, Nadir. I care for your well-being."

"Forgive me, dear one. But we must not consider failure. We must plan only for success. My job will be secure. We can have a bigger home." He glanced around at the cement walls and meager furnishings. "I will buy you a real table, not a big box, with a cloth over it. I want to do well for you."

"You will, Nadir, you will. If Mahdi is sending you, it is most certainly the will of Allah. We have no need to fear. Forgive me."

Nadir stepped toward Bashra, and she slipped into his embrace. He ran his fingers down her long, silky hair. "Your hair is finer than the mane of the grandest black stallion in the Mahdi's stable. You will always be my beautiful bride. How I wish you did not have to wear your burka always."

"Oh, do not say that too loudly. I wish it, too, but alas, I must. It is the law. It is who we are."

"Perhaps I should take you with me to the Jews' house and there you could wear your hair down and uncovered and pretend you are a Jew."

Bashra spat. "You go pretend. Do your job, husband. But forget not who you are. I will not pretend for the sake of my hair. I will not defile myself by eating food in the home of my enemy."

"Yes, you are right. However, I must. And I may have to go more than once."

"It is the will of Allah."

"Yes, and then we will be wealthy and never have to do such things again."

"May Allah bless your work."

"I must go. The driver should be here anytime."

Bashra pulled her burka over her head, tucking in any unruly strands of hair. When she was done, she walked behind her husband out the door to await the driver who would take him near to the Samuel Orbin home.

Bashra had to admit she loved the approving glances of the neighbors as they walked by when a car from the Mahdi came to pick up her husband. It was both a fearful and honorable position to have. She realized that if he failed or displeased the Mahdi, he might not come home one day. She knew also it was rumored that if one man was eliminated by the Mahdi, the family may well be eliminated as well. Once, in a very hushed conversation, Nadir told her that if he wasn't back by a certain time she must go to their secret place, not even to her sister's home for there she would be found.

As teens, when they first fell in love, before their parents had arranged for them to be together, they would secretly meet in an outcropping of rocks along a wooded hill. They were able to sneak into the woods from different points and wind around to the rocks. The rocks, several feet high and scattered about, sheltered a little dug out place where Nadir and Bashra could sit and hold hands and dream and talk. They wondered if other young couples had been there as well before them. Once they kissed and feared the wrath of Allah. When nothing happened, they decided to inform their parents of their affection one for the other.

Surprisingly, both sets of parents were fond of their child's choice. A meeting was set between the parents and arrangements made. Not long after, Nadir and Bashra became man and wife.

Now Bashra shivered as she remembered the time Nadir did not return and she thought she'd lost him. She'd gathered her few belongings and under the cover of darkness fled to the rocky hiding place. Terrified at every sound, she huddled and cried, asking Allah to protect her.

Then she heard a whisper. "Bashra, Bashra, are you here?"

Knowing it could be a trick, she said nothing and wrapped her arms tighter around herself as if it would hide her more sufficiently.

"Little Mare, Little Mare, I am here."

It was indeed Nadir, her man who compared her beauty to the sleekness of the stallions and wild mares they watched in the Mahdi's compound. She let out a little squeal and soon found herself in Nadir's arms, crying and laughing.

She hoped that this venture to steal the relic would not fail. To fall into the hands of an angry Mahdi would most likely be a fatal journey.

CHAPTER 7

Tassie stood by the fountain in Grant Park. The wind caught some of the spray and sprinkled her face. Moving a few feet away, she glanced around for an available bench, so she could munch her sandwich and decompress. High-powered lunches with senior partners and clients made her relish the days of simple lunches and walks to the fountain.

If she had extra time she could walk along Lake Michigan to lower her stress level, not to mention help her maintain fitness. Although she worked out at the gym near her office and in her apartment, nothing matched a fresh air walk.

She allowed the glistening rainbows the fountain created to mesmerize her. A familiar voice startled her from her reverie.

"Hello, Tassel. How are you?"

She almost dropped her sandwich. "Why, Hector, what a surprise. And disappointment."

"Have you done your background check of Omar?" The straggly little man acted like her boss.

"Where do you get off, telling me—"

"I know you're falling in love, Tassel."

"What of it? It's a free country."

"He's not from this country."

"So, what, Hector? He has every right to be here." Tassie threw her hands in the air. She didn't have time for him today.

72

"True, but the country of his heritage does not like Jews."

"Oh, please. We are both contemporary. In case you didn't know, multi-culturalism is in vogue right now."

"He covers his hatred well, Tassel."

Tassie struggled not to yell. "Hatred? What are you talking about."

"Before you give him your heart, Miss Tassel, press a little further."

Tassie shook her head and turned to stare at the fountain. Feeling the anger subside a bit, she turned back to Hector. He was gone. She stood, knowing in the vastness of this park, he should still be visible.

"Sheesh, he's like the invisible man."

Tassie sat back down to finish her sandwich but had lost her appetite. She tossed it in the trash can and walked back to her office.

"Honey, could I tell you a little bit more of what I've learned in my research? On Blood Moons?"

"Mother, I . . ."

"Sweetheart, just pretend I'm a boring witness, but you're required to listen."

Tassie closed her eyes and shook her head. "Fine, Mother, I'll be polite."

"Wonderful! You're a gracious daughter."

Tassie pulled out a chair, turned it around, and straddled it. "Hector will be glad."

Her mother whirled around. "Who? What did you say?"

"Did I say that aloud? It's nothing, Mother, nothing important."

"No, please, what was the name you used?"

Tassie lowered her eyebrows but said nothing.

"Did . . . did you say Hector?"

Tassie gripped the back of the chair. "Mother, quit begging. It was a frumpy old guy that they let into the office . . . why, I don't know. Said I needed to listen to the blood moon stuff from you."

Her mother plopped into a chair and fanned herself with her hand. "Did he have long straggly hair?"

"I knew it." Tassie stood up. "Mother, you can't just ask people to come to my office and persuade me to do something. It's . . . it's . . . it's unethical."

"I've never spoken to him." The color had drained out of her face.

"Of course, you did. He told me to listen to your research stuff. Who else even knows about that?"

"Well, actually, a number of people know. But Tassie . . . sit down, dear."

"This is so exasperating. It's like you sending the neighbor to school to remind me to behave. It's wrong, Mother, wrong." Tassie scraped the chair across the floor and sat down. "Okay, I'm sitting, but not for long."

Her father walked in, patted Tassie's shoulders, and kissed the top of her head. "Sweetheart, settle down. It is an interesting story. You should know."

Tassie leaned her head against her dad and took a deep breath. "Okay, Mother, how do you know Hector?"

Her mother locked eyes with her husband for a moment. "I was pregnant with you. I met a Lydia Abrams at the shower my friend Geraldine had for me. You remember Geraldine? Her daughter Annie and you ice skated together one winter when we lived in—"

"Yes, yes, go on. I remember."

"Sorry." Mother waved her hand which she often did when nervous.

Her father set down two cups of tea in front of Marge and Tassie. "Tea for my girls. Take your time, Marge. Tassie's in no hurry, are you, Tass?" He winked at her.

Rolling her eyes at her dad, Tassie picked up her cup. "Of course not . . . I'm never in a hurry."

Her mother reached across the table and patted Tassie's hand, then picked up her own cup. "Thank you."

"So . . ."

"So, Geraldine's friend Lydia was visiting from out of town, and when she heard that I studied archaeology, relics, history, she began telling me all about her study of her family history and the relics connected to it."

Tassie's voice rose a notch. "She told you about the bottle. Of course. Her name was Lydia. Hector is her husband."

Her mother ignored her tone. "No, she did not know about Hector. But she began to tell me the history of Christopher Columbus. I'd heard bits and pieces. I remember my grandparents talking about it, and of course, Uncle Rupert, but my parents were dismissive of it, so I was never curious. Which is surprising, because of my love of history."

"You were a lot like somebody we've watched grow up." Her father returned to stand behind Tassie and placed his hands on her shoulders. "Actually, Tassie, you are so like your mother." He rubbed her shoulders.

Tassie breathed deeply. "I get it, okay."

"When I told her about the memory of my grandparents discussing Columbus, she asked their names. She thought Winkelman just might be in the Columbus genealogy and promised to look it up. We became fast friends and wrote letters to each other often. Indeed my grandparents and I were in the genealogy. I began to do my research in earnest."

"So, where does Hector come in?" Tassie sipped her tea and quelled the urge to tap her foot.

"It was a dream, I think."

Tassie raised her eyebrows. *Oh, Mother, puh-leeze!*

"I was eight months pregnant with you and tired all the time. I gained so much weight with you." She looked at her husband and covered her mouth with her hand.

The judge pulled out a chair and sat down. He grinned at Tassie. "There was a time a lady asked her when she was due."

"Yes, yes, I was six and a half months."

"And your mother responded, 'two or three months'. This woman gasped and said, 'I thought you'd say two or three weeks. I hope you don't have to wear a sling'."

Tassie's dad was laughing with tears rolling down his face.

"I wanted to slap her." Marge grinned. "But I said nothing."

Tassie shook her head. "I think I would have kicked her. With sharp toed shoes."

"So anyway, I was big at eight months, waddling everywhere, and I sat down often for naps. It was one of those times. To this day, I've wondered if it actually happened, but I've always assumed it was a dream."

Marge brought her hands together against her face and stared across the room for a moment. "In the dream I woke from sleep to the doorbell ringing. Before I could get out of the lazy chair, the door opened a crack and an older man's voice called my name. I was groggy and must have assumed I knew him. So, I called, 'come in'."

Her mother paused and took a sip of her tea. "Well, this scraggly man came in. Slightly balding on top, he had long gray and blond hair, a few missing teeth, but the kindest eyes. He said, 'Margie, Margie, don't get up. I'll just sit and visit.' He told me his name was Hector Woodley."

The sound of Tassie's cup crashing to the floor startled all of them.

"Oh, my, Tassie, are you burned? Are you cut?"

"I'm . . . I'm okay."

Her father had already knelt, mopping up the mess and picking up the cup. "I'll get you another cup, sweetheart."

"No, no, Daddy. I'm fine, but . . . but, Mother, I never told you Hector's last name." Tassie's hand shook.

"Your Hector was Hector Woodley, too?" Her dad sat back down and laid his hand on his wife's hand. "Maybe it wasn't a dream."

"Daddy, how. . ."

"Well, look at the evidence, darling." He retrieved another cup of tea and set it in front of Tassie.

Tassie shifted in her seat. "Go on, Mother."

"Well he came in and sat right down. There was a bit of a smell. Reminded me of a farm we used to visit. It wasn't overwhelming, but I noticed it."

Tassie gulped but said nothing. *Good grief, he still smells.*

"'You're studying your family history', he said. I nodded, even though it wasn't a question. 'You need to know you are a direct descendant of Christopher Columbus, as is your little girl, here.' Now, Tassie, we didn't know if you were a boy or a girl. I was shocked that he said that and I was confused. But again, I just nodded. Then he said that you . . . " She paused and glanced at her husband.

"Go ahead, honey. It's time we told her." Her father tapped the table. "If it's true, it'll happen. If not, it's just a curious event."

Her mother reached over and took Tassie's hand. "He said, 'This little girl has been chosen to be influential in the last days' events of Israel.'"

Tassie stood up. "Whaaaat! Last days! Mother, that is ludicrous!"

"Let her finish, Sweetie. Sit down." Her dad nodded at her.

Tassie put her head in her hands.

"Then Hector said, 'She will bring back Lydia's tassel and provide blessing to Israel.' I just stared at him. I was speechless. Then he said, 'In fact, Tassel would be a fitting name for that wonderful child.' He reached over, squeezed my hand, and then walked out the door. The next thing I remembered was waking up as your dad came through the door. I told him the dream, even though it seemed so real."

"We didn't talk about it much." Her father's voice was hoarse. Tassie bit her lip. "We talked about other names, names already planned, but when you were born, we looked at each other and together we said, 'Her name is Tassel.' Your mother smiled and said, 'Tassel Lydia Stevens.'"

"When I was pregnant with Reuben we worried that we'd have to name him Hector."

Tears ran down Tassie's cheek and her tea sputtered out of her mouth as she began laughing. "Oh, oh, my."

Her father coughed and put his head in his arms on the table and his body jiggled all over.

"Jack, are you okay?"

He nodded his head. "Can . . . you imagine? Hector."

Tassie sniffed. "My side hurts. I can't stop laughing."

Marge blew her nose. "I know, I know."

Taking a deep breath, Tassie composed herself. "So, was it a dream or did Hector just walk into your house? I know I wasn't dreaming when he just walked into my office."

CHAPTER 8

Metro News Alert!

Tassie had just set her purse on the table and hugged her dad.

"You'd think the election was this year with all the fuss. Or did another young celebrity get arrested. Mother, you—"

"Wait, Tassie. Listen." Her mother shushed her with a wave of her hand and kept her gaze on the TV.

Jace Shepard, the afternoon news reporter, was a master of teasers. "This is an amazing story, one you don't hear very often. Well, I guess never. At least not in the last 2000 years." Shepard paused as the camera zoomed in on his face. "This is just in from Israel."

"Mother, don't hold your breath." Tassie plopped down on the couch.

"It seems that a group of rabbis, and quite prominent ones—but then all rabbis, I would think, are considered prominent." Jace Shepard smiled. "Anyway, this group of rabbis has declared that they believe Jesus is the Messiah."

Tassie's mother gasped. "Oh my."

"Now, there have been rabbis who have said this before. However, this group claims to represent over fifty percent of all rabbis in Israel. They have released a statement saying that many have believed this for years, but for obvious reasons have kept it under wraps, so to speak."

Tassie sat on the edge of the couch.

"These rabbis determined that once they crossed the fifty percent mark they would go public. Yesterday was Passover, a high holy day for all of the Jewish faith. It was also a lunar eclipse."

Her mother looked at her father and then at Tassie.

"Now these rabbis believe that lunar eclipses portend great meaning for Israel, sometimes positive and sometimes negative. This is the first of two lunar eclipses to fall on a high holy day this year." The reporter paused and looked at his paper. "Who keeps track of this stuff? Did anyone else know that?"

Her father answered. "I knew it, Jace. I'll send you an email."

"And, apparently there are two more to occur next year. That's cool, four lunar eclipses in a row on high holy days. Now the rabbis say that these will bring great persecution and great provision for the people of Israel."

Each member of the Stevens family was now sitting on the couch, leaning forward, giving Jace Shepard their full attention.

"I can tell you that this declaration is going to probably ignite a firestorm of opinion, both negative and positive. It must be a monumental announcement to all Jewish people who are looking for their Messiah, to hear their rabbis, their honored teachers, say the Messiah has come and He is Jesus. This will make for some fascinating panel discussions. But, I do believe it will be life-changing for many as well. Now, up next . . . "

"I'm dumbfounded." Tassie's mother stood up as she grabbed the remote and turned off the TV.

Her father nodded as he leaned back and put an arm around Tassie. "He's right. It'll be a firestorm. It's like they're rejecting their faith."

"Mother, your face is as white as a sheet." Tassie stood to take her arm and guide her to a chair.

Her dad came over and took her hand. "Are you all right? Why does this news shock you? It's odd and bound to stir up controversy."

"It's the blood moons."

Tassie turned around and threw her hands in the air in disgust. Turning back to her mother, she tried to not sound condescending. "Mother, please, this is an interest, not your life. It's like a TV series . . . exciting, suspenseful, but of no consequence."

Her mom's voice was steel. "Oh, it's significant. Nothing will be the same from this day on. Mark my words." She smiled and stood up. "This next year . . ." She shook her head. "Or two years . . ." She continued staring off. "Well, it will be different. Significantly different. Things are going to change in Israel and it will affect everything."

"Mother." Tassie's voice was gentle this time. "Events in Israel or concerning Israel are always changing, but in a way, it all stays the same."

"Not this time. You mark my words. Not this time."

"Mother, are you listening to those messianic Jews on TV? I mean, I know people say they are Christian Jews or Jewish Christians, whatever it is, and they have every right, but I never thought you had an inkling in that direction."

"Well, no, I never did, but, well . . ."

"Marge, really?" Tassie's dad pulled his head back. "That would surprise me."

"Oh, I did turn on a couple, just for research." She laughed. "No, that's nothing, but this report is definitely something. Believe me, this is something. But now we need to celebrate our Passover dinner, only a day late, but I don't think God will mind too much. Thank you Tassie for coming. It's so special to have you here."

"I still enjoy it, Mother. I do apologize for having to work so late yesterday. But, I did see part of the lunar eclipse out my window in the middle of the night. And it did look red. I wouldn't call it blood red, but it was red."

Marge Stevens hugged her daughter. "I love you, Tassie, so much. Thanks for putting up with me. Now let's eat."

———————

The news was tuned in on the restaurant TV when Tassie arrived. Omar sat staring at the table. "The Secretary of State is so misinformed it's ridiculous."

Tassie slid into the booth and placed her hand on Omar's. "He goes on and on and on. I don't believe a word he says. Do you really think Iran, or even North Korea, is negotiating and holding off development of a nuclear bomb?"

Omar raised his head. His eyes were steel points. "He says what he needs to." She detected a sneer in his voice. "Iran has never slowed down. The Secretary makes no one happy, except the . . . Americans."

Tassie was sure when he paused he was going to say 'stupid Americans'. "You don't like him, do you?"

"He's a stooge. Many people are." Omar smiled.

A forced smile.

"I'm having ribs. What about you, beautiful?" He reached over and drew his finger along Tassie's cheekbone.

"Ribs do sound wonderful." Her eyes held his. *Is this blossoming love or simply middle-eastern flattery?* "So, tell me about your childhood."

"Do I hear the investigative lawyer or the inquisitive lover?"

Tassie almost gulped. She wasn't sure. Hector's warning rang in her mind: 'Do the background check, Tassie.' Could Omar detect that?

"I'm naturally curious." She gave a coy smile. "Syria?"

"Yes, I was born in Damascus, a typical Arab boy, playing in the streets with my friends, beat up by my older brothers, taught Islam by my father. We moved to the country when I was ten. My father's business required travel and so we were sent to live with my grandfather. I resented it at first, but it was a good thing. My grandfather was quite wealthy and was able to pay for all of us to go to university here in America. I travel home once or twice a year to visit and . . . see friends as well as family. It has worked out well."

Tassie tipped her head. "How does that work with all the turmoil, the civil war?"

Omar closed his eyes and chuckled. "Well, I fly in and I fly out. War does go on in one section of the country, but where I go, it's safe." He placed his elbows on the table and rested his chin on his hands. "Actually, I have friends in high places."

Tassie widened her eyes, speechless.

"For a lawyer, you sure are gullible." Omar grabbed her hand and kissed it. "Anywhere in the Middle East is potentially dangerous. I time it well. Not to worry."

"Well our little trip to Door County begins in a few days." Tassie rubbed the back of Omar's hand. "I can leave work at noon on Friday."

"Perfect, I'll pick you up at one."

The drive from Chicago to Door County was just a few hours in length, one that Tassie always enjoyed. Tassie gave Omar details of the history and sights as they drove.

"Door County has over 200 miles of shoreline, and it's such a beautiful place. Sunsets, sunrises, wonderful shops, fabulous restaurants. It can be a quiet getaway or a totally busy adventure. I love it." Tassie patted Omar's arm as he drove. "The only problem is that almost everyone up here is a Green Bay Packers fan."

Omar squinted his eyes. "Really? They're big into it?"

"Maybe they have nothing else to do." Tassie chuckled. "Not really. The people are great. But there is a strong rivalry between the Bears and the Packers. It's fun."

"I guess I'm a Dolphins fan. But I don't have much time for football."

Tassie settled back in the seat. She was excited to share this weekend with Omar. Door County could be romantic and full of adventure. Her parents loved it and Tassie hoped Omar would as well. He intrigued her. He was charming, smart, financially well off, a hard worker. Muslim, yes, but what did that matter in this day and age.

They stayed at a resort of cottages right on the Bay of Green Bay in northern Door County in the tiny town of Ellison Bay. Omar held her hand as they walked out on the dock just after sunset. The hues thrilled her soul. She felt chills and warmth at the same time. Purples and oranges layered the sky and lapped the water as long as daylight held.

Walking back, they paused on the little sandy beach. Omar picked up a stone and expertly sent it skipping, grazing the surface of the calm waters five times.

"Oh, you are on. I'm good at skipping stones."

"Let's do it. Winner buys breakfast in the morning. Best of seven wins." Omar began gathering stones.

"Ah ha, the world series of stone skipping, best of seven. Where's my hat?"

A young family was preparing a fire in the grand stone firepit reserved for guests of the resort. Two young boys ran to Tassie. "Can we help you find stones?"

"You sure can." She bent over close to their ears. "I have to beat him. I need flat, smooth, sort of narrow stones."

"We know what kind. Our dad taught us."

Omar let out a belly laugh. "Now, don't help her too much, boys. We guys need to stick together."

The youngest boy looked up at Omar. "Can I help you, sir?" He seemed scared of Omar.

Omar ruffled his hair. "You sure can."

The contest went far beyond seven throws each. They were neck and neck, and then Omar scored nine skips. The boys were jumping up and down, and Tassie was holding her side from laughing so hard. The youngest boy and Omar high-fived and the little guy ran back to his mom by the fire. "We won! We won!"

Tassie and Omar warmed themselves by the fire, chatted briefly with the parents, and thanked the boys for their great assistance before returning to their cottage. Standing on the deck, Omar put his arms around Tassie as they gazed up at stars that seemed as close as any time she could remember.

Omar gently pulled Tassie's arm and guided her inside. As she placed her hand on the light switch, Omar closed his hand over hers and embraced her. As his lips found hers, Tassie melted into his arms and thought of nothing else.

———

The little restaurant was just a block's walk. The young man in the Green Bay Packer sweatshirt swept the sidewalk in front. Tassie paused as they walked by him. "Hi. I like your sweatshirt."

"Are you a Packers fan?" His face lit up as he asked the question, and Tassie could see the face of Down Syndrome. Growing up, the boy next door had been born with Down Syndrome and she always loved his openness and honesty with other people.

"I'm not a Packers fan." She leaned toward him and whispered. "I'm from Chicago. I'm a Bears fan."

He grinned. "We beat them all the time. And two weeks in a row right before the Super Bowl."

"Ouch, you know how to hurt a girl."

The young man laughed and held the door open for them.

"Two?"

Tassie nodded. A young woman led them to a booth and gave them menus. Tassie tilted her head. "That young man knows his Packers."

"Yes, Chris always has Packer clothes on . . . every day."

"Except when he has his Wisconsin Badger sweatshirt on." The man in the next booth spoke over his shoulder.

Small towns.

"But he always has a Packer t-shirt on underneath. I'll be right back with coffee."

Omar and Tassie had pancakes and eggs and discussed their plans for the day. They wanted to hike the parks, visit a few shops, and enjoy a fish boil later in the day. Omar had never been to one, and Tassie couldn't wait for him to try it.

"They pour kerosene on the fire after cooking the fish, potatoes, and onions. The pot boils over with any grease and the flames go fifteen feet in the air."

"And it actually tastes good? Boiled fish?"

"It's delicious. You won't be disappointed."

Chris walked by on his way to wipe off a table. Tassie caught his eye. "You really love your Packers, don't you?"

Chris put one finger in the air. "Actually, I love Jesus more. Do you love Jesus?"

Omar groaned and Tassie pursed her lips. "Well, Chris, I'm Jewish."

"How about you, sir."

"I'm Muslim. We believe Jesus was a prophet."

"But do you love Him?" Chris held up both hands. "Wait. God loves you, so I can pray." He put a hand on each of their shoulders. "Dear Jesus, come into their hearts. They need you. Amen. Okay, have a good day." He turned and walked away.

Omar and Tassie sat, not saying a word. The people at the neighboring tables and booths grinned and looked away. The man who had spoken earlier leaned over. "That's Chris, he's a good kid. Don't let him upset you."

Tassie nodded. "It's fine, just kind of a surprise."

They finished their breakfast, paid, and left the restaurant.

"Well, that was the most unique breakfast I have ever had." Omar put his arm around Tassie, and they walked back to the cottage.

CHAPTER 9

Tassie found a seat close to the water on the patio. This coffee shop was her favorite spot after a run.

The water rippled by, seemingly on a mission to somewhere. *At least it appears to have purpose. If I asked it, would it know where it was going?*

The breeze graced Tassie's face. Not cold, not refreshing, but, oh so pleasant. The wrought iron railing impeded the view a bit, but what could be better than sitting right next to the water? Quiet, peaceful. No demands, no timelines.

There were always things to get done at work. But now, sip the warm coffee. Warmth, comforting warmth flowed from the cup to her hands. *It warms my soul somehow.*

Slightly bitter, the taste made her tongue protest, but she sipped on. The moment was all important, the moment to feel still, to feel special, to be important to herself, to enjoy her little retreat.

The white of the clouds puffed higher and higher on the horizon. If they turned dark, they might deliver a storm, but for now they were friendly, pretty. The light teal blue of the sky was a treasure.

How far is the sky blue? Her dad would often ask her that when she was little. She would open her eyes as wide as she could, and she would stare, trying to see the end of the blue. She'd wonder and ponder, but finally she'd look into her dad's slightly scratchy face ... 'my all day shadow' he called it ... and into his deep set brown eyes that always had a twinkle.

She would say, "I don't know, Daddy. How far?"

"Forever, sweetie, and that's how far our God will provide for us."

Tassie never quite understood, but it sounded so profound that she never questioned further. She would just snuggle closer to her dad and feel safe.

Snapping out of her memory, Tassie glanced again at the clouds. They were a shade darker. *Umm, hmm, friendly fair-weather clouds about to become mean dark thunderheads.* A shiver ran down her arms and she pulled her sweater a little closer.

Is that what Omar is, a friendly cloud, beautiful and majestic, but beginning to darken into a fierce storm? She'd been avoiding that thought, avoiding her parents because they already sensed something was amiss.

Tassie looked above the clouds. The blue did go on forever. The blue was there even when a storm was raging. Hidden from sight, but there nonetheless. Could God really be there in this storm of life? Could He be there? Provision that lasts forever?

Tassie shook her head. *I must be really stressed, thinking about God.*

The water caught her attention. The ripples were still traveling one direction, but the rolls from a distant wake were coming in at an angle, making it difficult to discern the correct current. Looking like a thousand moles under a carpet scurrying in every direction, the water never stopped moving. Each ripple hurried to the next and told it to move on. The grays and whites of the little waves reflected the white of the clouds. Further out the whole surface was a pale turquoise.

Tassie sighed. *Oh, what am I to do? Where am I going? I do love my job. I do love my parents. Mother drives me a little nuts, but I love her. And I do love Omar.* Tassie stared at the water.

Do I, do I love him? Does he love me? Do I even need to know that?

A fish jumped near her. Its graceful body propelled itself out of the water and just as quickly reentered it, leaving a few ripples to add to the confusion at the water's surface.

Does it wonder where it's going? Probably not. Tassie pumped her shoulders up and down a few times and stretched her neck both ways. Time to go.

What sounded like running water gurgling down a drain startled her. She turned totally around, searching for the strange occurrence.

"Silly," she laughed. A string of ducks, wings flapping the water as they became airborne, passed before her. They gained lift and were soon dots in the distance.

Guess they know where they're going. Or at least when it's time to leave. That just might be the better thing . . . knowing when to leave.

Tassie gathered her things, returned to her car, and drove to her apartment. Turning off the music as she pulled into her parking spot, Tassie noticed her mother walking to her car.

Tassie stepped out of her car. "Mother, is everything okay?"

"Oh, Tassie, there you are. I tried to phone but there was no answer."

"Sorry, turned it down at the coffee shop." Tassie pulled out her phone and returned the volume level to high. "You thought something was wrong?" Tassie raised her eyebrows.

"Oh no, just was so eager to let you know Uncle Rupert passed." Her mother smiled. "Mr. Luney has left this world." She began to giggle. "Actually, we all thought he left years ago. I shouldn't laugh, but I bet he's so happy. He can prove all his theories now."

Tassie shook her head and stifled the laugh gurgling up inside. "Mother, you're terrible. That is just bad."

Her mother wrapped her arms around herself. "I know, I know. How can I laugh? He's probably watching me right now. He was ninety-six and just passed in his sleep, God rest his soul. It was a few days ago and my cousin lost our number. The funeral is this afternoon. Two hour drive. Do you want to go?" She sniffed and dabbed her eyes. "I am so bad. Your father has too much decorum to snicker like this. He's getting ready to go and suggested I come tell you in person since I couldn't get you on the phone."

Tassie sported a wry smile. "He probably wanted you to leave so he could have a good belly laugh. How are Aunt Margaret and your cousins?"

"Oh, everyone is fine. 'Best way to go,' they say. 'Live a good, long, funny life'. . . no they didn't say 'funny' . . . what is wrong with me?" She pretended to slap her own face. "'And then just go in your sleep.' I do agree with that. So we have good long-life genes, my dear Tassie. Now, would you like to join us? It'll be good to see family."

"You know, I think I would. Omar is out of town." A bit of a cloud seemed to pass across her mother's eyes. "And, I'm actually almost caught up on all my work. Want me to drive over as soon as I'm ready?"

"Why don't I just wait since I have to drive back home anyway. Then we'll just drop you off when we return."

"Sounds good." Tassie trotted up the stairs to her second floor apartment, and her mother followed. "I need a quick shower. I took a jog before the coffee shop. I should be ready in twenty or twenty-five minutes. Is that okay?"

"Certainly, darling. I'll let your dad know. I'll need to change, too, but I think if we're on the road in an hour we'll be fine."

"You're Tassie, right?" The freckled faced, red-headed young man stood in front of Tassie. He shifted from one foot to the other, and Tassie wanted to show him where the restrooms were. "I'm Jethro, Rupert's grandson. I think that makes us cousins twice removed or to some degree like that." He smiled at Tassie, and then sneezed. "So sorry. Allergies. You are Tassie?"

"I am. Nice to meet you, cousin Jethro."

"I'm glad you came. With your name and all, I figured you know all about the blood moons and well, the history." He twisted his hands and sighed.

Tassie groaned.

Jethro's eyes widened. "That bad? You're not interested? You think we're all crazy? Luney?"

Tassie reached out and touched Jethro's arm. "I'm sorry, Jethro. My mother is the one you need to talk to. She has studied all this, and truthfully, I'm not all that interested. I just got stuck with the name." She shook her head and laughed. "I would love to know nothing about this."

"But, but, but you have the name," Jethro sputtered.

Tassie stepped back. *Dad was right. Strange family.*

"Tassie, you are involved. There is some prophecy about you. It's the end time, and you need to be prepared."

"Oh puh-leeze, Jethro. It's family legend. There's a relic that's probably worth a fortune. And, I got stuck with the legend and the relic in my name, but that's it."

"No, no, no. My grandfather did the research, studied the blood moons. This next couple of years are so significant. You need to be ready."

"To do what."

"To bring back the relic and help Israel."

"I think Israel already has it."

"What? How do you know?"

Tassie blanched. *Privileged information, girl! You can't share this. You don't know this.* "Oh, I don't. But after all these years why wouldn't they? Wasn't it taken back after World War Two?"

"Well, that's what my Grandfather said. But it was stolen from the Orbin's shortly after it came to Israel. It is said that the Mahdi was behind it, and then he hid it. At this time no one knows where it is. But now that the four Blood Moons are here, it is supposed to return to a family member who will get it back to Israel. That has to be you, Tassel Lydia Stevens."

Just then Tassie's mother walked up. "Oh, Tassie, there you are. Hi Jethro. What a wonderful eulogy you gave your grandfather. It was like watching Rupert up there speaking. You are so like him." She turned to Tassie. "Sweetheart, we need to go. Your father wants to get home before dark."

"Mother, Jethro has taken up the study of the Blood Moons. He is indeed like his grandfather." Tassie tried to not smile, knowing she might laugh.

"Oh Jethro, that is so wonderful. I would love to talk with you, but I do have to go. Perhaps you could email us." Marge reached into her purse. "Here's my card." Without waiting for a response, she took Tassie's elbow and guided her away.

"Mother, sometimes you are terrible." Tassie's voice was a whisper.

"I know, I know." She put her arm around Tassie and shook with laughter.

Jethro's voice reached them, "But, I wanted to know if you met Hector."

Both women stopped. Slowly they each turned around to face Jethro. "What did you say?" Mother's voice was barely above a whisper.

"Hector. I want to know if you know Hector." Jethro moved closer and looked from Tassie's face to her mother's. He smiled. "Oh, good. I was hoping you had met him."

"Ladies, time to go." Tassie's dad walked up, tapping his watch. "Jethro, great job today." He shook Jethro's hand then looked at Tassie and her mom. "What? You look like you've seen a ghost."

"Daddy, it seems Jethro has met Hector as well." Tassie walked over and let her dad put his arm around her.

"Well, looks like we'll be driving after dark. I really do hate driving after dark."

The four of them sat down at a table, now empty. Many had already left after the funeral luncheon. Jethro fetched a coffee pot and four cups, pouring each a cup before sitting down.

"I'll start. It was the day Grandpa died. We were at the funeral home making arrangements and this man walked in. I thought he looked pretty rumpled for an assistant funeral director which is what I thought he was. He began talking about Grandpa and what a fine man he was, and then he turned to me. His eyes just pierced me. 'Young man,' he said, 'you need to carry the torch now for the blood moons and the tassel relic and the survival of Israel.' I was taken aback and asked who he was."

No one said anything. Jethro took a sip of coffee and looked at the questioning eyes in front of him. "He told me his name was Hector Woodley."

Tassie coughed. Mother cleared her throat. Her dad drummed his fingers on the table. "I guess this is a lot bigger than we thought." He reached over and put his hand over her mother's hand.

"Yes, Jack, it is." Jethro looked around. No one else was paying any attention to the four at the table. "He told me that Grandpa had actually seen the relic, the tassel in the bottle, when he was in Israel to watch the inauguration of Ben Gurion back in '48. Hector said Grandpa went to the Orbins who actually had brought the relic back to Israel. They came to Eretz-Israel, the land of Israel, on the boats that the British kept turning away. They married after arriving and opened their home to feed and encourage displaced Jews returning to their homeland. They were a very gracious couple and were deceived by a man who stole the relic for the Mahdi, the Arab leader in the area, and it was never seen again."

"So, it's real." Tassie's dad wiped his face with his hand. "I guess I believed it. I mean there was all the research you did, Marge. But this is more evidence."

"He also told me. . . " Jethro paused and bit his lip, "that I should look out for Tassie." Jethro looked at Tassie. "He calls you Tassel. I don't think I ever made that connection . . . that Tassie was short for Tassel. I don't remember Grandpa ever saying anything about your name. But Hector said you were very important in the end-time scenario around the blood moons and he was very concerned about you."

"Jethro, did Hector tell you anything about himself. Where he is from, who he is, why he's so involved." Tassie spread her hands. "I mean, maybe he has the relic and is just playing us all. I feel like he's stalking me. I really don't want any more connection with all this."

Mother patted her hand. "Tassie, have you seen him more than the time in your office?"

Tassie stretched her neck and then took a sip of coffee. "Yes, he's found me twice at the park. He tells me to pay attention to the blood moon research and do—" Tassie stopped.

"And do what, Tassie?" Her dad leaned forward. "Is he wanting money or something?"

"No, no, just do the research with Mother." *Shut up, Tassie. They already don't trust Omar.*

"So, do you know anything else about him?" Jethro looked at each of them. "He's a little odd." A smile crept across Jethro's face. "I know people think that about us . . . Grandpa and me especially."

Her dad smiled. "No, Marge met him years ago, and then Tassie in the last few weeks, but that's all. I don't think I've ever met him and I had no idea that Rupert met him. Did you, Marge?"

"No, never knew. But then everyone's experiences with him seem so odd that no one really talks about it."

He stood up. "Jethro, it's good to know that you know all this stuff. I don't perceive that there is anything else that can be done at this time. Thank you for your concern for Tassie, but we really should be going. I really do not like driving after dark. We should keep in touch."

"I gave him my card." Her mom went around the table and gave Jethro a quick hug. "You are a fine young man. Do keep in touch."

"Yes, thank you." Tassie held out her hand to shake Jethro's. *Can't do the hug. Sorry.* She slipped her arm into her dad's and walked down the hall.

CHAPTER 10

Gabe stomped the glass and then took his bride in his arms and twirled her around. Everyone cheered and called "Mazeltov, mazeltov!"

Lydia laughed and wondered at the marvelous joy she felt to become the wife of Rabbi Gabriel Goldman. "I promise not to batter you anymore," she whispered.

Gabe stopped, held her at an arm's length and said, "Are you sure?" Laughter rolled out of them both. Gabe placed his arms around her and proclaimed, "In Spain, as we fled the King and Queen's edict in the dark of night, I held the tassel that Lydia had retained and declared, 'I will be a rabbi when I grow up and I will marry you, Lydia Liebermann.'" Cheers rose throughout the synagogue. "And then she said she would hit me if I tried." Laughter replaced the cheers. "So now, after many such beatings and refusals, sweet, lovely Lydia is my wife and I am a rabbi." The foot stomping accompanied with clapping made the floor shake. "So, before the celebration goes any further we must say the 'shema' as we did that night."

Voices lifted in unison. "Hear, O Israel, the Lord is our God, the Lord is One. Blessed be the name of His glorious kingdom forever and ever."

As they danced and rejoiced into the night, Lydia recalled the gripping excitement and utter fear that swam within her when they arrived in the new land. Gabe rarely left her side, even as a boy, and by virtue of their journey together, they truly became best friends. Gabe's father and mother she called uncle and aunt. Aunt Anna stepped in without hesitation to nurture Lydia as a mother, from the moment Lydia's beautiful mother passed.

How wonderful it would be if Mama was here. There was a stirring within and Lydia felt she heard a voice, the voice of God whom she so loved and trusted. "She is with me here." Lydia sighed deeply.

She would take time tonight to honor Aunt Anna. She had stayed close when every thought of Lydia's screamed that she was leaving her mother behind in the ocean. She remembered her father holding her and praying for her.

And, now here she was, just fifteen years later, full of joy and hope, hope for a good future, and a long life.

————

The years flew by. As they passed, more colonists came from Spain and nearby areas, many of them Jews who had converted to Catholicism to escape death. Gabe and Lydia mentored and cared for them on a variety of islands in and around the Caribbean helping them find a financially feasible way of life and a life of freedom as Jews.

The year they married saw an epidemic of smallpox strike a huge number of the Europeans who found their way to Hispaniola and nearby islands. Gabe and Lydia spent much time ministering to those who suffered. Despite the devastation that smallpox wreaked on that population, the Goldmans did not become sick. Those of their congregation also were not struck down by the disease. Many associated it with the tassel in the bottle.

Family soon followed marriage for the young couple. Five children became the joy of their lives. Their first girl was given the name Esther after Lydia's mother.

In 1530, with children ranging in age from ten to twenty, the Goldmans determined that God would have them travel to Florida to minister to any Jews that might have preceded them. Life was never easy, but always meaningful and joyful for the Goldmans. Two years after they arrived in Florida, Rabbi Liebermann and Joseph and Anna Goldman joined their children.

CHAPTER 11

Judge Stevens raised his eyebrows when Marge walked through the door. Heaving her shopping bags onto the counter, she breathed a sigh of relief. She glanced at her husband. "What?"

"Listen to this." He looked down at his smart phone, scrolling it to the news story. "Russian President Nikoli Lemkrof has threatened to invade all of Ukraine, and troops are massing near the border of Czech Republic."

Marge shook her head and bit her lip. "This is just all too real. That's what appeasement does." She pulled the bread out of the bag and put it in the freezer. "It doesn't prevent war. It promotes war and all sorts of atrocities. What's Israel saying?"

"Haven't seen it yet, but probably, 'I told you so.' The State Department says it is having high level talks and the Secretary of State is on his way."

"To do what? Slap their hand? Say 'No, no, no'?"

The door was unlocked. Tassie smiled. She knocked as she opened it slowly. "Hi, Omar, I'm here." She heard a low voice in another room. *Must be on the phone.*

She set her things on the couch and walked to the windows. The panoramic view of Lake Michigan and bevy of parks, buildings, and scurrying people always took her breath away. There was nothing like a city on the water. The variations of color in the blues from teal to aqua to azure provided a feast for the eyes.

This is where I almost believe in God, seeing this grandeur.

"We cannot wait." Omar's voice was loud and clear now. Tassie turned from the window. Eyeing the meat on the counter, she decided to make herself busy in the kitchen. Perhaps she would surprise him by starting dinner. *He's probably dealing with a difficult case or deadlines.*

She opened the smoky glass inlaid cabinets and removed long-stem wine glasses. She poured two cups two-thirds full of the red wine on the counter.

After she set his glass on the little alcove table next to the windows with the panoramic view, she strode by the door to the office where Omar was on the phone. "You've got to be kidding! Israel must be stopped. If that's what Lemkrof wants, let him think he'll get it, but our timeline must be kept."

Tassie froze. Blood drained from her face. In her mind's eye, she saw Hector looking at her. She quickly hurried back into the kitchen and gulped her goblet of wine. She began pulling things out of the cupboard, making noise. *I just got here, just walked in—went right to the wine cabinet. Heard nothing. Should I run?*

She hurried back to the table with her wine glass to pretend she was just setting down his glass.

Omar peeked out the door, held up one finger, and closed the door. *Please think I just got here.* She heard him speaking in Arabic, first low and firm, then loudly again. He ended the conversation and came out with a sweet, big smile.

"When did you get here? I didn't hear you. My brother just called from Syria. My mother is ill. I may need to go."

"Oh, I am so sorry. Please send her my love."

Omar raised his eyebrows. "Of course. You just arrived?"

"Yes, yes—went right for the wine and wanted to see the view. It's so beautiful." She kissed him lightly and hurried over to the window.

Omar sipped the wine, set down the glass, and stood behind Tassie, wrapping both arms around her waist and nuzzling her neck. Tassie forced herself to relax and lean back into him. He chuckled, "You are a noisy cook."

"Oh, I knew I was late and saw the steaks already out, so I just started getting stuff ready. Then I knew I needed wine, so I poured us each a glass. I heard you on the phone."

She sensed the slightest change in his grip around her. "You heard my phone call?"

"I heard Arabic, so I wondered if you were talking to family." *Say no more. Shut up, Tassie.*

Omar turned her around to face him and kissed her gently on the lips. Then he held her at arm's length looking deeply into her eyes. She felt as though she was melting. *How does this man do this to me?*

"Shall we have dessert before dinner?" He smiled.

"Sounds delightful, but we'd better eat."

"Dessert after sounds even more delightful." He took her hand, and they returned to the kitchen and just gazed at each other as they sipped more wine. "All right, then. Let's make dinner."

Dinner was over, dishes done, and Omar lounged on the massive couch that faced the windows. Tassie curled up beside him. Now the stars twinkled back at the city lights below and the beauty of the night enthralled Tassie. Deep within, though, dwelt a jumble of unease.

That phone call. Lemkrof? Israel? Anger about plans and deadlines? Maybe Hector was right. Tassie determined to continue acting as though all she heard was Arabic. She could do that. Tassie sighed deeply to calm herself. *If he asks, I can truthfully say it's the beauty right out that window that makes me sigh.*

"I do hope your mother will be all right."

She felt Omar stiffen ever so slightly. "I do too. I'll call the airline in the morning and see if I can get a flight for the afternoon or evening. I have to take care of a few things before I go. She's in good hands. And so are you." Omar lifted her face to his. Little electric thrills coursed through Tassie, and despite her worry, she yielded to his persuasion.

An hour later, Tassie started gathering her things.

The door to the bathroom opened. Omar stood in the doorway, observing Tassie as she prepared to go. He strolled to her and pulled her onto his lap on the bed. "You're not thinking of leaving now? It's too late. It's not safe."

Tassie chuckled. "Oh, I've been around the block a few times. The parking garage is secure, and I know my way home." She tapped his nose. "I'll be fine. You have a long day tomorrow."

"I'll deal better with tomorrow if you're here tonight." Omar put his face in his best pout. "Please stay."

It wasn't the first night she'd spent with Omar. She knew it displeased her parents, but it was her choice. She had originally planned to stay the night, but now she was unsure of who this man was. Lemkrof, Israel... What could that mean? Did she misunderstand?

"Tassie, you in there?" Omar was laughing.

"Yes, yes, I'm here."

"Good. I need you here tonight." He kissed her again.

A few minutes later Tassie snuggled beside Omar and fell asleep before she had time to consider the situation again.

She heard voices. *Must be dreaming. It's too dark for conversation.* Tassie tried to shift her position. *How in the world did I get tangled in the sheets?*

"Hold her still."

Tassie felt hands press her arms to her side. She thrashed. She stole a peek at what was happening. There were two men in the room. In the bedroom! With Omar!

"Pull that bag back over her head." That was Omar's voice.

"A bag? Over my head? Omar, what..." Tassie felt a severe blow to the side of her head. Pain. A stunning realization that faded into nothingness.

––––––––––

Tassie awoke to low voices speaking a language she didn't know and to a throbbing headache.

Where am I? Did I have that much to drink that I'm hungover? She was in some kind of lounge chair that had a familiarity to it, but first she needed to open her eyes. Why did they not work? She needed to bring her hand up to rub her eyes and force them to awake.

She hesitated. Her head pounded. She slowly recalled being at Omar's, of staying the night, of dreaming she was wrapped up in the sheets and a bag. Tassie froze. Her heartbeat picked up pace and sweat formed on her brow. She reached up to wipe the perspiration while holding her eyes shut. Her forehead wasn't there. Instead, her hand met velvet cloth. It covered her face.

Claustrophobia engulfed her, and she tore the head piece from her body. The pain in her head was no match for the terror she felt as she realized she was on an airplane. She moaned and began coughing.

A door opened. Arabic voices. Then Omar appeared. He sat beside her, taking her hands into his and lightly kissing them. "I see you are awake. Would you like something to eat?"

"Omar, what are you?"

Omar slapped her face. The sting brought tears to her eyes and shock to her thinking. Tassie stared at him, letting the tears roll down her face.

"Oh, poor baby. I don't know what you heard, but you heard more than you should have. I should have noticed when you came in, but I didn't. So my only choice is to take you with me."

Tassie shook her head and tried to swallow the fear rising within.

Omar's voice was hard, his eyes piercing. "You will serve us well. Oh, by the way, I took the freedom to use your phone and text your mother that you were taking a few days off to go on a business trip. I texted your boss that there was a family emergency and they would be unable to contact you for a few days."

"That's unscrupulous and you know it, Omar." She placed her hand on her head. The pounding had not let up.

"Eat, and then sleep off your drunken stupor."

"I had two glasses of wine. You know I wasn't drunk. Someone hit me on the head."

"And if you don't shut up, you'll get another strike." Omar turned and left the cabin.

Tassie tasted bile. It hurt too much to think, but she had to think. *Quit crying. Hector was right. I should have done a background check, but it's too late now. I have to think about what I can do.*

"Omar?" She could still see him through the open door.

He looked at her with hard steel eyes but said nothing.

"Where are you taking me?"

He smiled and quickly raised his eyebrows. "Oh, I thought I told you. My mother is ill, and I have to go to Syria." Several voices laughed, and he closed the door.

Syria! She might never return. Despite the blood pounding in her head, Tassie willed the pain away. She needed to think clearly.

The door opened. A big burly man brought a tray of food to Tassie. "Eat," he ordered. "She is a pretty one, Omar." He grinned.

"I'm done with her." Omar laughed. "Perhaps I'll give her to you."

Fear constricted her throat, but Tassie refused to react. Her lawyer training helped her, but she knew it was more than that. *Perhaps there is a God and He is helping. I certainly need help now.*

The food was like a stew. She couldn't quite identify it as it held an unfamiliar taste. *It's the spices . . . cumin, thyme, but there are more. Oh wait, I didn't savor it.* She glanced around.

"Hey boss, she's polite like an Arab when she eats. Maybe you want to keep her. She'd look good in a burka."

"Believe me, she looks better with nothing." The laughter was cruel. "But you're right. She might be of some use. Then I'll give her to you."

Eat, Tassie, eat. And think.

"Boss, boss, check the window. What is that?"

"It's the northern Lights. Didn't you go to school?"

"Yea, but they're red. Are they supposed to be red?"

Tassie forgot the food and lifted the shade next to her. There in amazing brilliance was a curtain of lights dancing across the sky in reds and pinks and greens. She could see the full moon in the same direction with tints and shades of red. It made her think of the blood moon just the month before.

Mom was right. And Hector, and Jethro. Dear God, what is happening? Did I just pray? I don't know how to pray. But, God, I need help.

Tassie was mesmerized by the view of the red northern lights engulfing the moon. It was terrifying and beautiful at the same time.

"Hey, who said you could watch?" The burly man pulled her shade and leaned down to her face. "Eat!"

Avoiding his stare, she picked up her fork and began eating. The more she ate, the groggier she became. *Not a spice, a drug. Oh, Dear God, even Hector Woodley, please help me.*

Before she finished the food, her head dropped back, and she could think no more.

Tassie jolted awake. *What was that?*

It felt like a plane touching down. The shades were still pulled down, so she couldn't quite discern if it was daylight or dark. As her eyes adjusted, she became aware of a heaviness all around her. *Oh no, a burka. They have me in a burka.* She wanted to scream. Tears threatened to flood her eyes. *No, I'll be strong. There has to be a way. There must.*

CHAPTER 12

Nadir entered the house. *Oh Allah, guide my steps. Bless my deception.*

The young couple chatted joyfully with the people who entered before him. The smells of a plethora of food greeted his nostrils, and he breathed in. *Not only do I get the relic but delicious food as well. I am favored already.*

It was his third visit. He was pleased. They liked him. He must exercise caution for he didn't want them to like him so much they remembered him. The people were nice, for Jews. The food was marvelous. He would try to teach Bashra a few of the recipes.

The stone walls had paintings on them reflecting the landscapes of Israel, and a braided rug graced the floor. Mismatched chairs sat about the room. Wonderful smells wafted in from the kitchen. The house was small yet spacious. And Samuel and Sophie Orbin made all feel welcome.

Sophie approached Nadir. "Oh, hello. Benjamin, is it? Forgive me, I try to remember everyone's names, but I do get a few mixed up."

"That is correct. You remember very nicely." Nadir was pleased that he had given a Jewish sounding name far from his. No way to trace him.

"Oh my, this is it." A man in an officer's uniform stood in the doorway staring at the mantel where the bottle was displayed. He walked directly to it. "Oh my." He turned, looking at Sophie and Nadir. "May I touch it?"

"Certainly." Sophie walked over. "I am Sophie Orbin. My husband Samuel and I, with my father, brought the tassel back to Israel. Please pick it up, sir."

The officer turned back and gingerly picked it up. "Oh, blessed be God. This is so wonderful to hold. So many years, so many generations, so many blessings."

He carefully set it back on the mantel after kissing the bottle. Then he seemed to wake up. "Oh, forgive me. I have forgotten my manners. Thank you. Thank you for allowing me to be here. I am Rupert Winkelman. I am in the lineage of Christopher Columbus, so I must be related to you, Mrs. Orbin."

Samuel entered the small living room. "Sir, I am Samuel Orbin. I'm delighted to meet a family member. We carry a wonderful heritage. Oh, I see you have brought Benjamin with you."

"Oh no, we came separately, but I'm pleased to meet you." Mr. Winkelman held out his hand to shake Nadir's hand. "Benjamin, I am from the United States. Where are you from?"

Nadir backed up. This was a little too close, too personal. He wanted to only blend in, not stand out. These Americans, so direct, so rude. "I have recently returned to Eretz-Israel. It is a blessing of God, to be here, and see the bottle."

Nadir walked quickly over to the bottle, to avoid more conversation and possible exposure. The man and the couple talked animatedly. They were all Americans, Jews, and related. Nadir wanted to spit. He knew he needed to get the relic soon. He wanted to get it tonight. Would it be possible?

More people arrived, and Nadir was able to blend in more. He managed to avoid any more conversation with the American officer. Nadir heard him say he served in the American Air Force and had been stationed in Italy. He was the center of attention, which was just fine with Nadir. However, would this man be able to solve the mystery of the missing bottle if he absconded with it tonight?

Nadir put off his plans when the food was served. He bowed his head and mumbled so anyone standing near him would think he was doing the shema with them. *I must strengthen myself for the task. Bashra is a beautiful wife, but her cooking . . . well, it could be better. I will enjoy this food.*

All the people helped clean up. Nadir considered it below him. This was woman's work, but he would follow. Let them all think he was a Jew. Just the thought made him want to spit. But, no, he was chosen by Allah and sent by the Mahdi. He would complete his mission, and he and Bashra would be honored for years to come.

He looked up. The American officer was leaving. He went to the window to be sure. Indeed, he climbed into a vehicle and drove away. Would he come back? Was this the time?

"Benjamin." There was a tap on his shoulder. He jumped.

"Oh, Benjamin, I am so sorry." Sophie backed up. "I didn't mean to startle you. We are going outside for a time of prayer and thanksgiving to God. Tomorrow is Passover and we are so excited. Samuel built a fire in back. Please join us."

"Thank you, Mrs. Orbin. I would be honored to do that." Nadir followed her out and considered his options. *I am blessed. This will be easy. I will remain in the back while they bow their heads and close their eyes, and I will slip back in the house when it is dark. They will not notice. And because we are going out before it is very dark, they will not have light on in the house. Allah has blessed my work.*

Nadir sat on the ground near the back. He moved a couple times, so he wouldn't be noticed as leaving. The people sang songs that thanked their God. They were quite nice songs. *We should consider songs to bless Allah. I think that would be a good thing.*

Then the Jews prayed. That was not nice. They prayed protection from the Arabs, from the Mahdi. They prayed that they would increase. It was almost more than Nadir could take. He had never been exposed to such prayers before. Nausea churned in his stomach. He should leave before he gave himself away. He looked around. Everyone had their heads bowed and eyes closed as they mumbled along with the prayer being offered at the time.

Nadir put his feet underneath him, positioning himself into a crouch. He saw no one looking his way so he hurried toward a bush near the privy. He waited a few minutes and then realized it was dark enough that he could not even detect the forms of the people at the outside of the circle. Only those very close to the fire were visible.

He glanced at the house. It was dark, except for a dim light in the kitchen area. Nadir almost laughed aloud. He walked carefully around the house to the door into the living room where the bottle stood.

He walked in. No one was there. Only the bottle, the relic of antiquity, the bottle with protection properties. He grabbed it and placed it in an inner pocket and quickly removed himself from the premises.

It was all he could do not to run. He walked briskly. He had a three mile walk home in the dark. He could do it. It would be all right.

Headlights. A car coming his way. He lay down next to the road and rolled toward a ditch. The car drove by.

Nadir breathed. It continued past the Orbin home. Yes. It will not be returning. Bless Allah they were not picking up Jewish people from the home. Nadir picked himself up and ran until he could run no longer. Walking the rest of the way home with the light of a full moon, he considered singing a song of praise to Allah.

Undetected he entered his home and sat down on the rickety chair and laughed. Bashra snored lightly in the bedroom. Soon they would have a fine home with rugs and pillows, even couches. Bashra could take cooking lessons and feed him like a king. Better yet, they would hire a cook, and they would take walks and go horseback riding on their own beautiful stallions. He had the bottle, and soon he would place it in the hands of the Mahdi. What a glorious day that would be. He, Nadir, would have money and honor.

Nadir jolted awake. The relic! Where was it? Had he forgotten to go to the Orbins'? Then he saw the bottle in his hand. He laughed out loud. Bashra snored and turned over in the bed in the other room. Nadir sighed as he looked at the bottle. What wealth would soon be theirs! He stood and walked to the window, wondering if he could go back to sleep.

The sky was not right. He distinctly remembered a full moon as he walked and ran home with the relic. But now the moon was half gone, and the missing part was red. It wasn't normal. A heavy foreboding came over him and he stood watching the red completely engulf the moon over the next hour. He shook and sat down again, hoping that all would still be well.

He slept again and dreamed of great honor bestowed by the Mahdi. He awoke once more and looked out the window. The moon was normal again. Nadir relaxed and fell asleep once more.

————

Bashra found him asleep on the chair clutching the bottle with the tassel.

"Set it down, dear husband, and let me spit on it. Is this what you have risked our lives for?"

Nadir opened his eyes. Bashra stood with her hands on her hips and derision on her lips. A slow grin crossed his face. "Nay, nay, Little Mare, this is our path to wealth and fame." He stood and embraced his wife. Picking her up and swinging her around, he whispered, "Oh wife, we are so blessed. We will have everything we want and need. You need to rejoice."

"We shall see. Shall I prepare you a meal?"

"First I must hide this magic relic according to the Mahdi's instructions. Then I will inform our great leader of my blessed success to obtain it."

He hid the bottle deep within the narrow cave in the hiding place that he and Bashra thought of as their own. Nadir arrived at the Mahdi's palace with great anticipation and attempted great humility when given audience. "Oh, great Mahdi, Allah has blessed me, and I have taken the relic bottle from the terrible Jews. It now belongs to you and will add to your already magnificent powers. I thank you for letting me be of such great service to you."

"Yes, yes, where have you hidden it?" Mahdi did not look up from writing at his ornate wooden desk, piled with papers, books, and foods.

Nadir bowed. "It's in a favorite hiding place about a mile from here, a wonderful unnoticed place. There is an outcropping of rocks enclosing a narrow cave. Back in the cave there is a small cavern covered by a rock or two. The bottle sits there wrapped in a cloth to protect it from breaking."

"Thank you . . . your name again, young man?"

Nadir's shoulder slumped. *He remembers not my name?* "Nadir Mehmet, sir."

"Thank you, Nadir. That is all."

Nadir walked home with his head hung low. *Perhaps I should move it. Perhaps I should take it and run. I could probably sell it. Does he not know what great risk I suffered? Does he not know what great powers it has? He will still honor me, I know.*

Bashra stood at the window as he walked toward the house. As he came through the door. Bashra spat. "He did not care? Is that right?"

"No, no, he was very excited."

"You lie. I know you better than that. I have prepared food. Sit and eat. I must go to market."

Nadir sat and looked at the food. His appetite was gone. But then, Bashra's cooking did not ever help his appetite or attitude.

Nadir looked up. He had fallen asleep again. Bashra stood before him. "I have praised you in the market place, my dear husband."

Nadir jumped up, his eyes big. "What do you mean?" His voice was too loud.

Bashra spat. "You yell? I have honored you where the Mahdi did not. I have told how you were given great assignment with great success in stealing a relic from the Jews, giving you great approval from Allah, and hopefully great wealth from the Mahdi."

"We must run. Now, Bashra. We must leave." He wanted to strike her but could not bring himself to do such things. "This was to be a great secret. They will come after us."

In tears, Nadir's wife began to gather their meager belongings. Nadir paced back and forth in their little house trying to formulate a getaway plan. The hardest part was letting go of his earlier certainty of great wealth. Now he prayed for their lives to be spared.

"Nadir, look. A car from the Mahdi. Perhaps they come to honor you?"

"I fear they will no longer honor me, my Little Mare. Hurry, you go hide. I must go with them. Perhaps my fears are unnecessary. You should hide until I return. I love you, sweet Bashra."

Bashra's tears increased and she clung to him. "Nadir, I did not mean to dishonor you. I . . . "

"You must go quickly, Bashra. I will find you. Do not fear."

Nadir shook all the way to the palace. The driver and the bodyguard said not a word. Upon arriving, he was not ushered into the Mahdi's chambers. Instead they took him down stairs. He felt he was descending into water and the waves were washing over him. He gasped for breath. The cold embraced him within and without. Not a word was said. The guards simply placed him in a cell and left.

That morning he'd been confident of great reward, convinced he'd be the recipient of great treasures he could lavish upon his wife, the one person he loved more than himself. Now cold and hungry, he sat in a dungeon, wondering where his wife was and if she would survive.

The questions were short-lived. He heard the door clanking and familiar cries. Slaps and screams came closer and closer.

The guard who shoved Bashra in with Nadir, laughed. "Stupid man. Hide the relic and tell his wife to hide there as well."

Nadir's face fell into his hands. He looked up at his wife. Her face was tear-stained and red with welts from being slapped. He stood and embraced her.

"I did not know, Nadir. I did not know. They knew our hiding place."

Nadir began to sob. "I did not think I would need a hiding place anymore. I was so sure we'd be honored and rewarded. And I did not think that you would go there." He looked sadly at his wife. "I know. I should have thought of that. Perhaps there will be mercy given."

"The Mahdi is not known for mercy, dear husband."

The two sat, hungry and slumped over, for three days. The smell was worse than they thought possible and fear ate at their every fiber.

The clang of guards entering the dungeon sent Bashra into screams and writhing on the floor. Nadir could only shake his head and acknowledge that his wife's boasting had eclipsed their lives. He would not hate her for he truly loved his Little Mare.

The sunlight burned his eyes as they were dragged into the courtyard.

"You are being shot for deceiving the Mahdi."

"That cannot be." Nadir turned to the guard. He was met with a whip across the face. Nadir pulled himself up from the ground trying to resist the pain that seared his face. "Are we not being punished for bragging about stealing the bottle from the Jews?"

Bashra, even in her fear and depleted energy, managed to spit when her husband mentioned the Jews.

The guard sneered. "The bottle was not there. After they deposited you in the dungeon, they searched your home for the relic and then checked the site you named a second time. Your wife, only, was found. And she is not what the Mahdi was interested in."

"No, no, I told him exactly where to look. It must still be there. I gave him direct instructions."

"The Mahdi does not like lies."

Gunshots echoed.

———

A young boy skipped into a small house. "Look, Father, I have found buried treasure." He extended his hand.

"Hmmm, what have you found? A bottle? You think it is treasure?"

"I saw a man go into a cave where we like to play. After he left, I went in there and found another tiny cave I had not seen before and the bottle was in there."

"Avram, do you think it is anything? Son, did the man put it there, or was it already there?"

"I do not know, Mama, but it looks important. It looks like the strings at the bottom of the rabbi's shawls."

Avram's wife examined the bottle. "Why it does, and it looks well sealed. Should we give it to the Jews down the street?"

Avram rose from his seat. "Let us wait. Perhaps we will hear something in the marketplace. Perhaps we could sell it if, indeed, it has value."

"Can I play with it, Father? Can I take it apart?"

"No, son, I think we need to hide it for now and not say anything. Let us only listen. Do you understand, son? We don't want there to be trouble because of this."

The boy wrinkled his nose and lips. "Maybe I can find more treasure in that cave."

"No." His mother placed her hands on his shoulder. "Stay away from there for a few weeks."

The boy blew out air. "I have other places to play. Maybe I can find something that is of value somewhere else." He turned and ran out of the house to play.

CHAPTER 13

"Mom, it's Tassel. Yes, yes, I'm fine." Tassie kept her voice chipper. "Just decided to take a break with a business trip. Sunny Florida. It's wonderful." She paused. "Oh, yes, it was slow at work, so they actually suggested I go." Tassie glanced at Omar as her mother questioned her. "No, they are totally happy—this is like a reward." Omar put his finger to his neck and made a slashing motion and scowled at her. "Well, gotta run. It's happy hour. Give Dad and Uncle Hector my love." Tassie hit 'end' on the phone.

"Give me your phone." It wasn't a request.

Please, God, don't let Mother call back. Tassie dutifully followed Omar back to the room where the other women were. Tassie entered and went to a corner to sit. The other women tolerated Tassie, but she could feel their contempt. She'd tried to help with the cooking and cleaning, but they would have none of it. Tassie was sure they enjoyed ignoring her and seeing her ignored by the men when she served food.

She couldn't imagine what would happen if they knew she was Jewish.

Tassie hoped her mother noticed that she said 'Mom' when she always said 'Mother' and Tassel when she always went by Tassie. *Please, Mother, notice, think.* Tassie sighed. Even if she missed those things, surely she'd know when Tassie said 'Uncle Hector'.

"Did you hear? Ukraine took back the airport."

Omar cursed. "We'll need a different way to get Hakan in with the weapons."

Tassie set the food on the table, keeping her eyes downcast. Nobody paid any attention. She was invisible. What a way to live. Put on a burka and disappear.

An idea began to form. Disappear. Don't think now. Just be the robot. Formulate a plan after discovering their plan.

The room was dimly lit and filled with men in suits and men in Arabic robes. Men of importance and men who desperately wanted to be important. She set the variety of dishes before them. *At least I'm learning some good recipes.* The meze, a selection of several dishes to accompany alcoholic drinks, intrigued her. White cheese, melon, a walnut type paste, a heavy yogurt, and stuffed vine leaves covered the table. Thankfully, the women were able to eat the same food in the kitchen. Not the arak, the anise seed drink, however.

She really needed a drink. No, probably not. She needed to be clear-headed to figure out a way to escape.

"My cousin is Ukrainian."

Everyone laughed. "You have cousins from every country, Yusef."

Fortunately, the conversation was in English. *These guys must be from all over the world, or at least the Middle East and east of that.*

Tassie chided herself for not being able to detect correctly a Russian or Middle Eastern accent. She had always been so focused upon celebrating multi-culturalism that she did not take in distinctive attributes.

"Really. I'm serious. He is Ukrainian, and he is with us. Like a cousin. How's that?" Yusef pleaded his case.

"Lemkrof needs to move. These elections must go in our direction. Yusef, is Nikoli Lemkrof your cousin?"

The laughter around the table was derisive. Yusef hung his head and did not answer.

Omar raised his hand and the laughter stopped. "Lemkrof knows my power. I will speak, and he will hear."

Tassie heard no more as she left the room, her serving of food complete.

The door opened from the meeting room and one of the men waved his hand. "More drink, woman. Bring arak and wine!" The command was followed by Arabic words.

The other women thrust a bottle into each of Tassie's hands. She poured arak into Omar's cup and then set both bottles down as he waved his hand, dismissing her. As she was about to go through the door, a gun shot rang out.

Tassie fell to the floor with her hands over her ears. She could not stifle the scream. When she looked up she saw a man on the floor. She screamed again.

Omar was standing over her and slapped her. "Get the other women to help clean up this mess." Tassie couldn't move. She looked at Omar.

Omar laughed. "This is why women are only good for a few things." Hearty laughter was followed by faces that were tense. Tassie took the moment to scan the eyes as they all beheld Omar. She saw intense fear. Each one glanced at Yusef's dead body, then quickly looked back to Omar.

Omar yanked Tassie up by her arm. "His cousin is not Ukrainian. Now go get the women to clean this up." He slammed his fist on the wall. "Now, woman!"

Tassie hurried through the door. The women were all standing erect as if they were waiting. *They know. I'm now one of them.* She signaled for them to come with her. Two brought towels and a bucket. Three grabbed the man and hauled him out.

Tassie followed the bucket-woman's lead and knelt to mop up the blood with a towel. Vomit threatened to rise and she used every ounce of strength she had to keep it down. The cloths were quickly saturated, and the women placed them in the bucket and exited the room. Holding hands over their mouths they reached for more towels. Tassie nodded at them, took two clean towels and indicated she would complete the job. She fell to her knees as she returned to the meeting room and swabbed every last ounce of blood. She did not look up and kept her back to Omar, hoping she would again be invisible. It seemed she was.

"We have only a few years before the next U.S. election. The American public has no stomach to do anything. But, if the next presidency is more hardline, they will choose action. We must accomplish our goals before that time. Lemkrof needs to follow through on his threats to take Ukraine, so we can move into Slovakia and Czech Republic. As a result, Russia will get sanctions, but that is nothing." Omar's derisive tone felt like bites on Tassie's skin. She shivered, but wiped methodically, slowly, and she listened.

"We must all organize Moldova, Estonia, and Georgia. Ukraine should be having dreams of Russian occupation with memories of Nazi occupation. We need pro-Russian blood to be spilled in each of these countries so Lemkrof has reason to invade, to assist his people."

"The U.S. will see through his plans, don't you think, sir?"

"He has nothing to fear from the U.S. The White House will not even provide arms." Omar looked around. "You will find contacts from these countries who will pass information, weapons, and will stir up strife. We help Lemkrof. He helps us. Our goal to annihilate Israel continues to proceed.

"What will be fun is if we can get the U.S. to show any force. That will give us great pleasure to respond. Russia sends weapons openly to us which is why the U.S. won't show force. But, we get weapons anyway. Lemkrof can pretend to rescue Russian Israelis, or we have time to grow strong and go in ourselves. We must silence the U.S. and Israel through mocking intimidation and get more people there to voice support for us."

Omar paused. "Woman!"

Tassie jerked upward, but kept her head turned away from Omar.

"Get us tea and coffee!"

Tassie scurried to the kitchen.

Two women actually smiled at Tassie, each one handing her a pitcher, one black tea, the other cardamom coffee. Taking a deep breath, Tassie moved slowly through the door and gingerly set one pot down near Omar.

"Ukraine gave up nuclear facilities in 1994 on the premise that the U.S. would protect them." Omar laughed. "That was priceless. The U.S. did not protect them, and Russia will own Ukraine in just a matter of time. Then they will move into the surrounding countries."

One of the men raised a hand. "I do believe the U.S. is doing fly-overs. Is that not a threat?"

"Only a show of contempt. They think that will move us." Laughter rose up and several held up a cup for Tassie to pour tea.

"You may have heard the rumors about Jews having to register in Ukraine. There was a great outcry about it and then they found out it was only a rumor. Soon it was forgotten. When it actually happens, they will again think it a rumor and dismiss it. Lemkrof will wait for their high holy day in the fall and announce it. If there is an outcry, he will show balance and have the Christians and Muslims register, too. Then he will let it sit a while, and when the time is right, the Jews can be done away with."

The men nodded their approval.

"We are very near, my comrades. America partied and prospered. We made plans. And yes, Jordan's ambassador was kidnapped in Tripoli. In exchange, we will get back our brother who planned the bombing of the airport. Jordan thinks the U.S. will help them, but the U.S. will do nothing inside Jordan. Benghazi stopped them in their tracks. Instead of rising up in retaliation as any good Arab would do, they cower in the background. Even though Jordan is fighting al-Qaeda, the U.S. does nothing of importance to assist them."

Omar took a sip of coffee before he continued. "The Secretary of State is even informing the U.S. that Syria is fulfilling its commitment to destroy all chemical weapons." Omar paused and rolled his eyes, giving everyone permission to laugh and high-five each other.

"Everything is gone except eight percent which is behind insurgent lines." Omar's voice rose to a high pitch. He chuckled, and then his face went somber. "Those chemicals are here. We will use them if we need to. Lemkrof knows.

The U.S. can think what they want. We know. Now you know." Low gasps were heard around the room.

Tassie could not believe her ears. Chemical weapons in Syria. She must do something. She needed to get word to someone.

Who would believe her? And where would she begin? She realized she had stopped pouring and a few heads were turning her way. She set the pot on the table, put her head down, and returned to the kitchen.

It was a restless sleep. Tassie finally gave up and lay wide awake. But what tickled the back of her mind? What kept attempting to rise up in her thinking? She didn't need memories now. She needed strategies, a way of escape. Escape. Had she met a person that could help her? She mentally checked off all those she dealt with here. No one seemed to be a means of escape. Tassie closed her eyes. She longed for sleep.

That tickle introduced itself again. However, she was finally drifting off and she ignored the tickle. Dreaming almost immediately, she was back in Door County with Omar and falling in love. Even in the dream she cringed. *What was I thinking?*

She turned over to her side. *Background check, should have done that.*

Dreaming again. The little restaurant, breakfast, and there he was. The young man . . . Chris. 'Do you know Jesus. Well, I do, and I can pray for you'.

Tassie smiled. She was wide awake. Jesus . . . a way of escape? Was that the tickle? But she was Jewish. And in a burka. Well, why not Jesus?

Okay, Jesus, I am so in trouble here. Can You help me? I know You know I'm Jewish, but I guess You were Jewish, too. So, who better to know how I think?

Tassie opened her eyes. The eyes of the woman on the next bed penetrated hers. Tassie didn't know how she restrained herself from hollering in surprise, and then she realized she felt calm. It was uncanny. The other woman smiled. Was she the same one who had smiled at her when they were cleaning up after the shooting?

Glancing over again, the woman smiled and put her hands together in front of her mouth as if she were praying. Again, Tassie felt an uncanny peace. Was the woman praying for her?

Did I pray aloud? Did she hear me? As soon as that panicky thought filled her, the uncanny peace pushed it out. Tassie nodded to the woman and then turned over. *I can't handle too much more tonight. Jesus, if this is real and she can help, let us figure something out in the morning.*

———————

"Well, now, this is very interesting."

Tassie awoke. It took a moment to remember where she was and she wondered if she could ask the woman next to her the actual location. Also, were the women here just accepting of their cultural demeaning? Did they want change, even just one of them? And, did any speak English?

It slowly dawned on her that she was hearing Omar's voice in the bedroom. Fear rushed in and she stiffened. Not long ago, Omar's presence was all she wanted. Now she was wiser. She opened her eyes and pulled the covers close around herself. Omar was standing there with her phone in his hand.

Oh no, Mother called back, and revealed the clues I gave her. He might kill me. Tassie wanted to look over to see if the woman who smiled at her last night was awake, but she didn't dare.

"Get up. Get dressed. You have a message from your Mr. Goldman about a relic."

Tassie could hardly breathe.

CHAPTER 14

Reuben Liebermann Stevens stood gazing out at the Great Falls of the Potomac River. One mile from his home, this was his favorite spot to think, to walk, to show visiting friends and family, and make necessary contacts. At this moment he watched daring kayakers who rode those falls into the depths.

A couple near him on the rocky observation point took pictures and gasped. "They went completely under . . . it's too long . . . are they . . . there they are! Did you get the picture?"

"I videoed it. They were under sixteen seconds! That's just crazy! I could never do that."

Rube smiled. The amazing feat of traveling the falls by kayak could certainly be deemed ridiculous. He had gone over three times and that was enough, but what a ride.

Rube had started kayaking back in Chicago while growing up. The best times, though, were in Door County, Wisconsin. He never experienced waterfalls there, but waves had capsized him a few times. He and his friends learned the necessary skill of righting an overturned kayak. *Fearless, we were fearless.*

After moving to the Washington, D.C., area and settling in McLean, he often hiked to the Great Falls and discovered the kayak daredevils. He felt a scratching inside and began strength training. He soon joined the groups that rode the Great Falls.

His wife gave him a beautiful kayak but wrote on its floor, 'If you don't survive, I will kill you.' Rube chuckled thinking about it. Jill was always so funny and serious at the same time. *That's why her students love her.* A fifth-grade teacher, Jill was strict, fair, and oh, so funny. She could chew a kid out and make him laugh at the same time.

On his premier trek over the falls, his friend John went first. Rube resisted holding his breath as he watched.

He counted, fourteen, fifteen, sixteen. Cheers went up and bodies turned, and people pointed as John came up and continued triumphant down the river between the rocky outcroppings.

My turn. Focus. Straight. Paddle. Slightly to the right of center. This is it. No backing down. He glanced down. 'If you don't survive, I will kill you.' Rube smiled. *I will survive.* The kayak bow was sticking out over the falls. Rube held his breath. *No, take deep breaths, get full.* Kayak tipping. Vertical. *Now! Big breath and hold.* A rush of water and adrenaline.

Confusion. *Use the paddle to redirect up. Don't fight. Let the bow arise. Hard to think. Low on oxygen. I see the surface. Bow out and so am I. Yes! Breathe, balance, and paddle.*

The cheers of the onlookers reached his ears and he saw cameras capturing his moment. The best was seeing John on the side give a fist pump as Rube caught up to him.

Now, Rube joined the onlookers and relived those exhilarating moments flying over the falls and plummeting to the depths. Rube's phone interrupted his musings. It was his mother. She'd not called in a while and Rube chided himself for not calling her first.

"Mom, hello. How are you? Is it as beautiful there as it is here? I'm out at Great Falls on a hike, but Jill is home, if you need to talk to her."

"Rube . . . " Mom paused. Rube could hear the worry in her voice.

"What is it? Is Dad okay?" He walked over to a bench and sat down. He heard nothing. "Mom, are you there? Can you hear me? Did I lose you? The reception isn't that great here."

"Rube . . . called . . . not right."

"Mom, wait, say that again." Rube stood and walked closer to the river.

"Can you hear me now?" Mom's voice was full of concern.

"Yes, Mom. Who called? What's not right?"

"It's Tassie. She called yesterday. She called me 'mom'."

Rube waited.

"Rube, she never calls me mom, she only calls me mother. I think she was trying to warn me."

"Of what, what do you mean? Where was she?"

"That's the concern. She just left without warning. That's not like her. Said she was taking a break, that the firm was rewarding her, but she hasn't been there that long to be given a vacation as a reward. Said she was in Florida."

"Well, they like her. Maybe she was relaxed or had a couple drinks. This isn't like you, though, Mom. Anything else."

"She called herself Tassel."

"Okay, that may signal World War Three, Mom. I know she doesn't go by Tassel."

"Rube, don't make fun. I think something is wrong. She used a cheery voice to say, 'Hi, Mom, this is Tassel.' She did not sound tipsy."

Rube heard a roar of voices and turned. Another group of kayakers flew over the falls, and the onlookers were enthralled. He sat on one of the huge rocks that fenced the river.

"Okay, Mom, tell me the whole conversation and anything that was unusual, besides calling you mom and herself Tassel."

"Well, the cheeriness of her voice was overdone, and she also said to say hi to Uncle Hector."

"Hector? We don't have any Hectors in the family, do we?"

"Hector is the man who I thought was just a dream that told me to name you two after the Liebermanns from 1492."

Rube wiped his forehead with his hand. "Mom, that was a dream and apparently you told her about it."

"Yes, but she also met a Hector Woodley at work who told her to listen to my research of the four blood moons."

"Hmmm. Well, okay, so you think she was saying there was something about the blood moons thing or this Hector that was connected to why she is gone."

"I think that exactly, Rube, but I don't know what to do. I would feel foolish calling her firm and asking where she is, but I'm wondering what she told them. What if she's in some kind of trouble with them?"

"Okay, Mom, anything else? Is this Hector someone who would kidnap her?"

His mom began to cry. "Oh, Rube, you think she's been kidnapped? Jack, Rube thinks she's been kidnapped."

Immediately another phone picked up. "Son, you really think that?"

"No, Dad, I mean I don't know. I hear Mom's concern. I'm trying to walk through this concern with her."

Everyone was silent for a few moments. Rube looked out at the tumbling waters of the Potomac. He felt that same turmoil in his mother's voice. Obviously, something was amiss. Rube hoped he would not have to reveal his second life to his parents at this time. They only knew he worked as an IT guy at the electric grid consortium.

But his concern for Tassie was growing by the moment.

"Mom, tell me more about this Hector guy. Did she go out with him?"

"No, no, she didn't even like him. He's old and scraggly. She just kept running into him and he would tell her to listen to my research and well, I think there were some other things. She started to mention them and then changed the subject."

"If she didn't like him, would he react strongly enough to hurt her?"

His dad jumped in. "I don't think he's that kind of guy. In fact, I wonder if Hector was trying to warn her and she wouldn't listen. Marge, didn't she tell you to say hi to Uncle Hector."

"Yes. I just told Rube about that. It didn't make sense. Maybe what he said was the warning. Who or what could he have been warning her of?" Marge began to cry again.

"Okay, Mom, anybody else that could be a concern with her? Doesn't she have a new boyfriend? Can you talk to him? Is she with him?"

His mom sighed, and his dad groaned.

"What's the deal with the boyfriend?"

"Well, son. He's Muslim, which in and of itself is no big deal, but when we met him, it seemed he had a strong underlying disdain for all things Jewish."

"So why was he dating Tassie?"

"Well, either he didn't know at first, or perhaps he had ulterior motives from the first."

Jack cleared his throat. "He knew our connection with Christopher Columbus, too."

Rube shifted his position on the rock. "Well, maybe Tassie told him that."

"But she hates to talk about it, so I wonder how that came out. Rube, what if he took her someplace and now she's being held there against her will."

"Mom, Dad, I have some friends in high places, and I know a bit about technology searches, so let me do some checking around and make a few calls."

"You have connections, son?"

"Dad, I will say no more about that, but let me do some checking. Mom, think about the phone call. Did you hear anything else? Just close your eyes, remember the phone call. Listen and notice. Just listen and notice."

"Okay." His mom paused. Rube could picture her, eyes closed and mind darting. "She said 'Hi, Mom, this is Tassel.' That threw me a little, so I almost didn't hear the next part. 'I'm taking a break. In sunny Florida. Work said it was fine.' I asked if there was a problem and she said it was more like a reward and work was slow. Does that happen in a legal firm, Jack . . . things get slow?"

"You didn't tell me that part. That's unusual. There's always work, especially for the newer hires."

"Mom, tune back in. Listen to the phone call." Rube had pulled a notebook out of his jacket pocket and was taking notes. He would call Jared when he finished talking to his folks.

"OK. Sunny Florida, things are slow. Then she said it was happy hour and had to go."

"What time was the call, Mom?"

"It was morning. Seven or eight AM."

"Happy hour, in the morning? That doesn't sound right."

"I just took it as a way to get off the phone. I half assumed she was somewhere with Omar and didn't want to tell us about it but didn't want us to worry."

"Omar's the boyfriend?" Rube wrote down the name. "Do you have his last name?"

"Jack, what was it? It started with a T. Tartran, Tuscan, Tugran?"

"Tugan or Tugani, I think. Omar Tugani, or something like that."

"Okay, Mom, anything else, like sounds in the background? Wind, people laughing, doors closing, slamming, anything?"

"I do remember something like a horn blowing in the background."

"Cars, traffic?"

"No, no, not like that. Kind of long and mournful, but it was faint. Don't know."

"I'll think about that, Mom. I'll check out a few things. Hopefully, she'd just had a couple morning drinks, which she probably isn't used to and shouldn't have called till later." Rube was ready to change the subject. His first thought of a long mournful horn sound, was the Arab call to prayer every afternoon. He'd been to Saudi Arabia, Egypt, and Jordan a few times, something his parents did not know, and the prayer call was heard everywhere, every morning and every afternoon, and a few other times. Calculating the time change, morning in the States would be afternoon there.

"One more thing, do you know where Omar is from."

"I have no idea. Tassie never said anything. She knew we were a little concerned about him, so she probably told us even less than she might have normally."

"Mom, Dad, I'll check out a few things. I'm sure everything is just fine. Have you tried to call her?"

"She doesn't answer. I left one message to call me but didn't say anything more . . . just felt like that's all I should say. I'm worried, Rube."

"I know you are, Mom, but we'll figure it out . . . she'll figure it out and get in touch with us. Again, not to worry, Mom." Rube was writing notes of several possibilities as he assured his parents that Tassie was fine.

After hanging up with his parents, Rube sat for five minutes, thinking, writing scenarios, and listing people to check with. Why Tassie, what might she know? Was someone trying to get to him? Jared would be aware of any chatter from the Middle East.

Wish I could hear that phone call.

Fortunately, his CIA connections would bottom line this fairly quickly. If it was just a young woman on vacation from a high-stress job, wanting to drink and play all day, that was one thing. But if this was a kidnapping with Middle Eastern connections, that was altogether different, and a very dangerous situation. Rube walked home.

"Have a good walk? Do any kayaking?" Jill smiled and winked as Rube came in the house. She was in the kitchen putting dishes away.

Rube walked over and kissed her lightly on the lips. Her long brown hair was down, and he loved it that way. So often for school she pulled it straight back into a ponytail, so she didn't have to think about it. With her high cheekbones and gorgeous hazel brown eyes, she always looked good, but when her hair was down, Rube loved just gazing at her, which he did just now.

"Is something on your mind?" She tilted her head and paused with a plate in her hand.

"I just enjoy looking at you."

Jill laughed. "That's it? You were gone longer than usual and looked so deep in thought when you came in."

Rube opened the refrigerator and grabbed a water bottle. Leaning against the counter he took a big swig, then blew out his breath. "It seems Tassie is missing."

"What!" Jill whirled around almost dropping the platter in her hands. Setting it down, she gave Rube her full attention. "What do you mean?"

"I'm not sure. Need to call Jared."

"You think this is international, terrorist related? What can you tell me?"

Rube was glad his wife knew about his CIA connections. It was Jill in fact who was responsible for getting him recruited. Her father was a retired CIA operative and Jill had figured it out and told her dad in no uncertain terms that she wanted to be involved. She had done a few undercover missions while in college on the pretense of study in other countries. She was excellent at bringing people into her confidence and her observation powers were second to none. She always laughed that a little CIA experience was a great thing to have as a teacher. No one pulled the wool over her eyes.

When Rube got his IT job at Washington Electric, Jill realized that he might be an excellent person to recognize any tampering to take out electrical grids. Even though she was basically out of the business, she still had discussions with her dad about current concerns. He enjoyed getting her perspective on many issues. Jill had an uncanny way of thinking out of the box.

In one of those discussions, she told her dad about Rube. "I think he could be a great asset. Pull some strings, Dad. Send him on a humanitarian trip to assist with the technology on electrical grids. He really is an expert and his connections would be invaluable."

"Does he know anything about our CIA involvement?"

"No, he just wonders why I tend to interrogate him on details of anything going on . . . and he just thinks I'm a snoopy nut."

Soon Rube was being trained and sent to Saudi Arabia, Egypt, and Jordan. He told his parents he was going on vacation or taking a short sabbatical for study and research in his field.

"Rube, do you think she's been recruited?" Jill's eyes were big.

"That thought occurred to me. She'd probably be a great CIA operative. I think Jared could find that out."

"Want me to contact Dad?"

"Go in person. If she's been abducted in order to get to us, we don't want to be on the phone too much. And it may be nothing, just a silly vacation, and my mother is being a mother."

Jill smiled and put her arms around Rube. "I'll be the same way when we have kids and they grow up."

"No, Jill, they will never go anywhere without you knowing about it. You will stalk them. My mother stalks us with questions and lovey-dovey stuff. You will have GPS and other informants stalking our kids twenty-four seven."

"Yes, I will. And we can start right now." Jill patted her stomach and dipped her head looking a bit side-wise at her husband.

"What?" Rube froze for a split-second. "You . . . are you . . . are we?"

Jill nodded.

"We're pregnant!" Rube picked up Jill in a big hug and twirled her around. He planted a big kiss on her lips. "Terrific, this is terrific!"

Jill stepped back. "Rube, how about I call your folks and get your mom's mind off Tassie with our good news? You call Jared and maybe Frank, too, and I'll go see my dad."

"Yes, you talk to my folks and your dad, and I'll go see Jared."

CHAPTER 15

"Miss Stevens, this is Harvey Goldman. I believe you'll remember me. I visited you about a possible custody case. My wife was moving to Israel. I won't share anymore over the phone, but, well, I just came across your name and number on the paperwork we did, and realized . . . well, your family heritage, and felt you should know what is happening with my family as it relates to your family, not so much your profession. Please return my call. I would very much like to discuss some matters with you. You were quite helpful that day we talked. Thank you, Miss Stevens."

Tassie puffed out her cheeks, and then bit her lower lip. Why had he called now?

Omar put a finger under her chin and lifted her gaze to his. A wry smile greeted her. "So, this is the international custody case, the relic people, the oil people?"

Tassie turned her head and looked down. Omar would have none of it. The sting of the slap was enough for her to nod her head and look at him again.

"You will call him."

Tassie groaned.

"You'll find out about the relic. Then you'll tell him you're traveling in the Middle East with me, your fiancé, and you would love to visit."

———

The plane touched down in Tel Aviv and Tassie prayed. *Dear God, could You help me escape this man? Mr. Goldman would help me get home.*

She looked up. Omar stared at her. She gulped.

"Tassie, you look beautiful, just like the old days. I'll admit this is more appealing than the burkas. But when this is done, back to the burkas." He laughed. "You belong to me now. I own you, so don't get any ideas about escape here. I like you, but if you double cross me, you're dead. Understand?"

Tassie nodded.

"Right now, you are again the happy lover that you were back in the States. Let me see you smile."

Tassie started to grimace but realized it would accomplish nothing. *Play the game, Tassie, play the game.*

The heat and humidity lifted off the pavement in steamy tendrils as they exited the plane. The brightness of the sky assaulted her eyes and welcomed her at the same time. She'd not spent time outside since her abduction. *How far is the sky blue, Tassie. That's how far God will provide for you.*

Tassie looked up. *Is that You talking to me, God? Like a father talking to his little girl?*

Mr. Goldman waited just outside the terminal.

Tassie extended her hand. "Mr. Goldman, how nice to see you again." *You have no idea.* "This is my fiancé Omar from the States. You sounded like you may have the relic."

"I do, Ms. Stevens. And, I'm so glad I returned to Israel. I hope that did not come back to haunt you, that I dropped the case."

"They forgave me." Tassie smiled.

Mr. Goldman coughed. "So sorry. I do apologize. But I needed to be here."

Mr. Goldman took the handle of Tassie's luggage and began walking toward a waiting car. Omar slung the strap of his bag over his shoulder and placed his hand on Tassie's elbow, guiding her toward the car.

Horns honked, and people were everywhere. This was Israel. The land of her heritage, though she'd never had a desire to see it. The stone buildings, centuries old, mingled with new metal and glass buildings and seemed not to mind. Tassie had heard about all the dangers in Israel, why it was unsafe, but no one looked concerned. People were out and about just as in any U.S. city.

"Tassie has shared with me your great find of the relic. It sounds so fascinating. The fact that Columbus is related makes this such an interesting story."

You are such a jerk, Omar. "Yes, Mr. Goldman, I'm so excited to actually see it."

The door opened. "Jared, what do you have?" Rube was out of breath.

"Did you run or drive here? Don't think you've made it to Langley this quickly before, even though we're practically next door." Jared stood up and shook Rube's hand. Piles of folders and papers littered his desk. Three smart phones were within hand's reach and two laptops sat side by side. On the side wall were two mounted flat screens with maps and information streaming across each one. On the back wall hung a white board with Tassie's name and a few notes.

"Well, I called you on my way. I mean, this is my sister, definitely a priority for me. She's clever, brilliant in fact, but I don't think she had any idea this was coming."

"Does she know about you or Jill's dad?" Jared ran his hand through his red straight hair.

"No, Jill is the only one of the family that knows. Well, except my cousin, Jethro. He's been the quiet researcher on the family history and end time predictions. Everyone thinks he's as luney as his grandfather—who, by the way, recently died."

"That's right. I heard that. Sorry."

Rube moved a stack of books to a side table then sat down in a leather covered chair with wooden arms. "I think we need to get Jethro to Israel. I gave him a call on the way, as well. He thinks Tassie's boyfriend is after the relic."

"We got on it as soon as you called. Omar Tugani, with a legitimate U.S. passport, went to school in the States and serves admirably with a Chicago financial law firm. Told his office that his mother in Syria is dying and had to go."

Rube pounded his fist on the table. "Syria! What was Tassie thinking?"

"Apparently, he's a looker, and smooth. Of course, there are sleeper cells in Syria connected with Nikoli Lemkrof. As things heat up in Ukraine, we're picking up increased traffic between Syria and Lemkrof." Jared took off his glasses and laid them on the desk.

Rube shook his head. "Jethro may already be on a plane. If so, he'll arrive here in a couple hours. I think he has intel on the relic. He's convinced the blood moons play a big part."

Jared sighed and rubbed his head with his hands. He pulled out a pen and tablet. "Okay, we'll cover all angles. First, any word from your sister?"

"Just the call to our mom. Nothing since."

"Got a hold of Frank." Jared shuffled through some papers, found one, glanced at it, and handed it to Rube. "He's in the Mideast now and was able to get a read on her phone. She got a call from a Harvey Goldman about some case Tassie worked on and an indication of some family connection. Familiar with that name?"

"Goldman is the family that my family traveled with getting out of Spain with Columbus. The Goldman boy married my ancestor Lydia. So, they would be distant family. Did she call him back?"

"She did. Said she and her fiancé were traveling and would stop in Israel and meet him."

"Are you kidding me? Fiancé? Oh, man." Rube stood up and then sat down again.

"She said his name. So, it is confirmed she is with him." One of the smart phones dinged. Jared glanced at the text message. "Rube, this is from Frank. Just uncovered that this Tugani guy has big connections."

Rube nodded. "Figured."

"Okay, so here's the plan. You're going to Israel." He chuckled. "A lot easier than getting you into Syria. Extraction, if needed, will be a lot easier there."

"You think extraction is needed?"

"She's probably figured it out. She may be able to walk away from Tugani, with a few diversionary tactics."

"What about Jethro?"

"We'll keep him here for a while. I need a good debriefing on all this blood moon stuff and family history."

Jared stood up and extended his hand. "You leave Reagan airport in two hours. We have a cab for you. More info in a folder in the cab. Who picks you up, more intel, a secure phone. Use it to call Jill, but keep it brief."

Rube left the building and went to his car, removed his carry-on luggage, always packed, ready to go, turned his phone off after forwarding any calls that would come in to Jill's phone, stuck it in the glove compartment, and turned his keys over to the cab driver who would have it in his locker when he returned, hopefully with his sister. And who knows, maybe the relic.

CHAPTER 16

"Ms. Stevens, this is my wife, Sally Goldman. Sally, this is..." Mr. Goldman paused and raised his eyebrows, "this is Tassel Lydia Stevens." He gestured to Omar, "I guess soon to be Tassel Lydia Tugani. But she is the one named for our wonderful relic. And her fiancé, Mr. Omar Tugani."

Sally was short and blonde and exuded energy. She grabbed both of Tassie's hands. "So delighted Miss Stevens. May I call you Tassel?"

"Tassie, please."

"Tassie." Sally pulled her closer and gave her a hug. "I understand our marriage is still intact because of you."

Tassie shook her head, wide-eyed. "Oh no, I just listened to your husband and asked a few questions."

"Well they were the right questions. And then to find out that you were Tassel of the relic. We had no idea. Well, I'm just delighted to meet you. Our daughter Josie will be disappointed she didn't get to, but she's at camp for a few days."

Omar smiled his engaging smile throughout, but Tassie could tell he was impatient. Her mind raced. Beads of moisture formed on her forehead.

Sally looked at her and Tassie could see the question in her eyes. "Sally, could I get a drink of water?"

"But, of course. Forgive our rudeness. Harvey why don't you show Omar around while Tassie and I get some water." She glanced at Omar. "Unless, you as well would like some water, Mr. Tugani."

Omar smiled. "Yes, yes, water would be good. I'll come with you." He followed Tassie and Sally toward what looked like the kitchen.

Tassie's heart fell. *Okay, God, I need a time alone, so I can escape.*

The kitchen was small but well equipped. Tassie's heart was warmed by the Goldmans' welcome and their home. There were several little rooms connected in a haphazard fashion, with a garden and wooden trellis outside every window and door. Flagstone paths passed through the gardens such that you could just as easily go through a garden to get from the sitting room to the kitchen. Looking out one window she noticed a totally enclosed interior area that was a garden. She didn't know why but she felt at home. The fragrance of lavender floated throughout the little home and she noticed it hung from the trellises and also lay crushed in bowls in each room.

"We will have tea and a chilled drink with lunch in about an hour. If you would prefer that instead of water, you are more than welcome." Sally looked Tassie straight in the eyes.

Tassie wondered if she was just direct or if she was trying to discern what was going on. She allowed a plea to flow forth from her eyes followed by what she hoped indicated a warning to Sally to not ask with Omar in the room. The looks were but a split second, but they spoke volumes, as Tassie perceived understanding in Sally's eyes.

"Water is fine for me right now." Tassie placed her hand lightly on Omar's arm. "Darling, what do you prefer?" She batted her eyes at him.

His smile back to her was more of a smirk, and Tassie was sure Sally noticed it.

Thank God for discerning people. I sure am thinking about God a lot.

"Yes, I'll have water now as well. Thank you." Omar nodded in thanks.

Sally led them to the little inner garden, full of ornate benches, filtered light, and plants everywhere. Harvey was already there. Sally seated herself next to him and indicated another bench for Tassie and Omar. Tassie sensed Omar's impatience.

Omar took a few sips as Sally asked Tassie about their trip. Before Tassie could reveal too much, Omar interrupted. "I am amazed at the story of the relic for which my wonderful Tassie is named. To see it will be a thrill. Do you have it here?"

Harvey clapped his hands and threw back his head. "Oh my, no."

Tassie could feel the iron in his arms as Omar tensed. She did not need to look at him to know there was fire in his eyes.

Tassie took his hand in hers. "I don't think either of us realized the great status it holds here in Israel. Will we be able to see it?"

"Yes, yes, of course, yes. But it is under lock and key in a local museum." Harvey rubbed his hands together. "However, I have the key, and will let you hold it. Tassel Lydia Stevens must hold the tassel in her hands. Now, you do know that it is sealed in a glass jar. It never would have survived without that. It is amazing that it has even survived intact within the glass, and that the glass has never broken. I do not doubt that God, blessed be His name, has blessed it or that He blesses all those who have possession of it."

Tassie felt Omar relax and she let go of his hand. She hoped to never hold that hand again.

Omar took another sip of water. "Where did you find it?" He glanced at Tassie. "Wasn't it lost for some time?"

Harvey nodded. "Yes, it was stolen in 1949, recovered in 1967, and then lost again. Sally's uncle, a rabbi, will join us for lunch and give you more information."

Small talk continued as the Goldmans showed Tassie and Omar around their home and multiple gardens. Tassie desperately wanted to get Sally alone so she could reveal her situation, but Omar managed to remain with Tassie at all times playing the love-sick suitor who reveled in her presence. Tassie sensed that Sally might see through the ruse but was not sure.

They reentered the tiny dining area just as another guest arrived. Sally introduced him. "Here is my uncle, Rabbi Hermann Welcker."

A shiver ran down Tassie's back as she heard that familiar HW name. Hector Woodley, Harry Woodson, and now Hermann Welcker. She turned slowly.

He did not look just like Hector, but easily could have been related. He was short and slightly balding with tiny hair braids in the Hasidic Jew fashion. His eyes penetrated hers just like Hector's had, and it unnerved her.

Rabbi Welcker took Tassie's hand in both of his. "It is more than wonderful to meet the young lady named for the tassel in the bottle. The tassel has encountered amazing adventures, some that we know and some that we know not. I hope to share some of those adventures with you, but first . . ." Rabbi Welcker removed his jacket and laid it on a nearby chair. He turned toward Harvey and Sally Goldman, nodding only slightly toward Omar. "Have you had the news on?"

"No, uncle, we have been greeting our guests. You need to meet Tassie's fiancé, Omar Tugani." Sally touched Omar with one hand and Rabbi Welcker with the other. The two shook hands and nodded kindly to each other.

The Rabbi turned back to the Goldmans. "You must know what is happening. The Iraqi cities of Mosul and Tikrit have both been overrun by an offshoot of al-Qaeda. It's the ISIS. They have stolen uniforms and weapons of the Iraqi National Guard and are moving toward Baghdad. The Balad airport is evacuating the American personnel. It is great trouble, but we knew great trouble would come. The blood moons do not lie."

Tassie saw a quick smile sneak across Omar's face.

Harvey put both hands on his head. "Oh, dear God, blessed be Your name, have mercy on us. I thank You the tassel of Your Presence is with us and You give us protection."

"What's that?" Omar took a step toward Harvey. "You say the relic has powers?"

Rabbi Welcker held up his hands. "Now, now, not powers. God, our Father, has all the power needed. But, yes, the ownership of the relic has coincided with the blessing of God and His protection on the countries or the people that have had it in their possession."

Omar changed the subject. "Is this trouble you speak of just in Iraq?" Omar's voice sounded way too innocent.

"No, ISIS is the Islamic State of Iraq and Syria. So, this uprising is greatly supplied from Syria. All the oil reserves are being affected."

"Not our oil, Uncle." Sally began drawing the group toward the lunch table. "Let us sit and sup, before we continue our conversation."

A sweet soup was already at the table. As everyone quietly sipped the soup, Sally brought out cucumbers, avocados, hummus, and sourdough bread.

"This is wonderful, Sally. Thank you so much." Tassie smiled at her host.

"Yes, very nice." Omar looked at Sally. "Can you tell me what you mean about 'our oil'?

Harvey cleared his throat. "Well, yes, Israel has discovered oil and we are amassing means to get it out to the world."

"I suppose that will be helpful if Iraq's oil is delayed with this latest development." Tassie looked around, wondering if she really wanted to know all this.

Omar's phone beeped. Pulling it out he glanced at it. "That's my news app. Had it off on the flight. The U.S. is offering support to Iraq and so is Iran."

The rabbi bowed his head. He spoke in Hebrew, then looked around the table. "I fear that by the ninth of Av we too will see this at our door, but then we have always lived in a rough neighborhood."

"Uncle, what do you make of all this." Sally passed him the bread.

"Trouble for Israel. It has always happened around the blood moons. We will survive and come out the better for it in the long run, but the short run will be trouble for Israel."

Omar narrowed his eyes. "What do you mean, Israel will come out the better for it?"

"As you know, my friend, the countries around us would like nothing more than to totally annihilate Israel, and while they're at it, they would like to get rid of the U.S. But now, not only are the insurgents flooding Iraq, but many of them are coming from Syria. The pipeline is being overrun. Turkey is getting involved. So, we have Iraq, Syria, Iran, Turkey, and who knows who else in turmoil. I wish our little relic could thwart what they do, but I know it is the power of God Almighty that will alone deliver us. It is God who keeps Israel. The road is often bumpy, too bumpy, but God, blessed be He, always causes us to survive."

Tassie could feel Omar's rage bristling under the surface and wanted to change the subject. "I heard that many of the rabbis have turned to Jesus as their Messiah. Rabbi, is this something that surprises you."

A sweet smile crossed Rabbi Welcker's face and he closed his eyes momentarily. "Surprise? Yes. Surprise? No." He chuckled. "The claims of Jesus as the Messiah have always been far from my interest, no? But, current events, study of the Torah and the Prophets, and the hand of God Almighty, blessed be He, have strangely turned my heart and ears to listen to these claims. As other rabbis have persuaded my thinking, I, too, have given my heart to the One who always called Himself the Messiah of the Jews. Jesus has truly become my Lord and Savior, and I couldn't be more happy or more settled within my spirit."

"Uncle!" Sally stood up, came around the table, and hugged the rabbi. "Oh, I didn't know. I am so happy for you. This happened to me and Grandfather one year ago, and to Harvey shortly after he came to Israel."

"I suspected as much, Sally. I could see it in your countenance."

Tassie was dumbfounded. These were all Jews, now Christians? "So, you're Christians, now . . . not Jews."

"We like to think we are completed Jews. We have our Messiah now. We were all a little surprised that our Messiah was Jesus. It took us a long time, as Jews, to realize it, but hey, we're pretty pleased with it all." Sally had a smile that seemed to come from within even more than from her face. Her whole demeanor seemed to glow.

Tassie momentarily forgot Omar was a terrorist, ready to kill her or keep her in a burka the rest of her life, ready to turn her over to other men for whatever they wanted to do.

"Omar, remember the young man at the restaurant in Door County?"

"The Packer fan kid? Yea, what about him?" Omar looked at her and shook his head. Tassie just took it that he didn't remember.

"He prayed for us that we would find Jesus." Tassie laughed. *Is that what happened to me the other night when I prayed. Is Jesus my Messiah?*

Omar pushed his chair back from the table. It scraped on the floor. Everyone paused. "Thank you for the lunch. This conversation is not for me. I would like to hear about the relic. I would like to see the relic." His eyes bore into Harvey's. "Is not that for which you invited us?"

"Why, yes, Omar, my apologies." Harvey stood up. "Please be seated again. We have a fruit dessert. Then we will go."

Sally began to get up to retrieve the dessert. Harvey shook his head. "I'll get it. I'm already up."

The rabbi stood up. "My sincerest apologies, Omar. I did not mean to offend. I have much to tell you about the relic."

Rabbi Welcker remained standing until Omar sat. By then Harvey had returned with small bowls full of strawberries, pears, and grapes, cut in small pieces. He brought a small pitcher of cream to pour over if they desired.

"Rabbi, you mentioned the ninth of Av. What is that?" Tassie poured the cream over her fruit.

"Dear one, so many horrible things have happened on the ninth of Av, which occurs the end of July to the beginning days of August. The Temple was destroyed on that day. World War One started that day, the orders for the holocaust were given that day, and on and on. It has never been a good day for Israel.

"Now the blood moons are lunar eclipses that fall in groups of four that land on Jewish feast days. They occurred in 1493 and 1494, in 1949 and 1950, in

1967 and 1968, and right now. They began on Passover in April this year and continue to the Feast of Tabernacles next year. There will also be a total solar eclipse during this series. That also holds significance."

Tassie pressed her lips together and looked around. "Forgive me, Rabbi, my mother has told me all this, but I felt it was totally anecdotal, not prophetic or significant . . . more coincidental."

"That is how many look at it, but as one who studies the Scriptures continually and the writings of rabbis who have studied this throughout the ages, I and others are quite sure that these signs in the sky are God's signals. He writes this in the prophet Joel. It says, 'The sun shall be turned into darkness, and the moon into blood, Before the coming of the great and awesome day of the LORD.' Each of these times of the four blood moons on the feast days has indicated great trial and persecution for the Jews, but praise to our God, blessed be He, it is always followed by great triumph and provision."

Rabbi Welcker paused to sip his drink and take another spoonful of fruit. He looked all around, then continued. "In 1492, we were expelled from Spain, only to be given a whole new world via Columbus. In 1948, we received our nation Israel after the holocaust and we had to fight to keep our nation, for the British and the Arabs put up many barriers for us. In 1967, the whole world wanted to tell us what to do and the whole neighborhood around us decided to wipe us off the map. Instead, with the miracle-working hand of God, blessed be He, they were stopped. And we received Jerusalem, Gaza, and the West Bank back into our possession.

"So now, look what is happening. Lemkrof is moving into Ukraine. They are considering making Jews register. Register! That is what Hitler did before World War Two. No one confronts Lemkrof, they only appease, just as happened with Hitler. And now Iraq is being taken over by insurgents. It is not just Iraq, but Syria and Iran moving into this process. As I said, they may be at our door by the ninth of Av or before. But, the Scriptures also say that our God, blessed be He, will pour out of His spirit. The rabbis are realizing Jesus is the Messiah. Perhaps it is time that Israel will fully have their God in their hearts. Perhaps part of the provision is the oil that we now have with the promise of even more oil. And, just perhaps we will get our Temple back."

Omar jumped up. Tassie was sure he was going to pound his fist on the table or turn the table over. Instead he grabbed his knee and bent over. "I'm so sorry. Every once in a while my knee slips out of joint while just sitting. It's a sharp pain, but it subsides quickly. Please go on." Omar gingerly sat down rubbing his knee. Everyone watched him. "Please, go on. Tell us how the relic figures in."

Good recovery, Omar. What a lie! Hope you fooled no one.

Rabbi Welcker ran his fingers down one of his Hasidic braids. "I believe the relic is such a sign, a signal, of God's provision in little and big things. The Jews in 1492 lost all. The tassel, saved by little Lydia, was like their synagogue. It provided a point of worship, a gathering position. And then, it seemed that wherever it was, there was protection. As they traveled throughout those many years whether by land or by sea, they arrived safely, while others were not always safe. Coincidence, perhaps. The blessing of God, blessed be He, perhaps.

"In 1948, while many boats were turned back trying to bring Jews to Israel, the boat with the tassel had no problem. In 1967, as the six-day war was ending, and Jerusalem was recovered, a young soldier, who escaped as a child from the Nazis, was presented the relic by an Arab child at the Wailing Wall. As its story was told, many more believed that the relic was a signal of God's blessing and miracle-working power.

"But, alas, in the early 90s, it disappeared again, assumed stolen on the ninth of Av. Because of that date, many were convinced that the relic was definitely a sign of God's blessing and thus many relic hunters searched for it. It became like the movie, *Raiders of the Lost Ark*, and stories of its powers abounded."

Omar spoke up. "You think those stories are unfounded, that the relic carries no power."

"As a rabbi, the Lord's command to have no idols tells me to not put much stock into the powers of such a relic. The history and archaeological value of this tassel in the bottle is incredible, though." The rabbi put his elbows on the table and rested his chin in his hands. "The stories that go with it are sure hard to deny. Whoever has possession of it definitely has a treasure, that is for sure." Rabbi Welcker stood up. "Enough discussion. Would you like to see it?"

"Certainly." Omar stood up and pulled Tassie's chair out for her to stand up.

The drive to the museum took only a few minutes.

The museum appeared unprotected. It stood on a small residential street while children played nearby, and people walked along the worn sidewalks. Many carried bags with fruit and vegetables, even some flowers sticking out, apparently returning from a nearby market.

Tassie wondered if she could get a message to her parents through the Goldmans. Omar managed to not allow her out of his sight. Even visiting the restroom, Omar was just outside the door, as if he was concerned that she was ill, and he was ever present to assist her.

The museum was much like the Goldmans' house, small rooms, set in a haphazard fashion. Purposeful, perhaps. Endearing, but a little cluttered. Swords, shields, vases, paintings, maps from the many eras of the life of Israel. Holocaust items, war information, and Nobel Prize plaques displayed the accomplishments and the heartaches of the Jewish people. Tassie's head swiveled back and forth, taking in the comprehensive history that this little place held.

Why has this never interested me before? Mother would love this. And I studied world history. If I get out of this, I need to bring my parents here.

Very few people occupied the museum. Tassie wondered if those present were maintenance or research people. The quiet of the museum unsettled her. Everything had been noisy or tense since Omar kidnapped her. Now stillness enveloped them. Tassie wished she could relax.

They rounded a corner and there, in a little interior room, sat a pedestal with a bell jar on top. Inside the jar was a small glass bottle. It reminded Tassie of medicine bottles she'd seen in old movies. Square on the bottom, two inches across, and about six or seven inches tall, including the neck which was about an inch or so high. The top had a seal of dark brown wax. In the bottle hung a small tassel of an off-white color.

Tassie gasped and leaned in. What she beheld was over five hundred years old, and she was named for it. She counted five knots and observed the wrap of threads between the knots. A sense of reverence was in the room. Tassie could not take her eyes off it.

If it could only tell us of its adventures. All of a sudden, the tassel became blurry. Tassie stood up confused, until she realized tears were rolling down her cheeks. As she brushed them away, the Goldmans and the rabbi smiled.

Omar smiled, but she knew it was more of a smirk. The magic dissipated, and she knew he was probably waiting for a moment to remove it. *There are so many things here that he despises, but he wants this for its magical properties.*

Mr. Goldman walked over, entered a code in a small key pad on the side of the pedestal that Tassie hadn't noticed. Lifting the bell jar, he handed it to Sally and picked up the bottle with great care, as if it would shatter at any moment, and set it in Tassie's hands.

She cried. *Why is this doing this to me?*

She wiped her eyes on her sleeve as best she could, and then stared at the tassel, turning the bottle every which way. She looked at Mr. Goldman. "Thank you." Her voice was just a whisper. She glanced at Omar, fearful he would grab it, somehow shoot everybody, and run out.

He pulled out his phone and was about to take a picture when a hand reached in and removed it from Omar's possession. Omar jerked up and whirled around, eyes glaring. "What the . . ."

"Sorry, sir, no pictures."

Omar pulled himself erect and face to face with the young man who held his phone. "Excuse me. I am the fiancé for the namesake of this relic, and we are here at the request of the owners."

"Even so, I have my orders, sir."

Tassie saw five more men arrive and take positions all around the room. *Where in the world did they come from? I thought no one was here.* She looked at Harvey Goldman and shrugged her shoulders in question.

"IDF, Israeli Defense Forces. They know the value of this relic. Even a picture could be tracked by GPS and the location exposed. I'm sure you meant no harm, Mr. Tugani. I should have told you. I was so excited for Tassie to see it that I forgot. We are used to having the IDF ever ready, and we so appreciate it." He took the bottle and placed it back on the pedestal. After Sally returned the bell jar, he reentered a code in the tiny key pad.

Tassie tried not to let her smile show. She bent over to look again at the tassel, so Omar could not see her expression. She glanced sideways and could see the muscles rippling on his neck.

"No problem." His voice was strained. He reached out for the phone. "I need to answer a text."

The young man with the phone glanced at the face of it, handed it to him, and followed him as he headed toward the door. Tassie watched him dumbfounded. *Now is my chance. They'll help me. They're the IDF.*

Tassie turned to talk to the men. Before she could get a word out, Omar whirled around and locked eyes with her. "I'm so sorry, darling, forgive me. Did you see enough? If not, I can wait. Why don't you walk out with me?" He walked over to Tassie and held out his arm. She took it and walked out.

Just before getting to the door, Tassie turned. "Thank you. This means so much to me. My mother would so love to see the tassel." She brought her shoulders up and smiled. "She named me after that tassel and the little girl who kept it." A bubble of excitement rolled through Tassie. Never had she felt pride or happiness at her name, and now, here she was in Israel, being held by a terrorist, in the presence of the IDF, beholding the relic. And she was happy.

The Goldmans and the rabbi joined them outside. Tassie gushed about the relic and Omar texted.

"Will you spend the night, dear ones? We would love to have you. We have rooms for each of you. It would be no trouble at all."

"That's very kind of you, Mr. Goldman, but we must be moving on. Thank you for letting us see the relic. That was certainly an honor. And, Tassie loved it."

Tassie nodded. "I certainly did. I can't believe how blessed I feel."

Omar looked at Tassie with his face all screwed up and laughed. "Really?"

It was the first relaxed impression he gave her since that night in Chicago. It lasted only a moment. She remembered, and so did he, for his face immediately hardened and his eyes held no sparkle of love, only the image of hate.

Dear God, do the Goldmans or Rabbi Welcker see through this? Have I missed my opportunity to escape? Did the IDF figure it out?

CHAPTER 17

Omar all but shoved Tassie into the rental car. He was steaming, and she feared for her life. The excitement of moments before was gone. She tasted tension in every fiber of her being. She did not see the streets, the trees, the buildings. The people didn't see her. She was invisible again and everything was blurry. *No, don't cry Tassie. Don't let him see that. He'll kill you or beat you.*

Omar was cursing the traffic as he jerked the car through the streets on his way back to the airport. He glanced at the GPS map on the dashboard and groaned. Tassie realized he had made a wrong turn. As he tried to find a place to turn around, a car suddenly pulled in front of him just before a stop.

Tassie screamed. "Omar!"

The crunch of metal was loud enough, but Omar's cursing was louder. He threw the gear into park and jumped out, yelling at the man who was slowly climbing out of his car and rubbing his neck. The man looked at the dent and scratches Omar's car had caused and threw up his hands.

People gathered around and said it was Omar's fault. Omar denied it. He then pulled out his wallet and asked the man what the cost of repair would be, apparently realizing that he had no time to argue and have attention brought to him. The man and others gave their opinion and dickered back and forth. A car mechanic stepped forward and gave his rough estimate. It was equivalent to five hundred American dollars. The driver then reminded Omar that his neck was in a great deal of pain. Omar gave him one thousand

American dollars. The driver slapped him on the back. The crowd clapped and dispersed. The cars that had been waiting while all this occurred honked their horns for everyone to get moving.

Omar cursed again. He sighed and climbed back into the car.

Tassie was nowhere in sight. She'd left the rider's door wide open preventing Omar from driving away until he got out of the car and went around to close it. He slammed the steering wheel. Blood vessels popped out in his neck.

Horns were honking, preventing him from texting or calling at the moment for his bodyguards to assist him. He jerked the car over to the side before realizing he could not park anywhere on this thoroughfare. Not one of the side streets had an available parking slot. By the time he found a parking area, and got back to the place Tassie disappeared, she had been out of his sight for at least twenty minutes.

Tassie stumbled as she ran and skinned her knee, but she took no time to examine the wound. Where could she go? Were there police or Israeli Defense Forces? Who could she trust? This was Israel. She could probably trust everyone, but she needed to get far enough away. Omar could catch up and sweet talk anyone or shoot them. Either way she would be back in his clutches.

She found herself in Old Jaffa, now a part of Tel Aviv. The streets narrowed, and the stone steps rose to more narrow roads overlooking the sea. The brown bricks that made up the wall as she climbed the stairs felt rough on Tassie's hands. She paused and leaned against them to catch her breath. On the other side were uneven rows of roughhewn stones. They seemed to sway. Tassie half wondered if it was she that swayed. Fear oozed out of her. Maybe it was only sweat.

Rounding a corner at the summit of the stairs, Tassie lost her breath again. This time it was the sea. The beauty of the Mediterranean stole her breath. She gasped and wandered, not paying attention to where she was going. The slightly salty air was heavenly, and she began to relax just as she found herself near a market place with shops and cafes.

Thirst nudged her forward. A woman walked out the door of a cafe and observed Tassie. *I must look a sight.* The woman glanced back into her café and said. "Believe me, appeasement will never work."

Tassie recognized the European accent but could not decipher the specific country. She knew it was not Middle Eastern. "Are you Eastern European?"

The woman smiled and extended her hand. With her other hand she brushed a stray gray hair back behind her ear. "Yes, I am, my dear. And you? American?"

"Oh yes." Tassie plopped down in a wrought iron chair next to a glass topped table. She put her chin down and looked at the woman over the top of her sunglasses. "You wouldn't have a coke, would you?"

"But, of course. Americans always ask, so I always have. But come, you must have my pastry. Czech pastry is best and Czech beer is better." The woman put her hands on her hips, twisted slightly and tilted her head. "So, after your coke and pastry, we have a beer and talk."

Tassie laughed. "So, you are Czechoslovakian?"

The woman sighed. Her short chestnut hair framed her face giving her a young look. But the wrinkles on her neck and sleeveless arms revealed that she had seen many years. "We will talk with a beer." She turned and entered the small quaint building that boasted several signs in different languages. In English it said Best Bakery Ever.

The woman returned, setting an old-fashioned bottle of coke on the table with a glass of ice and a plate of kolaches, some with plum in the center, and some with poppy seed.

"Oh my, thank you so much." Tassie almost guzzled the coke and she failed in her attempt to not let any run down her face. Dabbing her face with a napkin she gulped a kolache in two bites. When she looked up, the woman was smiling broadly.

"If you burp, that will be a compliment."

"Oh, that would be so embarrassing."

"Not to the baker. It is a sign that you appreciate the food."

"Oh, I do. It's wonderful."

"My name is Yitka."

"This is so good, Yitka. My name is Tassie."

Yitka went back inside and returned with two bottles of beer, and a plate of Czech dumplings. "This has a little meat in the dumpling. You look a little thin. Don't want you to get drunk on my beer. So, eat. This is my treat for you."

Tassie tilted her head and gazed at Yitka. *Whatever does she see that she wants to sit and talk? Perhaps she needs to talk. Does she think I need to talk? I need to escape. Why am I not telling her I need help or at least a phone?*

"So now, beer is best. My treat. Besides, I need a break. I will tell you why I am not Czechoslovakian. One is either Czech or Slovak. Two different countries, because of Neville Chamberlain. He appeased Hitler. He did not stand firm. He made concessions, and Hitler came in and destroyed and divided the country. We are now one or the other. So, I am Czech."

Tassie bit her lip, then took another sip of beer. "I did not mean to offend."

"You did not offend. I like to explain. Americans used to understand. Now, your country, your administration, wants to appease. It doesn't work. My friend inside is from Ukraine. She would like to know why the U.S. lied to Ukraine. They gave up their nuclear facilities and signed a treaty with U.S. Your country promised to protect them from attack. Now they do nothing. They appease, and Ukraine suffers." Yitka threw up her hands in resignation. "How do you like the beer?"

"It's good." Tassie held it up, and Yitka tapped her bottle against Tassie's.

Yitka held up her hand. "To America. May they take a stand and help us all."

Tassie nodded. "You feel strongly about this, Yitka."

"Growing up, we lived in Lidice, just northwest of Prague, when World War Two began. Most of the men were massacred. The women and children were sent to concentration camps and were gassed. My parents saw it coming and got us out just before it happened. They talked our Jewish neighbors into leaving with us, but we were stopped at the border. Their children were blond like my mother, so the guards believed that they were my siblings. Their parents, though, were detained.

"The children began to cry as we crossed the border and their mother broke away as she was being led away and ran for her children, trying to get past the border. The husband ran after her to stop her. He knew it was hopeless for he and his wife but knew the children would survive with us. The Nazi guards shot her. The children saw it and began to scream. Their father threw his body over his wife and was also shot. In the confusion we ran. The guards perhaps realized their mistake in assuming the children belonged to our family and ordered us to halt. We did not, and they shot at us.

"I don't know how we managed to get away unscathed, but we did, at least physically. The children saw their parents shot. The son was brave and stoic, but the little girl withdrew. It was a month before she talked again.

"We traveled to Holland and were hidden along the way. Our family was marked because we harbored Jews, so we changed our name and were given false passports in Holland in order to travel to the States. We weren't Jewish, except for the two children that we claimed as our own, so travel to the United States was not too difficult.

"When we became teens, the boy and I fell in love and married. He was nineteen and I was just eighteen. We knew no one would ever understand either of us like we did each other."

Tassie had become engrossed in Yitka's story, placing her elbows on the table and holding the beer bottle with both hands. She occasionally took a sip as she listened.

"Right before we crossed that border as children, and my parents and my husband's parents were separated, I heard his mom tell my mother to never let him lose his coat. 'Promise,' she said. 'Never, ever, lose his coat. Keep it always.' At the time we thought she meant for it to keep him warm. We would be outside a great deal, and parents naturally worried about their children. I later realized my mother believed it would serve as a reminder of who he was, and the protecting love his parents had for him.

"When we arrived in the States and finally had a home, my mother put the coat in a glass topped box and hung it in his bedroom on the wall, almost like a painting.

"After we'd been married a few years and our first son was almost two, we planned to move to Israel and I decided it would be wonderful if our little boy wore his father's coat. I took it out of the box and saw it needed repair. As I separated the lining to fix the pocket and an interior seam, an envelope fell out.

"In it was a letter from the parents to my husband and his sister. It told of the story of Christopher Columbus."

Tassie's beer bottle bounced off the table shattering on the brick patio.

Yitka quickly grabbed a broom and dust pan while Tassie wiped up the spilled beer.

"I had a feeling you needed to hear this story."

Tassie wrung out the cloth in a bucket Yitka brought outside from the bakery and gave the cobblestone patio a final wipe before dropping herself back into her chair and wiping her hands dry on a napkin. "Yitka, I am so sorry. I . . . I just . . . well . . . Go on with your story."

"Here, another beer for you. Either you don't hold it well, or my story is connecting somewhere. I think the latter. Am I right?"

"Yes," Tassie mumbled. "Please, please, go on. Thank you. I'll pay for this beer." *Wait. I don't think I have any money. Where is Omar? Why am I just sitting here?*

"Did you know Christopher Columbus was part Jewish?"

Tassie nodded her head. Her hands shook, so she held onto the bottle but did not try to pick it up.

"Well the King and Queen did not. They financed his journey to the Americas with money stolen from wealthy Jews." Yitka chuckled and took a sip of beer. "I do love the irony of it. I wish I could see the look on the Queen's face when, in eternity, she found out that Columbus founded a new world where Jews could live free and prosper." Yitka shook her head and beamed at Tassie. "But that is just the beginning. Wait, let me get some more dumplings. You like?"

Tassie nodded.

"Have you lost your voice? Well I have not given you much time to talk. I will be right back."

Tassie sighed. *Next thing you know, Hector Woodley will walk around the corner. Or Omar. I should go or ask for a phone.*

Yitka returned with warm dumplings and marvelous bread. The aroma wafted around Tassie, and she wondered if she was just having an amazing dream. Surely, she would wake up soon.

"Now, where was I? Oh yes, the letter about Columbus that I found in my husband's little coat. The letter proceeded to explain that he, my husband, and his sister were direct descendants of Christopher Columbus."

Tassie stood up. She needed air. She couldn't breathe. She put her hands on her chest and pushed. Yitka watched her.

"It is warm. Shall I get you some water. Too much beer?"

"Yes, thank you." Tassie sat back down and wiped her forehead with the back of her hand.

After Tassie took a few sips of water, Yitka continued. "I am not Jewish, but I have learned to be a true storyteller like my husband." She laid her hand on Tassie's. "I know I am taking a long time. Forgive me."

Again, Tassie nodded.

"The letter informed us that the son of Columbus's cousin, Gabe Goldman, married the daughter of a Rabbi Liebermann. She, at the time of the dispersal from Spain, had kept the tassel of the Rabbi's tallith, his prayer shawl. This became the only physical representation they had of their faith. It became their synagogue and they decided to preserve it by placing it in a glass jar, sealing it with wax, and passing it on for a symbol of God's presence and blessing. It was kept with only descendants and was returned here to Israel in 1948 when Israel became a nation."

Tassie heard her mother's voice and her own echoing the story in her head. Yitka's voice blended with her mother's voice and the inner voice of Tassel Lydia Stevens telling the story together.

"In 1949 the tassel, the relic, was stolen. Then in 1967 during the Six Day War, it was recovered. There had been a total lunar eclipse on Passover, less than two months previous. The rabbis called it a Blood Moon, warning of great devastation followed by divine intervention. It seemed the whole world was against Israel, much like now. The greatest threat was the immediate neighbors." Yitka's smile was rueful. "We live in a rough neighborhood."

Yitka continued, and, as if in a dream, Tassie could hear the sounds and see the Six Day War with Yitka's husband, Aaron. She felt transported back to 1967.

1967, ISRAEL

"Shimon, this is what we are called to do." Aaron laid his hand on his friend's arm.

"I know, I know, I am ready to die for Israel, to die for you, Aaron. But I'm shaking. Those against us are so numerous."

Aaron slapped his back, "And there are more with us than with them. Remember the story of Elijah."

"I'm thinking David and Goliath."

"Either way, God, blessed be He, is with us. Now where is the enemy?"

"Probably just over the hill. Check the map. Is Syria the hill or are we already there?"

"This is the border, my friend. Guns ready. Other tanks behind us. God, can You make us invisible?"

"Be careful what you pray. We don't want to disappear."

"Right. Moshe and Ari are just to our left and a little back."

The cabin of the tank seemed tighter than ever. Sweat formed on Aaron's forehead and dripped into his eyes. It stung. Wiping across his face with his shirt sleeve, almost as wet with perspiration, Aaron stared into his gun sights. He had no time to consider the moisture and the heat. Shimon could swivel and move that tank faster than anyone he'd ever seen.

Just don't choke on me, friend. If he stayed sharp, Aaron was sure they could dodge and defend well. The rest of the fleet hidden behind him had guns ready as well.

The tank dipped and bumped up the rising ridge marking the line between Syria and Israel. Intelligence knew the biggest front could be right here. The entire Arab world had united against Israel, and now Aaron was part of the Israeli Defense Forces . . . his dream come true. He and Yitka, his wife, married as teens, moved to Israel three years previous, when their first child was two.

Now as Yitka was about to give birth, Aaron was heading into the enemy's camp. What was that children's song he heard as a child new to America after escaping the Nazis? *"I'm going into the enemy's camp, to take back what he stole from me." That's what I'm doing. Should be over the ridge in less than a minute. May God, blessed be His name, help us all.*

All citizens served two years in the Israeli Army, regardless of gender or ethnic affiliation, and Aaron was determined to be able to serve the nation of his heritage. He thought it would be difficult, but the process went smoothly and now he was beginning his second year in the military.

Shimon's voice was calm. "Nearing the crest of the ridge. Guns ready?"

"Ready." Fear and courage swelled inside. It smelled like sweat.

It took a few moments to process the scene before them as they came over that hill. Syrian tanks were in mass, gun heads pointed at them. As Aaron commenced to fire as many rounds as possible into the enemy before being decimated, he realized that dozens, perhaps hundreds of soldiers were running hands up away from them.

"Shimon, am I dreaming?"

"I am having the same dream."

"Moshe and Ari, are you seeing this, or are we dreaming?"

"We see it. Is there air cover coming behind us?"

Aaron swung around, noting all directions for anything that would make an entire army run. Nothing. At least nothing that he could see. Then he saw movement to the side.

"Driver, stop." Aaron aimed the guns at the lee side of a nearby tank. Two Syrian soldiers waved their hands and fell to their knees. Aaron glanced around. The soldiers' guns had been left behind them. *A trick? What is this?*

"Surrender. We surrender."

"Shimon, go tie their hands. I will keep the guns on them. Moshe, Ari, you see?"

"We're watching. Unbelievable."

Shimon scrambled out of the tank and tied the soldiers' hands. "Why are you surrendering?"

The two looked at each other. "You did not see?"

"See what?"

"Father Abraham. He rose over that ridge five minutes before you did. And with him an army of angels."

The second captive looked around. "We are warriors, soldiers, but we cannot withstand the heavens. You did not see it? Were they not with you?"

Aaron smiled. "Yes, those with us are more than those with you."

The tank radio bristled. "Aaron, Shimon, what is happening? We are ready with gun support. Are you meeting resistance? Are you still there?"

"We have taken two prisoners. The rest have run. There may be a few snipers left behind. Assist us in a sweep. And our tank arsenal has just grown. We need drivers more than gunners."

As the rest of the arsenal came over the hill, cheers went up. Many of them asked the captured soldiers again and again to describe Father Abraham and the angels. Soldiers cheered, a few sat stunned, and some cried. It took a few hours to sweep all the tanks to make sure no one was left behind and to move them all inside Israeli borders. It was a grand spoil.

The next day the news arrived that Jerusalem had been liberated. At this news, every soldier in Aaron's battalion fell to their knees, raised their hands, and prayed, "Blessed are you, oh King of the Universe . . . " They arose with a great cheer and danced.

Shimon shook Aaron's shoulders. "It is like a dream. Can you believe it?"

"I must go to the Temple Mount, to the Wall, as soon as we return."

"I will go as well. I must meet my father there. He was in the war in 1948. He was hit in the head by mortar. The surgery lasted all day removing bones and parts of his brain. His only prayer was that Jerusalem be liberated. When it was not, he wondered why he lived, why he was hit in the head, what he fought for, but he continued to pray. And now . . . now, Aaron . . . my father's prayers are answered. I cannot wait to see him."

Three days later, Aaron, Yitka, their five-year-old son and their newborn son, named Abraham, stood before the Wailing Wall and wept. Soon, Shimon and his father joined them, and they wrapped their arms around one another and prayed.

"Aaron, tell me what you saw, what you heard. Shimon has relayed the story to me, but I must hear it again from another voice."

Aaron laughed and clapped Shimon's father on the shoulder. He retold of the day in great detail and then introduced baby Abraham as the namesake of the battle that was not a battle.

A young boy ran up to Aaron. "Please, please, sir, I hear your story. You know the God of Abraham, Isaac, and Jacob. I fear Him but do not know Him, but I know that you should have this." From a pocket in his jacket, the boy presented Aaron a small bottle with a tassel from a prayer shawl in it. "My uncle, when he was a boy my age found this hidden in a cave not far from here. They say it is very old. That if you have it, the God of Abraham, Isaac, and Jacob will bless and protect you. I know that will only happen if you are a Jew. It did not help us in this short war. There are too many stories like you just told. Please, you should have it, for you are the blessed." The boy turned and ran away.

"May I?" Shimon's father reached out for the bottle. His eyes were big, and his breathing came in short breaths.

"Sir, are you ill?" Aaron gripped the arm of the elder man and looked him in the eyes. But the man's eyes were on the bottle. "What is it? You look like you've seen a ghost or gold." Aaron studied the bottle. "What is it?" He handed it to the older man.

Shimon's father held it gently and ran his fingers over the smooth glass, around the rounded corners, and over the wax that covered the top opening. He held it up and stared at the tassel inside. "Blessed are you, King of the Universe . . . " He recited the rest of the shema prayer as Aaron, Yitka, and Shimon bowed their heads and said it quietly with him.

The man looked up. Tears ran down his face. "There is another prayer I have prayed for many years. I have told few people. Shimon, you may remember it. I had friends who had come from the Americas. They married and opened their home to any and all, especially refugees just coming out of the holocaust. Such a kind couple. We shared wonderful food, prayed for the settling of the land and prosperity of Eretz-Israel, and had such joy as young adults with God's blessing. I had recovered from my injuries. My wife, young Shimon, his sisters, and I would visit at their house weekly. The best part was they brought with them from the Americas the relic that was as old as the famous ocean journey of Christopher Columbus.

"The Jews had been banished from Spain and they had lost all, except a tassel. The tassel represented God, the synagogue, and God's provision. It came to the Americas and was passed down through the generations to Sophie and Samuel. They returned it to Eretz-Israel. The ship they were on, full of refugees, was one of the few that met no resistance upon entering our homeland.

"While we were there one evening, having a wonderful time, and a big meal, the relic disappeared. Sophie and Samuel were remorseful. They realized they had been careless by their generosity of letting it sit on the mantel available for all to handle and look at it. Someone deceived them and stole the relic. I felt so bad for them, not to mention the loss of the relic that had represented God's blessing in so many ways, that I prayed that it would be returned or found. I had almost forgotten. Now, here it is."

Shimon and Aaron stood stock still.

"After all this time." Shimon's father let the tears roll freely. "We have Jerusalem and we have the relic. Indeed, this is a day to rejoice."

"Aaron, why do you think he gave it to you?" Shimon took the bottle from his father and examined it before handing it to Aaron.

"Just before the war, I too found out that I am a descendant of Christopher Columbus. Do you suppose this was meant to be handed down through his descendants?"

"How did the kid know?"

"God works in mysterious ways, blessed be He." Shimon's father put an arm around Aaron. "It is your turn now to be the keeper of the relic. If you are a descendant of Columbus then you are related to the Orbins. I have lost track of them but I'm sure we can find them. This is amazing."

"I think we should turn it over to the Israeli archaeological society. This should be available for all of Israel to see and learn the history. But with protection."

People were pouring in to the area of the Wailing Wall, falling on their knees and weeping. Some were dancing and shouting praise to the Almighty God. Several had gathered around Aaron, Shimon, and his father. They reached out and touched the bottle with reverence. Some passed it around and then returned it to Aaron.

The dust upon the stones rose up like a cloud with all the activity. A few coughed but did not mind. As the dust settled, the golden tone of the wall reflected in their faces from the glow of the setting sun.

———

PRESENT DAY, JAFFA

Tassie heard Yitka's voice again and seemed to wake up from the dream and return to the present. "So, Aaron, out of respect, turned it over to the authorities to place it on display, protect it, and bless all of Israel."

Tassie shook her head. This was her tassel, the one for which she was named. Hector told her mother that she, Tassel Lydia Stevens, would be influential in Israel in the last days. Could that still be? She was running for her life. Omar was after her. What if he just hired a sniper to take her out? What if he'd gone back and stolen the relic. If he was looking for her, he probably would have found her by now.

"Why there you are. Sweetheart I totally lost track of you. Did you get lost? You must be exhausted? We really should get back."

Stupid. I'm stupid. I didn't make a call or ask for help. Tassie hung her head. She couldn't even bring herself to look at Omar. He was probably smirking or seething. Smooth voice, hatred in his soul. She glanced at Yitka who simply looked at Tassie. Tassie saw the question in her eyes but could not answer.

She simply stood and said, "Thank you for the food and drink. It was wonderful." She turned to Omar and saw his bodyguards, his henchmen, a short distance away. No sense running or putting Yitka in danger. "Darling, I'm so glad you're here. I need to pay this dear woman for a lovely meal and drinks."

Yes, he's seething. But he paid and left a tip as well. As soon as they were out of sight, Tassie thought his grip would cut her arm in two.

"I should kill you. Why I let you live . . ."

CHAPTER 18

Before she could think it through, Tassie was back on a plane and changing into a burka. *How did I not escape? I think I'm so smart. Not so.* She could overhear Omar on his phone.

As the plane paused in its taxi along the runway preparing for takeoff, Tassie watched a plane unloading onto the tarmac. A young man looked her direction and Tassie almost fainted. It was Jethro, her distant cousin, grandson of Uncle Luney. Dressed in a suit coat and khaki pants, he looked so official. He was dressed nicely at the funeral, but now he looked almost in charge. Other people were handing him items and taking his luggage for him.

A car pulled up and a man stepped out and shook Jethro's hand. People began placing his luggage in the trunk. The man from the car turned and Tassie began to cry. It was her brother, Rube. How could this be? Why were they in Israel? Twenty minutes previous they might have seen her, but now she was in a burka, leaving in a plane. Twenty minutes ago, she could have called to them, run to them.

Now they would not see her or notice her, let alone recognize her. Were they here to rescue her? Mother must have called Rube, but how did he know to come to Israel? The Goldmans? No? Not enough time. Wait, Rube's an IT guy. Perhaps he could have tracked her phone. The tears almost engulfed her vision. She wiped the tears and put her hand on the window. Omar was paying no attention.

Jethro pointed her way, and in what seemed slow motion, Rube turned. He looked directly at the window and leaned forward. Rube placed a hand over his eyes to shield the sun and stared. Tassie waved and blew a kiss, all the while sobbing, trying to hold it in so Omar would not hear. Rube swiped his phone and began talking into it. He walked and then ran toward the plane.

What can he do? We are moving. We are leaving. Tassie's eyes hurt. She blew out her breath and covered her mouth with her hand. Twice now a chance to escape gone. The plane picked up speed and raced down the runway, leaving Rube and Jethro and rescue behind, and taking Tassie in a burka to a future she could not bear thinking about.

The grief engulfed Tassie's mind and she felt herself shut down. The world, the airplane, disappeared. Darkness descended on all that she was.

I am done, I have failed at that for which I was purposed, but I never understood or accepted that purpose anyway. Perhaps I can just kill myself. I should let Rube or the Goldmans know so no one looks for me. I have set them up for danger. Danger.

Danger is real. Mother was right. Forgive me. Someone, please forgive me. God, Jesus, please forgive me. I have failed. I will die. Please don't let anyone else be hurt or killed.

The darkness became a fog. It was almost worse than the darkness, because it seemed that she should be able to see, but she could not. It was hard to breathe. Perhaps she was dying. If so, she should just yield to it. Why did she resist? She'd failed. She deserved death.

There were no tears now. She would be brave. No, not brave, just accepting.

"Tassie, everyone deserves death. Everyone has failed."

Tassie heard the voice and looked around. Too foggy. Gray air. Rotten, moist smelling air. No life. Dead.

What? Everyone deserves death? Then why is anyone alive? She closed her eyes and slumped into the seat. Cradling her face in her hands, she let the tears begin again.

"Tassie, look at me."

Tassie blew out air from her cheeks and slightly shook her head. *Well, Omar is here to kill me now. Maybe if I keep my eyes closed it will just be over.*

"Tassie, please look at me."

Please? What? Already it seemed hard to lift her eyelids. *I can't open my eyes. Don't make me. Just kill me.*

"I am not here to kill you, but to show you life."

What? Tassie's eyes flew open. *What?* That voice. She recognized that voice. But who did it belong to? The fog ran through her mind. Focus left. She tried to catch it. *I know that voice. Who is it? Where is it?*

"Tassel."

Tassie whirled her head and looked across the aisle. There sat Hector Woodley in the fog. He had a strange light about him.

"Oh, Hector, don't tell me you are God." *Perhaps I've already died.*

"No, Tassel, only a messenger." He smiled that almost toothless grin, and the warmth crossed the aisle and wrapped itself around her.

"Am I alive?"

"You are, but only physically."

"What do you mean?"

The fog thinned and there was light in the cabin of the aircraft. Tassie could see Omar in the distance, still on the phone, but it seemed he was in a movie, not real, just visible to her.

"I mean it is time to receive forgiveness and live."

"I don't deserve that. I have failed."

"Everyone has failed. No one deserves forgiveness."

"Well that's a happy thought, Hector. And I thought perhaps you had good news." *I guess I am still alive. My cynicism has returned.*

"But God, in His great love for us all, sent us His Son as a provision to die in our place, that we might walk in newness of life."

An electric pulse began in Tassie's shoulders and traveled to her toes. Her mind snapped clear. Truth filled her thoughts. She was a lawyer. She always sensed that she could discern truth in a courtroom, in people. Somehow, she had remained clueless in terms of truth for herself. Now, she could see. The fog was gone from her mind.

The rabbi, the Goldmans, were right. Jesus was the Messiah. Wait. Jesus is the Messiah. He is my Messiah. He gave His life for me because He loved me. He still loves me. How can it be? Tears once more poured from her eyes.

"Hector?" Tassie's voice was soft. It was full of respect. She had only talked with disdain to this man, the messenger of God Almighty, blessed be He. "I believe. I receive Jesus as my Messiah, as my Lord. He died for me. I'm free. I'm forgiven. Forgiven. Thank you, Hector. Forgive me for my ugly attitude." Her eyes looked at his. "Thank you, for visiting my mother before I was born."

Hector smiled. "Praise God, Tassie. But now, this time will seem like a dream as it seemed to your mother. The fog will lift. I will be gone. Omar will be talking on his phone. In his mind, you have been asleep all this time." Hector chuckled. "That's because he hears you snoring. He will continue to consider you asleep, but you will be alert, more observant than you've ever imagined in the courtroom. Listen to his every word. Remember them. You will not die. You did not fail. You needed to remain with Omar to hear these plans. Listen, Tassie, listen."

———

"Jethro, get to the Goldmans and find out what they learned. I am already finding out where this plane is going. I'll get back to you later."

Rube trotted toward the terminal. His phone rang. Swiping it, he answered. "Jared, Jethro is here, but we just saw a plane leave. We're quite sure we saw Tassie on the plane and assume Tugani is with her. I'm heading toward the terminal to find out where the plane is going. Could blow my cover, though."

"Rube, Jethro already sent us the picture, the video, he took of the plane. Got the info."

"Whaaat?" Rube stopped and caught his breath.

"Jethro's good. The flight is scheduled to return to Damascus. The names are not authentic, but, you're right, it's most likely Tugani. And it is Tassie in the window. She's crying, Rube."

"Oh, man. How did this happen?" Rube bent over, placing one hand on his knee. The steam on the tarmac lifted and increased the perspiration on his face. "Okay, Jared, what now?"

"Get yourself over to the museum where the relic is kept. We're getting some chatter about an IDF soldier there getting a take on Tugani's phone. They were considering shooting down the plane. Frank is handling it, and talked them down, and Jill's dad is here, too. Jill will run interference with your folks. If this continues, she may have to reveal your CIA involvement."

"Yeah, I know." Another car arrived as the first had left with Jethro. Rube climbed in and gave instructions to go to the museum.

Rube showed his CIA identification to the IDF that met him at the door.

"Right this way, sir." The man ushered Rube into a small interior room. Just before entering, Rube glanced to his right.

"Is that it, the relic with the tassel? Is that it?" He walked toward it, eyes wide.

"Sir, it is, but let's look at it later."

Rube pulled his gaze from the bottle, and nodding his head, followed the soldier into the small room. Three more IDF greeted him.

"We got a take on Tugani's phone. He was about to take a picture, and we stopped him. James, here, grabbed the phone out of his hand and must have hit a button for when he glanced down just before returning it to the man, there were three texts." The soldier smiled. "It was good that it was James. He had our new copy chip strapped to the palm of his hand. He didn't have Tugani's phone long enough to get everything, and it took a while to get through his firewalls and encryptions, but what he did get was a gold mine and we sent it to the Mossad.

"One text was one of the five Gitmo prisoners recently released by the U.S. in exchange for a prisoner of war. Apparently, the guy is a cousin of Tugani. The second one was from The Ghost, the mastermind of the ISIS raid on Iraq. He was informing Tugani of the progress. Just on that alone, we scrambled jets to take him out, as the third text indicated that his plane was ready and waiting for him here in Tel Aviv.

"Upon informing the U.S., your lead man, Jared, requested a stand down through his operative, Frank, based on the U.S. citizen, your sister, on board that plane. Sir, there is no question that her life is in great danger. Tugani is a major player here. The texts seem to indicate that he is not just an informant but a decision maker, and these people are reporting to him. At first, we thought he was an info gatherer for ISIS. But as the back story is coming in, his family runs the Syrian part of the Islamic State of Iraq and Syria.

"As you may already know, ISIS plans to establish an Islamic Caliphate for the States of Syria, Iraq, Jordan, Lebanon, Palestine, and Israel. They are brutal and superstitious. They think the relic will give them extra powers, and if your sister is the namesake, they may feel she will serve them in some capacity. I fear to consider how. Perhaps they will return for the relic. Forgive me, sir, but they may sacrifice her for the relic or for some superstitious ritual for power."

Sweat poured from Rube's forehead and ran into his eyes. Wiping it with his hand did not stop it.

"Sir, perhaps you should not be here. I understand another man from the States familiar with the case of the relic and all the religious underpinnings is here as well. Perhaps he should be the point man."

"He's our cousin. I thank you for your consideration, but we are here, and we will perform. I trust all of you will remain involved. Please let us or Jared know whatever you need."

"Yes, sir. I believe your cousin has arrived."

One of the IDF soldiers opened the door. Rube did not get up but turned in his chair. Jethro stood one foot from the relic, stooped to look eye level at the tassel. He turned his head. "It's amazing, is it not? May I handle it, albeit carefully." He stood up and attempted to take the little boy admiration off his face as he saw the soldiers standing in the office and Rube appearing not well. "I'm sorry. I just, well . . . never mind. Forgive me." He walked over to the IDF. "I'm Jethro Winkelman."

"Yes, sir." The soldier shook his hand. "I'm Jonas Samuel. James, go ahead and let Mr. Stevens and Mr. Winkelman see the relic. They are part of the family that brought it to us."

Rube stood and patted Jethro on the back. "They just debriefed me. It's pretty bad. But let's see the relic."

The bell jar was removed, and the relic was carefully handed first to Rube. He gingerly held it, turning and noting everything. He counted the knots in the tassel as he handed it to Jethro.

"Your sister counted the knots, too." James smiled.

Rube shook his head. "When we were kids, I really teased her about her name. I told her that a real tassel had k-n-o-t-s but she had n-o-t-s. Not pretty, not smart, not nice."

Jethro nodded. "I remember that drove her crazy, and then she'd call you a Rubik's Cube and threaten to rearrange your face."

"She did sometimes. She's a fighter." Rube's face fell. "Maybe she can survive this."

Jethro returned the bottle to the pedestal. "Thank you so much. This is an honor, but now what?"

"Let's return to the office." James, Jethro, and Rube each found a seat in the small room jam-packed with papers and file boxes. The lead soldier, Jonas, sat down behind the desk. His square shoulders and his direct brown eyes displayed professionalism and respect. There was no question that he was in charge.

"We are getting more intel. Mossad has further infiltrated Tugani's cell phone and we are quite certain he is unaware. He has revealed nothing about the hostage, excuse me, your sister, Tassie. He is planning high-level meetings in Syria. He has connections with Lemkrof, with released terrorists from Gitmo, and with ISIS. He is a powerful man."

"Are we going after him?" Rube sat on the edge of the chair. Tassie was at the mercy of a monster.

"I am." Jethro's eyes met Rube's. "I've been on the phone with Jared, Frank, and even Jill's dad. You perhaps didn't know I've done a lot of field work. Jared wanted that time with me, not so much for the prophecy timeline. He already knew that. He wanted to get me ready in case something of this sort happened. Thankfully I saw and actually got the video of Tassie. And I talked to the Goldmans."

"Tell me. How was she when she was with them? Did he show his hand?"

"He did, in his disdain. They saw the pleading in her eyes and the steel in his, but they had no idea it was anything so serious. They just felt he was not very fond of the Jewish mindset, but that he really cared for Tassie. They thought they were just picking up on a basic disagreement between them concerning faith. And, they assumed he was simply a secular Jew, not a Muslim. When the soldier took his phone, the Goldmans were a bit afraid, saw real anger, but again had no idea."

Jonas stood up. "All right, Jethro is going to Syria with a Mossad operative."

Rube felt himself shaking. *Pull yourself together, man. It's your sister, but you can handle it. She can handle it. She can. She's a Stevens. She's tougher than me. We're of Columbus stock.* Rube realized his eyes were closed and his face rested in his hands with his elbows on his knees. He opened his eyes. Jethro and the soldier were looking at him.

Rube clapped his knees with his hands. "Okay, Jethro and a Mossad agent. Name?"

"Esras." Jonas smiled. "And he's my cousin, so Rube, you and I will be the info and intel guys here, keeping tabs, monitoring, and ready to go if need be."

"Is there a plan?"

Jethro and Jonas exchanged looks. Jethro stood up. "Rube, I'm taking the relic and am going to set up an exchange. Tassie for the relic."

"Wait. You do that, they'll kill her and you. They're ruthless, Jethro. Have you heard what ISIS is doing? They round up soldiers, cut off their heads, shoot them, and then post the video. They have kids using Uzis. He has no use for Tassie unless he thinks she can come back here and get the relic." Rube realized he was yelling.

Jethro put his hand on Rube's shoulder. Rube pushed it off. "Rube, it probably won't be a direct exchange, but that's the end result. We have some contacts there. They will be told I stole it or purchased it from someone who did. I know all the details here, so Tugani can't fool me with the minutiae of the place and background. We hope to sell it for a handsome price and in the meantime, free Tassie."

"Things don't always go as planned." Rube ran his hand over his face.

"That's true. That's why you will be here, monitoring every step. And that's why we need to go now." Jethro reached out and shook Rube's hand. "We'll get her, Rube. I'll have the relic of God's blessing with me."

Rube pinched the bridge of his nose. "But once they have the relic, you won't have it."

"True, but we'll get her, and we'll get back."

———

Tassie listened. Amazed, she could hear herself lightly snoring. She settled back in her seat and focused her mind and ears on Omar's conversation. Her hands rested on the heavy fabric of the black burka. *Not exactly my little black dress or my black power suit, but somehow, I sit in a powerful place right now.*

Omar sat in the front near the pilot's cab. His elbows were on his knee and one hand was on his chin. The other hand held the phone close to his ear. He nodded and shook his head. Occasionally he cast an eye toward Tassie, and even though she could see and hear him, he basically ignored her presence, somehow convinced she was asleep.

"No, that won't do. I don't care how long it takes. If they abandoned the weapons, I want them gathered. Most of them are American and we need their technology. This is not a short plan. We are in this for the long haul." There was a pause. Omar rubbed his eye while he listened.

"My cousin that just got released from Gitmo . . . Yes, get in touch with him in Qatar. He's already contacted me. They're already back on board. They can run interference and help ISIS map out the strategies. I know Baghdad is tough, but we can secure borders all around. He has some ideas on how to deal with Iran. America thinks Iran backs Al-Jamal in Iraq, but we have a lot of sleeper cells in Iran."

Omar stood and stretched. He grabbed a bottle of water, took a swig, and sat down. He waved his hand at one of his nearby men. The man walked past Tassie, paused to look at her, and went on. Shortly he returned with a plate of cheese, nuts, and grapes and set it on the tray table next to Omar.

"The Gitmo guys, one of them has connections in Iran. They'll get in touch with them . . . true, our calls would be suspicious. Let Lemkrof know that we have Russians in Iran and Iraq, as well as Syria. Tell him they have contacted us for assistance." Omar laughed. "Of course, I know, but what does it matter . . . if we tell Lemkrof, he'll believe us. All he needs is a 'concern' and he will act. Getting Russia's military moving our way will totally confuse the Americans. They have no idea who to work with right now, Sunni or Shia, Russia or Ukraine, so they do nothing. It's perfect."

Omar leaned back in his seat, stretching his legs out in front of him. "Let's activate all the separatist cells in Ukraine. If they're shooting down planes . . . or the Russian military is shooting them down . . . what difference does it make?

The Ukrainians will fight back and then Lemkrof can move in. So can we. Now, the Czech Republic is the only one who is gathering troops on their borders. They stand with the U.S. and unfortunately with Israel, not Hamas. We need to step up our plans to get in the Czech Republic and Slovakia. Lemkrof is too slow on that, but if we can rally even a few Russian Jews or any pro-Russian citizens, we can get Lemkrof or our own people in there to 'assist'."

Omar stood and sat down in a different seat. "Patience. We will attack the U.S. all in good time. Right now, we need them confused and arguing about everything and accomplishing nothing. Their president thinks he should just be able to do what he wants with his pen, with no Congress or anyone to stop him or slow him down. He has effectively thrown the economy and the whole country into a tailspin. Like I said before, we need to act before the next president takes over. But right now, we need to focus on the Middle East and Eastern Europe."

Omar stood up and walked the aisle. He paused next to Tassie and stared at her for a few seconds. Tassie could hear herself lightly snoring still and marveled. She wanted to smile but did not dare.

"Yes, yes, I almost forgot. We need to get out the information that Israel is finding good sources of oil . . . I know, who would've thought. However, that gives Russia another reason to go after Israel . . . for their oil. We need to find a few more Russians that will say Israel has not fulfilled their promise of prosperity to them and Lemkrof could almost take care of Israel for us. So, let ISIS know I said to get all the weapons they can and secure all borders out of Iraq, contact my cousin for more strategies to get those borders and to contact our people in Iran. Lemkrof needs to know there are abused Russians in all places, and that Israel is stealing their oil. What? Tell them you have proof that their oil reserves are connected to Russia's. And, let Lemkrof know again we might consider sharing our chemical weapons with him . . . right, or use them in exchange for a few favors."

Omar hit the end button on his phone. After taking a few more bites of cheese, he rubbed his eyes, glanced back at Tassie, and pulled out his laptop.

"Boss, weren't you going to send those American weapons into Israel?"

"Yeah, my Gitmo cousin is going to get some of them into Israel, and he has some American contacts that he'll also move into Israel. In addition, he's going to run some interference on the possible search and rescue of the woman here." He nodded toward Tassie. "She'll draw some Americans, perhaps Israelis, looking for her. We can take out some key people in Israel and then leave some dead Americans with the American weapons as evidence. That will increase suspicion and distrust between Israel and the U.S. which works for us." He crossed his arms and pulled his shoulders back. "The plan is working quite well."

At that, Omar focused on his laptop and seemed engrossed in whatever information it held the rest of the flight. Tassie felt the strange sleep lift as they touched down in Damascus. She had heard every word and actually watched though she appeared asleep to her captors.

CHAPTER 19

Jethro and Esras played the part of antiquities dealers who stopped at nothing to steal and make money on any antiquity they could find and sell. Jethro's flawless Arabic served him well in the ruse.

They stood near the portal entryways into the Four Seasons Hotel on the famed Barada River in the downtown district of Damascus. Slightly cluttered with marketplace treasures for sale outside, the inside displayed richness and class. Jethro haggled a bit with the sellers and kept an eye out for Omar while Esras gazed through the sale items making comments as well. Their contacts had little time to pave the way, so Jethro and Esras were on their own. When Jethro spotted Omar and Tassie, he and Esras quickly entered the impressive lobby area to wait.

Jethro walked up to Omar as he entered the hotel, Tassie in tow. "Excuse me, great sir Tugani." Jethro bowed.

Omar stopped. "There are places for hand-outs. This is not one of them." Omar turned away.

"Oh, you wound me, my great one. I have something you desire and only request an adequate remuneration."

Omar turned back, and Jethro bowed again. "I have little time for your entertainment. What is it you want?"

Jethro stood and smiled. "Oh, sir, it is what you want. Does the name Goldman sound familiar to you?"

Tassie stood with her head down. Discreetly she looked around at the elegant furniture, the heavy curtains, and tried to see the art that filled every available spot. Old world jeweled vases, exquisite paintings with ornate frames, and sculpture graced a lobby decorated in deep warm reds accented with gold and cream.

Then she heard the name Goldman. *What?* She looked up. The man looked familiar, but not. Could this be anyone she knew? She remembered her place and quickly looked down and studied the marble floor.

"Goldman? The Jew who holds the . . . ?" Omar had switched to English.

"A wise man you are, indeed. Yes, the Jew who holds the relic." The man swept his arms out again in a bow.

"Enough. What do you want?" Omar gripped Tassie's arm tighter.

"We deal in antiquities, sir. We have heard you were impressed with the Goldmans' relic. We have our ways, sir, to . . . how shall I say, to obtain certain items that are desired by men of means, such as you."

Omar looked around. "Are you telling me you have the Goldman relic."

Tassie swallowed a gasp and tilted her head to observe this man again.

He glanced over at his companion. "I told you he was a discerning man."

"Show me."

The pain in Tassie's arm intensified. She lowered her head again but sensed the steel in Omar's eyes.

"Let us discuss our remuneration first, Mr. Tugani."

"I could just take it. There are armed guards around."

"True, true. I have an armed guard as well." He signaled to his companion who revealed his Uzi under his coat. "But why make things messy. This can be an easy exchange."

"How did you obtain it?"

Tassie stole a glance as the man smiled. "We have our ways. We can be very persuasive. We can also be very stealthy. I think that is all we'll reveal about it."

"Where was it? Where did you steal it from?"

"Oh, the little museum, where it sat on the quaint pedestal under the bell jar. They thought it quite secure."

"How much?" Omar looked around noting his guards.

"One million would do."

"Too much."

"I understand you enjoy women, much as we do."

Tassie stifled a groan. Omar's grip tightened once more.

She looked at this snake of a man with her eyes wide. *No, No.* Suddenly a flashback filled her mind of the airport tarmac and seeing Jethro. She closed her eyes and turned away.

Omar jerked her around. "This is a pretty one. I'm about done with her. What would be the price for this relic if I throw her in?" Omar chuckled.

Tassie took advantage of the moment and looked at the man in the eyes. Yes, it was Jethro. Escape. They had come after her. She covered her mouth with her hands as if she were upset. *Please, God, don't let me blow his cover by being happy.*

"Five hundred thousand would do. She looks like a feisty one."

Jethro, I can beat you up.

Omar jerked her up again. "That she is. If indeed you have the relic, I will pay your price and include this woman."

"Excellent, how soon . . . "

"I have a meeting right now. I will see you here at ten tomorrow morning. If you do not have the relic, I will have you shot."

Jethro bowed. "A pleasure doing business with you, Mr. Tugani. We are staying here as well. We will see you in the morning." He and the other man turned and walked out into the marketplace.

Omar watched them for a moment, chuckled, and then went on to his meeting after making sure Tassie entered the women's quarters. She hoped that, indeed, Omar would release her. The relic would be gone, but at least she had seen the relic. And she had a lot of information about Omar's plans.

The hotel room was clean and elegant. The furniture sported an excellent combination of comfort and sleek lines. The charcoal gray, accented with golden tones and a few deep reds, provided an inviting ambiance. Esras worked on his reports and gazed at the view from their high floor.

Jethro paced. "It's warm. Let's walk along the river before it gets dark."

Esras smiled. "Americans. Can't sit still. It's fine. I like to walk."

Jethro hid the bottle in his clothing. Esras tucked his Uzi in his jacket, and they walked out into the beauty of the city. The warmth of the air wafted over them mixing with the smells of the outdoor restaurants and the market place. As they paused to examine the fruit in one of the kiosks, Jethro felt a gun in his side.

"Give me the relic."

Jethro turned. Three men, big men, stood behind him. Esras had his hand on his Uzi, but one of the men already had a gun in his side as well. Jethro heard a shuffling noise. The sellers in the market place quietly removed themselves from the area. There would be no support. They had slipped up. Blew it. Perspiration gathered on his forehead. *Will Tassie live, now?*

The gun was jammed further into his ribs. "The relic, now."

Jethro glanced at Esras. He nodded. Jethro reached inside his shirt to the pocket that held the precious antiquity that was to buy his cousin back. He carefully pulled it out and handed it to the men.

Each man looked closely at it. They looked at Jethro. "This is it? This bottle?"

"Yes, that's it. Mr. Tugani was to purchase it in the morning. He is powerful. He will not be happy that you have stolen it from us."

The men laughed. "We work for Mr. Tugani. This does not look like it is worth a half a million, but we have it and will take it to Mr. Tugani, the rightful owner."

Jethro coughed. He wanted to protest and demand it back. He wanted to tell them Tugani did not own it, ever. He stuffed the argument down. Life would be a good exchange right now.

"Tugani said not to kill you, at least not yet, so go, get out of here. Go back to where you came from. You have twenty-four hours. If you remain, you'll be dead."

Jethro and Esras walked, glancing over their shoulders at times, to the hotel.

Stopping just outside the hotel, Esras looked around. "That certainly didn't go well. However, we are alive, when they easily could have killed us. Must think we're not worth it. Should have known that once we revealed ourselves we would be targets. Foolish on my part. But God, blessed be He, has given us our lives. They may be watching us."

Esras faced Jethro and lowered his voice. "When we get back to the room, assume they've bugged it, so no talking, except for things unimportant. We'll need to examine our clothing in case they have placed indicators or microphones. Hopefully tomorrow we'll find our package and deliver it home."

Without speaking further, they returned to the room. The room had been ransacked.

Quickly stepping in and shutting the door, Esras took a deep breath. "Guess it was good we left. We'd be dead."

Twenty minutes later, their search discovered two listening devices. One was embedded into the heavy drapes on the window. The other was attached to the hinge of a closet door next the bathroom.

"I think I'll take a shower." Esras began running the water and shut the door to the bathroom but stayed in the main room. He found a piece of paper and wrote a note. 'If they realize we found their devices, they may return and kill us. Let's try to mislead them'.

Jethro walked over to the bathroom door and opened it. "Hey, man, that freaked me out. I'm going to bed. We need to leave by early afternoon tomorrow."

Esras walked through the door and turned off the water. "Yea, I hear you. I think I hear Qatar calling me."

———————

As morning peeked through the heavy curtains, the call to prayer sounded forth as it did in all the Islamic areas six times a day. Jethro and Esras left the room very quietly, hoping the listeners would think they still slept.

They found a quiet spot in the hotel restaurant and ordered breakfast. Elegance graced every section of the restaurant. Tablecloths and chairs were shades of gold and creams, and each table entertained tall narrow glass vases filled with yellow wild flowers. They examined the table for listening bugs and decided they were safe, at least for the moment, although it was most likely they were being watched and followed.

"We need a strategy to rescue her, but we've no leverage now. We can't separate. We'd be too easy to grab." Esras picked up his coffee cup. "Do you think she's here?"

Jethro pulled a notebook out of his briefcase. He sketched a map of the hotel, river, road, and office buildings. "This is where we saw them yesterday, walking to the hotel from the building on the other side of park. Now perhaps they drove and parked, but maybe they are housed over there."

"Or that was another meeting. Tugani has his fingers in every surge of Islamic takeover that's going on in the world. He's got his relic. He doesn't need Tassie."

Jethro swallowed and released a pent-up breath. "Will he just dispose of her?" He rubbed his neck.

"He might. We need to locate her first. They may be here at the hotel. Our room wasn't broken into. They must have had the key. Maybe he owns the hotel. He has the money."

"Makes sense."

They ate in silence for a few minutes. A group of businessmen sat in the tables near them and talked loudly about the contracts they'd signed, and the money exchanged. That afternoon they'd fly home, much more prosperous than when they arrived. And not only that, but the man had promised them some women to entertain them for a few hours before their flight.

Esras shook his head and glanced at Jethro. "Tassie might be included. She's here somewhere. This hotel or that other building or neighborhood."

The businessmen finished their breakfast and went outside with their coffee to sit on the veranda by the river. Jethro and Esras followed them. To any observer, they blended in with the businessmen. Their discussion revealed the women would arrive in about an hour. Seated at a wrought iron table near the river, Jethro and Esras watched for any glimpse of Omar or Tassie, hoping she might still be with him.

Jethro prayed she was okay. He only had that painful, tear-stained image of her on the plane and the look of total shock as she realized who he was the day before. He'd always admired Rube and Tassie growing up. Popularity followed them while he was the nerd. Grandad wore the moniker of nerd long before Jethro. Tagged as Mr. Luney because of his love of space and science, Jethro assumed his grandad's travels consisted of teacher conferences. However, they were CIA missions. Jethro never had a clue until he met Rube's father-in-law who recruited him on Grandad's recommendation. It was the most exciting day of his life. And, now he was tasked with saving Tassie's life.

Esras cleared his throat. "Visual at ten o'clock."

Jethro nodded and pulled out his phone and sent an encrypted text to Rube and Jonas back at the museum. They had not used the phones after the relic had been taken from them knowing it might be detected, but now it was essential. Contacts needed to be informed.

A few of the businessmen also noticed Omar and Tassie. "There he is. He's bringing one. More will follow." The men grinned and patted one another on the back. A few rose and headed toward a back entrance of the hotel.

Those behind stayed seated. "We go in five minutes. Guess we don't want to overwhelm the ladies by arriving all at once." They all snickered.

Jethro and Esras stood and walked to the river, then circled around the veranda, hoping the businessmen would block Omar's view of them.

Would Tassie see them and break and run. She was a smart woman, but what had Omar done to her in terms of control? Would they be able to get a shot off at him or did he have snipers hidden on roofs and in bushes? Even if they shot him, and retrieved Tassie, would they be able to get out of the city without being detected or captured? Would their contacts be able to help? It wouldn't be easy, but they had to follow her, get her attention. Maybe they could rescue her from the businessmen.

They paused to see if Omar offered her to the men, but he steered her away from the hotel as his bodyguards arrived on the veranda with several women and escorted the remaining businessmen into the hotel's back entrance.

Rube sat in the office with Jonas. He observed the computer screen placed on the desk. Jethro and Esras had been outfitted with an Israeli developed global positioning identification chip. "I didn't know that Jethro was fluent in all the Arab dialects."

"He's been in the field some time. I understand that he began studying languages in high school. His grandfather and your father-in-law connected at your wedding and recruitment followed."

Rube shook his head. "Where was I? How did I not know this? Was I in the field or something? Wait. Our wedding? No wonder, I wasn't even recruited then. I never would've dreamed Jethro had seniority on me."

"Is that a problem?" Jonas paused in his typing and dipped his head toward Rube.

"No, just makes me wonder if there are others in the family with CIA connections."

"I worked with your wife, her dad, and Jethro. I'm always the back-up assistant. I'm a tactician, and help operatives strategize routes and procedures."

"So, you're Mossad or IDF?"

"Technically, I'm IDF. That is where I put in my time. I do some training and tactics for the Mossad. So, actually I'm both." Jonas smiled.

A message feed came across the computer screen. Jonas quickly decrypted it.

"They have visual contact. Jethro's picture of Tassie on the plane has been inserted into his glasses, accessible through his phone. When he looks at a woman in a burka, the facial recognition app deciphers the image on the phone."

"Where in Damascus are they?"

"Downtown near the Barada River. Near the Four Seasons Hotel. Our operatives have stayed there before. The building is less than twenty years old. Jethro and Esras are on Shukri Al Quatli Street, near the Eastern Gate."

"I was there once. Can we zoom in on the street and see if we can locate Tassie ourselves?'

"Rube, our technology cannot be matched by anyone. However, too many eyes are detectable. We don't need any more eyes on the package if Jethro and Esras have a visual on her."

"Right. I just keep seeing my mother's eyes pleading with me to get her home."

"Believe me, Rube, I know exactly. That's why you're here, not there. Being such a small country, we deal with family connections all the time. No matter how great your ability, you sit it out, work with the technology, but not in the field." Jonas stood up and poured a cup of coffee from the little corner stand behind his desk. Setting it in front of Rube, he turned to get one for himself.

With the warm cup held in both hands, Rube studied the computer screen. The red and blue dots indicating Jethro and Esras were moving. He wanted to zoom in, but Jonas was right. "I think this is fairly close to the House of Saint Ananias. A guy I was undercover with wanted to visit it when we were there.

I think it's where the Christian Church got its strongest advocate other than Jesus, and it's amazing it's preserved from the first century."

"That would be the apostle Paul, right?" Jonas sat back down behind his desk and took a sip of the hot coffee. "Yeah, it's interesting being Jewish, living in the land, yet it's the Christians who want to visit all the sites. A bit ironic. But I don't mind. My brother-in-law is a tour guide, and it's amazing the Christians' love for Israel. I understand the Muslims' attachment to the land because so many have lived here so long, but the Christians are just in love with Israel."

"Tell me what you think about all the rabbis saying Jesus is the Messiah. My mom told me it was on the news. They went public."

"That's what I mean . . . it's all so interesting. I believe in God. I believe He wants to bless and protect Israel. I like being Jewish and I love being able to serve my country, but I'm not so sure about Jesus. I mean we're taught that the Messiah will come, hasn't yet come. And now the rabbis that taught us are saying, 'Oops, He's here. Actually, He was here.' It's a little strange."

"I hear ya." Silence settled on the two. Rube prayed for the safety of his sister.

Omar and Tassie walked along the road nearest the river. He'd had enough of Tassie and he had the relic now. It was time to be done with this woman. American women were so bossy, so irreverent. Sharia law was what they needed. They had an opinion on everything and expected to be treated with respect. Well, he'd played the game. It had been fun. But now it was time for the Islamic Caliphate. For Sharia Law. For conquering the Middle East for Allah. To blot out the little Satan, Israel. To someday wipe out the Great Satan, the U.S. Nothing could replace the pride he felt to be a part of it.

Omar pulled himself up straight. Not only a part of it, but a constructor of much of the plan. What delight that his cousin and the other Taliban had been let out of Gitmo. The American president thought they would be good . . . just talk about it and everyone would work together. Well the president had part of it right. The Taliban, the al-Qaeda, and the ISIS would talk and work together, thanks to the great skills of Omar Tugani, the mastermind of Allah's plans for this time and place.

His grandfather had seen it in him, from that fateful day Omar was sent to live with him, uprooted from the city and so resentful. His grandfather knew. He saw the fire in Omar then and the ability, and he had groomed it, shaped him, taught him, and then sent him to the U.S. to make contacts, to make inroads and plans. And now, victory. The bloodshed did not bother him. Those it bothered, he did away with quickly. There was no time for patience anymore. They had been patient and now the wait was over. The plans had been laid out and now fulfillment was coming.

Why had he put up with this woman so long? Perhaps to get the relic. *For some reason I need this relic. It will keep me safe. I am not dumb enough to think there won't be those who will attempt to take my place. And I will have the relic and I will be protected.* But now Tassel Lydia Stevens was dispensable. She always loved the water. Chicago. Grant Park. Door County. Water, water, water. Omar spat. *I will leave her in the river. A fitting end. I will let her see the relic and then dispose of her.*

A short distance from the hotel and the river, Omar stopped. He pulled out the relic. Shock covered Tassie's face. "How did you get that, Omar?"

He slapped her. She had no right to demand information from him. "I have my ways. I get what I want."

She said no more and lowered her head. That was better.

———

Jethro saw Omar and Tassie stop. He faced her and pulled out the relic. He was laughing. He held it, so she had to reach for it. Then a sizzle filled the air.

"Drone!"

Jethro and Esras dove over the veranda wall and rolled down a grass embankment toward the river as the explosion obliterated a car and anything near it. Debris and smoke filled the air. They both scrambled back up the hill and ran toward Tassie and Omar. But Tassie and Omar had disappeared.

Sirens pierced their ears. Screams and cries for help were everywhere. Running to the spot where they last saw Tassie, they found a small crater. It was surrounded by broken rock, pieces of cars, and pieces of people.

Jethro bit his lip. *Keep looking. Doesn't mean they have been blown up. Does it?*

A man lay like a rag doll about forty feet from the crater. Jethro went near and leaned in for a closer look. It was Omar. He was dead or close to it.

Jethro signaled to Esras. "It's him. Dead or almost. Check this distance in a perimeter. She may have been thrown just as far."

Jethro circled to the right, while Esras went to the left. They dodged people with broken or missing limbs, many deathly silent, others crying for help. Three ambulances arrived, and triage was being set up. Scanning every person in a burka, neither Jethro nor Esras saw Tassie.

Could she have survived? Did the relic survive? They surveyed the area with as much precision as the chaos would allow, making one more circle. Jethro wanted to cry himself. Prophecy had been spoken about her. He had to believe she was alive. Everything within him screamed that she was dead, but what if she survived? That was the premise they had to go by. Now they had to determine what she might do.

Jethro turned in a circle studying every direction. "If we assume she survived, she would try to escape. She had no idea, at least I don't think she did, where we were. Which way would she run?"

"On the chance she saw us over on the veranda, let's check that out and the river." Esras began to run. Jethro followed.

People were either actively searching for or assisting the injured. Others wandered. Confusion reigned. At least no one paid attention to Jethro and Esras.

Part of the triage was setting up on the veranda. Jethro's eyes took in everyone in a burka. No Tassie. Perhaps she had shed the burka . . . still no one resembled his cousin.

"River on this side. Business section there. Would she go to a residential area?" Esras stopped and looked at Jethro.

"Maybe someone would take her in if she was injured. Would they protect a woman injured or being given over to men's pleasure?"

"Jethro, injury yes, but man's discretion, no. This is not a woman friendly atmosphere. Few will give her shelter, but if she is injured, it's a possibility."

Jethro pulled his jacket off and wrapped it around his head. He coughed from the smoke and debris that continued to clog the air as they ran toward the residential section closest to the hotel. Esras kept his head down and his hand over his mouth and nose as they dodged the broken concrete. The cries grew more faint as they put distance between them and the site of the explosion, but the traffic increased as ambulances and service personnel hurried to assist.

CHAPTER 20

A FEW MINUTES EARLIER, DAMASCUS

"Now, Tassie. Look at it." They stood near the street, just a short distance from the hotel on a sidewalk leading to the river.

Carefully Tassie lifted her head. Omar shoved the relic in her face and then held it two inches away. "Ha, namesake, Tassel. But it's mine, so I don't need you. I'll let you touch it one last time. Go ahead."

Tassie reached up and placed her hands on the bottle. At that instant there was a sizzle followed by an explosion. The drone hit the nearby car, but the force of the explosion sent the two of them flying, as well as anyone in the vicinity.

Omar landed on the paved sidewalk on his head and rolled, cracking his face against a small stone fence. He immediately found himself standing on the other side of the fence, looking at a man who most likely was dead and laying right where he thought he had landed. He looked around. No one else moved. He alone survived. Well, that was only right. He was the most important man in the country. Allah had blessed him and chosen him. And he had the relic. He began to feel for the relic. He must have dropped it.

It was gone and so was Tassie. He needed to find the relic. Perhaps she grabbed it when the explosion took place. *It protected me. I hope it didn't protect her.*

Omar stepped over the fence, but when he looked down, his other foot seemed to pass through the fence. That was weird. He paused and looked at the man lying dead beside him. He looked strangely familiar. He could be his brother. Omar paused. Something was not right here. He bent down to turn the body over and his hand passed through the body. He screamed and jumped.

Omar heard footsteps. Coming toward him was a regal man with robes of glorious fabric and colors. A light seemed to surround him, emanate from him. Omar remembered stories of the Twelfth Imam and how he would come in great elegance and richness. Could this be him? This was no head of state that he knew. He wanted to fall on his knees before this man, but he could not move.

Omar ordered himself to look down. He could not. The light mesmerized him making him feel dizzy yet more stable than he'd ever felt before. He could not remove his eyes from this dazzling authority and feared he would be struck down for his disrespect, his insubordination. The man, the king, advanced toward him. There was nothing else. No sound. In fact, the silence was engulfing. It confused Omar, yet his mind felt so clear. *Who, indeed, is this?*

A fragrance. A slight odor of lavender. It was light, effervescent. Omar quickly glanced around, still no sound, no movement, only this man, this king, walking regally toward him. He stood and waited. He could not move.

"Omar." The voice was rich, so authoritative, yet almost melodic. Omar couldn't quite comprehend the quality.

"You . . . you know my name?" Omar fell to one knee.

"I knew you before you were born."

Omar felt his head would explode. This was too much to grasp. This must be the Twelfth Imam.

"I am not the Imam, Omar."

Omar's head jerked up. His mind jerked to attention. "Then who . . . what . . . I mean, if . . . I may humbly . . . ask, who, sir . . . are you?" Drums were going off in Omar's chest and he could barely breathe. If this was not the Twelfth Imam, it must . . . it couldn't . . . be . . .

"I am Jesus, the Christ."

Omar fell to the ground and pounded his fists. "Nooooo! This cannot be. I will not see this." He jumped up and turned away. He walked and clenched his fists with every step.

I have heard of these visions and dreams. They are from the great Satan, not from Allah. I will not succumb. I will not.

Omar stopped and looked down. There on the ground lay the body that was killed in the explosion. Was this someone else? He knew he should be several blocks from the bomb site by now. He glanced behind him. The horrible glorious man was still there. The man's eyes bore through him. Now there was pain. This man must be evil.

He tortures me. I will not bow to him. I will not submit to his ways. Never.

"Then you may die, Omar. That is you on the ground. If you remain there and die, you will not go to paradise. I am the door to life, not Islamic jihad. You love death. This is death. It is pain and fire for eternity. I am the way, the truth, the life. Choose life, Omar."

Omar threw himself to the ground, falling on top of the man. Pain engulfed him. "No, no, this cannot be true. I choose life, but my life, not yours."

Darkness. Nothing. *Am I done? Am I dead? No paradise. Pain. Fire. I'm burning up.*

Omar could think no more.

————

The explosion sent Tassie flying through the air. Whatever she landed on penetrated her burka. There were stinging scratches everywhere. Bees, ants, shrapnel? She had trouble seeing. A liquid ran into her eye and darkened her vision.

Cries, she heard cries for help, cries of loss everywhere. Sirens screamed, and smoke rose.

Omar had been beside her. He'd taunted her with the relic, held it to her face, said she would never have it. For some reason he let her reach up for it. She knew he would pull it away and laugh or hit her with it. But she had wrapped her fingers around it, felt the cool smooth glass.

Then the crack, the boom, the bomb, she didn't know what it was. She brought her arm up and bent her head to wipe her eye.

Everything hurt, but she was alive. The liquid she felt was sticky. She opened her eye and touched her forehead. A bloody gash. Searing pain rolled through her.

She looked around. She had landed in a very prickly shrub, and stickers were stuck in every square inch of her. It would have been worse without the burka. She smiled as best she could. At least for once she was thankful for the burka.

Then she glanced down. Tassie stared through a haze. It was the relic! The explosion must have occurred just as her hands closed on it.

Tassie wanted to laugh but cried. The salty tears stung. She, like Lydia in a time of expulsion, had saved the tassel. Perhaps there would be a Columbus to rescue her as he rescued little Lydia.

Tassie caressed the bottle and kissed it. Tears made it hard to see, but she studied it, counted the five knots and thought of her brother Rube. Did he see her that day in Israel?

Get up, Tassie, you need to leave now.

She obeyed. Gingerly she rolled over and out of the bush. Every part of her felt scratched, but she had the relic. She had it, and Omar was . . . well she didn't know where he was. He could show up anytime, so it was time to move. She reached inside the burka to a pocket and placed the bottle in it.

She stood straight and turned. Devastation was everywhere. Injuries and death met her eyes. She wanted to help, but the voice inside had said to leave, and she needed to obey. Which way?

A little girl ran up to her. She pulled Tassie's hand. Tassie let the child lead her.

It seemed right. Tassie ran with the girl. People parted and let them go because of the child. People were crying out to anyone that was ambulatory, but no one requested help from Tassie and the child. In a matter of minutes, they were in a residential area and no one was around.

The child ran Tassie right up to a house. The door opened quickly, and a woman conducted Tassie into the house. She looked familiar.

"Quickly. Come with me. We need to clean you up and put ointment on your injuries. We have little time. You must get out of Syria." She ushered Tassie into a back room and began washing her face.

"But, you, who . . . "

"Remember the servants for Tugani's big meeting, the shooting?"

"You were there?"

"Look at me."

"Yes, yes, you smiled. I didn't understand."

"I am with Mossad. Undercover in the Muslim world for the glory of God."

"You have your daughter with you, under cover?" It didn't seem quite right.

"She is a neighbor. Her family does not serve Allah. We keep each other's secret and watch each other's back. She is able to go places where many cannot go. Her father works as a guard and brings me secrets. Her mother is a cook and got me the job with Tugani."

"How did the girl know it was me?"

"She saw you cry and tuck the relic in your pocket. Had that not happened, I'm not sure we would have found you."

"I'm crying again. What should I do now?"

"I have a clean burka that you can put on until you are safe. I have street clothes to put on under, and I have a safer pocket that you can wrap around yourself with the relic right next to you, so you don't lose it." She smiled. "I've heard that anyone that has it is kept safe."

Tassie took her hand. "I have no idea what to do, where to go, but thank you for taking care of me, helping me to escape." Tassie began to cry as the anguish of the past days oozed out of her pores.

The woman placed her arms around her and rocked her like a mother with her child. "There, there, we have a way for you."

"You do? I don't even know your name."

"And we will keep it that way. I believe God will bring us together again someday. But my name you do not need. It is the umbrella of secrecy that protects us." She brought out the clothes and a burka.

"Please tell me, if you are Mossad, why we weren't rescued, or Omar caught when we were at the meeting."

"I was undercover, as you know, and could not have technological communication. We were trying to get more information on the Russian connections and discover if Tugani was the informant or a decision-maker. I filed my report yesterday, which is when I was informed of your situation."

"I have learned a great deal of information about his plans." Tassie removed the burka she had on and the woman helped her wash and apply ointment to the many scratches and the small gash on her forehead. Thankfully, most had not penetrated the skin deeply. They were simply scratches.

Washing and applying cream was heaven to Tassie. She dressed and admired the street clothes briefly in the mirror. Next, she wrapped a scarf around her waist made of a sturdy material. It held two pockets. The bottle was placed in one and false identification was placed in the other in case she needed it. The burka was placed over all.

While Tassie dressed, the woman wrapped cheese and bread in a small bag that Tassie could put over her shoulder and tuck under the folds of the burka. Tassie took a long drink of water before she said, "I'm ready."

"I have been contacted by another Mossad operative who is here looking for you. He and another man of the CIA will intercept you and hopefully get you back to Israel."

Tassie felt her pulse quicken. Might her brother or Jethro be along? CIA? Did they come to help? Had the CIA been onto Omar all along? She couldn't quite put the pieces together.

I simply want to go home. If this woman is caught, she could be shot or hung. Oh God, keep us safe. Keep her safe for helping me.

"We will leave now."

Tassie nodded and followed.

———————

Rube sat with his head in his hands. Jonas was immersed in technology. His screen had Hebrew sentences running across the top. He was typing, texting, and speaking Hebrew into his mouthpiece which was connected to several inputs.

They had been chatting and watching Esras and Jethro moving toward Omar and Tassie. They had a visual and were on the move. And then, the explosion. The drone was visible on the screen. Rube couldn't breathe. His sister. Possibly blown up by a terrorist. How would he tell his mother? How would he live? Why hadn't he gone? He couldn't have protected her, could he? He groaned.

Jonas glanced over at him, and then went back to his communications. After several minutes he turned to Rube.

"She's okay, Rube."

Rube's head popped up. "Tassie?"

"We have contact with a female undercover Mossad who was able to recover her after the explosion."

Rube closed his eyes. "Recover?"

"Alive, Rube, she's alive with minimal injuries. Just scratches. Amazing, yes. And she has the bottle. Most importantly, she has a lot of information on Omar Tugani. We are sending a Mossad agent to intercept and debrief her."

"I need . . . can I . . . " Rube's hands were sweaty.

"You're going along, Rube."

Rube just stared.

"Rube, did you hear me. You are going along, not just because we like you and you're her brother, but she may well be severely traumatized and not know who to trust. We need you to give her the level of safety she needs to tell us everything. Jethro will also be there. Is that clear, Rube? Are you hearing me?"

Rube nodded. "Yes, I'm good. I hear you. When do we leave?"

"Now. We have a cargo plane flying into Damascus. You will dress as a businessman, while our Mossad agent will be in traditional Arab dress. They will lay the ground rules on the flight, but just so you know, Rube . . . " Jonas grinned. "He will do the talking. And you need to pull yourself together."

"Yes, sir."

"Can you tell me where we are going?" Tassie and her handler walked briskly along the road that traveled toward the river.

The handler took Tassie's arm. Her face showed concern, but Tassie could not detect fear. "Church of Ananias. Are you familiar with it?"

"No, I know of synagogues, but no churches. Why there?"

"No more questions. It is better you do not know."

Tassie hurried through the streets beside the woman. Whenever possible, they went in the same direction as other people in the streets. People were running toward the explosion, either to protest and demonstrate, or to assist the wounded.

After several blocks they ducked into an alleyway and stepped through an open door in a stone wall. Tassie thought it seemed more like a low window. She thought she would find herself in a courtyard or another alley, but they went down a set of stone stairs just out of sight of the wall opening. At the foot of the stairs were three tunnels spanning out from a tiny room. The woman led Tassie into the left tunnel. It was dark, but there were small lights tucked into the wall that provided enough light to allow them to find their way. The coolness wafted around Tassie. She gingerly touched the wall. The bricks were slightly bumpy but worn almost smooth. Despite the cooler air, the bricks had a slight warmth to them.

The tunnel ended at another set of stairs. Tassie was about to go up the steps, but the woman tugged her arm. She crossed to the other side of a small room and pulled out two different bricks in the wall. It seemed surreal, as if she was in a movie hunting for archaeological treasure.

A section of the wall opened just enough for them to slip through. Before entering, the woman carefully returned the two bricks and then quickly followed Tassie to the other side. The door closed. The quietness of it surprised Tassie.

The woman smiled. "We are safe now. We are under the river and near the church. Centuries of building and rebuilding has caused there to be layers of rooms underground. Tunnels allow us to traverse safely when the weather is unkind or there is danger in the streets. Very few know this place that we are in now, but it is connected to the church. Someone there will help you return to Israel. Miss Stevens, it is a pleasure to serve you, the lady of the bottle. You are helping to keep evil from taking over the world."

Tassie stopped. "I don't know what to say. I thank you and I thank God for keeping me alive, so I can return to my family."

"Not just to your family, but the family of God. You let the God of Israel and His Son speak to you and guide you. We are honored to be a part of that plan."

Tassie began to shake all over. The other woman hugged her, took her hand, and led her down another tunnel.

At the end, she tapped on one brick. A small window opened, and two eyes beheld the two of them. "Who are you?"

Tassie's guide smiled. "The genie is here."

The door swung opened and they stepped in. Immediately they were whisked up a set of stairs and around a corner. Ushered into a small room, Tassie was met by the heavenly smell of a sweet soup and fresh bread. Seated at an ornate wooden table on one side of the stone room were four people. The two with their backs to Tassie swiveled around upon hearing the door.

Tassie squealed and fell into her brother's arms.

Rube squeezed her long and hard. Tears coursed down his cheeks. He finally loosened his grip and stood back with his hands on her shoulders. "Tassie, I thought I might never see you again."

Tassie buried her face in his shoulder and mumbled, "Me, too."

Jethro placed a hand on her back. "Tassie, I am so sorry we weren't able to get you before the explosion. We were over on the veranda, watching and waiting for the right moment." He looked down and shook his head. "We obviously waited too long. I'm so sorry."

Tassie looked at Jethro and saw the man, whereas at his grandfather's funeral she saw a boy. "It's okay, Jethro. You were there. Seeing you yesterday gave me hope. Thank you." She put her arms around him and hugged him and cried. Pulling back, she wiped her eyes with her sleeve. "Did Omar get away?"

Jethro looked over at Rube and then back at Tassie. "We think he's dead, but not quite sure. He was lying limp on the side of the road and you were our priority. The body was gone when we checked back with our surveillance eyes at IDF. And we didn't find the relic bottle either. We're so sorry."

Tassie stood still. She brought her hands up to her mouth and ran them across her face. "Omar's dead? I should be glad, I guess. He was awful, and he was planning terrible things. Oh, I have a whole list of plans that ISIS and Lemkrof and Omar are plotting. He thought I was sleeping on the plane and I heard it all. But, he's dead?" She bit her lip. "Wait, I have the bottle. The relic, my tassel. He was taunting me with it and made me reach for it right before the explosion. Somehow it ended up in my hands." She reached inside her burka and pulled it out and placed it in Jethro's hands.

"You know, my grandfather held this bottle in his hands in Israel not long before it was stolen. The history of God's purposes and blessings so amaze me." Jethro passed the bottle to Rube, who just held it and turned it.

Rube glanced at Tassie. "Five knots."

"Rube."

"Tassie, not dead, not missing, not afraid, not injured, and . . . not pretty in a burka." He grinned at her.

Tassie laughed. "Rube, that is so true. Someone help me get this thing off." Tassie looked around again. "And, was I called a genie?"

Jethro answered. "Think about it. Genie in a bottle."

Tassie shook her head. "Am I supposed to give you three wishes? I would love to. Wait. Where is the woman who brought me here?"

Rube stood up to help his sister. "She's gone, Tassie. Her mission was to deliver you to us safely and that she did."

"Oh, I wanted to thank her again, Rube."

"She saw you and your brother hugging. That was thanks enough." Jethro smiled. "A lot of people have been trying to rescue you, including these new friends, here. This is Rabbi Joshua and Pastor David."

A short, stout man extended his hand to Tassie. His deep brown eyes held kindness. His clothing was rumpled. Tassie wondered if he too had just arrived or if perhaps he had to sleep in them.

"Tassie we want to welcome you. We are here undercover as you might presume. I am actually a part of Aman, Israeli Military Intelligence, as well as a Rabbi. I am here to find out what you have learned from Omar Tugani, a man whose family has great influence in many anti-Israeli events as well as strong leadership with ISIS. We have been trying to find the layers of networks that he is in charge of and getting a take on his phone was key. Your personal information will fill that in."

The other gentleman stepped forward and took both her hands in his. "Tassie, I too am pleased to meet you. I know you have been through an ordeal the last few days. I am a pastor stationed here in Damascus providing information as I can to both Aman and the Mossad. Where we sit is one floor lower than the famed Church of Ananias. Ananias was the man God sent to Saul to restore his vision and tell him of what great things God would do through him. Saul, later known as Paul . . . who wrote the majority of the New Testament in the Bible . . . was on the road to Damascus to arrest the Christians. God did not like that idea and knocked Saul off his horse, spoke to him, and struck him blind. He sent him to this place to receive his healing and find out God's plans for him." Pastor David pulled a chair out from the table. "Please sit down. You must be worn out. We have food and drink for you."

Tassie sat down and sighed. She looked from one gentleman to the other, then back to her brother. "I didn't pay much attention to the Jewish stories, and I don't think I heard too many Christian ones. I'm glad you're here, though. Are you in danger, now? Have I put you in a more dangerous position than you were?"

The rabbi smiled. "We are always in danger. David and I rather thrive on it. We believe God, blessed be He, has called us to these places. We are continually watched, a bit like the cat and mouse game, but to make the metaphor a little more modernistic, the mouse is what is connected to the computer, the technology. Israel is the leader in technological innovation, so we have many methods to avoid the cat that would rip us to shreds."

The Pastor poured and handed a cup of tea to Tassie. "We also have a lot of people praying for us and we spend a good deal of time in prayer. We believe God knows the way we take and the way we need to take, so we pray and then trust the instincts, the leading, that we sense that He gives us."

The rabbi set soup and bread in front of Tassie. She picked up a spoon and a shudder of relief coursed through her. She practically inhaled the food.

As soon as she finished, the rabbi gestured to Rube, Tassie, and Jethro to follow the pastor through a door they had not even seen before. A winding stairway led downward to a large cavern lit only by LED lights and computer screens filled with streaming videos of scenes from Iraq, Israel, Syria, Jordan, Lebanon, Egypt, Gaza, and Iran. One large screen was divided into sections showing border crossing points. Three men and two women kept their eyes riveted to the screens. Every few seconds they typed information into laptops on tables before them. Each one briefly acknowledged the visitors but kept their eyes on the screens.

Tassie was invited to sit at one of the kiosks of computer keyboards. The rabbi punched a few buttons and before Tassie on the screens were three men in uniform. Rabbi Joshua informed Tassie that the three represented the Shin Bet, the Aman, and the Mossad, similar to the U.S. FBI, Military Intelligence, and CIA.

"Tassie Stevens, you were on the airplane with Omar Tugani and with him at other times. Will you now reveal what you have learned to these men?"

CHAPTER 21

Rube sat on one of the couches across from his mother. She sat with her hand over her mouth. Her eyes were directed at Rube, but he sensed she did not see him but instead saw fears, saw terror, and Rube wished he could spare her. His dad walked over and sat down. He placed his arm around her and she buried her face in his shoulder. She began to shake, and the sobs convulsed out of her.

Her sobs lessened, and she looked at Rube. "I know Tassie's strong. But she's my daughter, my little girl. Oh, I know she's okay, but what awfulness she's endured. Will she be able to recover, Rube? Oh, we tried to warn her." She looked up. "Is that man in jail? He truly belongs there." She looked up into her husband's eyes. "Don't you agree, Jack."

"I do. We were unsure of him, but never dreamed it was this bad. What have you heard about him, son?"

"He may be dead."

"Oh, well . . . " His mom wrung her hands. "I suppose . . . oh, I don't know. I just want to know Tassie's really okay."

His dad sat up straighter as his mom stood to go make a cup of tea. "You said 'may be'. Do you know if he's dead?"

"Well, Jethro saw him and thought he might be, but then they went to find Tassie. When they checked into it, they couldn't find out for sure if he was dead or just seriously injured. Best case scenario is he's hospitalized."

His mom stopped, turned, and stared at him. His dad tilted his head and squinted his eyes.

Rube looked around. "What?"

"Jethro? Our Jethro? Winkelman Jethro?"

Rube took a deep breath and shook his head. "Man, I am so slipping up. I shouldn't be on the case when it's my sister. They tried to tell me, but I wouldn't hear it. Mom, sit back down. I have a lot to tell you."

"No, I'll get us all a cup of tea. I have a feeling this will be a long conversation."

"Dad, I . . . "

"Let's wait for the tea. I'll get the cheese and crackers. We'll sit at the table." He looked sideways at his son. "Rube, should I take notes?"

"I'd rather you didn't, Dad. Why do I feel like I got caught with my hand in the cookie jar?"

"Sorry, son, but we just need to know what's going on."

His mom brought in the tea. His dad set the cheese and crackers on the table and sat down across from Rube. They both picked up their tea and waited for Rube to explain.

Rube bit his lip, then looked at both parents. "Okay, bottom line, right away, and it stays here. Is that clear?"

His father shook his head. "Okay, but what . . . "

"Stays here, Dad, you guys know too much already."

"All right."

"Please, Rube, just tell us." His mother set her cup down and took a deep breath.

"Bottom line, Jethro and I are both CIA."

His dad looked at Rube over his glasses and held his breath.

His mother looked up at the ceiling. "Well, I'm glad I set my cup down." She placed her elbow on the table and rubbed her forehead against her hand. "Does Jill know this?"

Rube's grin was sheepish. "Jill was CIA before me but is basically retired."

"How did this happen?" His dad put both hands on the table and stood up. He turned around and then sat down again. "How did I not see this? Jethro, too?"

"Yes, Jethro was recruited at our wedding . . . before I was."

"What? Did Rupert know this?"

Rube laughed. It was a nervous laugh. "Well . . . Rupert was CIA as well and good friends with Jill's dad who is also retired CIA. Jill's dad recruited both Jethro and me. Actually, Jill told her dad I needed to be in after I got the Washington Electric job."

"So, those training sessions in other countries weren't for the electrical grid job?"

"Training and missions."

"Oh, my. And I thought we had such a quiet, nicely boring, family." His mom sliced a piece of cheese, placed it on a cracker, and ate it.

"So, you were there in Israel, looking for Tassie?" His dad leaned back in his chair and ran his fingers through his hair.

"I was in Israel. Jethro went to Syria. I wanted to go, but they made me stay back and do tactical because I was pretty emotional. Jethro and Es . . . the guy from Israel he was with almost lost her when the explosion happened."

"Son, was she hurt? Truth, please."

"Scratched from a bush she landed in, shaken up, cut on her forehead, but for the most part, amazingly okay."

"And where is she now?" His mother leaned forward.

Rube looked down. "In Israel."

"Why?" It was in unison from both parents. His dad put his arm around his wife.

Rube stood up and walked around his chair, placing his hands on the back of the chair. "She's working for the Goldmans and the Israeli law firm that handles their oil permits."

His dad gave a little chuckle and put his hands up. "Well, that makes perfect sense. What in the world is she thinking? What is going on, here? She should be home. Isn't she still in danger? Wouldn't Omar's people come after her? This is crazy."

Tears ran down his mom's face. "This can't be!"

"It's her choice, Mom."

"But, she's been traumatized. She's not thinking clearly." His mom dabbed at her eyes with a tissue.

"She believes the prophecy about her."

His parents looked at each other and then at Rube. His mom put her head in her hand before looking up again. "The prophecy about her being influential in Israel's future?"

"Yup." Rube reached over for a piece of cheese.

"So now what? I miss my girl." His dad placed his hand over his wife's hand.

"Well, Dad, she wants you and Mom to join her."

His dad rolled his eyes. "Well now, that sounds reasonable."

His mom tilted her head. "We could, you know."

His dad shook his head again. "Oh, boy, here we go."

———

MEANWHILE IN DAMASCUS

Omar's eyes flew open. His body convulsed in pain. Groans were everywhere. He realized the groans belonged to him. A young woman came into focus. Beautiful, long flowing hair, face close to his filled with sweetness.

Omar's voice struggled. "Paradise?"

The sweet face smiled and giggled. "No, Mr. Tugani, Damascus General Hospital. We thought we might not get you back. You were severely hurt and burned in the explosion. But you are alive."

"The explosion?" Omar's mind tried to comprehend. Thinking was so difficult. He attempted to sit up. Searing pain across his mid-section screamed at him.

"Oh, sir. You cannot move. You are injured. Please lay still."

Omar closed his eyes and searched his mind. Memories came in waves. *A beautiful woman. Her name? Tassie. A Jew. Why would I remember a Jew? Chicago. Oh, yes. A bottle. Magical powers. Really? ISIS. Conquest. Meetings. Decisions. The woman again. The explosion? The explosion. That man. No. I'm alive. I'm here. I'm not dreaming now. That was a dream. The explosion was real. The man was not.*

"How are you, Omar? Are you awake?"

That voice he knew. Omar opened his eyes. An old and wizened man stood there. His face was stern, yet there was compassion in his eyes. He gripped Omar's hand. Omar winced and tried to make it a smile. "Grandfather, so good to see you." Out of the corner of his eye, Omar saw the young nurse leave the room.

The old man's laugh unsettled Omar. "It is good to see you alive, but not so incapacitated."

"I'm awake now. How long was I out?"

"Two days, son, two days. At least your enemies think you are dead. But your subordinates have feared you are dead." Omar's grandfather turned and nodded to two men that now stood in the doorway. They walked over to Omar. They were Omar's brothers, Saiim and Daran. Grandfather closed the door.

Again, Omar grimaced. This was not a good sign. "Brothers, what brings you to Damascus?"

"You, Omar. Well, actually, Grandfather and the Brotherhood. Decisions still have to be made. ISIS needs some guidance and help. The fighting has been stymied moving south. Baghdad has fortified itself. The U.S. reentered in the name of support. Iran has sent militia against us. Russia is sending us fighter planes and weapons. Egypt has contacted us and will consider assistance, albeit discreetly."

Omar shook his head and thought it would fall off. He closed his eyes until the dizziness left. "No, not Egypt, not now. It would show our hand too early. We need Lemkrof moving Russia through Ukraine, Slovakia, and Czech

Republic while everyone focuses on Iraq. If Egypt enters the ring, all will know, and if we haven't closed enough borders, the U.S. or Israel will attack. We can't have that happen."

"Brother, you fear the U.S. and Israel?" Saiim tipped his head to his grandfather. "I told you it was too much time in the U.S. and with his pretty little Jew. He's gone soft. Perhaps we should pull these plugs."

Omar bit his tongue. He had been so proud of his rise to power, ahead of his older brothers. Grandfather had preferred him, he was sure, but now he was not so certain. He looked at the old man who looked away.

"Omar, I think we need to put Saiim in charge. Daran will be his right-hand man until you are well."

The bile rose in Omar's throat. The protest rose in his whole being. "No, Grandfather, I will pick up right where I left off." Every ounce of his body hurt, but to be trounced by his brothers was not acceptable.

Grandfather gave an almost imperceptible nod to the brothers. They left the room without a word. Grandfather reached out and gripped Omar's shoulder. Pain shot through every fiber of his body. "Son, you've done good work, but you are unable right now. You are a great loss to the cause, but I think your brothers will do an acceptable job. I will stay right beside them, but we need the two of them. You could do it alone. I hope you survive. Perhaps there will still be a spot for you."

"Grandfather. Please. I . . ."

The old man shook his head. "The decision is made, Omar. It saddens me. You made me proud. But now your brothers will take over. Do get well." He squared his shoulders and left the room without looking back at Omar.

Tears filled Omar's eyes and he squeezed them shut. *How can this be? I'm the man. I run the show. They can't do it without me. I must get well quickly.*

A sharpness penetrated his arm. Turning his head, he saw the sweet young nurse pulling a needle from his arm. "You need to sleep, Mr. Tugani. You will heal faster."

"No!" The sound was gurgled. He thrashed.

The nurse laid her hand on his arm. "Yes, it will be better."

No. I must get up. I have decisions to make. Why is no sound coming out of my mouth? Why can I not think? Omar felt himself sinking. Was it quicksand? Was it death? It did not feel like sleep.

The pain left. The nurse left. No, the room left. Grandfather let him die. It was wrong, but he certainly deserved Paradise. The light and glory that seemed to descend upon him and around him was more wonderful than any had ever told him. He glanced to his side. A throne. Yes. He had served Allah well and was being rewarded. But why did Allah, or anyone, have sandals on? A sensation of fear crept up his body. Omar hesitated then turned fully.

The King smiled at Omar. "Yes, we meet again."

Omar convulsed. The King reached over and touched his shoulder. The shaking stopped. The strangest peace filled him. He'd felt pride; he'd felt power; he'd felt satisfaction. Peace, however, was a stranger. Omar was not sure if he liked it. He looked at the King. "Who are you, really?"

"Omar, I am Jesus, whom you despise. Even so, I desire to show you where you will live in your spirit if you follow me, the place you will go when you die."

Omar coughed.

Jesus smiled. "I know your thoughts, Omar. All is made plain to me."

Omar said nothing. He looked around and saw the most magnificent streets of gold below him. Gold. And fields, mountains, rivers, trees, and flowers of every color in a vast panorama before him. He sat above this scene so that nothing hindered his view.

"You would sit with me in the heavenlies, Omar, and all this would be yours to enjoy."

I like the gold.

"I thought you would." Jesus laughed. "Remember, I know your thoughts. Now, Omar, this is not your Paradise with seventy virgins. I would like to show you what that is actually like."

Omar looked over and studied Jesus.

"Look there, Omar." He gestured to his left. "That is where your friends go when they assume they are going to Paradise."

Omar turned. A black cloud stood in front of him. As Omar watched, it thinned and revealed a pit filled with fiery stones. The stench of burning flesh assaulted his nose. The red glow of the stones provided the only light. A sound of agonized cries rose to Omar's ears. He felt rather than heard a voice calling his name. The weight and the screech of the voice unnerved him. Shivers ran down his spine as he felt the heat of the place.

Omar squinted his eyes and stood. He walked to the edge of the cavern. He saw no one, but he felt a chaotic spirit and grimaced as he felt pain. The pain enveloped him, and tendrils of flames licked at his feet. "No, this is not Paradise. This is not where my friends go."

Jesus stood beside him. "Yes, Omar, it is. It is tragic and doesn't have to be." Jesus pointed. Omar saw his hospital bed. Doctors and nurses stood around shaking their heads. He saw in the hallway his grandfather seated with his head in his hands.

"Omar, you can live or die. You will die now, if I don't intervene. The doctors cannot help you. Your grandfather, as much as he loves you, cannot help you. If you die now, without making me your Lord, you will not go to Paradise. You will go to this awful place I just showed you. But, if you take me as your Lord, you will come to be with me when you die, and in this life you will know peace and freedom in your spirit."

Omar jerked his head around. "This can't be happening, because it is not true. You don't exist. It's just a dream."

"Yes, it is a dream, but it's true, Omar. I have loved you since before you were born." Omar whirled to face Jesus. "I am not a God of hate, as you have been raised to believe. I gave my life for all those who dwell in the world whether they respond to me or not. But I stand before you today and give you a choice between life and death. Choose life, Omar, choose life."

"I can't . . . I mean . . . why . . . ? What do you expect of me? What do you have in it for me?"

"I have set plans for you, Omar. They are not what you have done or what your family has taught you. If you follow me, you will discover these plans. And if you follow me, you will have peace now and forever."

"I am gifted at war, not peace. I lead. I command. I receive respect. I don't need peace or love . . . that is temporary. I have responsibility. That is the mark of a man. I will have peace and love in Paradi—" Omar stopped.

"There is no peace or love there, Omar. Only pain and regret and hate. Your fuel now is hate, is it not?"

"Yes, hate is good fuel and for good reason." Omar looked into Jesus' eyes. It stunned him. What was it? His eyes were pools. Deep, calm. Omar had never seen anything like it. It transfixed him. It held him. *Is that peace? Love?*

Omar wanted to be cynical, but he felt cynicism leave. The void was quickly filled with a remarkable understanding that life was good, that people had worth, that men had a purpose to benefit others. It was almost more than he could bear. Yet it felt good. It fit. That surprised him. It fit.

Omar looked around. Jesus was fading, and the hospital room was moving closer. He heard the voice of Jesus one more time. "I will pursue you, Omar, until you choose to pursue me. I have given my life that you might know me. I did it because I love you and have given you a great purpose."

Omar shivered and then all went dark once more.

———

Omar coughed. The nurse screamed. Something fell and clattered on the floor. Someone called a name. Another called a number. Omar could hear people running and yelling. He opened his eyes. His grandfather had tears in his eyes. His brothers stood back with eyes wide. They were not smiling.

Doctors were taking his pulse and shining lights in his eyes. Then he realized it. The pain was gone. His mind was clear.

"I think I'm okay." His voice was clear. He sat up. With all the IVs it was difficult, but there was no pain.

"Your skin is no longer burned. Look at this!" The doctors pulled his hospital gown sleeve up, so all could see. "These were serious burns. There's fresh skin here now." They backed up. Everyone was silent.

Grandfather stepped even closer. "Allah has raised his leader up. We will win this war. We will conquer. You are all witnesses to the amazing power of Allah. I don't believe you need to be here anymore, son. We have work to do."

Saiim and Daran locked eyes and sighed deeply. Grandfather saw it. "Your time will come. It is not yet. We have Allah's seal on Omar now and we must submit to his plan."

The doctors unhooked all tubes and monitors from Omar. He stood up thinking he would be shaky, but instead he felt strong and agile, not even stiff. There was a niggling in the back of his mind, but he ignored it. Allah had raised him up for his purpose. That dream he had . . . it was a dream.

CHAPTER 22

A FEW DAYS LATER, CHICAGO

Marge set a plate of fresh baked oatmeal raisin cookies on the table with two cups of steaming decaf coffee.

Jack raised his eyebrows and set the newspaper aside. "A bribe? Comfort food? What's up?"

"I think I'm nervous." Marge's smile was weak.

"Comfort food, then. What's on your mind?"

"Are we thinking of moving to Israel or just going to visit?" Marge plopped into the chair and popped half a cookie into her mouth. "I mean, fif wis um good ijea."

Jack reached over and took her hand. "Translation? With your mouth empty."

"I'm sorry, Jack." She wiped her mouth with a napkin and took a sip of her coffee. "I just wonder if this is really a good idea."

"Going to Israel or moving to Israel?" He broke off a piece of cookie and put it in his mouth.

"Either. I'm worried for Tassie's safety. What if Omar is still alive and comes after her?" Marge started to wring the napkin around her fingers. "I mean Rube didn't tell us everything. If he's CIA, then he knows a lot that he isn't telling. I know Jethro is watching her and so is the IDF, but Jethro seems so young . . . I can hardly believe he's CIA."

"He just looks young, hon. Remember what I used to ask Tassie when she was little about the sky?"

"How far is the sky blue, Tassie? Forever. That's how far God will protect you. I know but look what she went through." Marge set her elbows on the table and rested her chin against her clasped hands. She closed her eyes.

"Marge, God delivered her and used her, and He will keep her safe now. She sent me a text this afternoon."

"She did? Oh, what did she say?"

"'Hi Dad, how far is the sky blue?' It was followed by a smiley face."

"That's it? My sweet girl. I miss her, Jack." A tear rolled down her face.

"I think we should go. We can decide whether to stay after we get there."

Marge sighed. "But then we'd have to come back to sell everything."

Jack sat for a moment chewing another cookie. "Great cookies, sweetheart. Look, the economy is taking a dive. Argentina defaulted, and the U.S. holds the note. China could call our note in. The stock market is down, and anti-Semitism is rising. I never thought we'd come up against this. I totally love my country, but our daughter is in Israel now. Perhaps it's time for us to go there, too."

Marge set her cup down, leaned back in the chair, and stared at Jack. "Go, as in move? Really, Jack, how could we? I mean I know I considered it, but I didn't think you would. I expected you to just say it would be safe enough to visit. I never dreamed you would want to actually go. I don't think I can sell all our stuff. I mean . . . " Marge put her head down on her arms and sobbed.

Jack stood and walked over to Marge and caressed her shoulders. As the sobbing lessened, Marge lifted her head. Jack pulled his chair over to face hers. He took her hands in his. "Marge, I have come to a conclusion about all this." Marge nodded and sniffled. Jack continued. "Israel is not the problem. Israel is the solution. Israel honors its people. It protects its people. It honors God. And I believe God honors Israel. They have so much pressure from the rest of the world, but they are innovative, smart, caring, and blessed. The U.S. used to be the same way, but so many things have changed. The Psalms say that God will prosper those who love Israel."

He paused. "And, Marge, you know I love to study the history of the U.S. just like you love world history."

Tears continued to run down Marge's face. She dabbed her eyes and nodded again.

"Well, recently I learned that the United States Navy was developed in order to stop the Barbary Pirates. Thomas Jefferson and John Adams, as Presidents, studied the Koran to understand the mindset of the pirates. Today our leaders don't do that. They don't understand the threat to the freedom principles we live by. Some do, but they're shamed into thinking they are narrow minded and bigoted. Israel, however, simply understands and realizes what must be done to protect themselves. And, if Hector were here, I think he'd tell us to go."

Marge hung her head and began to giggle. "Oh my, I think he would."

Jack dipped his head. "He's been right so far, and I think we should go."

Marge closed her eyes and sighed. "I guess I can do this." She looked around. "All my antiquities, all my artifacts, my collections. I shouldn't feel this way."

"They are precious to you, Marge. I understand that. Select a few to bring. We can store the rest, donate some, sell some."

"Rube and Jill might want them. Oh Jack, the baby is coming into all this. How can I leave with the baby coming?"

Jack reached over and picked up another cookie. "These are too good." He took a bite. "You know, a few weeks ago, I would have worried about them and the baby, but now that I know they are CIA . . . " He chuckled. "I think they can take care of themselves. And, we can come see them often. Maybe they'll come to Israel, too. He worked pretty well with the IDF or the Mossad or whoever it was."

———

PRESENT DAY, ISRAEL

The plane touched down and Marge had her face plastered to the window. "Oh, Jack, I can't believe it. Israel. Tassie. This is so exciting."

Jack patted her hand and smiled.

As they stepped off the plane onto the walkway, the steam from the asphalt of the runway, rose and wafted all around them.

"Oh, there she is." Marge saw Tassie and tears glistened in her eyes.

Tassie spotted them at that very moment. A big grin spread across her face and she ran to meet them, hugging Jack first and then Marge. "Daddy, Mother, I'm so glad you're here."

"Tassie, are you okay? All that you've been through. Did he hurt you?" Marge couldn't stop blubbering. Tears coursed down her face.

"Mother, it was scary, and I had some scratches and cuts from the explosion. But I'm okay. Emotionally, it was hard, but the sky is blue." Tassie reached over and grabbed her dad's arm.

"Tassie, we really were worried." Jack's voice was gruff. "But we knew God would be with you."

Tassie's face lit up. "Yes, He was." She stepped back and looked each parent in the eye. "And I have come to know the Messiah of the Jews."

Marge stopped. She leaned slightly forward and stared off in the distance. "Tassie, do you mean Jesus? Like the rabbis?"

"Yes, Mother, and I couldn't be happier or feel more complete. I hope you're okay with this."

Marge placed her arms around her daughter while the tears streamed again. "I don't know why, Tassie, but now I truly know you are all right." She stepped back and put her hand over her mouth while tears once more pooled in her eyes. "I'm happy for you, so happy."

Jack handed his wife some tissues. "Well, my girl, looks like we have some interesting discussions in our future."

"Yes, we do, Daddy. Now we have an apartment for you not far from the Goldmans. Jethro is in the same building." She stopped and turned to her parents. "Jethro is a gem. He's such a good friend. Who would've thought?"

Harvey and Sally arrived with her uncle, Rabbi Hermann Welcker, and his wife, Joannie. Tassie and her parents were already having coffee as they sat at the outdoor café. The sun was warm. Tassie grinned. "Sally, get cream in your coffee. They draw flowers on the surface of your coffee with the cream."

Sally laughed as she sat down. "I know. I love it." She looked across the small table at Tassie's parents. "Welcome to Israel. May this always be home for you."

"I can't believe how at home I feel here." Tassie's mom reached over and patted her hand. "I was so nervous about coming and so worried about Tassie."

"I'm really glad you came, Mother. I'm just as amazed that I'm here."

Her mother glanced at Tassie's dad. "When we were deciding whether to move, we actually thought about what Hector would say. We agreed that he would encourage us to come."

Her dad nodded. "We did."

Rabbi Welcker had a quizzical look on his face. "Did you say Hector."

Tassie and her parents burst out laughing.

Just then the waitress arrived and took coffee and pastry orders from the rabbi, Joannie, Sally, and Harvey. "You are a happy bunch."

Tassie smiled. "Yes, we are." As she walked away, Tassie turned to the rabbi. "So, you know Hector, too? Hector Woodley?"

"I do, but I'd decided that maybe he was an angel."

"Maybe he is an angel to the descendants of Gabe and Lydia Goldman." Tassie's mom leaned forward. "Tell us how you met him."

"Well, it begins with my father-in-law. When all those involved in the oil drilling were about to give up, he had a dream, at least he thought it was a dream."

Tassie and her parents exchanged looks. Her mom responded. "Yes, I thought mine a dream as well."

"I didn't." Tassie rolled her eyes. "It was real, but a nightmare, I thought."

The rabbi continued. "Well, in the dream, John, Joannie's father, was reading in Deuteronomy, chapter 33, where Moses blessed the children of Israel before he died. As my father-in-law read, he became aware of a man standing near him. John commented that normally that would have startled him, but since it was a dream, he was fine with it."

Her mom chuckled and took a sip of coffee.

"This man pointed out the verse that said Asher will dip his foot in oil and said, 'Did you ever look at a map as to where Asher's land is?' John shook his head. The stranger reached in and turned a few pages in John's Torah book and there was a map of the twelve tribes of Israel. He pointed at Asher's land. 'What does that look like, John?' John just stared at it for a minute and then he saw that it was like an extended foot. 'Oh, I see it,' John said. 'Dip his foot. The toe? Is that where the oil is?'

"'Does the verse say toe' he asked John. 'No, it says foot'. Then the man pointed to a spot along the shore line north of where the toe would be. 'If I were you, I'd look right here.' John told him that was near where they already had drilled and actually produced a little bit and that he only had enough to drill one more place before they closed down the company. 'Go out there tomorrow. Do your soil samples in exactly this spot. Check it out.' John agreed and fell asleep, except it was a dream so he continued sleeping until morning."

The waitress returned with coffee and pastry.

"The next day he told his crew they were going to check out a different place. They replied, 'Yeah, Hector already told us we were to do soil samples at one more location.' John looked at them. 'What, who? Hector?' They pointed and there was the man in his dream. He'd not taken a good look at him, but he knew it was him."

Tassie picked up a piece of pastry. "What did he look like?"

"Well, I arrived a short time later with Joannie. John had called us, and we weren't quite sure what to make of it, but I knew dreams were Biblical. Hector was standing there talking to John. He was not very tall, had kind of long, sort of scraggly hair. It was gray, blond, a little of both, and balding on top."

"That's him," Tassie and her parents said in unison.

Rabbi Welcker took a sip of coffee, then winked at his wife. "We actually noticed that he resembled me enough to be a distant cousin."

Joannie grinned and took up the story. "We had the necessary paperwork ready as Dad had called us early about his new venture. Seemed a little hair-brained to me. We arrived just as the second soil sample was coming up. The first looked promising. I walked over to Dad just as Hector turned to him and said, 'This is the one you're looking for.' He smiled at me and said, 'Joannie, this is the best find of all. By the way, I'm Hector.'

"The crew was bringing up the auger with the soil sample tube and a chunk fell off. Hector pointed at it and said, 'That's what you need.' Hermann and I walked over and picked it up. John and Hector joined us as we pawed through the muddy chunk. A bottle fell out. Hermann had heard stories about it and recognized it immediately. Hector said, 'This is where you need to drill.' We were pretty blown away. And I guess you know it was almost a gusher."

"And now, here we all are." Tassie's dad set his coffee down. "We're all descendants of Columbus or married to them. The world is pretty crazy, but I think more and more we are perfectly in God's will. I said before, I believe Israel is the solution or at least part of the solution. That's why we're here. I don't know what's going to happen, but I think it's big."

Rabbi Welcker placed his arm around his wife. "Well, if I may quote David Ben Gurion who, right here in Tel Aviv, proclaimed the birth of the state of Israel and soon became Israel's first prime minister . . . he said, 'In Israel, in order to be a realist, you must believe in miracles.'"

"Hear, hear." Tassie's mother lifted up her coffee cup and tapped Tassie's cup. "I heard someone say the other day, 'God performs miracles in such a way that you can choose to believe or not.' I thought that was so good. I want to believe in all His miracles. And I am so glad to be here with you all." She wiped a small tear from her eye.

Sally lifted her cup. "I think my favorite quote along that line is: God has made us strong and smart and wise enough to know it is He that has done it."

Tassie pushed her hair behind her ear. "Rabbi, could you fill in one more piece of the puzzle?"

"I'll try."

"I've been following the path of the bottle. It came across on the Santa Maria with Lydia and Columbus. Well, the tassel did. Who knows about the bottle? And there were four blood moons right after that journey. Then it remained in the family until 1949 when it was stolen from the Orbins' house on the night of a blood moon. A young boy found it not long after and it remained with that family, not related to any of the descendants, until his nephew returned it to a family member at the end of the Six Day War. At that time there were also four blood moons. And now, a short time before the blood moons we're already in, you guys find it. Omar steals it for a short time and steals me a longer time. And now we are back here. But where between 1967 and a few months ago did it go missing?"

"It occurred on the ninth of Av in 1994, a day that is traditionally known for bad things happening in Israel. Talk about signs in the heavens . . . the comet Shoemaker-Levy 9 collided with Jupiter and broke into twenty-one pieces at that time. Beforehand, the tassel of the bottle was displayed at another museum in Tel Aviv, the same art museum where Ben Gurion proclaimed the birth of the State of Israel. Even though the museum was guarded sufficiently, the relic was not. It's thought that perhaps a museum worker, who had studied what was considered its protection blessings, decided to steal it. How it ended up in the soil miles north of here, we're not sure. I think it must have been thrown off a ship somewhere."

Joannie smiled. "Okay, my theory is that the thief saw the movie *Titanic* when the lady throws the jewel off the ship at the end, so no one would have it, and decided to throw the bottle overboard."

Harvey laughed. "And there was a lot of farming going on for a while near our oil drilling locations, so maybe it washed ashore. Maybe a kid found it and buried it and then it was plowed up and under. Who knows, but it was there and signified where to drill for oil."

The sun was high. The rabbi looked at his watch. "Should we order lunch? We've been here a long time."

"Could I just ask one more question of you, Rabbi?"

"Of course, Jack."

"Why does God use blood moons?"

"In the prophets of the Bible, it says in the book of Joel that He will show wonders in the heavens and the earth, that the sun shall be turned to darkness, and the moon into blood before the coming of the great and awesome day of the Lord. In Genesis, the book of beginnings, we are told that the lights in the skies would be for signs or signals and seasons. So, we see these blood moons as signs that signal both God's judgment and the accomplishment of His great purposes in the earth. Now in 1492 after great persecution, the Jews were given a new world to live in. In 1948 after terrible tragedy, the Jews gained Israel. In 1967 there was incredible pressure followed by the triumph of retaking Jerusalem. Now here we are again. Perhaps the Temple will be rebuilt or perhaps the temple of God will be rebuilt in the hearts of men."

The waitress came and removed the plates and some of the cups.

"Well, I for one can't wait to see what God is going to do." Tassie's mother reached across the table and patted and squeezed everyone's hands. "I will admit I'm still a bit nervous, but excited."

"Forgive me, but I must get back out to the oil site." Joannie stood up. "I'm so delighted to have had this time with you."

Harvey picked up the bill. "This one is on me. And I should get going as well."

Soon they all had departed except for Tassie. She remembered sitting at the coffee shop by the water in Chicago, wondering where she was going. *I feel like I've lived a lifetime since then. I wonder what is still ahead.*

CHAPTER 23

The morning dawned bright and beautiful. The sun rising over the Israeli countryside soon cast its golden glaze upon the stones of Jerusalem. It was as if internal flames lit each stone that made up the buildings and walls of Jerusalem. For Benjamin Akeena it never grew old. Every morning he praised the God Almighty, blessed be He, that he, Benjamin, the most blessed of all men, could live in such a place. Yes, a rough neighborhood, no doubt, but never a place more anointed by God in the whole world.

Arriving in Israel from Russia as a young man was the most joyous day of his life. From the time he could perceive anything he had heard his father pray, beg God, speak out, believe, and cry for an open door to Israel. The government would not let them leave, but his father and mother would not let go. Then the day came that they were told to go, just drop everything, leave their belongings, all their cattle but one milk cow, and go. They left with almost nothing, but themselves, the cow, and their faith, their belief in the one true God, blessed be He. The arduous journey wore on them and lasted a month.

When they arrived, they were welcomed, and a place to live and learn and grow opened up. They were home, and life just got better. Benjamin was nearing the end of his three years in the military. He had been training in the technological field and wanted to always work in the IDF, to always guard and protect this land that he loved and that he was so sure loved him.

Today was the ninth of Av, a bad day in the history of Israel. Terrible things happened on this day so many times and everyone was on high alert. Still the beauty of the sunrise could not be dampened by the concern of the day.

Then the beeping began on his smart phone. He glanced at his compatriots. They had heard it as well and were taking their places at their missiles. Benjamin checked his orders. Syrian missiles were in-bound for Jerusalem. Were they crazy? Jerusalem?

Benjamin barked the orders and missiles fired over Jerusalem to intercept the IEDs. F151s were on their way. The Iron Dome was ready. Benjamin and his crew were first cover. They were able to take out three. The fourth continued. Benjamin sent out coordinates of possible impact. Another team destroyed it just before it entered the city, exploding over the Kidron valley. By then F151s were deployed and Benjamin listened to the chatter.

Syria had ordered the destruction of Jerusalem. They figured they could rebuild the city if it was destroyed. They just wanted to annihilate Israel. Benjamin shook his head. Syria had no idea what a sleeping giant they had just awakened. Did they know it was the ninth of Av? Did they care?

Benjamin reloaded. He knew that the first intercept was all that was needed. The Iron Dome of automatic missile response and the F151s would take over and part of Syria would be no more. He waited for the news. It was only a matter of minutes before he heard half of Damascus was gone. The sun was well above the horizon, but in essence, it had set on Damascus, and in world opinion it would soon set over Israel. Somehow, Israel would be the bad guy.

It always happened. Someone, anyone, would attack Israel. If Israel retaliated, world opinion was swift. Israel should show restraint. Israel promoted violence they said. Israel should stand down. It was said often in Israel that if those against Israel would lay down their arms there would be peace. If Israel, however, laid down their arms, they would be wiped off the face of the earth.

Hamas had built tunnels into Israel from Gaza in order to execute terror. They denied it. Israel used ground troops to destroy the tunnels. The U.S. told Israel to use restraint. Hamas regularly shot their rockets into Israel elementary schools and residential neighborhoods, knowing that Israel would try to take the shooters or at least the launcher site out. Invariably the retaliation would take the life of an innocent or cause damage in homes, hospitals, and schools, even though Israel would send texts, robo calls, and drop leaflets to warn the residents to leave.

The press would then take up the diatribe against the audacity and violence of Israel against the young, helpless, and unarmed, making them out to be monsters and the world would agree. Blinders, they had blinders over their eyes. They never looked to see that Hamas had set it all up and were the aggressors.

"Sir, are you listening. Everyone is being placed on high alert. Syrian forces and ISIS are mobilizing against Israel. Our team just started World War Three."

Benjamin looked over at his friend and team member. Rani was about to begin his university training and was making plans for marriage. Rani's eyes were big, and Benjamin knew he was afraid.

"Rani, we did not start this. It is the ninth of Av, and the Syrians did this. If half of Jerusalem had just perished, they would have rejoiced, and the world would say we brought it on ourselves. Perhaps it is just time to see our God, blessed be He, stand in our defense as He did in the Six Day War and the Yom Kippur war." Benjamin reached over and clapped his friend on the back. "But, my friend, I do not think we will be done with our three-year commitment this week."

Rani's face fell. "And what do I think of that? I think not much. I fear you are right, my friend. May God, blessed be He, intercede on our behalf."

———

That same day Hamas added to the fray. They started sending a barrage of Iranian FAJR-5 missiles. The rockets had a range of 47 miles, so they could reach Jerusalem and Tel Aviv. The Syrian-made M-302s, recently smuggled into Gaza, had a range of 93 miles, placing five million Israelis in danger.

Benjamin and Rani saw the Iron Dome take out the majority of them. It was late in the day, and they would remain on duty well into the night. The orders came for an extra twenty thousand troops to take up positions on the border of Gaza. Benjamin and Rani would remain on the outskirts of Jerusalem as eyes and ears for the Iron Dome and be prepared for any Hamas sleepers trying to penetrate the city.

With Syria on one side and Hamas on the other side in Gaza, the Iron Dome was stretched to capacity. Benjamin would soon order return fire to strike where Hamas missiles had been launched. "Touchy business."

"Muttering again?" Rani grinned.

"It's so frustrating. We're launching into neighborhoods to take out their launchers, but they set it up where kids and the sick are. Then they blame us."

"We know that already."

"But the world doesn't see it. They twist it."

"Benjamin, we drop the flyers, send text messages, and robo phone calls to let them know the retaliation is coming."

Benjamin blew the air out of his cheeks as his phone buzzed. "Orders. Flyers have been dropped. O God of Israel, help us take out the launchers and the terrorists, not the children."

Rani patted his back. "Amen."

Immediately after the ninth of Av Damascus war, the U.S., Britain, France, and Germany roundly condemned Israel for going on the offensive.

Israel, however, did not regret their swift and almost automatic response to the Syrian missiles. Perhaps it was the straw that broke the camel's back. But Israel refused to be broken. They were going to stop the nonsense. When ISIS and Syria mobilized against Israel, the IDF stood ready. The IDF was always ready. They prepared for just such a scenario on a daily basis. Meeting the threats against them militarily topped their priority list. Many thought they should have taken out Damascus, Baghdad, and Tehran years ago. Why put up with the constant threat, the endless rockets, and mindless hatred sent their way daily.

For three weeks Israel remained under siege and had lost fifty-one innocents. Thirty-six soldiers died, and countless buildings suffered destruction. When the dust cleared, though, more stories of victory and miracles arose than those of tragedy.

Syria had been judged. That was Israel's conclusion. Its military was almost decimated. Russia sent weapons, but Israel intercepted them. The story was too amazing. Two Israeli F15s had been shot down. The four flyers parachuted safely to the ground. They kept their Uzis with them and escaped into a wooded mountainous region. Nearing a cave, they heard sounds and took cover nearby. Within minutes, jeeps with covered trailers drove out of the cave. They recognized Arabic and Russian as the camouflaged men shouted to one another.

One of the flight crew was fluent in both languages. He turned to his team. "These are weapons, bombs, and missiles from Russia to assist the offensive against Israel."

They had little time to fire on the vehicles and were greatly outnumbered. Their top gunman, the one who never missed, used a silencer and took out the tire on the first jeep as it covered a rocky area of the road. Thinking it was simply a flat tire, the rest of the men stopped and smoked cigarettes while the soldiers in the first jeep repaired the tire.

Realizing that God had presented them favor and position, they quickly moved ahead of the caravan and found a ravine in which the jeeps and trailers must pass through. Taking up position on both sides of the road the four men prepared to take out the shipment of weapons on its way to Syrian military outposts. Just as they were about to fire, the explosion of the F15s lit up the sky.

The IDF soldiers had triggered the self-destruct portion of the fighter jets on the chance that enemy combatants would try to apprehend the machines.

As the explosion sounded, the convoy participants had just entered the ravine. They dove out of their jeeps with guns ready. The IDF now had a target that was stationary even though the enemy soldiers were ready for trouble. One by one, one side after the other, the IDF shot a round into each jeep and trailer. After firing, each one ran to another position. With the combination of varying positions and right-on shooting, the convoy soldiers thought they were being ambushed by a hundred troops. When only three convoy soldiers were left, they stood up waving a white shirt for surrender.

CHAPTER 24

PRESENT DAY, IRAQ

Omar was back in full strength. The room was stark. Surrounding the large table sat those in leadership from every jihadist group connected to ISIS and those with vested interests. Several wore traditional Arab keyiffas and white thobes. Most were in business suits.

A large screen next to a huge map covered the wall behind Omar. He commanded respect. All present recognized his power and ability. His recent healing by Allah gave him unmitigated rule. He knew it and he used it. A worldwide caliphate was still possible, and he was anointed to make it happen.

Omar stood regally and looked each man in the eye. "I believe the shooting down of the Malaysia plane has accomplished several goals. Malaysia, as you know, is one of our first caliphates. Because some rebelled and became Christians . . . " Omar spat. "We dumped them in the ocean." The men chuckled and smiled. "No one can figure out why a plane just disappeared. Well, now we've shot one down over Ukraine as well."

Omar forced no emotion to show on his face. "I want this to continue. It has taken the world's attention away from ISIS. It has stirred up the Ukrainians, and they try to defend themselves from world opinion. We want continued skirmishes between Ukraine and the pro-Russian separatists." He tossed a file at one of the men. "Yugol, I want the Russian military to get those separatists more weapons." Pointing to a spot on the map in eastern Ukraine, Omar continued. "Right here, Yugol. This is the tunnel. Just like the Hamas, I want these completed. Let Lemkrof know we will assist with the funding. He needs to step it up and shoot from Russia, as well."

Omar took a drink from the water bottle sitting in front of him. "Speaking of tunnels . . . those Jews in Israel have found some of them. Yemi, you're adding tunnels into Israel, is that correct?"

A young man in a thobe and checkered keffiyeh stood. He walked around and tapped the screen. A map came up and with each tap increased the size of Israel and Gaza. Red lines revealed the tunnels already built. Yemi pointed out the eight discovered by IDF ground troops and cursed. He then pointed to those just completed outlined in blue. "This one here is the most promising. It gives us the ability to fire on the airport in Tel Aviv. It will only take a few missiles to cause the U.S. and other countries to stop all traffic in and out of the airport. That will kill the economy of Israel." He laughed. "Whatever works, right?" The young man sat down.

Omar smiled. "Not only that but having missile launchers in the residential areas definitely helps turn world opinion against Israel when they retaliate."

Omar nodded at one of the other men. He stood up and zoomed the map into the countries of Iraq and Syria. "As you know, Israel decimated half of Damascus with their strike and much of Syria's military. They think they have the upper hand. They have no idea of our resources. Fortunately, ISIS was not deterred by that. We had moved our headquarters to Mosul. Again, we have expelled or killed"—Omar smiled and raised his eyebrows—"or tortured before we killed, all the Christians. Mosul is now totally Muslim. And I rather like it here." The men clapped.

"We know we'll run into resistance, but we're well prepared. The U.S. trained Iraqi soldiers are weak. We torture, they run away. They have fortified Baghdad, but we have time, we have weapons, chemical and military, and we have money. They think Iran will help them, but we will eventually take over

Iran as well, or . . . " He tilted his head. "Maybe Israel will take out Iran for us." Everyone laughed. "Whatever works."

"So, in summary, we will take Ukraine and move into Slovakia and Czech Republic, cutting off a lot of U.S. assistance in the European theater. The U.S. President will continue to vacillate while assuming that his words accomplish great things." Omar rolled his eyes. "By the time they assist Ukraine as they promised years ago when Ukraine got rid of their nuclear facilities, we will have taken over through Lemkrof. ISIS is just waiting for the right time and we will have all of Iraq and possibly Iran. If we don't get Israel in the next few months, I'm confident Hamas will destroy their economy. I want more planes shot down, more missiles shot, more land taken over."

Omar spread his hands. "This is what we were born to do. This is the plan of Allah. This is the caliphate. This will usher in the Twelfth Imam." A shiver went through Omar. Deep within he felt the words. *"Remember I will pursue you until you pursue Me."* Omar bent over and coughed.

Two men jumped up to assist, but he straightened himself and lifted his voice. "Men, you know your assignments. We will have our caliphate!" All the men stood up and cheered.

The men filed out to honor prayer time and get something to eat. Omar gathered his papers and files, placing them in his brief case, and glanced up. An older man stood just inside the door opposite where the others left. The shiver he felt just moments before returned.

"Grandfather, what brings you here? I'm feeling fine, no need to check up on me." Few people could make Omar's knees shake. Actually no one could intimidate him except this one man. Grandfather had the heart of a lion, but it was surrounded with steel. Omar knew his love, but he knew even better his authority.

"It's your brothers." Grandfather stayed where he was. There was no movement toward Omar. Somehow this was not a good sign.

Omar bolstered all his strength, feeling like a little boy in trouble at school. "What has happened? Are they okay? What is it?"

Grandfather did not answer until Omar stood just two feet away. "They have left. Gone to Qatar."

Omar smiled, hoping to hear good news. "Joining our cousin released from Gitmo to get some terror events started in the U.S. That'll be great. I haven't heard from our cousin and planned to contact him later today."

Grandfather shook his head. "No, son, Daran and Saiim got a small taste of power and liked it. Your returning from the dead did not sit well with them. They want you to go back there. Yes, they want you dead. Your cousin was only too happy to accommodate their desires. Whether he will work with them to take you out or he will just use their energy to accomplish his own plans, I don't know. But you are on their list."

Omar glared. "Theirs and everybody else's. I will get a couple of my guys on their tail. Should I take them out, Grandfather?"

"They are your brothers. But, we shall see."

"What do you think is their plan? Hamas is with us and Qatar is funding Hamas."

Grandfather stepped toward Omar and placed a hand on his shoulder. "You know how slippery loyalty can be. Hamas only wants money, next to Israel's demise, and if Qatar or Turkey provides it, or your brothers, they will do anything. Let's walk. You need to know something."

The sigh rose up within Omar and it came out. He tried to hold it back. He did not have time for a lecture. He, Omar, was the lecturer now, but this was Grandfather and as a grandson, he could not dissuade the old man from what he set his mind to do. He walked.

"The drone. Remember the drone."

"Yes, well, no. I don't remember it, but I remember that it happened, and I almost died."

"You did die, Omar."

The shiver again. Omar ignored it. "Are you hungry, Grandfather? Food is being served down the hall."

Grandfather stopped. "Omar. Look at me."

Omar stopped, sighed again, turned and looked at the old man. He wanted to look at his watch. He had business to do. This was not the time for . . .

"The drone was from your brothers."

Omar saw white. Then he saw black. Red rose in front of him next. Then he took a breath. He turned and slammed his fist into the wall. Every blood vessel in his neck pulsed.

"I should have known. I should have known. Why are you just telling me this?"

Grandfather shrugged. "Omar, believe me, I just found out myself. When they left, I went through their technology. They didn't know I had access. However," Grandfather looked at Omar. "I know. I should have been checking before. I could have stopped it, but I didn't check it. Please forgive me. They tricked me into thinking they were totally with me, with you."

"Grandfather, I forgive you. Do you have anything that can help me now?"

"Only that they are in constant contact with your cousin in Qatar. I assume that is where they have gone. You are welcome to go through the technology."

"I will send someone home with you to check it. Right now, I need to return to the meeting room. I have much business to conduct today. Thank you, Grandfather for letting me know. I'm sorry I cannot spend more time with you."

Grandfather nodded, then grimaced. He placed his hand on his chest and breathed in deeply. The old man momentarily slumped against the wall and sweat poured down his face. Omar grabbed his arms, but his grandfather shook his head. He straightened himself with much effort. "You do your work, Omar. Be careful. I am fine, simply old."

Omar called to his assistant coming down the hall to attend to his grandfather and examine the technological secrets of his brothers.

Omar watched his grandfather walk slowly down the hall with the assistant, then turned and retraced his steps to the meeting room. He signaled to another of his men, who had already returned from prayers and eating, to find him some food.

Glad to know it was his brothers, vying for power, who tried to oust him that day in Damascus, Omar still felt unsettled. They were at it again, and with the Gitmo terrorists who had a lot of methods up their sleeves. And who knew which of his assistants may have been won over or bought by his brothers. Omar cursed under his breath. He hated living suspiciously. He wanted to be in control. He was in control, but who in this room wanted his brothers in control.

He informed his body guards, hoping none of them had been bought out while he was in the hospital. He told them to be constantly doubly vigilant. He would not live afraid. He would live alert and in charge. That's it. It was settled. He made a couple phone calls. There. His brothers would be history very soon.

He'd like to take out his cousin, as well. But he would wait to learn what the technology information revealed. His brothers had to go now. Omar did not have time to worry about them. He knew it would grieve his grandfather as he loved them as well, but this was now necessary business. Grandfather had not been effective in controlling them, so it was Omar's decision. Omar was in charge.

His grandfather died of a heart attack that night. Omar's assistant had just finished searching through the computer connection his grandfather had maintained. One person in Omar's circle had been revealed as joining the brothers. Omar shot him the moment he found out. There was no evidence that his cousin in Qatar was with them. Perhaps his cousin thought the brothers were bringing information from Omar. Well, hopefully they wouldn't arrive.

Omar had no time to properly bury his grandfather. He left it to other members of the family. His oldest brother maintained a business and had a family. Omar asked Mustafa to take care of the arrangements. Mustafa was even-tempered like his grandfather and understood Omar's predicament. He had never shown jealousy over the favoritism shown to Omar. He would take care of matters.

In the early morning, at the time of pre-dawn prayers, Omar slipped out to see his grandfather's body and confess his love and respect for him. Instead of two bodyguards, he allowed four to accompany him. He did not know if his other assistants had taken out his brothers yet, and he did not want to find out for a while. He would not be able to look his eldest brother in the eye if Mustafa found out about Daran and Saiim at this time. In war, that loss would be just what happens. But, in a family honoring the patriarch, the death of younger men would not sit well.

Grandfather was laid out in a grand room. The body guards remained outside the door. Omar went in and stood still by his grandfather. The emotions rose up and Omar tried to stuff them down. Respect was all he needed to show, not feelings. Grandfather might even frown on emotions. Still they rose up and leaked out his eyes. He could taste the grief. What would he do, now? Grandfather was his strength.

Omar began to shake and fell to one knee. The tears were flowing freely now. *You are my help, Grandfather. You are my strength. I owe everything to you, Grandfather. How will I be able to lead well? You had my back. You were my main advisor. I will trust Allah. I'm anointed by Allah, now, aren't I?*

Omar found himself on all fours, overcome by grief. *I don't have time for this. I will grieve another day. I must go.*

The room seemed foggy. He wiped his eyes, chiding himself for being so emotional. Then the shivers began.

Omar closed his eyes and shook himself. He stood up and found himself face to face with the King.

"Noooo! I am alive and well. I do not need to see you. I don't need to talk to you."

"Your grandfather loved you Omar. He loved you intensely."

"I know that."

"I love you more."

"That's preposterous. You are a hater. You don't exist. Don't talk to me."

"Look where your grandfather is, Omar."

There before him was the black cloud again. As it thinned, the pit became visible. Flames flew out trying to lap at Omar. He jumped back. Cries of anguish arose from the pit. Then Omar heard it. His grandfather's voice. It held fear and pain. Grandfather was calling Omar's name.

Omar shook and walked to the edge of the pit. A look of hope briefly crossed Grandfather's face. "Omar, Omar, listen to him, listen to the King. Omar, we were wrong. This is not paradise. It is the place the Christians call hell. Omar, we were wrong. Forgive me Omar. Believe this man. Do not come here. Do not let your brothers come here. Follow Him, Omar. He loves you. He will guide you."

"No, no, this is a trick. This is not true. My brothers must have drugged me. I am hallucinating. This is not happening."

Grandfather extended his hands toward Omar. "It is not a hallucination. Your brothers do not know that you sent out your assistants to kill them. I did not know that until I got here. I know also that you put Mustafa in charge of honoring me. Am I not telling you the truth?"

"Of course, that's true, but this is a hallucination of my mind. I know all that, so you know it."

"Well, you don't know this. Your brothers got word of my death and turned back. They encountered your vigilantes and killed them. They are arriving in a few minutes with every intention to murder you. That is not in your mind. Listen to this King. He is the true God. Follow him, son, follow Him. You don't want to come here."

The flames got hotter and higher and the black cloud rose up as well. Omar fell back, and the room returned. He took a deep breath and looked around. There was his grandfather lying without life where he had been before. *Good, this is over. I must leave if my brothers are here. Thank you, Allah, for letting me know.*

"No, Omar, it wasn't Allah, it was me. Come with me, Omar. I will once more save your life. Your brothers are here."

Omar wanted to protest but heard the struggle outside and knew his body guards and his brothers were clashing.

The King walked over to Omar and guided him over to another wall. Omar wondered if he would have to punch the wall out, but before he could prepare himself, they passed through the wall, then another and another. They were outside, and he saw his car and driver, but the driver was dead. The King waved his hand and Omar was back in his headquarters in his safe room.

The King sat down. "Now, Omar, you are safe from your brothers. They will be shaken that you are nowhere to be found as there is no other way out of that room. And you have a message for them when you next see them."

"What?" Omar was confused. He did not feel strong or safe or even sane.

"Your grandfather told you to tell them to follow me."

"They want to kill me. I need to kill them. I have work to do. I murder your followers."

The King frowned. "I know. That's one reason I'm here. You will not murder one more follower of mine. Their blood cries out to me."

The shivers began again. The room became foggy. Omar saw a screen, like a TV, but bigger, vibrating. It seemed alive. On it he saw the city of Mosul. He saw Christians being thrown from their homes, heads being cut off, hands being cut off. And he heard their cries. "Father God, Lord Jesus, deliver us, set us free, make this stop. We praise You. We trust You."

Omar sneered. "Their cries are unanswered. We will not stop. These people are unnecessary. You didn't help them."

"They are in the true paradise now. Heaven is a glorious place. And many Christians have escaped your henchmen. Look here."

The scene changed slightly. Omar recognized it as a rocky area outside of Mosul. It was as if there was a remote control in his hand and he zoomed in. He saw Christians being led by IDF soldiers into a tunnel.

"No! That can't be happening. How did IDF get in there? Why should they care?"

"The IDF are well able to locate tunnels with their new technology. They care for anyone suffering."

Omar's countenance returned to the sneer. "Well, thanks for showing me that. I'll let my men know. We can close that up quickly."

"Your phone doesn't work, Omar."

Omar quickly pulled out his phone. 'No Service' blinked off and on. He swiped and tapped, turned it off and back on, got up and walked around the room. Nothing changed.

"Sit down, Omar."

He obeyed. He looked at the King. "You said the Christians in Mosul were one reason you were here. What are the others?"

"Oh, this is one of my favorites." The King actually rubbed His hands together. The screen returned.

There was the little restaurant in Door County where he and Tassie ate breakfast. The young man stood with hands on each of their shoulders and prayed, "Dear Jesus, bring them to You."

Omar shook his head and looked at the King.

"I love to answer his prayers. Simple faith. That's what he has. That's all it takes."

Omar narrowed his eyes. "That kid is just a . . ."

It was like a lightning strike. Pulling back, Omar felt a singe on his lips. He felt the King's eyes boring through him.

"You will not deride my people, especially him, ever again."

Opening his mouth, Omar had a retort. Nothing came out. He tried to make his mouth speak. His voice was gone. With wide eyes, he looked at the King.

"It's time to listen one more time, Omar. I have plans for you. Your grandfather had plans for you. You have plans for you. Your grandfather knows now that his plans and your plans are wrong. You have touched My people, Jews and Christians alike. If you read My book, you will find out that I win. It's time for you to make the right choice, Omar. I set before you life and death. Choose life, Omar."

The King stood and walked over to Omar. Glorious colors and shafts of light flowed from His being and filled the room. Warmth and love embraced Omar. He saw himself walking down a street with a beautiful woman and three children. They entered a building filled with people and music. Omar and this family began singing with the group, lifting their hands in praise. To his surprise, he then got up and began reading from the Bible and talking to the people.

The vision faded. Then he saw himself standing before the men he was with the day before. He was once again ordering planes shot down, people killed, armies to advance, rockets to fly. His brothers walked in and he shot them. Shortly thereafter his cousin arrived. Omar went to greet him, and his cousin shot him. Then the flames were licking at him. His grandfather cried out, "Omar, did you not hear me? Did you not tell your brothers? Did you not listen to the King? Oh, Omar, my son, why did you not listen? You always listened before? Now we will all live in this agony forever." Cries of agony echoed off the walls that were covered with scorpion looking creatures. Pain filled his body.

Omar waited for the vision to fade as the first one did. It did not. The heat, the pain, the regret, and agony continued to build in and around him. He looked around for the King. Why didn't He stop this and tell him to make a choice again? He had no voice and he could not call out. He began to tremble. Perhaps this was it. Perhaps he had been killed. Perhaps this was actually happening. Fear engulfed him. Grandfather lay on the floor of this awful place writhing in agony.

Omar fell to his knees to help Grandfather. No matter how hard he tried he could not reach him, could not touch him. Only inches away, he could not get there, he could not help the only person he truly loved.

Why? Why? Why can't I get there? Why isn't this ending?

Nothing. *Please, please, King, get me out of this.* Omar placed his forehead on the floor. "I choose life. I don't understand all this. But I will follow you. I do not want to be here. I want life. Please help me, King Jesus. Forgive me."

The heat lessened. The flames disappeared. His grandfather saw him leaving and whispered, "Yes, yes, thank you, son. Follow the King. Tell your brothers. Don't come here. Live, son, live."

Omar called back. "I will, Grandfather. I will live. I will tell my brothers. Thank you." His voice was back. The room was clear. The King stood before him.

"Omar Tugani, I will now live inside you. I will never leave or forsake you. I will give you wisdom that you could never attain on your own. I will first guide you safely out of here. You will encounter your brothers in a few days and you will share with them. They will make their own choice whether to follow me or not. Pray for them as the young man prayed for you. Your most important mission now is to assist the U.S. and Israel in stopping the plans that you have set in motion."

Omar listened and then looked down. "I am to betray my people?"

"Omar, your people have chosen a path of death. You will stop as much of the evil as you can, and you will help them choose life."

"They will kill me."

The King smiled. "If they do, you have seen where you will go. Heaven is quite nice. But, Omar, I have great plans for you, and you will not die anytime soon."

The next day, the remaining half of Damascus and most of Syria was destroyed by an earthquake.

CHAPTER 25

The earthquake shook everything right before dawn. Tassie had just rolled over in bed and almost fell out. Barely catching herself, she swung her feet out and stood up. She allowed herself to fall back on to the bed which felt like a raft in the water. Cups, glasses, bowls clattered to the floor in the kitchen.

Dear God, please keep my parents safe.

Just as quickly as it began, it stopped. Sirens sounded in the distance. She waited a few moments to see if the rocking would start once more, and then grabbed her robe and placed her arms in the sleeves. She walked into the kitchen as she tied the belt of her robe and found Sally Goldman picking up bits of glass and pottery.

"Be careful, Tassie, there's broken glass." She smiled through sleepy eyes. Tassie liked how her hair was down on her shoulders and somewhat in her face. Sally kept pushing it behind her ears, but every time she bent over to pick up another item, the hair came loose again. As she stood up, she blew some hair out of her face. With hands full, she set the broken pieces on the counter. "Are you okay, Tassie? We don't have too many earthquakes. We both almost fell out of bed."

"I almost did, too. I've never been in one before."

"We've had a few tremors. This was stronger. We know there's a big fault under Israel. That's where our oil well is." Sally stopped. Her free hand flew to her mouth. "Oh my, I wonder if the oil well survived. Harvey needs to

238

check that if he hasn't already." She turned toward their bedroom and called. "Harvey! Harvey!"

Tassie waved her hand. "Go check. I'll pick this up, and I know where the broom is."

"Thank you, Tassie."

Tassie heard Sally's voice all the way down the hall calling out to Harvey.

She dumped the last dustpan full after sweeping the whole kitchen when Sally returned. Tassie waited for Sally to say something. She didn't. "Sally, is everything okay?"

"Harvey says, 'You think I didn't think about the well. Of course, I think. I worry. Of course, I call. And you know what?' So, I said, 'Of course I don't know what. So, what?' And he says, 'So what! You ask me so what? You don't care what happens? Did you hit your head?' So, I said, 'Of course I didn't hit my head. You asked me if I know what, so I ask you what. Tell me what, Harvey.'"

Tassie placed both hands on Sally's shoulders. "Sally, tell me what happened."

"Well, he told me. I love that man, but when he goes on like that, I know why I came to Israel and let him make the choice whether or not to come. Do I love him? Of course, I do, but when he won't answer a simple question . . . "

Tassie shook Sally's shoulders. "Sally, tell me if the oil well is all right."

Sally stepped back and pushed her hair behind her ears. "Well, let me tell you, Tassie."

Where's the crevice. I'm going to jump in. Tassie hung her head.

"They're having a gusher, Tassie. Not only is the well just fine, but the earthquake must have jarred something loose or opened up the artery. Fortunately, the night crew was still there, and the morning crew was just arriving. We have two wells there, Tassie. One had quit and that's when we thought it was all over.

"Then Grandfather found the bottle and drilled right there. It looks right now like that well is going to produce sixty percent more, and the other one that we thought was defunct is looking like it will be fifty percent by the end of the day, and who knows how much more than that. The night crew is on one rig and the day crew is on the other. Harvey is already calling in those who have wanted to work for us. Apparently, there are only a few disruptions with traffic, so they should be able to get the extra help."

Sally paused and looked around. "Oh, Tassie, you cleaned it all up. Thank you so much."

There was a yell from Harvey in the bedroom. "Sally, Tassie, get in here, you must see this." A clatter followed along with another yell. "It's okay, I'm okay, just knocked the chair over. Hurry, hurry."

Tassie chased Sally into the room. Harvey stood with one hand on the chair he had picked up and the other hand on the remote. He stood in rumpled night clothes staring at the TV. "The Dome of the Rock . . . it's . . . it's . . . " He turned and looked at the women. "It's gone, Sally. The earthquake swallowed it."

"Oh my." Sally's hand went to her heart and she moved slowly to the chair next to her husband and gingerly sat down. "I don't think I can breathe."

Tassie ran to her. "Sally, shall I call for help. I'll get my phone. Is it 911 here?"

"No, no, I'm all right. I'm just so stunned. God Almighty, blessed be He, has removed the Dome of the Rock, the place we could not approach, that we could not go." She turned and grabbed her husband's hand. "Does this mean we can go there, that we can rebuild the Temple?"

Harvey said nothing for a full minute. "Can we rebuild? Do I know? I do not know. How could I know? Who am I? Sally, Sally, call your uncle. The rabbi will know."

"Yes, yes, I will do that." But neither of them moved.

Tassie stood transfixed with the Goldmans watching the television video of the place of the Temple Mount. It wasn't a pile of rubble. When the cameras zoomed in, she went as close as she could to the flat screen without impairing the view of the others. She hunted for the gold of the dome. Even though the Jews did not like that it belonged to the Muslims, none could deny the exquisite beauty of the golden dome, as it glistened in the sun and announced to the whole world that this indeed was Jerusalem.

"I don't see any pieces of the gold dome. I don't see any pieces at all."

Harvey turned to her. "That's what I mean. It didn't collapse. It was swallowed up. It is gone."

"What does this mean?" Tassie sat down in another chair as the import of the Dome of the Rock disappearing began to sink in. She knew it grated at so many Jews to not have a temple, to only have the Wailing Wall. She also knew she had no idea how deep the longing was to be able to go into the area of the Temple Mount.

———————

The phone rang in Tassie's purse. She hurried to retrieve it and saw that Jethro was calling. She had so enjoyed getting to know him during this time in Israel. He had chosen to stay and attend yeshiva school and sit under rabbinical teaching. He wanted to see how all the prophecy, economics, and political upheaval played out. He also spent several hours a day as a liaison between the CIA and the Mossad. He was in his glory and he loved sharing from the rabbinical teachings with Tassie.

She was amazed at how much she appreciated the teaching. It rang with such logic and legal clarity that it appealed to her thinking, but it was changing her heart as well. She felt she was only now coming to know who she was.

"Tassie, something's happened. Can you get over to the museum?"

"Jethro, did you see the Temple Mount?"

Jethro paused. He sounded out of breath. "I did. I saw it disappear. With my own eyes. It was incredible. No one can believe it. We were in Jerusalem and had just lifted off in an IDF helicopter to return to Tel Aviv. I saw the Golden Dome with just a hint of the morning sunrise glinting off the top. The Dome swayed. It didn't make sense and then we heard a swoosh sound and a thunder type rumble. The Dome and the Mosque just sunk and disappeared. I rubbed my eyes and wondered if I was dreaming. Then the vibration shook the helicopter . . . and it floated up like a balloon. There was a moment when everything was still and silent. Then the sirens started, and people ran to the area. We didn't see any fires or accidents, but watching the Dome disappear was so amazing. God, blessed be He, allowed us to see it."

"Jethro, did you get pictures?"

"It was so fast, Tassie, but yes, one of the IDF guys got it. That is one of the videos you might be seeing on the TV. It was so stunning that we could hardly talk. And it's such a short flight. I think we were all in shock when we landed."

"Incredible." Tassie turned to the Goldmans. "Jethro saw the Dome disappear from the helicopter."

Jethro took a deep breath. "But there is something else. Come to the museum ASAP. Bring the Goldmans if you can."

"Okay." Tassie put her phone back in her purse. "Jethro wants us all over at the museum. Says it's big, and it's not the Temple Mount."

Harvey Goldman picked up his car keys. "Let's go. And then I need to go out to the oil well site. In the twinkling of an eye, all seems to be changing. And did anyone consider that the Feast of the Tabernacles is this week? I don't know if anyone remembered. I knew it yesterday, but today, who can think of anything?"

Tassie stopped. She placed her hands on the counter to steady herself. "The Feast of Tabernacles. That's the next blood moon, isn't it? Tonight? It's tonight!"

Sally stood in front of her husband. "Harvey, I love you. Of course you know, and we must hurry, but put your clothes on. We're all in our night clothes."

The Goldmans' car pulled up in front of the museum. Tassie's parents were just getting out of their car. A small planter that stood next to the door was toppled over and the sidewalk lay crumpled and cracked.

"Looks like the earthquake went right by here." Tassie hugged her parents. "Did you see the Temple Mount?"

"The Dome of the Rock is gone. Swallowed right up. Glad to see the museum is still standing. Wouldn't want the bottle with the tassel to get swallowed."'

Tassie's eyes widened. "Oh my, why didn't I think of that? Now I don't want to go in. What if something happened to it?"

Her dad placed an arm around her. "Chin up, probably some info on the Temple Mount."

Tassie's mom grabbed one of her hands. "I can hardly contain myself that tonight is the next blood moon. I'm so nervous and excited. And now, with the Temple Mount empty . . . what is going to happen?"

The door opened, and Jethro stood there gesturing for them to hurry in. They hurried through the door. He stopped them before they continued to the back of the museum. "Do you want the good news or the bad news first?"

Harvey and Sally just looked at each other and shrugged their shoulders. Tassie's parents said nothing.

Tassie looked at each face and back to Jethro. "You're serious?"

"I am."

"Okay, I guess the good news."

Jethro clapped his hands. "We have found buried treasure. Great funding for great projects."

Harvey Goldman cleared his throat. "Jethro we already know about the second oil well and the first one becoming a gusher."

Tassie's mom hugged Sally. "Oh my, how wonderful! With all the tensions, now Israel can produce its own energy." She looked back at Jethro.

"Congratulations. I had not heard that yet. But we have even more treasures to add to that. However—"

"However, what?" Tassie narrowed her eyes. "Spill it, Jethro."

"The bottle broke in the earthquake." Jethro opened the door and led them to the back where the bottle was kept.

Tassie's mom covered her face with her hands, and a tear tracked down Tassie's face. Harvey and Sally hugged each other.

Tassie's dad hung his head. "The earthquake, Jethro?"

"Yes, sir, but come see. We have moved nothing until you could come."

The bell jar lay shattered with glass everywhere on one side of the pedestal. On the other side, the bottle rested on the floor in five pieces. The neck, where the tassel was still attached, lay in two pieces. The base was broken from the rest of the bottle and the main section of the bottle was also broken into two pieces.

"We have taken pictures. We will videotape our examination of it now. Please put on gloves so you don't get cut or damage the tassel with body oils." Jethro handed each of them thick plastic gloves.

Harvey Goldman was on his knees, leaning in to peer at the base of the bottle. "The base was covered in wax, which I had not really noticed before, but look here."

Marge gasped and fell to her knees beside Mr. Goldman. "Is that what I think it is?" She glanced at Harvey and then back. "Can we have a magnifying glass?"

Jethro quickly retrieved one and handed it to her. Marge and Harvey took turns examining and sighing.

"Mother, what is it?"

Harvey rocked back so he was sitting on his heels. He shook his head and laughed. "It's diamonds. Diamonds, I tell you. Where from you say. I will tell you. They are from Spain. But, of course they are. Where else could they be from?" He paused. "Well, I suppose from America, but obviously from the 1400s. Marge, what do you think?"

"I think they are Spanish diamonds, smuggled over just like the tassel. Probably worth millions. Oh my."

"Mother, Harvey, do I see a ring or something in the neck? Is it just to connect the tassel?" Now Tassie perched on her knees and peered at the tassel. She looked up at Jethro. "May I pick it up?"

"You may."

Tassel Lydia Stevens grasped the neck of the bottle. She ran her gloved fingers over the tassel, the first person to do so in over five hundred years. She looked at her mother again. "This just blows me away."

"Can you pull it out of the neck?" Jethro handed her a pair of tweezers.

Tassie carefully dug at the wax a bit and it slipped out of the neck exposing a solid gold ring.

"I think I'm going to faint." Harvey sat back on the floor and put his head in his hands.

Tassie held the tassel in one hand and with the other hand worked at the gold ring. "Oh my . . . " She looked up, bit her lip, and shook her head. Everyone held their breath and could not break their gaze from the history being dug out in Tassie's hands.

"There are two rings here." She displayed the rings and it became clear that the tassel was looped around the rings. She held out her hands cradling the rings and tassel for the others to see. Jethro snapped a picture.

Her mother scooted across the floor closer to Tassie. "May I?" Tassie placed the relic in her hands.

"I thank You God Almighty for bringing us to this moment. For determining this moment to reveal the treasures of the tassel." She passed the tassel to her husband.

"The Psalmist has said, 'It is the set time to favor Israel'. The Dome of the Rock is swallowed up and perhaps this is the time to rebuild the Temple of the God of Abraham, Isaac, and Jacob. And these gems and precious gold, along with the oil, could probably pay for the building of this Temple."

Harvey Goldman stood up and held out his hands for his turn to hold the precious tassel. "Hear, O Israel, the Lord our God is one . . . " The others stood and prayed the shema with him.

Halfway through the shema, Rabbi Welcker came in and joined his deep baritone voice to the prayer. He seemed to almost sing it and Tassie sensed the moment had forever etched itself in each mind.

As everyone talked at once, Tassie's mother fell to her knees again. "Wait, I think there is more."

Immediately it was silent. Harvey knelt beside her. The two relic experts poked at a rather large piece of wax that had held the diamonds.

"Jethro, make sure you video this."

"Yes, ma'am, I'm here."

The two looked like kids digging in the sand. Harvey examined what was being uncovered in her hand.

"Is it a coin? I think it's a coin. Oh my, it has the image of Queen Isabella on it. Ooooh, look at this. I think again I'm going to faint." Harvey sat back and rubbed his face.

Tassie's mother held out the coin. "See, this side is Queen Isabella, and on this side . . . " Marge shook her head. "On this side is the name and image of Cristobal Colombo and the date 1492. The Queen must have had this made to go with him on the journey to authenticate his authority or just to commemorate or honor him and the journey."

Harvey nodded his head. "This is the documentation, the certification, for the age and place of the diamonds. It will increase their value. We have millions here."

Rabbi Welcker examined the coin. "One of my fellow rabbis is also a diamond and gold appraiser. With your permission, I will contact him. I'm sure he can be here in a few minutes."

Tassie realized the rabbi was looking at her. "Most definitely. Call him."

––––––––––––

Rabbi Yosef arrived ten minutes later. The diamonds, tassel, rings, and coin lay on the table. The wax was in one pile while the glass was in another. Harvey and Tassie's mother insisted that every piece be preserved and examined. Eyes wide, the Rabbi opened his mouth, and nothing came out. Regaining control, he glanced around at the others and then sat down. He put on gloves, placed the eyepiece in his eye and picked up one diamond and began mumbling.

Tassie whispered. "Is he saying something? Is he talking to us?"

Rabbi Welcker smiled. "Hebrew, and yes, he's mumbling."

There were eleven diamonds in all. The cut was a unique and simple cut that most certainly traced back to the time of Queen Isabella and King Ferdinand in Spain when the Jews were the main diamond cutters and sellers. "How did these get out? I have read about these priceless jewels. When they kicked out the Jews in the Spanish Inquisition, they cut some of them open if they suspected they had jewels, thinking they had swallowed them. It was barbaric."

He took a deep breath. "Just look at the brilliance. These are colorless and flawless, such rarity. Three of them have inclusions or blemishes to the side, but they would be graded very, very slightly included. The cut is exquisite giving them a brightness and fire that is outstanding. These two," Rabbi Yosef looked up and sighed. "These two are the rarest blue with such depth of color I've never seen. I'm almost beside myself. I've rarely seen anything like these. I am so honored to examine them."

Tassie and her dad put their arms around each other and said together, "How far is the sky blue? That's how far God will provide for us."

Rabbi Welcker pointed to the coin. "My friend, see the coin. Queen Isabella on one side, Cristobal Colombo, 1492, on the other. Is this sufficient documentation?"

Rabbi Yosef sat back. "I must catch my breath." He examined the coin. "This was in the wax with the diamonds?"

Everyone nodded.

"Do not destroy the wax. There are means to date it, to further document it." He studied the coin again. "This coin provides necessary certification as to the age of the diamonds."

Rabbi Welcker placed his hand on Rabbi Yosef's shoulder. "Did I tell you my niece's husband, Harvey, here, is an antiquities dealer, and Tassie's mother, Marge, is an antiquity expert?"

Rabbi Yosef stood up. "Oh, that's wonderful. Do assist me in calculating the worth of these. The connection to Spain, Queen Isabella, and Christopher Columbus definitely puts these in a high worth bracket."

The three sat down together and put pencil to paper. Fifteen minutes later, Rabbi Yosef looked at the others. "My honorable friends, I believe these diamonds are worth at least one point two million dollars."

A collective sigh went through the room.

Jethro stepped forward. "What about the gold rings?"

The diamond appraiser looked up. "Gold rings? Really? Oh my. All I was looking at was the diamonds. Are they solid gold?"

Harvey spoke up. "I would think that from that time, there would be very few alloys, so more than likely. Marge?"

"I would agree."

"Then, well . . . " Rabbi Yosef ran his hands over his face. "These are priceless, of course." He looked away. "Of course, priceless, but they need a worth, yes? A price. Of course, a price."

Tassie placed her hand over her mouth to stifle a giggle. She did not allow her eyes to meet her mother's knowing they would not be able not to laugh.

After another deep sigh, the rabbi examined the rings. "I would guess these two rings are of equal worth to the diamonds, assuming they are solid gold. A million dollars would be a minimum in my humble opinion."

Harvey and Sally looked at each other. "Tassie." Sally took both of her hands. "All of this is what you are named for, not just on a whim of Marge and Jack." She smiled at Tassie's parents. "But as a result of God's intention for you. Jethro, Marge, Tassie, and Harvey are all the descendants of Christopher Columbus, Lydia Liebermann, and Gabe Goldman. The choice is yours as to what to do with the items or the funds."

Tassie looked at her mother, Jethro, and Harvey, and realized they were looking at her. "What? What do all of you think?"

"We think you are the decider." Harvey placed an arm around Tassie.

Tassie's mother and Jethro nodded.

"I . . . ah . . . " Tassie then heard her voice strong. "I think we need to use the funds from the diamonds and rings . . . not the tassel or the coin . . . they should be preserved . . . but the diamonds and the rings should finance the oil wells."

Harvey squeezed Sally's hand.

Tassie continued. "It's time for Israel to become a huge oil supplier for not just Israel, but the U.S. and other countries. We need to build more wells to accommodate the veins that opened up. I believe that the oil wells will then do so well, that they can finance the rebuilding of the Temple on the now vacant Temple Mount."

The two rabbis placed their hands over their hearts.

"God Almighty, Blessed be He, has given you wisdom beyond your years, my dear Tassie." Rabbi Welcker took her hands in his. "I believe you have been given the words of God."

Jethro stepped forward. "I concur, but now we need to get these in airtight bags, take more pictures, and get something to eat."

Sally went into the small kitchen in the back of the museum as Marge, Harvey, and Jethro, according to antiquity protocol, bagged and labeled the diamonds, rings, tassel, wax, and the glass. Upon finishing they walked back to the kitchen, expecting to see food. Instead, Sally stood there crying.

Harvey ran to her. "My dear, what is wrong."

Sally simply pointed at the TV. The group stood mesmerized. It was like a dream. Like a dream come true.

––––––––––

Benjamin Akeena shook himself and stood up. Confusion reigned in his mind. Dust was everywhere. He examined himself. A lump on his head and a bit dizzy. Other than that, he thought he was okay. What in the world had happened? Then it came back. A rocking, a rumbling noise. Must have been an earthquake.

"Rani, you all right? Where are you?"

Rani sat on the ground grinning. "I always liked roller coasters, but that was a little weird. How about you?"

"Must have landed on my head. Got a little lump, feel a little dizzy."

"Sure hope it knocked some sense into you." Rani laughed and stood up. The dust was clearing, and sirens were beginning to sound in the distance. "Oh, man, what just happened?"

Ben was brushing the dust off. "C'mon, Rani. An earthquake just happened. Did you bump your head, too?"

"Look, Ben . . . where is the Dome of the Rock?"

"What? You lost your sense of direction, too?"

"No, Ben, look."

Ben looked in the direction of the Dome, expecting to see the reflection of the rising sun pierce through the dust of the earthquake. "Where is it? Why can't I see it?"

"It's gone. Swallowed up."

The two stood there, just staring. Then they heard the beep. Snapping back to military readiness, Ben read the orders on his phone. He let out a low whistle.

"Rani, we're to storm the Temple Mount. The Prime Minister said this is the time to take it back."

"This is God's time to restore, blessed be He. Let's go, bro."

All Israeli Defense Forces in the area were surrounding the Temple Mount. Considered a holy place by Jews, Muslims, and Christians, this would not be an easy task. IDF guards were already on the grounds, to protect the Dome, an Islamic shrine built in the seventh century, from anyone of any belief who wanted to destroy it. Two hundred meters to the south, also on the

Temple Mount, was the Al Aqsa Mosque, one of Islam's most holy places. It had been built originally in 715 A.D. but had been destroyed by earthquakes several times.

Individual Jewish groups, attempting to force Israel's hand or even God's hand, had planned elaborate, but ill-thought-out, take-overs in years past. All had been thwarted, some with loss of life and all with lengthy jail terms. This time, though, the Dome and the Mosque were just gone, swallowed up, as if they had never been.

Benjamin Akeena had never been to the Temple Mount. Even though IDF soldiers were posted there, the duty was never his assignment. Tourists had been allowed, but only if they were Muslim. He knew that this was the place where Muslims believed Mohammed had risen to heaven. He also knew that Abraham had come here to sacrifice Isaac, only to be stopped by God from killing his son. God wanted to know if Abraham would obey Him. Recently Ben had heard a most interesting comparison on a TV program.

He had been switching channels and heard a talk about Abraham and Isaac. They said that after stopping Abraham from injuring his son, God promised to sacrifice His own son, just like Abraham had almost sacrificed Isaac. It stunned Ben to realize this was the same place, Mt. Moriah, the Temple Mount, where Jesus was crucified. He never gave much credence to Jesus, but he knew that this promise from God to sacrifice His son was covenant talk. Ben's father always talked about the covenant God made with man, and that it was more binding than any contract men could make with each other.

God had exchanged His name with Abraham . . . He was known as the God of Abraham, Isaac, and Jacob. And Abram and his wife Sarai had God's name inserted into theirs and became Abr-Ah-ham and Sar-Ah. God was known as Yah, blessed be He. Benjamin knew there was an abundant supply of protection, provision, commitment, and blessing in the covenant. This was how his parents taught him the Holy Scriptures. The connection to Christianity and Jesus intrigued and drew him.

Now, the Temple Mount could be retaken for the Jews. He would be part of history. The moment was surreal.

Ben heard himself saying the shema as he ran toward the Mount. "Blessed art Thou, King of the Universe . . . " He heard Rani in tandem with him. He expected a firestorm. Surely there were hundreds, if not dozens, of Muslims having their morning prayers when the earthquake occurred and ready to stop a takeover. Had the IDF guards perished? What about the Muslim guards? Did they survive?

Ben adjusted the wireless earpiece to be sure he could hear any commands and all the chatter. They slowed to a trot as commanders sought to get everyone in place. Many IDF were still on Gaza's borders and searching out the Hamas missile-running tunnels and therefore unavailable for this mission.

Ben and Rani traversed the ground leading to the ascent of the Dome of the Rock. *History. We're making history. If we don't succeed, we will be history.* Ben coughed. *That's a sobering thought.*

The streets were thick with people. Some had been up for hours getting their market stands open, attending the Muslim prayer time, or preparing for work. Many were just waking up. All were experiencing the shock of the earthquake and the reality that the Dome of the Rock and the Al-Aqsa Mosque were gone. Not demolished but gone.

A smattering of colors reflected the rising sun, but it was not as bright as usual. Who knew that the Dome reflected so much light? Still, there was a patchwork of vibrating colors as droves of people ran toward the site. Shouting and screams accompanied the sirens.

Ben did not know if and how many civilians or soldiers had perished. IDF soldiers moved steadily and quickly in the throngs of people. Seeing IDF with guns in the streets was not unusual. Most would assume they were rendering assistance, not ready for a historical and dramatic take-over of the world-famous site.

It felt like a cloud. Perhaps it was dust. Perhaps it was reality that felt like a dream. Ben saw faces. Concern. Wonder. Fear. He heard orders . . . no one was to cross where the barriers had been . . . those on site already were to maintain the perimeter.

Sweat ran down his face. Or was it tears? The Jews would have ownership of the Temple Mount after centuries of waiting and prayers and agony. They could rebuild the Temple. They would, of course they would. Messiah could come. Ben knew there were stone streets beneath his feet, knew there were stairs he was climbing, but he couldn't feel them. He knew he was jostling others with his gear, but no one seemed to notice.

Was he breathing? Even at the height of fitness, he should be breathing heavily now. He did not feel winded.

Is this a dream? Will I wake up soon? Will my buzzer go off in a few minutes? Then he heard it. Beep. Beep. *Oh no, a dream. Time to wake up.* But, no, it was followed by orders. 'Report location'.

He and Rani were approaching the holy site. It was flat, no rubble, as if the Dome and the Mosque had been picked up and removed. Ben could see a crevice, but it appeared only a foot wide. How could the earth, the concrete, open and close with no other damage? He glanced at Rani. His eyes were wide, and he slowly shook his head. He mouthed the word 'unbelievable'.

Not one person was being resuscitated. No one was being carried off in stretchers. Ben could see the whole perimeter and there was not one Muslim guard.

His phone beeped again. Orders. Take up positions. There was no need to storm. No one was there to fight, to dispute, the Israeli takeover. They would post a contingent of round-the-clock guards in case the Muslims arrived to retake the Temple Mount.

An Israeli Jewish priest came forward. He walked slowly and made eye contact with each soldier he passed. He went to the center of the site. He stood next to the crevice and placed a shofar, the ram's horn trumpet, to his mouth. As he lifted the curved cream and brown instrument, a strong, steady, slightly mournful, sound rang forth. As he blew, he turned, facing east, north, west, south. The shofar was held upright, level, and every degree in between. The sound, meant to be an alarm or an announcement, came in short bursts and long notes.

Chills ran up and down Ben's spine. He wanted to fall to his knees but knew he could not as he was on duty. Israelis just outside the perimeter, though, were on their knees, arms upraised. The shofar continued for two minutes straight. As the priest removed the shofar from his lips, the shouts of rejoicing from the crowds were deafening.

Suddenly the shouts faded, and the air was filled with gasps and whispering. Ben looked around. The prime minister was ascending the steps to the Temple Mount. Ben could have reached out and touched him. The prime minister paused. Ben looked into his eyes. There were tears. The prime minister turned and smiled at Ben, reaching out to shake his hand. Ben was overwhelmed. The honor to be here. He wondered again if he would wake up from this dream.

The prime minister walked to the priest and they embraced. The first words out of his mouth were Hebrew. "The Lord is good, and His mercy is everlasting."

The crowds went wild with cheering. The prime minister repeated the phrase again and again. The crowds shouted it. After several times he stopped. "Good people of Israel. Our God, blessed be He, has seen fit to return this blessed place to the Jewish people. It is what we have prayed for, worked for, and fought for. You must know that not one life was lost in this disappearance of the Dome of the Rock and the Al-Aqsa Mosque." The crowds were silent. Ben could see people leaning forward to hear every word of the historic moment.

"Apparently," Prime Minister Gavi Ben-Aharon continued, "there was a water leak, a problem with the pipes, perhaps caused by the ground beginning to shift before the earthquake. For that reason, all personnel had left, Muslim prayers were held out of doors, and the repairmen had not yet arrived. The guards, both IDF and Muslim, were here. When the rumbling began, all those near, including the guards, ran for protection. We have taken the opportune moment to retake the site. World opinion will challenge us, and the Muslims may return to fight, but we believe this is our possession, and I hereby proclaim that the Temple Mount is now under the control of the Israeli Jewish people. I repeat, the Temple Mount is once more in our hands!"

Ben recalled the history of the 1967 recapture of Jerusalem when Lt. General Motta Gur, Commander of the IDF brigade said those same words. "The Temple Mount is in our hands! I repeat the Temple Mount is in our hands!"

Now the people danced and sang and shouted praises to God. Ben watched the proceedings and wept. His breathing came in short gasps and he thanked God for letting him be a witness to this. Rani stood next to him and sang Hebrew songs with the crowd.

Gavi Ben-Aharon raised his arm once more and the crowds went silent. "Today we believe the Psalms have fittingly described what is before us. 'When the Lord brought back the captivity of Zion, we were like those who dream. Then our mouth was filled with laughter, and our tongue with singing. Then they said among the nations, "The Lord has done great things for them." The Lord has done great things for us. And we are glad.' Let us hope the nations do say that."

Everyone went wild again. Dancing, leaping, shouting, and singing engulfed the Temple Mount and the streets of Jerusalem.

Once more Prime Minister Ben-Aharon raised his hands. "And our prophet Isaiah has told us that the Lord, our Redeemer, says to the Temple, 'Your foundation shall be laid.' Perhaps, my friends, that day has arrived."

At that, many fell to their knees and wept. Others shouted praises and the singing continued.

His phone beeped. Orders. Rejoice, but keep your eyes open. There could be suicide bombers, Hamas missile rockets, or crazies who want to be on the news. Ben quickly wiped his eyes and took up a guard stance. He and Rani high-fived each other, then stood with backs almost together. That way the two of them could observe the whole perimeter. Other IDF did the same. Several escorted Mr. Ben-Aharon and the priest safely through the crowds. Ben-Aharon would be answering questions from the world leaders and commentators the rest of the day, probably the week. But the people would rejoice. This day, the first of Sukkoth, the Feast of Tabernacles, would become a key holiday for the rest of time.

The days passed, and Israel rejoiced while the world condemned their takeover of the Temple Mount. They had taken advantage of a natural disaster and had no right. The amazing part was that, though the talking heads spoke out loudly against Israel, the Muslims who were in charge of the Dome of the Rock and the Al-Aqsa Mosque did not come out against the take-over. Gradually, it leaked out that the morning worshippers and the administrators and imams saw Father Abraham, huge and glowing, and heard him tell them, in no uncertain terms, to leave, that their time was up. Some claimed it was just before the earthquake, a few said they saw him after the earthquake. They all agreed that it was terrifying and powerful. No Jew saw the vision, only the Muslims.

If true, the IDF knew that, in time, the Muslim leadership may well choose to ignore that command and return, but for now they were impotent in fighting back.

The Hamas decided it should step up. The Iron Dome and the IDF were ready.

CHAPTER 26

Rube hung up the phone and turned to Jill. "That was dad. Sheez, he sounds so happy. Who would've thought they'd love Israel. They're hoping to come as soon as the baby arrives. He says Mom is loving it there, but says her arms are already aching to hold her grandbaby."

Jill smiled as she rubbed her belly. "Oh, I can't wait to see them. I'm so happy they love it there and to be there at such a monumental time." She arched her eyebrows. "Maybe we should go to Israel after this little guy arrives. Jared could transfer you, couldn't he?"

Rube sat down next to Jill. "So much happening . . . who knows what's next." He picked up the remote and turned on the news.

"This is Jace Shepard with breaking news. The third Jewish temple on Mt. Moriah may soon be underway, and it's causing dancing in the streets." Jace looked to the side. "Is this right? Yes, that's it. Dancing in the streets. What a roller coaster Israel has been on the last few months. First, all the attacks, then the earthquake which swallowed up the Muslim mosque and the Dome of the Rock on the Temple Mount. Israel reacted quickly, storming and retaking the area. Now they are rebuilding, and, as I said, literally dancing in the streets."

Jace walked over to his map. "Okay, take a look at this." A photo came up on the screen of the temple site. "Now remember, they did not have to clear away debris. The Golden Dome and the al-Aqsa Mosque were literally swallowed up, not demolished. And no lives were lost in the takeover. The Muslim guards swore they saw huge soldiers . . . angels, anyone? . . . and they ran. I guess a few guards returned and some were injured, but this was pretty seamless, and the Jews wasted no time in starting plans to build the new Temple patterned after directions in the Old Testament for the Temple that Solomon built."

Jace looked at the camera. "Solomon or David? Didn't David build it? What's that? Oh, I guess David was going to, but God told him Solomon was to do it. That's great. Get the kids involved." Jace smiled. "Now, get this, in today's economy, the old temple would have cost four billion dollars. So now how does Israel or Jerusalem fund this? Long story here. We reported on the four blood moons and prophecy and all that, but a little-known story connected to it is about a relic that came all the way from Spain with Columbus, as well as the little-known fact that Columbus was at least part Jewish—who knew? Anyway, this relic had a tassel from a prayer shawl along with diamonds and gold rings—what a treasure hunt. It's brought in millions or at least one or two million and reports tell us that will finance the oil wells in Israel."

Rube patted Jill's knee. "We knew that, Jace."

Jace took a drink. "I hope you're taking notes. If not, you can go to Metro News online and get the details. Israel now has a huge oil boom . . . I can tell you that helps the U.S. The funds from these oil wells are planned to pay for a big portion of the Temple. In case you haven't been listening to the news lately, the oil boom was helped by the earthquake . . . yes, the same one that swallowed the structures at the Temple Mount.

"Now this is interesting, too. The Israelis are funding and sending troops to protect the Christians in Iraq . . . Mosul, specifically. I hope you're recording this program, because this is all so amazing." Jace sat down at his table. "Let me give you some background. There is an organization that is several years old, called Christians United for Israel. They have lobbied Congress to have policies to help Israel. They have spoken out, loud and clear, their support for Israel to be independent and to be able to protect themselves, and they have worked diligently to stop anti-Semitism. They have a big conference in Washington, D.C., every year to promote Israel by lobbying Senators and Representatives. Many other Christian organizations have also supported Israel. Books have actually been written that when the United States policies have worked against Israel, natural disasters have occurred in the United States. Quite stunning connections."

Jace took another drink of water. "With all this going on, many Israeli Jews have said that the U.S. Christians are their best friends. They used to say the U.S. was their best friend, but administrative policies of late changed some of that. These same Christians are the ones who began informing us of the blood moons and all the changes that we have seen . . . they told us this would happen.

"Now, back to the Christians in Mosul. Israel said that since the Christians in the U.S. have given them such support, they did not hesitate to help the Iraqi Christians who are suffering unspeakable atrocities. Truth be told, Israel has helped anyone that is injured or in need, no matter their creed, background, or anything. They will work as hard to save the life of their enemy as they will their friends. But this is so special that they are going to the aid of the Mosul Christians."

Jace put his finger to his ear. "Is that right? Well, who knew? I was just informed that in the Israeli charter they pledge to help and protect any and all Christians within their borders. Hmmm. Now they're expanding it. I like a charter dedicated to the protection of people not destruction.

"One more thing before we have to go to break. With all the news about the rebuilding of the Temple and the amazing events going on in Israel, you'd think the secular Jews would become religious Jews, but what's happening is that many Jews, secular and religious, are recognizing Jesus as their Messiah.

"I reported on the Jewish rabbis doing so months ago and now the general populace is doing it. The rabbis announced more than fifty percent of them believed Jesus to be Messiah last April. Anyone know what it is now? Really? They just told me it's sixty-three percent. I mean if this was an election for Jesus to be Messiah, this would be a landslide. Incredible. You can't make this up folks, so hold on to your seats. I think a lot more is coming. We'll be right back."

CHAPTER 27

The world's attention stayed on Israel, the Temple, the earthquake, and the continued attempts of Hamas. Almost everyone forgot Iran. Except Israel. The world's top technological innovators worked for Israel and Israel remained the most important player in the field of technology. The U.S. Silicon Valley was on the decline because of tax codes and sundry policies, and the only edge the U.S. military held depended on new technology coming from Israel.

The newest developments belonged to the drones. Israel's Dr. Yahid Horowitz had finally completed his work on a system using drones that could detect enriched uranium, the necessary ingredient for Iran's nuclear capability. Dr. Horowitz had been responsible for the computer worm that was able to infiltrate and mess-up the computer files that held formulas and plans for Iran's nuclear work several years previous. Iran had since improved their ability to protect that information. The worm had slowed them down but did not totally cripple them.

It was the day before the earthquake that tests were complete on the drones. The plan moved close to readiness. The Israeli government prayed for a distraction, so they could go forward and finish the job before world opinion weighed in and stopped them. Usually the U.S. was informed of plans, but in recent months, even years, the U.S. pressed for restraint and verbal negotiations, not action. This action with the drones would be pin-point and swift. Mossad was directed to leak the information only to the CIA contacts that stood by Israel in all points.

Several weeks after the earthquake as world opinion continued to surge out both for and against the retaking of the Temple Mount, Horowitz's small group of technicians gathered near Haifa. World attention focused on the audacity of the Israelis to even consider plans for the rebuilding of the Temple. Meanwhile, the secret underground laboratory was ready, and the doors opened. A platform rose, and coordinates were triple-checked. Three drones left with little fanfare in a matter of ten minutes at two a.m. The platform returned to underground and then the tracking screens were in full gear.

Rube's phone chimed at five o'clock in the evening. A text from Jared. "Tonight will be great for star-gazing. Get over here." Rube showed it to Jill.

"Let's both go. We'll grab some fast food on the way. Traffic will be crazy, but this sounds like we need to be there."

Rube texted back. "Jill and I love the stars. Shall we bring you some food?" Jared's reply was one word. "YES!!!!!!!"

By six-fifteen Jill and Rube cleared security at Langley and arrived in Jared's cluttered office. Jared hugged Jill. "It's been a long time and I heard about the baby . . . I see it's not far off. Congratulations. Exciting."

Jill sat down, shifting her weight a bit gingerly. "We are so excited. A little tough with Rube's parents in Israel but we're good. We brought you food." She grinned. "And food for me and the baby. Traffic was crazy, so it took a little longer."

"We're okay, things don't start hopping until seven. I'm starved." Jared peeked in the bags and started pulling out burgers and fries. "Thanks!"

"So why are we here? What's happening?" Rube started shifting piles of files from the chairs to the desk.

"What's not happening? The whole world is happening. But who has been under the radar with so many other things in the news?"

Rube unwrapped a hamburger. "Iran."

"Exactly."

Jill groaned. "Don't tell me they're ready to fire on Israel."

"No, Israel is about to take out their nuclear capability." Jared held up his hand and high-fived Rube. "With your family so involved, you need to see this."

"Israel is going to bomb Iran?" Jill covered her face with her hands.

"Drones, Jill, drones. And these seek out enriched uranium. Ingenious. Israel's technology is amazing."

"Our administration isn't screaming about it?"

"They don't know. Frank was informed. He let me know. I let you know. We'll watch, then report. No one is paying attention right now. It's the perfect time."

"How can it be the perfect time?" Jill popped a french fry in her mouth. "Everyone is watching Israel."

"But no one is watching Iran, except the Israelis right now. They're striking while the iron is hot." Jared punched in a code on his computer. "Zero hour is two a.m. there, seven p.m. here."

"What if Iran retaliates?"

"Israel's military is on full alert. They've just added to their Iron Dome. Their F15s are on the tarmacs now. But they have been ready since they retook the Temple Mount. So, no one is noticing their alert. Sheez, the Israelis live in alert status."

Jared punched in a few more numbers on his computer. "Okay, here's the feed. Man, only three drones, and they can neutralize this Iranian nuclear threat. Dear God, help them."

Rube placed all his attention on the screen. "Do you think any radar can pick them up in these other countries?"

"Not likely. They are so hard to detect on radar. It's possible that people on the ground could see them, but they make so little sound." Jared grabbed another hamburger. "Jill, are you done? There are a few in here."

Jill laughed. "We know you, Jared. We got plenty extra. Eat all you want. I'm good."

Silence followed as they watched the blips representing the drones edge closer to Iran.

Rube interrupted the silence. "Jared, you just said 'Dear God'. Was that a prayer?"

Jared grinned. "You won't believe this. If I wasn't here watching this tonight, which I wouldn't miss, and technically I need to be here, I would be with Deb at church."

"Deb's at church on a Wednesday night. I thought church was just Sunday morning. How is she?"

"She's great. We both are." Jared paused and punched in some coordinates on the computer. The screen image zoomed in on Iran. "Oh, look, they are starting to split off. This is amazing. We thought they had three main centers, but we could determine only the locations of two for sure. Apparently, Israel found the third one. Praise God."

Rube turned. "Praise God? Who are you and what have you done with the Jared I know?"

"It's incredible, you guys, just incredible. You know, Deb and I have been on the verge of breaking up a few times. This CIA work wears on a marriage, as you well know. But Deb's sister invited us to this special thing to honor Israel at their church. Well, we went. Wait, wait, I think the drones are about to strike."

They stood shoulder to shoulder in front of the screen. Simultaneously the drones struck three locations in Iran. The satellite feed was close enough to tell they were exactly on mark. The explosions were significant and the fires high in the sky.

Jared turned up the volume of the Haifa laboratory technicians. There was Hebrew with English translations. "We have hit. They are direct on target. The uranium has been nullified and the buildings are on fire."

"I forgot to tell you. The drones were able to nullify nuclear detonation with a chemical powder, like a dust that was expelled moments before the explosion blew up the buildings. The innovation of the Israeli chemists is unprecedented."

Jared sat down and sent out an encrypted message to the White House. He looked up. "Well, now the real fireworks are about to start. I'm so glad, though, that Israel has the upper hand. If they could just stop ISIS and Russia, they'd be all set. Hamas is weakening, Israel has the Temple Mount, Iran has just lost nuclear capability, and Syria basically has no more power."

Jared typed a few more items. "Okay, now back to Deb and me." He took a big gulp of soda. "Well, we just fell in love with this church, and before we knew it, we prayed to make Jesus our Lord." He looked from Jill to Rube and back. "I'm sorry if that offends you, being Jewish, but there are a lot of people at the church who say they are Jewish and that they are now realizing that Jesus is their Messiah. Is that crazy or what?"

Rube leaned back and took Jill's hand. "It seems like that is happening all over Israel, too. My folks and Tassie have told us, and it's even on the news. I think Tassie has gone that route. It's strange, but I feel kind of drawn to it. Somehow it sounds right."

"And I hear it's happening all over our country. People are turning their lives over to God." Jared grabbed a few more fries.

Jill took a deep breath. "Yeah, being pregnant . . . I don't know if you get more serious or feel more responsible or what. You just want to make sure you do everything right." She looked at Rube and then back to Jared. "Maybe we should visit your church sometime."

"That would be great. I need to give you something else to consider. Frank has been our man on the ground in Israel for a long time. He's getting closer to retirement. Because of your expertise and keen abilities, Rube, I've been authorized to offer you a position as Frank's assistant with the plan that you take over for him when he steps down. It seemed to be a great fit as your family is there."

Rube sat open mouthed, with his soda in his hand. "You're serious, Jared. Seriously?"

"Yeah, I am. We are. It's a big decision. No hurry. You might want to wait till after the baby arrives, but it's open and will remain open."

Rube looked at Jill. Her eyes were wide. "We have a lot to think about."

CHAPTER 28

The three-day mourning period had ended for Omar's grandfather. Omar had missed most of it, but he walked to the burial site to watch his brother Mustafa, the oldest male descendant, place the soil blocks under Grandfather in the cemetery. The shroud was traditional white. Omar, under promise from the King that he would not be killed, and with his four bodyguards, walked to the body and threw soil on the grave. Although others had already said the Janazah prayer, he stood before his grandfather and said the traditional prayer. Inside his heart though, he saw his beloved grandfather in the pit of hell, pleading with him to tell his brothers that their Paradise didn't exist.

He could feel the tension in the air at his very presence. Some were glad to see he finally arrived to pay proper respect, not understanding why he would not have been there the whole time. Others, specifically Saiim and Daran, were angry that he remained alive.

There could be snipers around, but he trusted the King. Why, he wasn't sure, but he did. As everyone drifted off, he called Mustafa, Saiim, and Daran to him just a short distance from the gravesite.

"I know there is an inheritance that is sizeable." Daran and Saiim's eyes grew wide. Mustafa nodded his head. "I am here to say that I will give up my portion. You may split it or use it for a worthy cause as you see fit."

"Are you well? You don't look yourself." Mustafa, the quiet one, was usually the most perceptive.

Saiim and Daran were hot-headed, always. Daran's eyes revealed his hatred for Omar. "What are you up to? Why would you disrespect Grandfather? We returned as soon as we heard, and you were gone. We looked for you."

Omar smiled. "I'm sure you wondered where I went. I knew you came to kill me."

Saiim lunged at Omar, but Mustafa stepped between them. "This is not the time, brothers. Omar, you have something to say, so say it."

"I have come to know the Jewish King."

Daran rolled his eyes. "Did you get hit in the head? Do you mean the prime minister, Ben-Aharon?"

"No, I mean King Jesus."

Each brother stepped back as if pushed. Mustafa rubbed his forehead. "Are you sick, brother? What are you trying to tell us?"

Omar sighed. "Just listen." He related the details of his experiences from the time of the explosion to the present, focusing strongly on the pleas of their grandfather to tell them to follow the King and not go to the pit.

Daran and Saiim seemed at a loss for words. Mustafa shook his head. "I have heard of such things. I have not wanted to believe any of it. But, unless you sustained irreparable damage to your brain, I find it hard to dismiss what you say. And I see a light in your eyes that I have never seen before. I will consider it."

Omar gave Mustafa an embrace. "That is all I can ask."

Daran spat. "This is nonsense."

"I understand, Daran. I responded the same way at first."

Saiim looked Omar in the eye. "If this is true, you are an infidel, therefore a dead man."

"I know, Saiim, but I have chosen this, and you will probably never see me again."

"Yeah, because you will be dead, and I will not mourn you." Daran waved his finger in Omar's face.

"I don't think I'll be killed, but I understand, Daran."

"Only because it is you, Omar, will I consider it." Mustafa stepped back and hung his head. "I pray you will not be killed."

"Only because Grandfather told you things you could not know, I may consider it, but not necessarily. I do wish you well, Omar." Saiim stepped forward and embraced him.

Daran spat again. "I wish you dead, Omar. It is only right. Saiim said it. You are now an infidel. Death to the infidels." He turned and walked away.

"I must go. You must make your own decisions. I will not forget you, my brothers, our time growing together, and our grandfather to whom we owe so much."

Saiim looked in Omar's eyes once more and walked away without a word.

Mustafa nodded to Omar and handed him a card. "When you can, let me know how you are, and if this new allegiance is working for you. Even if you are under a different name, I will know it is you. Thank you for returning. Grandfather always loved you so much."

"Mustafa, I think you are most like him."

"Perhaps that is why I am not jealous of you and am concerned for your welfare. I wish you well, my little brother. I will miss you." He turned and walked away.

Omar stayed for a few minutes. The sky was darkening to a deep purple. Omar walked over to the grave. "I'm sorry, Grandfather, that you are in that place. I so wish I could get you out. But I will now live for the King. I warned them, Grandfather, like you asked me to do. I think Mustafa may follow the King, and maybe Saiim. Daran does not seem like he will at all, but I felt the same way at first. Perhaps. Perhaps. Thank you, Grandfather."

———————

Omar dismissed his bodyguards. He paid them a handsome sum and thanked them for their service. They were dumbfounded.

Omar left in the night and walked the three miles to the place of the tunnel through which the Christians were escaping. He waited till just before dawn and walked up to an IDF soldier. The soldier pulled his gun. "Who goes there?"

"I would like to pass through the tunnel with you."

"Who are you?"

"I have asked Jesus to be my Lord and I know my life is in great danger here."

"Your name."

Omar coughed. "Omar."

"Homer?"

Omar nodded.

"I need to search you." The soldier found nothing. Omar had transferred everything from his phone and computer to a small chip that he placed in his sock. Despite obvious suspicion, the soldier checked Omar's shoes but not his socks.

The man led him through. The tunnel came out near the airport. A cargo plane was loaded with crates of Christians for transport to Israel. "This is dangerous, sir, but we have not yet been detected. We believe the God of Israel, blessed be He, has given us grace. We have only one flight per day, but we have transported several hundred who have suffered greatly from the ISIS take over."

"Yes, I am only recently a believer, but have already been called an infidel. I do believe it is time for me to go."

"Most have already been through the tunnel under the cover of darkness. It looks like we got you here in time to join today's flight."

Omar breathed a sigh of relief as he sat inside a crate as the plane took off for Israel. Apparently, the manifest indicated it was a transport plane from Jordan, and so far, they had been able to keep up the deception. The IDF felt they would make only a few more flights as most of the Christians still alive had been located and evacuated.

Omar could hear the others talking, praying, and singing songs of praise to Jesus. He knew he was responsible for most of their grief, and yet they worshipped their God, now his God. He also knew he was destined for prison, but hoped he'd do some good beforehand. If he survived and ever got out of prison he would hopefully do more good. He thought of the image he had of being married with three children and speaking about God. It was hard to imagine but he would trust the King.

What sat so strangely on his mind was not just the peace and strength he felt inside but that he could almost hear the King's voice within himself telling him what to do. He knew he was doing the right thing and he prayed that turning himself over to the IDF or the Mossad in Israel would go smoothly.

The plane touched down. IDF came aboard and opened the crates. The people were instructed that they would be temporarily placed in a building near the airport. At this place they would be fed and provided medical assistance if needed. If they had family they were looking for, people would provide help. If they needed to start over, options would be provided.

Omar joined the group, hoping to blend in for a few more minutes. He was hungry and ready to eat. He sat with the others but did not make conversation. They did not know him, and he didn't want to make anyone uncomfortable nor was he ready to draw attention to himself.

He stood and walked toward the door. He could walk out and disappear. Instead he approached three IDF soldiers standing just inside the door keeping an eye on everything.

"How can we be of service?" One of the IDF men held out a hand to shake Omar's.

Omar took it. "Sirs, I want you to know I have just converted to Christianity from Islam."

One of the men patted him on the back. "That is a big step. We respect all religions here in Israel. I want you to know that."

"Thank you, but now I would like to turn myself in. I believe the Mossad would like to talk to me."

The soldiers slightly stiffened. "Were you involved in the take-over of Mosul?"

"Yes, and more."

"Sir, let us step outside so we can search you. We have many suicide bombers in this neck of the woods."

Omar held his hands up and walked outside. "The only thing I have on me is a computer chip in my sock that will give you all the information you need to stop ISIS and to thwart Lemkrof."

One of the soldiers let out a low whistle. "Who are you?"

"I am Omar Tugani."

"We are going to handcuff you now and turn you over to Mossad."

"Thank you."

Mossad was incredulous that Omar Tugani had voluntarily turned himself in. Not only did they have the Temple Mount, but they had stopped Iran's nuclear option against Israel, and now they had Tugani, lead man for ISIS and big contact of Lemkrof.

Omar was quickly transferred to a maximum-security building. From the computer chip they downloaded a treasure trove of information. They interrogated him, but found they simply had to ask him and he revealed all the information he was asked. The only place he hesitated was revealing the location of his brothers. After all was said and done, he appreciated family, and truly didn't want them taken out. A few days before he had ordered their killings, and now he prayed they would live, at least long enough to know the King.

Israel did not broadcast this great coup. They simply took his information and used it to infiltrate ISIS and remove key people. They had already used Tassie's debriefing information to locate the chemicals in Syria. The earthquake and the drones did the necessary destruction for them. They also fed a great deal of information about Russia's plans in Ukraine, Slovakia, and Czech Republic to the U.S. They knew the U.S. might still sit on it, so they also informed the countries involved and offered tactical support.

The U.S. had been publicly apoplectic about Israel taking out Iran's nuclear capability, even though they knew the world was much better off. Israel had become a star. World opinion slowly and surprisingly turned in favor of Israel, and the U.S. wisely chose to thank Israel for their drone strike, albeit undercover. The U.S. remained reluctant to believe that the Gitmo guys, one of which was Omar's cousin, had their fingers and their money in so many terrorist plans. Again, wisely they realized Israel should be given free hand to send drones after them. They informed them of this decision, again undercover.

Because Omar was so helpful and thorough in his interrogations, and so real in his new faith, Israel determined to hold him in maximum detention with top security for only two years. After that time, they promised to release him to live his life. They hinted that he might be welcome into their information gathering process if he truly proved his worth over the two-year time. Omar knew such a short sentence was a gift. He would cooperate and learn.

CHAPTER 29

Tassie, Jethro, and Tassie's parents walked the steps to the Temple Mount. The crevice had been covered over and people were allowed to walk over a portion of the area. It was the first time any of Tassie's family had been there, but what delighted their senses was watching the Israelis who had lived so close but had never in their lives visited this most holy site.

People regularly walked with their hands over their mouths. Part was the amazement of being there. Part was the amazement that the former buildings were simply gone. Many stood in one spot and just turned and gazed in every direction. Some did so with cameras, videoing history in the making.

Tassie and her family stood to the side and marveled. They had no words. An IDF soldier stood nearby. "May I answer any questions? We are here to guard, but also to inform."

Tassie shrugged. "I know so little. I don't really know what to ask."

"Are you American?"

"I am, does it show that much?" Tassie squinted at the soldier.

"Oh, no, just your accent. I am very appreciative of all that America has done for Israel. My name is Ben Akeena."

Tassie held out her hand. "I am Tassie Stevens. Those are my parents over there and my cousin, Jethro."

Jethro nodded to Ben. "Pleased to meet you. We appreciate the IDF and are amazed at this. Did you see it disappear?"

"I did, I was among those who stormed to retake it, but there was no resistance. You?"

"I had just taken off in a helicopter and watched it from the sky. Incredible."

"An IDF helicopter?" Ben Akeena studied Jethro.

"Yes, I've done some work with them. Did you hear about the relic with the tassel?"

"My parents told me that story, a young woman is the namesake, got kidnapped, but gained important knowledge of Israel's enemies."

As Ben talked and listened, Tassie noticed he occasionally turned and took in those who walked the Temple Mount, looking each person in the eyes. She had learned Israel trusted their soldiers' trained ability to detect motives in the eyes.

Jethro smiled. "This is the namesake, Tassel Lydia Stevens, right here." He put his arm around Tassie. "But call her Tassie or she might punch you."

Ben faced Tassie. "This is marvelous. I'm delighted to meet you. And I will be sure to call you Tassie."

"I usually don't punch strangers or soldiers, so you're safe."

Ben laughed. "Americans. You are so comfortable talking and joking with people. I like that."

"It's so nice to meet you, Ben. I should let you get back to your work."

Ben looked down, then took a step closer to Tassie. "Miss Stevens, my parents are quite taken with your story. Would you do the honor of coming to our home for dinner? They would love to meet with you and hear more of your story."

"That's very nice of you." Tassie glanced at Jethro, who quickly turned and walked away. "I would be happy to do that. Perhaps by then I will have more questions about this place and what is going to happen here in the future."

Ben looked at his phone. "Well, my shift is over in about five minutes. If you will still be here, I can share the history of the place without interruption."

"I would like that."

Tassie excused herself and found her parents who were busy taking pictures and chatting with Jethro.

Her dad put his arm around Tassie. "You ready to go, girl? We thought we'd walk back through the marketplace and just eat as we go."

Tassie hesitated. "Ben's shift will be over in a few minutes. He wanted to tell me some of the history here. He also invited me to dinner with his parents, so they can hear my story."

Her mom raised her eyebrows. "Who's Ben?"

Jethro smiled. "That good-looking soldier over there who can't take his eyes off Tassie."

"Jethro, I can still punch you out."

Tassie's dad laughed. "Well, that's fine. Do I dare ask that he walk you back to the hotel, so you don't get kidnapped again?"

"Daddy, I think I'll be fine. I'll call you if I need an escort."

He kissed Tassie on the forehead. "See you later, sweetheart." He put his arm around his wife, signaled Jethro to go with them, and walked off.

Tassie walked over to Ben. "My folks just left."

"Do you need to go?"

"No, I'm good."

"Well, I'm done so let me tell you the history of the Temple Mount. My mom is a great cook and loves company, so if you are free, we can go over as soon as we are done here."

Tassie's eyes widened. "Should you call her? I don't want to surprise her."

"I already called her. She was already cooking. One more is no problem. And she can't wait to hear your story."

"I guess it's settled, then."

"Well, this place, the Temple Mount, is where Abraham was instructed to sacrifice his son Isaac, many, many years ago." Ben continued telling Tassie the amazing history of the storied Temple Mount.

Afterwards, they walked to Ben's home. Tassie was immediately charmed by Ben's parents and their home. Hospitality existed as part of the fiber of Israel, and Tassie hoped she never tired of the welcome she received in this land of the Bible.

The stone house and its terrace looked out over the city. The hills of Jerusalem held so many homes, but they did not seem crowded. Perhaps it was the view. Each terrace was graced with plants, beautiful flowers, small trees, and a view that was expansive. Decorated simply but with such taste, Tassie took in each piece of art and furniture. By the end of the evening she knew that the people were the greatest resource of Israel. Such kindness, such understanding, such wisdom and practicality.

Ben walked Tassie back to the hotel. "Tell your father that it only makes sense for me to walk you home. I am a soldier."

Tassie and her parents along with Jethro remained in Jerusalem for a week. She and Ben saw each other each day, sightseeing, dinner with her parents and Jethro, and dinner and shopping with Ben's parents with whom they also discussed the claims of Jesus and how many Jews were claiming him as Messiah. Upon returning to Tel Aviv, Tassie and Ben texted often, and Ben traveled the thirty miles to Tel Aviv when he was off a few days. Tassie often went to Jerusalem as well, sometimes with her parents who were deciding if they wanted to move to Jerusalem, and sometimes alone.

Much of world opinion still raged against Israel, but they moved forward preparing the Temple Mount for the rebuilding of the third Temple. All of Israel made ready, and celebrations occurred throughout the country and especially in Jerusalem. The oil well company started by Sally Goldman's grandfather was expanding by the week, providing Israel and several countries with abundant supplies of oil. The profits grew, and the top fifty percent immediately went into an account for the funding of the Temple.

The IDF, the Mossad, the Shin Bet, and the Aman kept their technology innovative and their eyes on all avenues of attack against Israel. Most threats had been nullified. Russia however continued to complain that Israel had tapped into reserves from their oil veins. Russia claimed that Israel did not treat their Jewish Russians well and demanded access to all Israeli citizens that had Russian background. Israel refused. They had Omar's playbook from his own testimony and his computer files and the earlier information from Tassie. Israel also had the word of families like Ben's who had emigrated from Russia and were delighted to be in Israel.

Passover and the third Blood Moon were quickly approaching.

CHAPTER 30

Tassie stood with Ben Akeena on the terrace of his parents' home in the hills of Jerusalem. No longer did the golden dome of the mosque reflect the sun, but the walls and stones of Jerusalem glowed with the amber of the sun's luminescence. It warmed her heart. Ben Akeena warmed her heart, but the best lay in front of them: the foundation for the new Temple, the third Jewish Temple, also known as the Temple of prophecy, the Temple of the last days, was being laid. The excitement at every phase infused the Jewish people with laughter and joy.

"As our prime minister said, the Scripture tells us in the Psalms that our mouths would be filled laughter as we see our captivity disappearing. Seeing this makes me want to shout and dance and sing." Ben picked up Tassie in his arms and swung her around before gently setting her down and placing a kiss on her cheek. "Oh, Tassie, here we are, almost Passover, and the Temple is being built. And your family, with the relic diamonds and gold, and your oil wells, have financed the lion's share of it."

Tassie smiled. "I'm so happy to be a part of it. God really did all of this."

"True enough, but to be a part of it, to be able to see it . . . it's history and prophecy all together." He reached down and took her hand.

"Ben, I know the Bible indicates, or prophecy does . . . " Tassie paused. "I don't know enough . . . but I think the Christians believe that Jesus will return when the Temple is built, and the Jews believe that the Messiah can't come until the Temple is built. Is that right?"

"Well, my parents always told me God's ways are higher than our ways. That's in Isaiah. And all through the Holy Writings, God talks about His wonders. I think it's all culminating right now into God's plan from the beginning of time." Ben chuckled. "And it's a little different than everybody thought, but it's pretty much what we hoped would happen. What so amazes me is that so much of our country is starting to see that Jesus is the Messiah, that He already came."

"So, does that mess up the rebuilding of the temple? I mean, if the Jews are Christians now, do they want or need the Temple?"

Ben put his arm around Tassie. "Interesting, huh? Your uncle, Rabbi Welcker, said that it is something only God could do."

"Wait, wait, we want to hear this."

The young couple turned to see Ben's mom carrying a plate of bread and hummus and fruit, while his dad brought a pitcher of iced tea to the little table on the terrace.

"Please, come sit with us. We want to hear as well."

Tassie hugged Ben's mother and sat in the chair his dad pulled out for her. Mr. Akeena squeezed her shoulder and sat down.

Ben continued after having a sip of tea. "Rabbi Welcker said 'Only God could fulfill everyone's hopes and dreams and theology, as well as His own plans, in such a short time'."

"We're listening, son."

"The Temple provides the means for sacrifice. That is the work of the Temple. Sacrifice covered our sins, so the Jews believe we are still in our sins until the sacrifice is restored. But they know that the Messiah will fulfill all the requirement of the law, which is sacrifice. Now they are beginning to see . . . their eyes are being opened . . . to what the Christians held, that Jesus' death on the cross was the sacrifice needed once for all."

"So, will they still do animal sacrifice like we've been taught?" Ben's mother sat with her elbows on the table and her chin in her hands.

"Rabbi Welcker says . . . he's been studying the New Testament of the Bible . . . that our sacrifice now is praise."

"Praise? You mean like singing?" Tassie now mirrored Ben's mother with her chin in her hands.

"Think of the Psalms. Praise was singing, praying with shouts, dancing, bowing, lifting hands. It's exuberant and reverent at the same time. Kind of what people are doing as they see the foundation coming together."

Tassie pursed her lips. "Okay, but what about Jesus returning or the Messiah coming?"

"Well, the Messiah is coming . . . into the hearts of the Jews. Maybe when the temple is rebuilt it will signal the time for what they call the second coming of Jesus."

"Son, I think where we Jews got hung up was that we thought the Messiah had to come in power and glory. We missed the humility and sacrifice part. And don't the Christians believe the second coming is in power and glory?"

"Yes, Dad, that's pretty much it."

Everyone sat and stared off into the distance for a while. Tassie shook her head. "A year ago, I was only interested in being a powerful, rich lawyer, and I scoffed at anything religious. Now I live in Israel, a completed Jew, amazed that I know Jesus and love the Bible, and I'm a part of God's plan. Does it get any better than this?"

Ben glanced at his parents. His father winked. His mother smiled and wiped a tear from her eye. "Perhaps, Tassie."

Tassie looked at each one and squinted her eyes. "What . . . you mean, it does get better?"

Ben scooted his chair back and placed one knee on the terrace. He reached into his pocket and looked up at Tassie. Her eyes widened, and her mouth dropped open. "Tassie, I know time may be short, and it may be chaotic, but I believe it will be glorious if you will spend it with me as my wife. Would you do the honor of marrying me?"

Tassie gulped. "Oh, Ben." Tears ran down her cheeks. "I . . . I . . . "

Ben turned his head slightly and looked at her out of the corners of his eyes. "Is it too soon?"

"No, no, it's just that . . . I'm, I'm . . . "

"What?" All three Akeenas asked it together.

"Speechless, I'm speechless."

Ben's dad reached over and patted her hand. "Just one word, Tassie, a yes or a no."

Tassie put her hand over her mouth. Then pulling it away, she blubbered, "Yes, yes, of course yes, a thousand times yes."

At the 'of course, yes' everyone laughed, and Ben picked her up again, twirled her around and kissed her. Then his parents hugged her.

"Welcome to the family, Tassel Lydia Stevens. We are delighted."

"Wait, wait, the ring!" It was still in his pocket. Ben pulled it out. With tears coursing down her face, Tassie held out her hand. Ben brought her hand to his lips and gently kissed it and placed the ring on her finger.

Tassie wiped her eyes and looked at the ring. She wiped her eyes again and brought her hand closer and studied it. Ben and his parents just stood with smiles on their faces.

"Why does this look familiar?" Tassie noticed their grins and stepped back. "What?"

Ben's mother put her hands to her mouth. "This is so exciting." She turned to her husband as he placed his arm around her.

Ben took Tassie's hand. "I went to visit your parents to ask their permission to marry you. Rabbi Welcker was there and he told me a little story."

"Another story?" Tassie pretended to punch him in the stomach.

"Oh, oh, get engaged and now I get beaten up." Ben laughed and sat down at the table.

"Okay, tell me the story." Tassie sat down and picked up the bread, dipped it in the hummus, and took a bite. The sun was high in the sky and the day warm with a slight breeze. She could smell the fragrance of the flowers Ben's mother planted all around the terrace wall.

"Well, when they went to officially appraise the gold rings, they discovered that a smaller third ring was inside one of the bigger ones. Perhaps it was the wedding ring of the Goldmans or the Liebermanns. Rabbi Welcker asked if they could keep it and place one of the diamonds on it and give it to you since you are the namesake for so much of this."

Tears filled Tassie's eyes. She pulled her hand with the ring close to her face. "Are you telling me . . . " She looked at each of them.

"When I asked permission to marry you . . . by the way, your parents said yes." Ben laughed. Tassie smiled. "Well, the rabbi got this twinkle in his eye and rubbed his hands together. He told me about the ring and his idea, so we got the ring size from your mother, had it sized, and the diamond placed into the ring. The other rings, and diamonds, per your family's request, funded the extra oil wells, and they are helping fund the new temple. So, Tassie, does it get any better than this?"

"I'm overwhelmed." Tassie stood to embrace her fiancé.

"We'll leave you two lovebirds alone. Tassie, we love you. You are now our daughter. In Jewish tradition, once you are betrothed, you are family. What is ours, is yours, and we are so happy."

Tassie hugged them both and then walked over to the wall to again gaze across at the temple foundation. Ben stood behind her with his arms around her waist and kissed her neck. "I love you, Tassel Lydia Stevens."

"And I you, Benjamin Isaiah Akeena."

EPILOGUE

SEVEN YEARS LATER, VIRGINIA

Ben and Tassie, two children in tow, walked into the church that Rube and Jill had attended with Jared and his wife, Deb, before moving to Israel. It was the second time they had been back to visit in the States. Tassie and Deb walked down the hall to drop the kids off in children's church. Tassie started back down the hall and almost bumped into a man.

"Oh, excuse me. . . " The words died on her lips and, as if in a dream, Tassie remembered when she first met Mr. Green Eyes. This man stood with a beautiful woman. She had that gorgeous Middle Eastern tone of skin, slightly dark, slightly tan. Three small children clung to him.

"Om . . . " He shook his head. It was almost imperceptible. She recovered. "Oh my, I'm so sorry I almost ran into you." A wash of emotions swept over her, from fear to delight. "I remember you, but not your name. It's been a long time."

"Yes, a long time. My name is Rafael Koban. My wife, Emrah, and my children."

Tassie held out her hand to Omar's wife. "I'm Tassie Akeena. My husband Ben, our two children, and I are visiting with friends here. Rafael and I worked together years ago." She looked back to Omar. "You've changed."

"Yes, I have. Totally. Someday, in Heaven, we'll meet that young man from Door County and tell him his prayer was truly answered."

At that moment, two things happened. First, down the hall a short slightly balding man with long straggly hair waved at Tassie. Second, a piercing light filled the hallway. Electric shivers filled Tassie's being. Everything disappeared as she looked up into a brilliant blue sky and heard the whisper, "How far is the sky blue, Tassie?"

Then it was only glory, forever.

THE END

For more information about

Judy DuCharme
and
Blood Moon Redemption
please visit:

www.judithducharme.com
www.facebook.com/judy.ducharme.18
@packerjudy

For more information about
AMBASSADOR INTERNATIONAL
please visit:

www.ambassador-international.com
@AmbassadorIntl
www.facebook.com/AmbassadorIntl

*If you enjoyed this book, please consider leaving us a review on
Amazon, Goodreads, or our website.*

Made in the USA
Lexington, KY
21 November 2018